Penguin Books

The Pothunters and Other School Stories

P. G. Wodehouse was born in Guildford in 1881 and educated at
Dulwich College. After working for the Hong Kong and Shanghai
Bank for two years, he left to earn his living as a journalist and story-
writer, writing the 'By the Way' column in the old *Globe*. He also
contributed a series of school stories to a magazine for boys, *The Captain*, in one of which Psmith made his first appearance. Going to
America before the First World War, he sold a serial to the *Saturday
Evening Post* and for the next twenty-five years almost all his books
appeared first in this magazine. He was part author and writer of the
lyrics of eighteen musical comedies, including *Kissing Time*; he married in 1914 and in 1955 took American citizenship. He wrote over
ninety books and his work has won world-wide acclaim, being trans-
lated into many languages. *The Times* hailed him as 'a comic genius
recognized in his lifetime as a classic and an old master of farce.'

P. G. Wodehouse said, 'I believe there are two ways of writing novels.
One is mine, making a sort of musical comedy without music and
ignoring real life altogether; the other is going right deep down into
life and not caring a damn . . .' He was created a Knight of the British
Empire in the New Year's Honours List in 1975. In a BBC interview
he said that he had no ambitions left, now that he had been knighted
and there was a waxwork of him in Madame Tussaud's. He died on St
Valentine's Day in 1975 at the age of ninety-three.

THE POTHUNTERS
AND
OTHER SCHOOL STORIES

P. G. Wodehouse

PENGUIN BOOKS

PENGUIN BOOKS

Published by the Penguin Group
Penguin Books Ltd, 27 Wrights Lane, London w8 5TZ, England
Viking Penguin, a division of Penguin Books USA Inc.
375 Hudson Street, New York, New York 10014, USA
Penguin Books Australia Ltd, Ringwood, Victoria, Australia
Penguin Books Canada Ltd, 2801 John Street, Markham, Ontario, Canada L3R 1B4
Penguin Books (NZ) Ltd, 182–190 Wairau Road, Auckland 10, New Zealand

Penguin Books Ltd, Registered Offices: Harmondsworth, Middlesex, England

The Pothunters first published by A. & C. Black Ltd 1902
Published in this edition simultaneously by Souvenir Press Ltd and
J. M. Dent & Sons (Canada) Ltd 1972
Copyright © Souvenir Press, 1972

A Prefect's Uncle first published by A. & C. Black Ltd 1903
Published in this edition simultaneously by Souvenir Press Ltd and
J. M. Dent & Sons (Canada) Ltd 1972
Copyright © Souvenir Press, 1972

Tales of St Austin's first published by A. & C. Black Ltd 1903
Published in this edition simultaneously by Souvenir Press Ltd and
J. M. Dent & Sons (Canada) Ltd 1972
Published in Puffin Books 1983
Copyright © Souvenir Press, 1972

This collection first published as *The Pothunters and Other School
Stories* in Penguin Books 1985
5 7 9 10 8 6

All rights reserved

Printed in England by Clays Ltd, St Ives plc
Set in Plantin

Contents

THE POTHUNTERS

TO JOAN, EFFIE

AND ERNESTINE BOWES-LYON

Contents

[1]

Patient Perseverance
Produces Pugilistic Prodigies

'Where *have* I seen that face before?' said a voice. Tony Graham looked up from his bag.

'Hullo, Allen,' he said, 'what the dickens are you up here for?'

'I was rather thinking of doing a little boxing. If you've no objection, of course.'

'But you ought to be on a bed of sickness, and that sort of thing. I heard you'd crocked yourself.'

'So I did. Nothing much, though. Trod on myself during a game of fives, and twisted my ankle a bit.'

'In for the middles, of course?'

'Yes.'

'So am I.'

'Yes, so I saw in the *Sportsman*. It says you weigh eleven-three.'

'Bit more, really, I believe. Shan't be able to have any lunch, or I shall have to go in for the heavies. What are you?'

'Just eleven. Well, let's hope we meet in the final.'

'Rather,' said Tony.

It was at Aldershot – to be more exact, in the dressing-room of the Queen's Avenue Gymnasium at Aldershot – that the conversation took place. From east and west, and north and south, from Dan even unto Beersheba, the representatives of the public schools had assembled to box, fence, and perform gymnastic prodigies for fame and silver medals. The room was full of all sorts and sizes of them, heavy-weights looking ponderous and muscular, feather-weights diminutive but wiry, light-weights, middle-weights, fencers, and gymnasts in scores, some wearing the unmistakable air of the veteran, for whom Aldershot has no mysteries, others nervous, and wishing themselves back again at school.

Tony Graham had chosen a corner near the door. This was his first appearance at Aldershot. St Austin's was his School, and he was by far the best middle-weight there. But his doubts as to his ability to hold his own against all-comers were extreme, nor were they lessened by the knowledge that his cousin, Allen Thomson, was to be one of his opponents. Indeed, if he had not been a man of mettle, he might well have thought that with Allen's advent his chances were at an end.

Allen was at Rugby. He was the son of a baronet who owned many acres in Wiltshire, and held fixed opinions on the subject of the whole duty of man, who, he held, should be before anything else a sportsman. Both the Thomsons – Allen's brother Jim was at St Austin's in the same House as Tony – were good at most forms of sport. Jim, however, had never taken to the art of boxing very kindly, but, by way of compensation, Allen had skill enough for two. He was a splendid boxer, quick, neat, scientific. He had been up to Aldershot three times, once as a feather-weight and twice as a light-weight, and each time he had returned with the silver medal.

As for Tony, he was more a fighter than a sparrer. When he paid a visit to his uncle's house he boxed with Allen daily, and invariably got the worst of it. Allen was too quick for him. But he was clever with his hands. His supply of pluck was inexhaustible, and physically he was as hard as nails.

'Is your ankle all right again, now?' he asked.

'Pretty well. It wasn't much of a sprain. Interfered with my training a good bit, though. I ought by rights to be well under eleven stone. You're all right, I suppose?'

'Not bad. Boxing takes it out of you more than footer or a race. I was in good footer training long before I started to get fit for Aldershot. But I think I ought to get along fairly well. Any idea who's in against us?'

'Harrow, Felsted, Wellington. That's all, I think.'

'St Paul's?'

'No.'

'Good. Well, I hope your first man mops you up. I've a conscientious objection to scrapping with you.'

Allen laughed. 'You'd be all right,' he said, 'if you weren't so beastly slow with your guard. Why don't you wake up? You hit like blazes.'

'I think I shall start guarding two seconds before you lead. By the way, don't have any false delicacy about spoiling my aristocratic features. On the ground of relationship, you know.'

'Rather not. Let auld acquaintance be forgot. I'm not Thomson for the present. I'm Rugby.'

'Just so, and I'm St Austin's. Personally, I'm going for the knock-out. You won't feel hurt?'

This was in the days before the Headmasters' Conference had abolished the knock-out blow, and a boxer might still pay attentions to the point of his opponent's jaw with an easy conscience.

'I probably shall if it comes off,' said Allen. 'I say, it occurs to me that we shall be weighing-in in a couple of minutes, and I haven't started to change yet. Good, I've not brought evening dress or somebody else's footer clothes, as usually happens on these festive occasions.'

He was just pulling on his last boot when a Gymnasium official appeared in the doorway.

'Will all those who are entering for the boxing get ready for the weighing-in, please?' he said, and a general exodus ensued.

The weighing-in at the Public Schools' Boxing Competition is something in the nature of a religious ceremony, but even religious ceremonies come to an end, and after a quarter of an hour or so Tony was weighed in the balance and found correct. He strolled off on a tour of inspection.

After a time he lighted upon the St Austin's Gym Instructor, whom he had not seen since they had parted that morning, the one on his way to the dressing-room, the other to the refreshment-bar for a modest quencher.

'Well, Mr Graham?'

'Hullo, Dawkins. What time does this show start? Do you know when the middle-weights come on?'

'Well, you can't say for certain. They may keep 'em back a bit or they may make a start with 'em first thing. No, the light-weights are going to start. What number did you draw, sir?'

'One.'

'Then you'll be in the first middle-weight pair. That'll be after these two gentlemen.'

'These two gentlemen', the first of the light-weights, were by this time in the middle of a warmish opening round. Tony watched them with interest and envy. 'How beastly nippy they are,' he said.

'Wish I could duck like that,' he added.

'Well, the 'ole thing there is you 'ave to watch the other man's eyes. But light-weights is always quicker at the duck than what heavier men are. You get the best boxing in the light-weights, though the feathers spar quicker.'

Soon afterwards the contest finished, amidst volleys of applause. It had been a spirited battle, and an exceedingly close thing. The umpires disagreed. After a short consultation, the referee gave it as his opinion that on the whole R. Cloverdale, of Bedford, had had a shade the worse of the exchanges, and that in consequence J. Robinson, of St Paul's, was the victor. This was what he meant. What he said was, 'Robinson wins,' in a sharp voice, as if somebody were arguing about it. The pair then shook hands and retired.

'First bout, middle-weights,' shrilled the M.C. 'W. P. Ross (Wellington) and A. C. R. Graham (St Austin's).'

Tony and his opponent retired for a moment to the changing-room, and then made their way amidst applause on to the raised stage on which the ring was pitched. Mr W. P. Ross proceeded to the farther corner of the ring, where he sat down and was vigorously massaged by his two seconds. Tony took the opposite corner and submitted himself to the same process. It is a very cheering thing at any time to have one's arms and legs kneaded like bread, and it is especially pleasant if one is at all nervous. It sends a glow through the entire frame. Like somebody's something it is both grateful and comforting.

Tony's seconds were curious specimens of humanity. One was a gigantic soldier, very gruff and taciturn, and with decided leanings towards pessimism. The other was also a soldier. He was in every way his colleague's opposite. He was half his size, had red hair, and was bubbling over with conversation. The other could not interfere with his hair or his size, but he could with his conversation, and whenever he attempted a remark, he was promptly silenced, much to his disgust.

'Plenty o' moosle 'ere, Fred,' he began, as he rubbed Tony's left arm.

'Moosle ain't everything,' said the other, gloomily, and there was silence again.

'Are you ready? Seconds away,' said the referee.

'Time!'

The two stood up to one another.

The Wellington representative was a plucky boxer, but he was not in the same class as Tony. After a few exchanges, the latter got to work, and after that there was only one man in the ring. In the middle of the second round the referee stopped the fight, and gave it to Tony, who came away as fresh as he had started, and a great deal happier and more confident.

'Did us proud, Fred,' began the garrulous man.

'Yes, but that 'un ain't nothing. You wait till he meets young Thomson. I've seen 'im box 'ere three years, and never bin beat yet. Three bloomin' years. Yus.'

This might have depressed anybody else, but as Tony already knew all there was to be known about Allen's skill with the gloves, it had no effect upon him.

A sanguinary heavy-weight encounter was followed by the first bout of the feathers and the second of the light-weights, and then it was Allen's turn to fight the Harrow representative.

It was not a very exciting bout. Allen took things very easily. He knew his training was by no means all it should have been, and it was not his game to take it out of himself with any firework business in the trial heats. He would reserve that for the final. So he sparred three gentle rounds with the Harrow sportsman, just doing sufficient to keep the lead and obtain the verdict after the last round. He finished without having turned a hair. He had only received one really hard blow, and that had done no damage. After this came a long series of fights. The heavy-weights shed their blood in gallons for name and fame. The feather-weights gave excellent exhibitions of science, and the light-weight pairs were fought off until there remained only the final to be decided, Robinson, of St Paul's, against a Charterhouse boxer.

In the middle-weights there were three competitors still in the running, Allen, Tony, and a Felsted man. They drew lots, and the bye fell to Tony, who put up an uninteresting three rounds with one of the soldiers, neither fatiguing himself very much. Henderson, of Felsted, proved a much tougher nut to crack than Allen's first opponent. He was a rushing boxer, and in the first round had, if anything, the best of it. In the last two, however, Allen gradually forged ahead, gaining many points by his perfect style alone. He was declared the winner, but he felt much more tired than he had done after his first fight.

By the time he was required again, however, he had had plenty of breathing space. The final of the light-weights had been decided, and Robinson, of St Paul's, after the custom of Paulines, had set the crown upon his afternoon's work by fighting the Carthusian to a standstill in the first round. There only remained now the finals of the heavies and middles.

It was decided to take the latter first.

Tony had his former seconds, and Dawkins had come to his corner to see him through the ordeal.

'The 'ole thing 'ere,' he kept repeating, 'is to keep goin' 'ard all the time and wear 'im out. He's too quick for you to try any sparrin' with.'

'Yes,' said Tony.

'The 'ole thing,' continued the expert, 'is to feint with your left and 'it with your right.' This was excellent in theory, no doubt, but Tony felt that when he came to put it into practice Allen might have other schemes on hand and bring them off first. '

'Are you ready? Seconds out of the ring . . . Time!'

'Go in, sir, 'ard,' whispered the red-haired man as Tony rose from his place.

Allen came up looking pleased with matters in general. He gave Tony a cousinly grin as they shook hands. Tony did not respond. He was feeling serious, and wondering if he could bring off his knock-out before the three rounds were over. He had his doubts.

The fight opened slowly. Both were cautious, for each knew the other's powers. Suddenly, just as Tony was thinking of leading, Allen came in like a flash. A straight left between the eyes, a right on the side of the head, and a second left on the exact tip of the nose, and he was out again, leaving Tony with a helpless feeling of impotence and disgust.

Then followed more sparring. Tony could never get in exactly the right position for a rush. Allen circled round him with an occasional feint. Then he hit out with the left. Tony ducked. Again he hit, and again Tony ducked, but this time the left stopped halfway, and his right caught Tony on the cheek just as he swayed to one side. It staggered him, and before he could recover himself, in darted Allen again with another trio of blows, ducked a belated left counter, got in two stinging hits on the ribs, and finished with a left drive which took Tony clean off his feet and deposited him on the floor beside the ropes.

'Silence, *please*,' said the referee, as a burst of applause greeted this feat.

Tony was up again in a moment. He began to feel savage. He had expected something like this, but that gave him no consolation. He made up his mind that he really would rush this time, but just as he was coming in, Allen came in instead. It seemed to Tony for the next half-minute that his cousin's fists were never out of his face. He looked on the world through a brown haze of boxing-glove. Occasionally his hand met something solid which he took to be Allen, but this was seldom, and, whenever it happened, it only seemed to bring him back again like a boomerang. Just at the most exciting point, 'Time' was called.

The pessimist shook his head gloomily as he sponged Tony's face.

'You must lead if you want to 'it 'im,' said the garrulous man. 'You're too slow. Go in at 'im, sir, wiv both 'ands, an' you'll be all right. Won't 'e, Fred?'

'I said 'ow it 'ud be,' was the only reply Fred would vouchsafe.

Tony was half afraid the referee would give the fight against him without another round, but to his joy 'Time' was duly called. He came up to the scratch as game as ever, though his head was singing. He meant to go in for all he was worth this round.

And go in he did. Allen had managed, in performing a complicated manoeuvre, to place himself in a corner, and Tony rushed. He was sent out again with a flush hit on the face. He rushed again, and again met Allen's left. Then he got past, and in the confined space had it all his own way. Science did not tell here. Strength was the thing that scored, hard half-arm smashes, left and right, at face and body, and the guard could look after itself.

Allen upper-cut him twice, but after that he was nowhere. Tony went in with both hands. There was a prolonged rally, and it was not until 'Time' had been called that Allen was able to extricate himself. Tony's blows had been mostly body blows, and very warm ones at that.

'That's right, sir,' was the comment of the red-headed second. 'Keep 'em both goin' hard, and you'll win yet. You 'ad 'im proper then. 'Adn't 'e, Fred?'

And even the pessimist was obliged to admit that Tony could fight, even if he was not quick with his guard.

Allen took the ring slowly. His want of training had begun to tell on him, and some of Tony's blows had landed in very tender spots. He knew that he could win if his wind held out, but he had misgivings. The gloves seemed to weigh down his hands. Tony opened the ball with a tremendous rush. Allen stopped him neatly. There was an interval while the two sparred for an opening. Then Allen feinted and dashed in. Tony did not hit him once. It was the first round over again. Left right, left right, and, finally, as had happened before, a tremendously hot shot which sent him under the ropes. He got up, and again Allen darted in. Tony met him with a straight left. A rapid exchange of blows, and the end came. Allen lashed out with his left. Tony ducked sharply, and brought his right across with every ounce of his weight behind it, fairly on to the point of the jaw. The right cross-counter is distinctly one of those things which it is more blessed to give than to receive. Allen collapsed.

'. . . nine . . . ten.'

The time-keeper closed his watch.

'Graham wins,' said the referee, 'look after that man there.'

[2]

Thieves Break in and Steal

It was always the custom for such Austinians as went up to represent the School at the annual competition to stop the night in the town. It was not, therefore, till just before breakfast on the following day that Tony arrived back at his House. The boarding Houses at St Austin's formed a fringe to the School grounds. The two largest were the School House and Merevale's. Tony was at Merevale's. He was walking up from the station with Welch, another member of Merevale's, who had been up to Aldershot as a fencer, when, at the entrance to the School grounds, he fell in with Robinson, his fag. Robinson was supposed by many (including himself) to be a very warm man for the Junior Quarter, which was a handicap race, especially as an injudicious Sports Committee had given him ten yards' start on Simpson, whom he would have backed himself to beat, even if the positions had been reversed. Being a wise youth, however, and knowing that the best of runners may fail through under-training, he had for the last week or so been going in for a steady course of over-training, getting up in the small hours and going for before-breakfast spins round the track on a glass of milk and a piece of bread. Master R. Robinson was nothing if not thorough in matters of this kind.

But today things of greater moment than the Sports occupied his mind. He had news. He had great news. He was bursting with news, and he hailed the approach of Tony and Welch with pleasure. With any other leading light of the School he might have felt less at ease, but with Tony it was different. When you have underdone a fellow's eggs and overdone his toast and eaten the remainder for a term or two, you begin to feel that mere social distinctions and differences of age no longer form a barrier.

Besides, he had news which was absolutely fresh, news to which no one could say pityingly: 'What! Have you only just heard *that*!'

'Hullo, Graham,' he said. 'Have you come back?' Tony admitted that he had. 'Jolly good for getting the Middles.' (A telegram had, of course, preceded Tony.) 'I say, Graham, do you know what's happened? There'll be an awful row about it. Someone's been and broken into the Pav.'

'Rot! How do you know?'

'There's a pane taken clean out. I booked it in a second as I was going past to the track.'

'Which room?'

'First Fifteen. The window facing away from the Houses.'

'That's rum,' said Welch. 'Wonder what a burglar wanted in the First room. Isn't even a hair-brush there generally.'

Robinson's eyes dilated with honest pride. This was good. This was better than he had looked for. Not only were they unaware of the burglary, but they had not even an idea as to the recent event which had made the First room so fit a hunting-ground for the burgling industry. There are few pleasures keener than the pleasure of telling somebody something he didn't know before.

'Great Scott,' he remarked, 'haven't you heard? No, of course you went up to Aldershot before they did it. By Jove.'

'Did what?'

'Why, they shunted all the Sports prizes from the Board Room to the Pav. and shot 'em into the First room. I don't suppose there's one left now. I should like to see the Old Man's face when he hears about it. Good mind to go and tell him now, only he'd have a fit. Jolly exciting, though, isn't it?'

'Well,' said Tony, 'of all the absolutely idiotic things to do! Fancy putting – there must have been at least fifty pounds' worth of silver and things. Fancy going and leaving all that overnight in the Pav!'

'Rotten!' agreed Welch. 'Wonder whose idea it was.'

'Look here, Robinson,' said Tony, 'you'd better buck up and change, or you'll be late for brekker. Come on, Welch, we'll go and inspect the scene of battle.'

Robinson trotted off, and Welch and Tony made their way to the Pavilion. There, sure enough, was the window, or rather the absence of window. A pane had been neatly removed, evidently in the orthodox way by means of a diamond.

'May as well climb up and see if there's anything to be seen,' said Welch.

'All right,' said Tony, 'give us a leg up. Right-ho. By Jove, I'm stiff.'

'See anything?'

'No. There's a cloth sort of thing covering what I suppose are the prizes. I see how the chap, whoever he was, got in. You've only got to break the window, draw a couple of bolts, and there you are. Shall I go in and investigate?'

'Better not. It's rather the thing, I fancy, in these sorts of cases, to leave everything just as it is.'

'Rum business,' said Tony, as he rejoined Welch on terra firma. 'Wonder if they'll catch the chap. We'd better be getting back to the House now. It struck the quarter years ago.'

When Tony, some twenty minutes later, shook off the admiring crowd who wanted a full description of yesterday's proceedings, and reached his study, he found there James Thomson, brother to Allen Thomson, as the playbills say. Jim was looking worried. Tony had noticed it during breakfast, and had wondered at the cause. He was soon enlightened.

'Hullo, Jim,' said he. 'What's up with you this morning? Feeling chippy?'

'No. No, I'm all right. I'm in a beastly hole though. I wanted to talk to you about it.'

'Weigh in, then. We've got plenty of time before school.'

'It's about this Aldershot business. How on earth did you manage to lick Allen like that? I thought he was a cert.'

'Yes, so did I. The 'ole thing there, as Dawkins 'ud say, was, I knocked him out. It's the sort of thing that's always happening. I wasn't in it at all except during the second round, when I gave him beans rather in one of the corners. My aunt, it was warm while it lasted. First round, I didn't hit him once. He was better than I thought he'd be, and I knew from experience he was pretty good.'

'Yes, you look a bit bashed.'

'Yes. Feel it too. But what's the row with you?'

'Just this. I had a couple of quid on Allen, and the rotter goes and gets licked.'

'Good Lord. Whom did you bet with?'

'With Allen himself.'

'Mean to say Allen was crock enough to bet against himself? He must have known he was miles better than anyone else in. He's got three medals there already.'

'No, you see his bet with me was only a hedge. He'd got five to four or something in quids on with a chap in his House at Rugby on himself. He wanted a hedge because he wasn't sure about his ankle being all right. You know he hurt it. So I gave him four to one in half-sovereigns. I thought he was a cert, with apologies to you.'

'Don't mention it. So he was a cert. It was only the merest fluke I managed to out him when I did. If he'd hung on to the end, he'd have won easy. He'd been scoring points all through.'

'I know. So *The Sportsman* says. Just like my luck.'

'I can't see what you want to bet at all for. You're bound to come a mucker sooner or later. Can't you raise the two quid?'

'I'm broke except for half a crown.'

'I'd lend it to you like a shot if I had it, of course. But you don't find me with two quid to my name at the end of term. Won't Allen wait?'

'He would if it was only him. But this other chap wants his oof badly for something and he's leaving and going abroad or something at the end of term. Anyhow, I know he's keen on getting it. Allen told me.'

Tony pondered for a moment. 'Look here,' he said at last, 'can't you ask your pater? He usually heaves his money about pretty readily, doesn't he?'

'Well, you see, he wouldn't send me two quid off the reel without wanting to know all about it, and why I couldn't get on to the holidays with five bob, and I'd either have to fake up a lot of lies, which I'm not going to do –'

'Of course not.'

'Or else I must tell him I've been betting.'

'Well, he bets himself, doesn't he?'

'That's just where the whole business slips up,' replied Jim, prodding the table with a pen in a misanthropic manner. 'Betting's the one thing he's absolutely down on. He got done rather badly once a few years ago. Believe he betted on Orme that year he got poisoned. Anyhow he's always sworn to lynch us if we made fools of ourselves that way. So if I asked him, I'd not only get beans myself, besides not getting any money out of him, but Allen would get scalped too, which he wouldn't see at all.'

'Yes, it's no good doing that. Haven't you any other source of revenue?'

'Yes, there's just one chance. If that doesn't come off, I'm done. My pater said he'd give me a quid for every race I won at the sports. I got the half yesterday all right when you were up at Aldershot.'

'Good man. I didn't hear about that. What time? Anything good?'

'Nothing special. 2 – 7 and three-fifths.'

'That's awfully good. You ought to pull off the mile, too, I should think.'

'Yes, with luck. Drake's the man I'm afraid of. He's done it in 4 – 48 twice during training. He was second in the half yesterday by about three yards, but you can't tell anything from that. He sprinted too late.'

'What's your best for the mile?'

'I have done 4 – 47, but only once. 4 – 48's my average, so there's nothing to choose between us on paper.'

'Well, you've got more to make you buck up than he has. There must be something in that.'

'Yes, by Jove. I'll win if I expire on the tape. I shan't spare myself with that quid on the horizon.'

'No. Hullo, there's the bell. We must buck up. Going to Charteris' gorge tonight?'

'Yes, but I shan't eat anything. No risks for me.'

'Rusks are more in your line now. Come on.'

And, in the excitement of these more personal matters, Tony entirely forgot to impart the news of the Pavilion burglary to him.

[3]

An Unimportant By-product

The news, however, was not long in spreading. Robinson took care of
that. On the way to school he overtook his friend Morrison, a young
gentleman who had the unique distinction of being the rowdiest fag
in Ward's House, which, as any Austinian could have told you, was
the rowdiest house in the School.

'I say, Morrison, heard the latest?'

'No, what?'

'Chap broke into the Pav. last night.'

'Who, you?'

'No, you ass, a regular burglar. After the Sports prizes.'

'Look here, Robinson, try that on the kids.'

'Just what I am doing,' said Robinson.

This delicate reference to Morrison's tender years had the effect of
creating a disturbance. Two School House juniors, who happened to
be passing, naturally forsook all their other aims and objects and joined
the battle.

'What's up?' asked one of them, dusting himself hastily as they
stopped to take breath. It was always his habit to take up any business
that might attract his attention, and ask for explanations afterwards.

'This kid –' began Morrison.

'Kid yourself, Morrison.'

'This lunatic, then.' Robinson allowed the emendation to pass.
'This lunatic's got some yarn on about the Pav. being burgled.'

'So it is. Tell you I saw it myself.'

'Did it yourself, probably.'

'How do you know, anyway? You seem so jolly certain about it.'

'Why, there's a pane of glass cut out of the window in the First
room.'

'Shouldn't wonder, you know,' said Dimsdale, one of the two School
House fags, judicially, 'if the kid wasn't telling the truth for once in

his life. Those pots must be worth something. Don't you think so, Scott?'

Scott admitted that there might be something in the idea, and that, however foreign to his usual habits, Robinson might on this occasion be confining himself more or less to strict fact.

'There you are, then,' said Robinson, vengefully. 'Shows what a fat lot you know what you're talking about, Morrison.'

'Morrison's a fool,' said Scott. 'Ever since he got off the bottom bench in form there's been no holding him.'

'All the same,' said Morrison, feeling that matters were going against him, 'I shan't believe it till I see it.'

'What'll you bet?' said Robinson.

'I never bet,' replied Morrison with scorn.

'You daren't. You know you'd lose.'

'All right, then, I'll bet a penny I'm right.' He drew a deep breath, as who should say, 'It's a lot of money, but it's worth risking it.'

'You'll lose that penny, old chap,' said Robinson. 'That's to say,' he added thoughtfully, 'if you ever pay up.'

'You've got us as witnesses,' said Dimsdale. 'We'll see that he shells out. Scott, remember you're a witness.

'Right-ho,' said Scott.

At this moment the clock struck nine, and as each of the principals in this financial transaction, and both the witnesses, were expected to be in their places to answer their names at 8.58, they were late. And as they had all been late the day before and the day before that, they were presented with two hundred lines apiece. Which shows more than ever how wrong it is to bet.

The news continuing to circulate, by the end of morning school it was generally known that a gang of desperadoes, numbering at least a hundred, had taken the Pavilion down, brick by brick, till only the foundations were left standing, and had gone off with every jot and tittle of the unfortunately placed Sports prizes.

At the quarter-to-eleven interval, the School had gone *en masse* to see what it could see, and had stared at the window with much the same interest as they were wont to use in inspecting the First Eleven pitch on the morning of a match – a curious custom, by the way, but one very generally observed.

Then the official news of the extent of the robbery was spread abroad. It appeared that the burglar had by no means done the profession credit, for out of a vast collection of prizes ranging from the vast and silver Mile Challenge Cup to the pair of fives-gloves with which the 'under twelve' disciple of Deerfoot was to be rewarded, he had selected only three. Two of these were worth having, being the challenge cup for the quarter and the non-challenge cup for the hundred yards, both silver, but the third was a valueless flask, and the general voice of the School was loud in condemning the business abilities of one who could select his swag in so haphazard a manner. It was felt to detract from the merit of the performance. The knowing ones, however, gave it as their opinion that the man must have been frightened by something, and so was unable to give the matter his best attention and do himself justice as a connoisseur.

'We had a burglary at my place once,' began Reade, of Philpott's House. 'The man –'

'That rotter, Reade,' said Barrett, also of Philpott's, 'has been telling us that burglary chestnut of his all the morning. I wish you chaps wouldn't encourage him.'

'Why, what was it? First I've heard of it, at any rate.' Dallas and Vaughan, of Ward's, added themselves to the group. 'Out with it, Reade,' said Vaughan.

'It's only a beastly reminiscence of Reade's childhood,' said Barrett. 'A burglar got into the wine-cellar and collared all the coals.'

'He didn't. He was in the hall, and my pater got his revolver –'

'While you hid under the bed.'

'– and potted at him over the banisters.'

'The last time but three you told the story, your pater fired through the keyhole of the dining-room.'

'You idiot, that was afterwards.'

'Oh, well, what does it matter? Tell us something fresh.'

'It's my opinion,' said Dallas, 'that Ward did it. A man of the vilest antecedents. He's capable of anything from burglary –'

'To attempted poisoning. You should see what we get to eat in Ward's House,' said Vaughan.

'Ward's the worst type of beak. He simply lives for the sake of booking chaps. If he books a chap out of bounds it keeps him happy for a week.'

'A man like that's bound to be a criminal of sorts in his spare time. It's action and reaction,' said Vaughan.

Mr Ward happening to pass at this moment, the speaker went on to ask Dallas audibly if life was worth living, and Dallas replied that under certain conditions and in some Houses it was not.

Dallas and Vaughan did not like Mr Ward. Mr Ward was not the sort of man who inspires affection. He had an unpleasant habit of 'jarring', as it was called. That is to say, his conversation was shaped to one single end, that of trying to make the person to whom he talked feel uncomfortable. Many of his jars had become part of the School history. There was a legend that on one occasion he had invited his prefects to supper, and regaled them with sausages. There was still one prefect unhelped. To him he addressed himself.

'A sausage, Jones?'

'If you please, sir.'

'No, you won't, then, because I'm going to have half myself.'

This story may or may not be true. Suffice it to say, that Mr Ward was not popular.

The discussion was interrupted by the sound of the bell ringing for second lesson. The problem was left unsolved. It was evident that the burglar had been interrupted, but how or why nobody knew. The suggestion that he had heard Master R. Robinson training for his quarter-mile, and had thought it was an earthquake, found much favour with the junior portion of the assembly. Simpson, on whom Robinson had been given start in the race, expressed an opinion that he, Robinson, ran like a cow. At which Robinson smiled darkly, and advised the other to wait till Sports Day and then he'd see, remarking that, meanwhile, if he gave him any of his cheek he might not be well enough to run at all.

'This sort of thing,' said Barrett to Reade, as they walked to their form-room, 'always makes me feel beastly. Once start a row like this, and all the beaks turn into regular detectives and go ferreting about all over the place, and it's ten to one they knock up against something one doesn't want them to know about.'

Reade was feeling hurt. He had objected to the way in which Barrett had spoiled a story that might easily have been true, and really was true in parts. His dignity was offended. He said 'Yes' to Barrett's observation in a tone of reserved *hauteur*. Barrett did not notice.

'It's an awful nuisance. For one thing it makes them so jolly strict about bounds.'

'Yes.'

'I wanted to go for a bike ride this afternoon. There's nothing on at the School.'

'Why don't you?'

'What's the good if you can't break bounds? A ride of about a quarter of a mile's no good. There's a ripping place about ten miles down the Stapleton Road. Big wood, with a ripping little hollow in the middle, all ferns and moss. I was thinking of taking a book out there for the afternoon. Only there's roll-call.'

He paused. Ordinarily, this would have been the cue for Reade to say, 'Oh, I'll answer your name at roll-call.' But Reade said nothing. Barrett looked surprised and disappointed.

'I say, Reade,' he said.

'Well?'

'Would you like to answer my name at roll-call?' It was the first time he had ever had occasion to make the request.

'No,' said Reade.

Barrett could hardly believe his ears. Did he sleep? Did he dream? Or were visions about?

'What!' he said.

No answer.

'Do you mean to say you won't?'

'Of course I won't. Why the deuce should I do your beastly dirty work for you?'

Barrett did not know what to make of this. Curiosity urged him to ask for explanations. Dignity threw cold water on such a scheme. In the end dignity had the best of it.

'Oh, very well,' he said, and they went on in silence. In all the three years of their acquaintance they had never before happened upon such a crisis.

The silence lasted until they reached the form-room. Then Barrett determined, in the interests of the common good – he and Reade shared a study, and icy coolness in a small study is unpleasant – to chain up Dignity for the moment, and give Curiosity a trial.

'What's up with you today?' he asked.

He could hardly have chosen a worse formula. The question has on most people precisely the same effect as that which the query, 'Do you know where you lost it?' has on one who is engaged in looking for mislaid property.

'Nothing,' said Reade. Probably at the same moment hundreds of other people were making the same reply, in the same tone of voice, to the same question.

'Oh,' said Barrett.

There was another silence.

'You might as well answer my name this afternoon,' said Barrett, tentatively.

Reade walked off without replying, and Barrett went to his place feeling that curiosity was a fraud, and resolving to confine his attentions for the future to dignity. This was by-product number one of the Pavilion burglary.

[4]

Certain Revelations

During the last hour of morning school, Tony got a note from Jim.

'Graham,' said Mr Thompson, the master of the Sixth, sadly, just as Tony was about to open it.

'Yes, sir?'

'Kindly tear that note up, Graham.'

'Note, sir?'

'Kindly tear that note up, Graham. Come, you are keeping us waiting.'

As the hero of the novel says, further concealment was useless. Tony tore the note up unread.

'Hope it didn't want an answer,' he said to Jim after school. 'Constant practice has made Thompson a sort of amateur lynx.'

'No. It was only to ask you to be in the study directly after lunch. There's a most unholy row going to occur shortly, as far as I can see.'

'What, about this burglary business?'

'Yes. Haven't time to tell you now. See you after lunch.'

After lunch, having closed the study door, Jim embarked on the following statement.

It appeared that on the previous night he had left a book of notes, which were of absolutely vital importance for the examination which the Sixth had been doing in the earlier part of the morning, in the identical room in which the prizes had been placed. Or rather, he had left it there several days before, and had not needed it till that night. At half-past six the Pavilion had been locked up, and Biffen, the ground-man, had taken the key away with him, and it was only after tea had been consumed and the evening paper read, that Jim, thinking it about time to begin work, had discovered his loss. This was about half-past seven.

Being a House-prefect, Jim did not attend preparation in the Great Hall with the common herd of the Houses, but was part-owner with Tony of a study.

31

The difficulties of the situation soon presented themselves to him. It was only possible to obtain the notes in three ways – firstly, by going to the rooms of the Sixth Form master, who lived out of College; secondly, by borrowing from one of the other Sixth Form members of the House; and thirdly, by the desperate expedient of burgling the Pavilion. The objections to the first course were two. In the first place Merevale was taking prep. over in the Hall, and it was strictly forbidden for anyone to quit the House after lock-up without leave. And, besides, it was long odds that Thompson, the Sixth Form master, would not have the notes, as he had dictated them partly out of his head and partly from the works of various eminent scholars. The second course was out of the question. The only other Sixth Form boy in the House, Tony and Welch being away at Aldershot, was Charteris, and Charteris, who never worked much except the night before an exam. but worked then under forced draught, was appalled at the mere suggestion of letting his note-book out of his hands. Jim had sounded him on the subject and had met with the reply, 'Kill my father and burn my ancestral home, and I will look on and smile. But touch these notes and you rouse the British Lion.' After which he had given up the borrowing idea.

There remained the third course, and there was an excitement and sporting interest about it that took him immensely. But how was he to get out to start with? He opened his study-window and calculated the risks of a drop to the ground. No, it was too far. Not worth risking a sprained ankle on the eve of the mile. Then he thought of the Matron's sitting-room. This was on the ground-floor, and if its owner happened to be out, exit would be easy. As luck would have it she was out, and in another minute Jim had crossed the Rubicon and was standing on the gravel drive which led to the front gate.

A sharp sprint took him to the Pavilion. Now the difficulty was not how to get out, but how to get in. Theoretically, it should have been the easiest of tasks, but in practice there were plenty of obstacles to success. He tried the lower windows, but they were firmly fixed. There had been a time when one of them would yield to a hard kick and fly bodily out of its frame, but somebody had been caught playing that game not long before, and Jim remembered with a pang that not only had the window been securely fastened up, but the culprit had had a spell of extra tuition and other punishments which had turned him for the time into a hater of his species. His own fate, he knew, would be even worse, for a prefect is supposed to have something better to do in his spare time than breaking into pavilions. It would mean expulsion perhaps, or, at the least, the loss of his prefect's cap, and Jim did not want to lose that. Still the thing had to be done if he meant to score any marks at all in the forthcoming exam. He wavered a while between a choice of methods, and finally fixed on the crudest of all. No one was likely to be within earshot, thought he, so he picked up the largest stone he could find, took as careful aim as the dim light would allow, and hove it. There was a sickening crash, loud enough, he thought, to bring the whole School down on him, followed by a prolonged rattle as the broken pieces of glass fell to the ground.

He held his breath and listened. For a moment all was still, uncannily still. He could hear the tops of the trees groaning in the slight breeze that had sprung up, and far away the distant roar of a train. Then a queer thing happened. He heard a quiet thud, as if somebody had jumped from a height on to grass, and then quick footsteps.

He waited breathless and rigid, expecting every moment to see a form loom up beside him in the darkness. It was useless to run. His only chance was to stay perfectly quiet.

Then it dawned upon him that the man was running away from him, not towards him. His first impulse was to give chase, but prudence restrained him. Catching burglars is an exhilarating sport, but it is best to indulge in it when one is not on a burgling expedition oneself.

Besides he had come out to get his book, and business is business.

There was no time to be lost now, for someone might have heard one or both of the noises and given the alarm.

Once the window was broken the rest was fairly easy, the only danger being the pieces of glass. He took off his coat and flung it on to the sill of the upper window. In a few seconds he was up himself without injury. He found it a trifle hard to keep his balance, as there was nothing to hold on to, but he managed it long enough to enable him to thrust an arm through the gap and turn the handle. After this there was a bolt to draw, which he managed without difficulty.

The window swung open. Jim jumped in, and groped his way round the room till he found his book. The other window of the room was wide open. He shut it for no definite reason, and noticed that a pane had been cut out entire. The professional cracksman had done his work more neatly than the amateur.

'Poor chap,' thought Jim, with a chuckle, as he effected a retreat, 'I must have given him a bit of a start with my half-brick.' After bolting the window behind him, he climbed down.

As he reached earth again the clock struck a quarter to nine. In another quarter of an hour prep. would be over and the House door unlocked, and he would be able to get in again. Nor would the fact of his being out excite remark, for it was the custom of the House-prefects to take the air for the few minutes which elapsed between the opening of the door and the final locking-up for the night.

The rest of his adventures ran too smoothly to require a detailed description. Everything succeeded excellently. The only reminiscences of his escapade were a few cuts in his coat, which went unnoticed, and the precious book of notes, to which he applied himself with such vigour in the watches of the night, with a surreptitious candle and a hamper of apples as aids to study, that, though tired next day, he managed to do quite well enough in the exam. to pass muster. And, as he had never had the least prospect of coming out top, or even in the first five, this satisfied him completely.

Tony listened with breathless interest to Jim's recital of his adventures, and at the conclusion laughed.

'What a mad thing to go and do,' he said. 'Jolly sporting, though.'

Jim did not join in his laughter.

'Yes, but don't you see,' he said, ruefully, 'what a mess I'm in? If they find out that I was in the Pav. at the time when the cups were bagged, how on earth am I to prove I didn't take them myself?'

'By Jove, I never thought of that. But, hang it all, they'd never dream of accusing a Coll. chap of stealing Sports prizes. This isn't a reformatory for juvenile hooligans.'

'No, perhaps not.'

'Of course not.'

'Well, even if they didn't, the Old Man would be frightfully sick if he got to know about it. I'd lose my prefect's cap for a cert.'

'You might, certainly.'

'I should. There wouldn't be any question about it. Why, don't you remember that business last summer about Cairns? He used to stay out after lock-up. That was absolutely all he did. Well, the Old 'Un dropped on him like a hundredweight of bricks. Multiply that by about ten and you get what he'll do to me if he books me over this job.'

Tony looked thoughtful. The case of Cairns *versus* The Powers that were, was too recent to have escaped his memory. Even now Cairns was to be seen on the grounds with a common School House cap at the back of his head in place of the prefect's cap which had once adorned it.

'Yes,' he said, 'you'd lose your cap all right, I'm afraid.'

'Rather. And the sickening part of the business is that this real, copper-bottomed burglary'll make them hunt about all over the shop for clues and things, and the odds are they'll find me out, even if they don't book the real man. Shouldn't wonder if they had a detective down for a big thing of this sort.'

'They are having one, I heard.'

'There you are, then,' said Jim, dejectedly. 'I'm done, you see.'

'I don't know. I don't believe detectives are much class.'

'Anyhow, he'll probably have gumption enough to spot me.'

Jim's respect for the abilities of our national sleuth-hounds was greater than Tony's, and a good deal greater than that of most people.

[5]

Concerning the Mutual Friend

'I wonder where the dear Mutual gets to these afternoons,' said Dallas.

'The who?' asked MacArthur. MacArthur, commonly known as the Babe, was a day boy. Dallas and Vaughan had invited him to tea in their study.

'Plunkett, you know.'

'Why the Mutual?'

'Mutual Friend, Vaughan's and mine. Shares this study with us. I call him dear partly because he's head of the House, and therefore, of course, we respect and admire him.'

'And partly,' put in Vaughan, beaming at the Babe over a frying-pan full of sausages, 'partly because we love him so. Oh, he's a beauty.'

'No, but rotting apart,' said the Babe, 'what sort of a chap is he? I hardly know him by sight, even.'

'Should describe him roughly,' said Dallas, 'as a hopeless, forsaken unspeakable worm.'

'Understates it considerably,' remarked Vaughan. 'His manners are patronizing, and his customs beastly.'

'He wears spectacles, and reads Herodotus in the original Greek for pleasure.'

'He sneers at footer, and jeers at cricket. Croquet is his form, I should say. Should doubt, though, if he even plays that.'

'But why on earth,' said the Babe, 'do you have him in your study?'

Vaughan looked wildly and speechlessly at Dallas, who looked helplessly back at Vaughan.

'Don't, Babe, please!' said Dallas. 'You've no idea how a remark of that sort infuriates us. You surely don't suppose we'd have the man in the study if we could help it?'

'It's another instance of Ward at his worst,' said Vaughan. 'Have you never heard the story of the Mutual Friend's arrival?'

'No.'

'It was like this. At the beginning of this term I came back expecting

36

to be head of this show. You see, Richards left at Christmas and I was next man in. Dallas and I had made all sorts of arrangements for having a good time. Well, I got back on the last evening of the holidays. When I got into this study, there was the man Plunkett sitting in the best chair, reading.'

'Probably reading Herodotus in the original Greek,' snorted Dallas.

'He didn't take the slightest notice of me. I stood in the doorway like Patience on a monument for about a quarter of an hour. Then I coughed. He took absolutely no notice. I coughed again, loud enough to crack the windows. Then I got tired of it, and said "Hullo". He did look up at that. "Hullo," he said, "you've got rather a nasty cough." I said "Yes", and waited for him to throw himself on my bosom and explain everything, you know.'

'Did he?' asked the Babe, deeply interested.

'Not a bit,' said Dallas, 'he – sorry, Vaughan, fire ahead.'

'He went on reading. After a bit I said I hoped he was fairly comfortable. He said he was. Conversation languished again. I made another shot. "Looking for anybody?" I said. "No," he said, "are you?" "No." "Then why the dickens should I be?" he said. I didn't quite follow his argument. In fact, I don't even now. "Look here," I said, "tell me one thing. Have you or have you not bought this place? If you have, all right. If you haven't, I'm going to sling you out, and jolly soon, too." He looked at me in his superior sort of way, and observed without blenching that he was head of the House.'

'Just another of Ward's jars,' said Dallas. 'Knowing that Vaughan was keen on being head of the House he actually went to the Old Man and persuaded him that it would be better to bring in some day boy who was a School-prefect than let Vaughan boss the show. What do you think of that?'

'Pretty low,' said the Babe.

'Said I was thoughtless and headstrong,' cut in Vaughan, spearing a sausage as if it were Mr Ward's body. 'Muffins up, Dallas, old man. When the sausages are done to a turn. "Thoughtless and headstrong." Those were his very words.'

'Can't you imagine the old beast?' said Dallas, pathetically, 'Can't you see him getting round the Old Man? A capital lad at heart, I am sure, distinctly a capital lad, but thoughtless and headstrong, far too thoughtless for a position so important as that of head of my House. The abandoned old wreck!'

Tea put an end for the moment to conversation, but when the last sausage had gone the way of all flesh, Vaughan returned to the sore subject like a moth to a candle.

'It isn't only the not being head of the House that I bar. It's the man himself. You say you haven't studied Plunkett much. When you get to know him better, you'll appreciate his finer qualities more. There are so few of them.'

'The only fine quality I've ever seen in him,' said Dallas, 'is his habit of slinking off in the afternoons when he ought to be playing games, and not coming back till lock-up.'

'Which brings us back to where we started,' put in the Babe. 'You were wondering what he did with himself.'

'Yes, it can't be anything good so we'll put beetles and butterflies out of the question right away. He might go and poach. There's heaps of opportunity round here for a chap who wants to try his hand at that. I remember, when I was a kid, Morton-Smith, who used to be in this House – remember him? – took me to old what's-his-name's place. Who's that frantic blood who owns all that land along the Badgwick road? The M.P. man.'

'Milord Sir Alfred Venner, M.P., of Badgwick Hall.'

'That's the man. Generally very much of Badgwick Hall. Came down last summer on Prize Day. One would have thought from the side on him that he was all sorts of dooks. Anyhow, Morton-Smith took me rabbiting there. I didn't know it was against the rules or anything. Had a grand time. A few days afterwards, Milord Sir Venner copped him on the hop and he got sacked. There was an awful row. I thought my hair would have turned white.'

'I shouldn't think the Mutual poaches,' said Vaughan. 'He hasn't got the enterprise to poach an egg even. No, it can't be that.'

'Perhaps he bikes?' said the Babe.

'No, he's not got a bike. He's the sort of chap, though, to borrow somebody else's without asking. Possibly he does bike.'

'If he does,' said Dallas, 'it's only so as to get well away from the Coll., before starting on his career of crime. I'll swear he does break rules like an ordinary human being when he thinks it's safe. Those aggressively pious fellows generally do.'

'I didn't know he was that sort,' said the Babe. 'Don't you find it rather a jar?'

'Just a bit. He jaws us sometimes till we turn and rend him.'

'Yes, he's an awful man,' said Vaughan.

'Don't stop,' said the Babe, encouragingly, after the silence had lasted some time. 'It's a treat picking a fellow to pieces like this.'

'I don't know if that's your beastly sarcasm, Babe,' said Vaughan, 'but, speaking for self and partner, I don't know how we should get on if we didn't blow off steam occasionally in this style.'

'We should probably last out for a week, and then there would be a sharp shriek, a hollow groan, and all that would be left of the Mutual Friend would be a slight discolouration on the study carpet.'

'Coupled with an aroma of fresh gore.'

'Perhaps that's why he goes off in the afternoons,' suggested the Babe. 'Doesn't want to run any risks.'

'Shouldn't wonder.'

'He's such a rotten head of the House, too,' said Vaughan. 'Ward may gas about my being headstrong and thoughtless, but I'm dashed if I would make a bally exhibition of myself like the Mutual.'

'What's he do?' enquired the Babe.

'It's not so much what he does. It's what he doesn't do that sickens me,' said Dallas. 'I may be a bit of a crock in some ways – for further details apply to Ward – but I can stop a couple of fags ragging if I try.'

'Can't Plunkett?'

'Not for nuts. He's simply helpless when there's anything going on that he ought to stop. Why, the other day there was a row in the fags' room that you could almost have heard at your place, Babe. We were up here working. The Mutual was jawing as usual on the subject of cramming tips for the Aeschylus exam. Said it wasn't scholarship, or some rot. What business is it of his how a chap works, I should like to know. Just as he had got under way, the fags began kicking up more row than ever.'

'I said', cut in Vaughan, 'that instead of minding other people's business, he'd better mind his own for a change, and go down and stop the row.'

'He looked a bit green at that,' said Dallas. 'Said the row didn't interfere with him. "Does with us," I said. "It's all very well for you. You aren't doing a stroke of work. No amount of row matters to a chap who's only delivering a rotten sermon on scholarship. Vaughan and I happen to be trying to do some work." "All right," he said, "if you want the row stopped, why don't you go and stop it? What's it got to do with me?" '

'Rotter!' interpolated the Babe.

'Wasn't he? Well, of course we couldn't stand that.'

'We crushed him,' said Vaughan.

'I said: "In my young days the head of the House used to keep order for himself." I asked him what he thought he was here for. Because he isn't ornamental. So he went down after that.'

'Well?' said the Babe. Being a miserable day boy he had had no experience of the inner life of a boarding House, which is the real life of a public school. His experience of life at St Austin's was limited to doing his work and playing centre-three-quarter for the fifteen. Which, it may be remarked in passing, he did extremely well.

Dallas took up the narrative. 'Well, after he'd been gone about five minutes, and the row seemed to be getting worse than ever, we thought we'd better go down and investigate. So we did.'

'And when we got to the fags' room,' said Vaughan, pointing the toasting-fork at the Babe by way of emphasis, 'there was the Mutual standing in the middle of the room gassing away with an expression on his face a cross between a village idiot and an unintelligent fried egg. And all round him was a seething mass of fags, half of them playing soccer with a top-hat and the other half cheering wildly whenever the Mutual opened his mouth.'

'What did you do?'

'We made an aggressive movement in force. Collared the hat, brained every fag within reach, and swore we'd report them to the beak and so on. They quieted down in about three and a quarter seconds by stopwatch, and we retired, taking the hat as a prize of war, and followed by the Mutual Friend.'

'He looked worried, rather,' said Vaughan. 'And, thank goodness, he let us alone for the rest of the evening.'

'That's only a sample, though,' explained Dallas. 'That sort of thing has been going on the whole term. If the head of a House is an abject lunatic, there's bound to be ructions. Fags simply live for the sake of kicking up rows. It's meat and drink to them.'

'I wish the Mutual would leave,' said Vaughan. 'Only that sort of chap always lingers on until he dies or gets sacked.'

'He's not the sort of fellow to get sacked, I should say,' said the Babe.

' 'Fraid not. I wish I could shunt into some other House. Between Ward and the Mutual life here isn't worth living.'

'There's Merevale's, now,' said Vaughan. 'I wish I was in there. In the first place you've got Merevale. He gets as near perfection as a beak ever does. Coaches the House footer and cricket, and takes an intelligent interest in things generally. Then there are some decent fellows in Merevale's. Charteris, Welch, Graham, Thomson, heaps of them.'

'Pity you came to Ward's,' said the Babe. 'Why did you?'

'My pater knew Ward a bit. If he'd known him well, he'd have sent me somewhere else.'

'My pater knew Vaughan's pater well, who knew Ward slightly and there you are. *Voilà comme des accidents arrivent.*'

'If Ward wanted to lug in a day boy to be head of the House,' said Vaughan, harping once more on the old string, 'he might at least have got somebody decent.'

'There's the great Babe himself. Babe, why don't you come in next term?'

'Not much,' said the Babe, with a shudder.

'Well, even barring present company, there are lots of chaps who would have jumped at the chance of being head of a House. But nothing would satisfy Ward but lugging the Mutual from the bosom of his beastly family.'

'We haven't decided that point about where he goes to,' said the Babe.

At this moment the door of the study opened, and the gentleman in question appeared in person. He stood in the doorway for a few seconds, gasping and throwing his arms about as if he found a difficulty in making his way in.

'I wish you two wouldn't make such an awful froust in the study *every* afternoon,' he observed, pleasantly. 'Have you been having a little tea-party? How nice!'

'We've been brewing, if that's what you mean,' said Vaughan, shortly.

'Oh,' said Plunkett, 'I hope you enjoyed yourselves. It's nearly lock-up, MacArthur.'

'That's Plunkett's delicate way of telling you you're not wanted, Babe.'

'Well, I suppose I ought to be going,' said the Babe. 'So long.'

And he went, feeling grateful to Providence for not having made his father, like the fathers of Vaughan and Dallas, a casual acquaintance of Mr Ward.

The Mutual Friend really was a trial to Vaughan and Dallas. Only those whose fate it is or has been to share a study with an uncongenial companion can appreciate their feelings to the full. Three in a study is always something of a tight fit, and when the three are in a state of perpetual warfare, or, at the best, of armed truce, things become very bad indeed.

'Do you find it necessary to have tea-parties every evening?'

enquired Plunkett, after he had collected his books for the night's work. 'The smell of burnt meat –'

'Fried sausages,' said Vaughan. 'Perfectly healthy smell. Do you good.'

'It's quite disgusting. Really, the air in here is hardly fit to breathe.'

'You'll find an excellent brand of air down in the senior study,' said Dallas, pointedly. 'Don't stay and poison yourself here on *our* account,' he added. 'Think of your family.'

'I shall work where I choose,' said the Mutual Friend, with dignity.

'Of course, so long as you do work. You mustn't talk. Vaughan and I have got some Livy to do.'

Plunkett snorted, and the passage of arms ended, as it usually did, in his retiring with his books to the senior study, leaving Dallas and Vaughan to discuss his character once more in case there might be any points of it left upon which they had not touched in previous conversations.

'This robbery of the pots is a rum thing,' said Vaughan, thoughtfully, when the last shreds of Plunkett's character had been put through the mincing-machine to the satisfaction of all concerned.

'Yes. It's the sort of thing one doesn't think possible till it actually happens.'

'What the dickens made them put the things in the Pav. at all? They must have known it wouldn't be safe.'

'Well, you see, they usually cart them into the Board Room, I believe, only this time the governors were going to have a meeting there. They couldn't very well meet in a room with the table all covered with silver pots.'

'Don't see why.'

'Well, I suppose they could, really, but some of the governors are fairly nuts on strict form. There's that crock who makes the two-hour vote of thanks speeches on Prize Day. You can see him rising to a point of order, and fixing the Old 'Un with a fishy eye.'

'Well, anyhow, I don't see that they can blame a burglar for taking the pots if they simply chuck them in his way like that.'

'No. I say, we'd better weigh in with the Livy. The man Ward'll be round directly. Where's the dic? *And* our invaluable friend, Mr Bohn? Right. Now, you reel it off, and I'll keep an eye on the notes.' And they settled down to the business of the day.

After a while Vaughan looked up.

'Who's going to win the mile?' he asked.

'What's the matter with Thomson?'

'How about Drake then?'

'Thomson won the half.'

'I knew you'd say that. The half isn't a test of a chap's mile form. Besides, did you happen to see Drake's sprint?'

'Jolly good one.'

'I know, but look how late he started for it. Thomson crammed on the pace directly he got into the straight. Drake only began to put it on when he got to the Pav. Even then he wasn't far behind at the tape.'

'No. Well, I'm not plunging either way. Ought to be a good race.'

'Rather. I say, I wonder Welch doesn't try his hand at the mile. I believe he would do some rattling times if he'd only try.'

'Why, Welch is a sprinter.'

'I know. But I believe for all that that the mile's his distance. He's always well up in the cross-country runs.'

'Anyhow, he's not in for it this year. Thomson's my man. It'll be a near thing, though.'

'Jolly near thing. With Drake in front.'

'Thomson.'

'Drake.'

'All right, we'll see. Wonder why the beak doesn't come up. I can't sit here doing Livy all the evening. And yet if we stop he's bound to look in.'

'Oh Lord, is that what you've been worrying about? I thought you'd developed the work habit or something. Ward's all right. He's out on the tiles tonight. Gone to a dinner at Philpott's.'

'Good man, how do you know? Are you certain?'

'Heard him telling Prater this morning. Half the staff have gone. Good opportunity for a chap to go for a stroll if he wanted to. Shall we, by the way?'

'Not for me, thanks. I'm in the middle of a rather special book. Ever read *Great Expectations*? Dickens, you know.'

'I know. Haven't read it, though. Always rather funk starting on a classic, somehow. Good?'

'My dear chap! Good's not the word.'

'Well, after you. Exit Livy, then. And a good job, too. You might pass us the great Sherlock. Thanks.'

He plunged with the great detective into the mystery of the speckled band, while Vaughan opened *Great Expectations* at the place where he had left off the night before. And a silence fell upon the study.

Curiously enough, Dallas was not the only member of Ward's House to whom it occurred that evening that the absence of the House-master supplied a good opportunity for a stroll. The idea had also struck Plunkett favourably. He was not feeling very comfortable down-stairs. On entering the senior study he found Galloway, an Upper Fourth member of the House, already in possession. Galloway had managed that evening to insinuate himself with such success into the good graces of the matron, that he had been allowed to stay in the House instead of proceeding with the rest of the study to the Great Hall for preparation. The palpable failure of his attempt to hide the book he was reading under the table when he was disturbed led him to cast at the Mutual Friend, the cause of his panic, so severe and forbidding a look, that that gentleman retired, and made for the junior study.

The atmosphere in the junior study was close, and heavy with a blend of several strange odours. Plunkett went to the window. Then he noticed what he had never noticed before, that there were no bars to the window. Only the glass stood between him and the outer world. He threw up the sash as far as it would go. There was plenty of room to get out. So he got out. He stood for a moment inhaling the fresh air. Then, taking something from his coat-pocket, he dived into the shadows. An hour passed. In the study above, Dallas, surfeited with mysteries and villainy, put down his book and stretched himself.

'I say, Vaughan,' he said. 'Have you settled the House gym. team yet? It's about time the list went up.'

'Eh? What?' said Vaughan, coming slowly out of his book.

Dallas repeated his question.

'Yes,' said Vaughan, 'got it somewhere on me. Haynes, Jarvis, and myself are going in. Only, the Mutual has to stick up the list.'

It was the unwritten rule in Ward's, as in most of the other Houses at the School, that none but the head of the House had the right of placing notices on the House board.

'I know,' said Dallas. 'I'll go and buck him up now.'

'Don't trouble. After prayers'll do.'

'It's all right. No trouble. Whom did you say? Yourself, Haynes –'

'And Jarvis. Not that he's any good. But the third string never matters much, and it'll do him good to represent the House.'

'Right. I'll go and unearth the Mutual.'

The result was that Galloway received another shock to his system.

'Don't glare, Galloway. It's rude,' said Dallas.

'Where's Plunkett got to?' he added.

'Junior study,' said Galloway.

Dallas went to the junior study. There were Plunkett's books on the table, but of their owner no signs were to be seen. The Mutual Friend had had the good sense to close the window after he had climbed through it, and Dallas did not suspect what had actually happened. He returned to Vaughan.

'The Mutual isn't in either of the studies,' he said. 'I didn't want to spend the evening playing hide-and-seek with him, so I've come back.'

'It doesn't matter, thanks all the same. Later on'll do just as well.'

'Do you object to the window going up?' asked Dallas. 'There's a bit of a froust on in here.'

'Rather not. Heave it up.'

Dallas hove it. He stood leaning out, looking towards the College buildings, which stood out black and clear against the April sky. From out of the darkness in the direction of Stapleton sounded the monotonous note of a corn-crake.

'Jove,' he said, 'it's a grand night. If I was at home now I shouldn't be cooped up indoors like this.'

'Holidays in another week,' said Vaughan, joining him. 'It is ripping, isn't it? There's something not half bad in the Coll. buildings on a night like this. I shall be jolly sorry to leave, in spite of Ward and the Mutual.'

'Same here, by Jove. We've each got a couple more years, though, if it comes to that. Hullo, prep.'s over.'

The sound of footsteps began to be heard from the direction of the College. Nine had struck from the School clock, and the Great Hall was emptying.

'Your turn to read at prayers, Vaughan. Hullo, there's the Mutual. Didn't hear him unlock the door. Glad he has, though. Saves us trouble.'

'I must be going down to look up a bit to read. Do you remember when Harper read the same bit six days running? I shall never forget Ward's pained expression. Harper explained that he thought the passage so beautiful that he couldn't leave it.'

'Why don't you try that tip?'

'Hardly. My reputation hasn't quite the stamina for the test.'

Vaughan left the room. At the foot of the stairs he was met by the matron.

'Will you unlock the door, please, Vaughan,' she said, handing him a bunch of keys. 'The boys will be coming in in a minute.'

'Unlock the door?' repeated Vaughan. 'I thought it was unlocked. All right.'

'By Jove,' he thought, 'the plot thickens. What is our only Plunkett doing out of the House when the door is locked, I wonder.'

Plunkett strolled in with the last batch of the returning crowd, wearing on his face the virtuous look of one who has been snatching a whiff of fresh air after a hard evening's preparation.

'Oh, I say, Plunkett,' said Vaughan, when they met in the study after prayers, 'I wanted to see you. Where have you been?'

'I have been in the junior study. Where did you think I had been?'

'Oh.'

'Do you doubt my word?'

'I've the most exaggerated respect for your word, but you weren't in the junior study at five to nine.'

'No, I went up to my dormitory about that time. You seem remarkably interested in my movements.'

'Only wanted to see you about the House gym. team. You might shove up the list tonight. Haynes, Jarvis, and myself.'

'Very well.'

'I didn't say anything to him,' said Vaughan to Dallas as they were going to their dormitories, 'but, you know, there's something jolly fishy about the Mutual. That door wasn't unlocked when we saw him outside. I unlocked it myself. Seems to me the Mutual's been having a little private bust of his own on the quiet.'

'That's rum. He might have been out by the front way to see one of the beaks, though.'

'Well, even then he would be breaking rules. You aren't allowed to go out after lock-up without House beak's leave. No, I find him guilty.'

'If only he'd go and get booked!' said Vaughan. 'Then he might have to leave. But he won't. No such luck.'

'No,' said Dallas. 'Good-night.'

'Good-night.'

Certainly there was something mysterious about the matter.

[6]

A Literary Banquet

Charteris and Welch were conversing in the study of which they were the joint proprietors. That is to say, Charteris was talking and playing the banjo alternately, while Welch was deep in a book and refused to be drawn out of it under any pretext. Charteris' banjo was the joy of his fellows and the bane of his House-master. Being of a musical turn and owning a good deal of pocket-money, he had, at the end of the summer holidays, introduced the delights of a phonograph into the House. This being vetoed by the House-master, he had returned at the beginning of the following term with a penny whistle, which had suffered a similar fate. Upon this he had invested in a banjo, and the dazed Merevale, feeling that matters were getting beyond his grip, had effected a compromise with him. Having ascertained that there was no specific rule at St Austin's against the use of musical instruments, he had informed Charteris that if he saw fit to play the banjo before prep. only, and regarded the hours between seven and eleven as a close time, all should be forgiven, and he might play, if so disposed, till the crack of doom. To this reasonable request Charteris had promptly acceded, and peace had been restored. Charteris and Welch were a curious pair. Welch spoke very little. Charteris was seldom silent. They were both in the Sixth – Welch high up, Charteris rather low down. In games, Welch was one of those fortunate individuals who are good at everything. He was captain of cricket, and not only captain, but also the best all-round man in the team, which is often a very different matter. He was the best wing three-quarter the School possessed; played fives and racquets like a professor, and only the day before had shared Tony's glory by winning the silver medal for fencing in the Aldershot competition.

The abilities of Charteris were more ordinary. He was a sound bat, and went in first for the Eleven, and played half for the Fifteen. As regards work, he might have been brilliant if he had chosen, but his energies were mainly devoted to the compilation of a monthly magazine (strictly unofficial) entitled *The Glow Worm*. This he edited, and for the most part wrote himself. It was a clever periodical, and rarely failed to bring him in at least ten shillings per number, after deducting the expenses which the College bookseller, who acted as sole agent, did his best to make as big as possible. Only a very few of the elect knew the identity of the editor, and they were bound to strict secrecy. On the day before the publication of each number, a notice was placed in the desk of the captain of each form, notifying him of what the morrow would bring forth, and asking him to pass it round the form. That was all. The School did the rest. *The Glow Worm* always sold well, principally because of the personal nature of its contents. If the average mortal is told that there is something about him in a paper, he will buy that paper at your own price.

Today he was giving his monthly tea in honour of the new number. Only contributors were invited, and the menu was always of the best. It was a *Punch* dinner, only more so, for these teas were celebrated with musical honours, and Charteris on the banjo was worth hearing. His rendering of extracts from the works of Messrs Gilbert and Sullivan was an intellectual treat.

'When I take the chair at our harmonic club!' he chanted, fixing the unconscious Welch with a fiery glance. 'Welch!'

'Yes.'

'If this is your idea of a harmonic club, it isn't mine. Put down that book, and try and be sociable.'

'One second,' said Welch, burrowing still deeper.

'That's what you always say,' said Charteris. 'Look here – Come in.'

There had been a knock at the door as he was speaking. Tony entered, accompanied by Jim. They were regular attendants at these banquets, for between them they wrote most of what was left of the magazine when Charteris had done with it. There was only one other contributor, Jackson, of Dawson's House, and he came in a few minutes later. Welch was the athletics expert of the paper, and did most of the match reports.

'Now we're complete,' said Charteris, as Jackson presented himself. 'Gentlemen – your seats. There are only four chairs, and we, as Wordsworth might have said, but didn't, are five. All right, I'll sit on the table. Welch, you worm, away with melancholy. Take away his book, somebody. That's right. Who says what? Tea already made. Coffee published shortly. If anybody wants cocoa, I've got some, only you'll have to boil more water. I regret the absence of menu-cards, but as the entire feast is visible to the naked eye, our loss is immaterial. The offertory will be for the Church expenses fund. Biscuits, please.'

'I wish you'd given this tea after next Saturday, Alderman,' said Jim. Charteris was called the Alderman on account of his figure, which was inclined to stoutness, and his general capacity for consuming food.

'Never put off till tomorrow – Why?'

'I simply must keep fit for the mile. How's Welch to run, too, if he eats this sort of thing?' He pointed to the well-spread board.

'Yes, there's something in that,' said Tony. 'Thank goodness, my little entertainment's over. I think I *will* try one of those chocolate things. Thanks.'

'Welch is all right,' said Jackson. 'He could win the hundred and the quarter on sausage-rolls. But think of the times.'

'And there,' observed Charteris, 'there, my young friend, you have touched upon a sore subject. Before you came in I was administering a few wholesome words of censure to that miserable object on your right. What is a fifth of a second more or less that it should make a man insult his digestion as Welch does? You'll hardly credit it, but for the last three weeks or more I have been forced to look on a fellow-being refusing pastry and drinking beastly extracts of meat, all for the sake of winning a couple of races. It quite put me off my feed. Cake, please. Good robust slice. Thanks.'

'It's rather funny when you come to think of it,' said Tony. 'Welch lives on Bovril for a month, and then, just as he thinks he's going to score, a burglar with a sense of humour strolls into the Pav., carefully selects the only two cups he had a chance of winning, and so to bed.'

'Leaving Master J. G. Welch an awful example of what comes of training,' said Jim. 'Welch, you're a rotter.'

'It isn't *my* fault,' observed Welch, plaintively. 'You chaps seem to think I've committed some sort of crime, just because a man I didn't know from Adam has bagged a cup or two.'

'It looks to me,' said Charteris, 'as if Welch, thinking his chances of the quarter rather rocky, hired one of his low acquaintances to steal the cup for him.'

'Shouldn't wonder. Welch knows some jolly low characters in Stapleton.'

'Welch is a jolly low character himself,' said Tony, judicially. 'I wonder you associate with him, Alderman.'

'Stand *in loco parentis*. Aunt of his asked me to keep an eye on him. "Dear George is so wild," ' she said.

49

Before Welch could find words to refute this hideous slander, Tony cut in once more.

'The only reason he doesn't drink gin and play billiards at the "Blue Lion" is that gin makes him ill and his best break at pills is six, including two flukes.'

'As a matter of fact,' said Welch, changing the conversation with a jerk, 'I don't much care if the cups are stolen. One doesn't only run for the sake of the pot.'

Charteris groaned. 'Oh, well,' said he, 'if you're going to take the high moral standpoint, and descend to brazen platitudes like that, I give you up.'

'It's a rum thing about those pots,' said Welch, meditatively.

'Seems to me,' Jim rejoined, 'the rum thing is that a man who considers the Pav. a safe place to keep a lot of valuable prizes in should be allowed at large. Why couldn't they keep them in the Board Room as they used to?'

'Thought it 'ud save trouble, I suppose. Save them carting the things over to the Pav. on Sports Day,' hazarded Tony.

'Saved the burglar a lot of trouble, I should say,' observed Jackson, 'I could break into the Pav. myself in five minutes.'

'Good old Jackson,' said Charteris, 'have a shot tonight. I'll hold the watch. I'm doing a leader on the melancholy incident for next month's *Glow Worm*. It appears that Master Reginald Robinson, a member of Mr Merevale's celebrated boarding-establishment, was passing by the Pavilion at an early hour on the morning of the second of April – that's today – when his eye was attracted by an excavation or incision in one of the windows of that imposing edifice. His narrative appears on another page. Interviewed by a *Glow Worm* representative, Master Robinson, who is a fine, healthy, bronzed young Englishman of some thirteen summers, with a delightful, boyish flow of speech, not wholly free from a suspicion of cheek, gave it as his opinion that the outrage was the work of a burglar – a remarkable display of sagacity in one so young. A portrait of Master Robinson appears on another page.'

'Everything seems to appear on another page,' said Jim. 'Am I to do the portrait?'

'I think it would be best. You can never trust a photo to caricature a person enough. Your facial H.B.'s the thing.'

'Have you heard whether anything else was bagged besides the cups?' asked Welch.

'Not that I know of,' said Jim.

'Yes there was,' said Jackson. 'It further appears that that lunatic, Adamson, had left some money in the pocket of his blazer, which he had left in the Pav. overnight. On enquiry it was found that the money had also left.'

Adamson was in the same House as Jackson, and had talked of nothing else throughout the whole of lunch. He was an abnormally wealthy individual, however, and it was generally felt, though he himself thought otherwise, that he could afford to lose some of the surplus.

'How much?' asked Jim.

'Two pounds.'

At this Jim gave vent to the exclamation which Mr Barry Pain calls the Englishman's shortest prayer.

'My dear sir,' said Charteris. 'My very dear sir. We blush for you. Might I ask *why* you take the matter to heart so?'

Jim hesitated.

'Better have it out, Jim,' said Tony. 'These chaps'll keep it dark all right.' And Jim entered once again upon the recital of his doings on the previous night.

'So you see,' he concluded, 'this two pound business makes it all the worse.'

'I don't see why,' said Welch.

'Well, you see, money's a thing everybody wants, whereas cups wouldn't be any good to a fellow at school. So that I should find it much harder to prove that I didn't take the two pounds, than I should have done to prove that I didn't take the cups.'

'But there's no earthly need for you to prove anything,' said Tony. 'There's not the slightest chance of your being found out.'

'Exactly,' observed Charteris. 'We will certainly respect your incog. if you wish it. Wild horses shall draw no evidence from us. It is, of course, very distressing, but what is man after all? Are we not as the beasts that perish, and is not our little life rounded by a sleep? Indeed, yes. And now – with full chorus, please.

> ' "We-e take him from the city or the plough.
> We-e dress him up in uniform so ne-e-e-at." '

And at the third line some plaster came down from the ceiling, and Merevale came up, and the meeting dispersed without the customary cheers.

[7]

Barrett Explores

Barrett stood at the window of his study with his hands in his pockets, looking thoughtfully at the football field. Now and then he whistled. That was to show that he was very much at his ease. He whistled a popular melody of the day three times as slowly as its talented composer had originally intended it to be whistled, and in a strange minor key. Some people, when offended, invariably whistle in this manner, and these are just the people with whom, if you happen to share a study with them, it is rash to have differences of opinion. Reade, who was deep in a book – though not so deep as he would have liked the casual observer to fancy him to be – would have given much to stop Barrett's musical experiments. To ask him to stop in so many words was, of course, impossible. Offended dignity must draw the line somewhere. That is one of the curious results of a polite education. When two gentlemen of Hoxton or the Borough have a misunderstanding, they address one another with even more freedom than is their usual custom. When one member of a public school falls out with another member, his politeness in dealing with him becomes so Chesterfieldian, that one cannot help being afraid that he will sustain a strain from which he will never recover.

After a time the tension became too much for Barrett. He picked up his cap and left the room. Reade continued to be absorbed in his book.

It was a splendid day outside, warm for April, and with just that freshness in the air which gets into the blood and makes Spring the best time of the whole year. Barrett had not the æsthetic soul to any appreciable extent, but he did know a fine day when he saw one, and even he realized that a day like this was not to be wasted in pottering about the School grounds watching the 'under thirteen' hundred yards (trial heats) and the 'under fourteen' broad jump, or doing occasional exercises in the gymnasium. It was a day for going far afield and not returning till lock-up. He had an object, too. Everything seemed to shout 'eggs' at him, to remind him that he was an enthusiast on the subject and had a collection to which he ought to seize this excellent opportunity of adding. The only question was, where to go. The surrounding country was a Paradise for the naturalist who had no absurd scruples on the subject of trespassing. To the west, in the direction of Stapleton, the woods and hedges were thick with nests. But then, so they were to the east along the Badgwick road. He wavered, but a recollection that there was water in the Badgwick direction, and that he might with luck beard a water-wagtail in its lair, decided him. What is life without a water-wagtail's egg? A mere mockery. He turned east.

'Hullo, Barrett, where are you off to?' Grey, of Prater's House, intercepted him as he was passing.

'Going to see if I can get some eggs. Are you coming?'

Grey hesitated. He was a keen naturalist, too.

'No, I don't think I will, thanks. Got an uncle coming down to see me.'

'Well, cut off before he comes.'

'No, he'd be too sick. Besides,' he added, ingenuously, 'there's a possible tip. Don't want to miss that. I'm simply stony. Always am at end of term.'

'Oh,' said Barrett, realizing that further argument would be thrown away. 'Well, so long, then.'

'So long. Hope you have luck.'

'Thanks. I say.'

'Well?'

'Roll-call, you know. If you don't see me anywhere about, you might answer my name.'

'All right. And if you find anything decent, you might remember me. You know pretty well what I've got already.'

'Right, I will.'

'Magpie's what I want particularly. Where are you going, by the way?'

'Thought of having a shot at old Venner's woods. I'm after a water-wagtail myself. Ought to be one or two in the Dingle.'

'Heaps, probably. But I should advise you to look out, you know. Venner's awfully down on trespassing.'

'Yes, the bounder. But I don't think he'll get me. One gets the knack of keeping fairly quiet with practice.'

'He's got thousands of keepers.'

'Millions.'

'Dogs, too.'

'Dash his beastly dogs. I like dogs. Why are you such a croaker today, Grey?'

'Well, you know he's had two chaps sacked for going in his woods to my certain knowledge, Morton-Smith and Ainsworth. That's only since I've been at the Coll., too. Probably lots more before that.'

'Ainsworth was booked smoking there. That's why he was sacked. And Venner caught Morton-Smith himself simply staggering under dead rabbits. They sack any chap for poaching.'

'Well, I don't see how you're going to show you've not been poaching. Besides, it's miles out of bounds.'

'Grey,' said Barrett, severely, 'I'm surprised at you. Go away and meet your beastly uncle. Fancy talking about bounds at your time of life.'

'Well, don't forget me when you're hauling in the eggs.'

'Right you are. So long.'

Barrett proceeded on his way, his last difficulty safely removed. He could rely on Grey not to bungle that matter of roll-call. Grey had been there before.

A long white ribbon of dusty road separated St Austin's from the lodge gates of Badgwick Hall, the country seat of Sir Alfred Venner, M.P., also of 49A Lancaster Gate, London. Barrett walked rapidly for over half-an-hour before he came in sight of the great iron gates, flanked on the one side by a trim little lodge and green meadows, and on the other by woods of a darker green. Having got so far, he went on up the hill till at last he arrived at his destination. A small hedge, a sloping strip of green, and then the famous Dingle. I am loath to inflict any scenic rhapsodies on the reader, but really the Dingle deserves a line or two. It was the most beautiful spot in a country noted for its fine scenery. Dense woods were its chief feature. And by dense I mean well-supplied not only with trees (excellent things in themselves, but for the most part useless to the nest hunter), but also with a fascinating tangle of undergrowth, where every bush seemed to harbour eggs. All carefully preserved, too. That was the chief charm of the place. Since the sad episodes of Morton-Smith and Ainsworth, the School for the most part had looked askance at the Dingle. Once a select party from Dacre's House, headed by Babington, who always got himself into hot water when possible, had ventured into the forbidden land, and had returned hurriedly later in the afternoon with every sign of exhaustion, hinting breathlessly at keepers, dogs, and a pursuit that had lasted fifty minutes without a check. Since then no one had been daring enough to brave the terrors so carefully prepared for them by Milord Sir Venner and his minions, and the proud owner of the Dingle walked his woods in solitary state. Occasionally he would personally conduct some favoured guest thither and show him the wonders of the place. But this was not a frequent occurrence. On still-less frequent occasions, there were large shooting parties in the Dingle. But, as a rule, the word was 'Keepers only. No others need apply'.

A futile iron railing, some three feet in height, shut in the Dingle. Barrett jumped this lightly, and entered forthwith into Paradise. The place was full of nests. As Barrett took a step forward there was a sudden whirring of wings, and a bird rose from a bush close beside him. He went to inspect, and found a nest with seven eggs in it. Only a thrush, of course. As no one ever wants thrushes' eggs the world is over-stocked with them. Still, it gave promise of good things to come. Barrett pushed on through the bushes and the promise was fulfilled. He came upon another nest. Five eggs this time, of a variety he was unable with his moderate knowledge to classify. At any rate, he had not got them in his collection. Nor, to the best of his belief, had Grey. He took one for each of them.

Now this was all very well, thought Barrett, but what he had come for was the ovular deposit of the water-wagtail. Through the trees he could see the silver gleam of the brook at the foot of the hill. The woods sloped down to the very edge. Then came the brook, widening out here into the size of a small river. Then woods again all up the side of the opposite hill. Barrett hurried down the slope.

He had put on flannels for this emergency. He was prepared to wade, to swim if necessary. He hoped that it would not be necessary, for in April water is generally inclined to be chilly. Of keepers he had up till now seen no sign. Once he had heard the distant bark of a dog. It seemed to come from far across the stream and he had not troubled about it.

In the midst of the bushes on the bank stood a tree. It was not tall compared to the other trees of the Dingle, but standing alone as it did amongst the undergrowth it attracted the eye at once. Barrett, looking at it, saw something which made him forget water-wagtails for the moment. In a fork in one of the upper branches was a nest, an enormous nest, roughly constructed of sticks. It was a very jerry-built residence, evidently run up for the season by some prudent bird who knew by experience that no nest could last through the winter, and so had declined to waste his time in useless decorative work. But what bird was it? No doubt there are experts to whom a wood-pigeon's nest is something apart and distinct from the nest of the magpie, but to your unsophisticated amateur a nest that is large may be anything – rook's, magpie's, pigeon's, or great auk's. To such an one the only true test lies in the eggs. *Solvitur ambulando.* Barret laid the pill-boxes, containing the precious specimens he had found in the nest at the top of the hill, at the foot of the tree, and began to climb.

It was to be a day of surprises for him. When he had got half way up he found himself on a kind of ledge, which appeared to be a kind of junction at which the tree branched off into two parts. To the left was the nest, high up in its fork. To the right was another shoot. He realized at once, with keen disappointment, that it would be useless to go further. The branches were obviously not strong enough to bear his weight. He looked down, preparatory to commencing the descent, and to his astonishment found himself looking into a black cavern. In his eagerness to reach the nest he had not noticed before that the tree was hollow.

This made up for a great many things. His disappointment became less keen. Few things are more interesting than a hollow tree.

'Wonder how deep it goes down,' he said to himself. He broke off a piece of wood and dropped it down the hollow. It seemed to reach the ground uncommonly soon. He tried another piece. The sound of its fall came up to him almost simultaneously. Evidently the hole was not deep. He placed his hands on the edge, and let himself gently down into the darkness. His feet touched something solid almost immediately. As far as he could judge, the depth of the cavity was not more than five feet. Standing up at his full height he could just rest his chin on the edge.

He seemed to be standing on some sort of a floor, roughly made, but too regular to be the work of nature. Evidently someone had been here before. He bent down to make certain. There was more room to move about in than he suspected. A man sitting down would find it not uncomfortable.

He brushed his hand along the floor. Certainly it seemed to be constructed of boards. Then his hand hit something small and hard. He groped about until his fingers closed on it. It was – what was it? He could hardly make out for the moment. Suddenly, as he moved it, something inside it rattled. Now he knew what it was. It was the very thing he most needed, a box of matches.

The first match he struck promptly and naturally went out. No first match ever stays alight for more than three-fifths of a second. The second was more successful. The sudden light dazzled him for a moment. When his eyes had grown accustomed to it, the match went out. He lit a third, and this time he saw all round the little chamber.

'Great Scott,' he said, 'the place is a regular poultry shop.'

All round the sides were hung pheasants and partridges in various stages of maturity. Here and there the fur of a rabbit or a hare showed up amongst the feathers. Barrett hit on the solution of the problem directly. He had been shown a similar collection once in a tree on his father's land. The place was the headquarters of some poacher. Barrett was full of admiration for the ingenuity of the man in finding so safe a hiding-place.

He continued his search. In one angle of the tree was a piece of sacking. Barrett lifted it. He caught a glimpse of something bright, but before he could confirm the vague suspicion that flashed upon him, his match burnt down and lay smouldering on the floor. His hand trembled with excitement as he started to light another. It broke off in his hand. At last he succeeded. The light flashed up, and there beside the piece of sacking which had covered them were two cups. He recognized them instantly.

'Jove,' he gasped. 'The Sports pots! Now, how on earth –'

At this moment something happened which took his attention away from his discovery with painful suddenness. From beneath him came the muffled whine of a dog. He listened, holding his breath. No, he was not mistaken. The dog whined again, and broke into an excited bark. Somebody at the foot of the tree began to speak.

Barrett Ceases to Explore

'Fetchimout!' said the voice, all in one word.

'Nice cheery remark to make!' thought Barrett. 'He'll have to do a good bit of digging before he fetches *me* out. I'm a fixture for the present.'

There was a sound of scratching as if the dog, in his eagerness to oblige, were trying to uproot the tree. Barrett, realizing that unless the keeper took it into his head to climb, which was unlikely, he was as safe as if he had been in his study at Philpott's, chuckled within himself, and listened intently.

'What is it, then?' said the keeper. 'Good dog, at 'em! Fetch him out, Jack.'

Jack barked excitedly, and redoubled his efforts.

The sound of scratching proceeded.

'R-r-r-ats-s-s!' said the mendacious keeper. Jack had evidently paused for breath. Barrett began quite to sympathize with him. The thought that the animal was getting farther away from the object of his search with every ounce of earth he removed, tickled him hugely. He would have liked to have been able to see the operations, though. At present it was like listening to a conversation through a telephone. He could only guess at what was going on.

Then he heard somebody whistling 'The Lincolnshire Poacher', a strangely inappropriate air in the mouth of a keeper. The sound was too far away to be the work of Jack's owner, unless he had gone for a stroll since his last remark. No, it was another keeper. A new voice came up to him.

' 'Ullo, Ned, what's the dog after?'

'Thinks 'e's smelt a rabbit, seems to me.'

' 'Ain't a rabbit hole 'ere.'

'Thinks there is, anyhow. Look at the pore beast!'

They both laughed. Jack meanwhile, unaware that he was turning himself into an exhibition to make a keeper's holiday, dug assiduously.

'Come away, Jack,' said the first keeper at length. 'Ain't nothin' there. Ought to know that, clever dog like you.'

There was a sound as if he had pulled Jack bodily from his hole.

'Wait! 'Ere, Ned, what's that on the ground there?' Barrett gasped. His pill-boxes had been discovered. Surely they would put two and two together now, and climb the tree after him.

'Eggs. Two of 'em. 'Ow did they get 'ere, then?'

'It's one of them young devils from the School. Master says to me this morning, "Look out," 'e says, "Saunders, for them boys as come in 'ere after eggs, and frighten all the birds out of the dratted place. You keep your eyes open, Saunders," 'e says.'

'Well, if 'e's still in the woods, we'll 'ave 'im safe.'

'*If* he's still in the woods!' thought Barrett with a shiver.

After this there was silence. Barrett waited for what he thought was a quarter of an hour – it was really five minutes or less – then he peeped cautiously over the edge of his hiding-place. Yes, they had certainly gone, unless – horrible thought – they were waiting so close to the trunk of the tree as to be invisible from where he stood. He decided that the possibility must be risked. He was down on the ground in record time. Nothing happened. No hand shot out from its ambush to clutch him. He breathed more freely, and began to debate within himself which way to go. Up the hill it must be, of course, but should he go straight up, or to the left or to the right? He would have given much to know which way the keepers had gone, particularly he of the dog. They had separated, he knew. He began to reason the thing out. In the first place if they had separated, they must have gone different ways. It did not take him long to arrive at that conclusion. The odds, therefore, were that one had gone to the right up-stream, the other down-stream to the left. His knowledge of human nature told him that nobody would willingly walk up-hill if it was possible for him to walk on the flat. Therefore, assuming the two keepers to be human, they had gone along the valley. Therefore, his best plan would be to make straight for the top of the hill, as straight as he could steer, and risk it. Just as he was about to start, his eye caught the two pill-boxes, lying on the turf a few yards from where he had placed them.

'May as well take what I can get,' he thought. He placed them carefully in his pocket. As he did so a faint bark came to him on the breeze from down-stream. That must be friend Jack. He waited no longer, but dived into the bushes in the direction of the summit. He was congratulating himself on being out of danger – already he was more than half way up the hill – when suddenly he received a terrible shock. From the bushes to his left, not ten yards from where he stood, came the clear, sharp sound of a whistle. The sound was repeated, and this time an answer came from far out to his right. Before he could move another whistle joined in, again from the left, but farther off and higher up the hill than the first he had heard. He recalled what Grey had said about 'millions' of keepers. The expression, he thought, had understated the true facts, if anything. He remembered the case of Babington. It was a moment for action. No guile could save him now. It must be a stern chase for the rest of the distance. He drew a breath, and was off like an arrow. The noise he made was appalling. No one in the wood could help hearing it.

'Stop, there!' shouted someone. The voice came from behind, a fact which he noted almost automatically and rejoiced at. He had a start at any rate.

'Stop!' shouted the voice once again. The whistle blew like a steam siren, and once more the other two answered it. They were all behind him now. Surely a man of the public schools in flannels and gymnasium shoes, and trained to the last ounce for just such a sprint as this, could beat a handful of keepers in their leggings and heavy boots. Barrett raced on. Close behind him a crashing in the undergrowth and the sound of heavy breathing told him that keeper number one was doing his best. To left and right similar sounds were to be heard. But Barrett had placed these competitors out of the running at once. The race was between him and the man behind.

Fifty yards of difficult country, bushes which caught his clothes as if they were trying to stop him in the interests of law and order, branches which lashed him across the face, and rabbit-holes half hidden in the bracken, and still he kept his lead. He was increasing it. He must win now. The man behind was panting in deep gasps, for the pace had been warm and he was not in training. Barrett cast a glance over his shoulder, and as he looked the keeper's foot caught in a hole and he fell heavily. Barrett uttered a shout of triumph. Victory was his.

In front of him was a small hollow fringed with bushes. Collecting his strength he cleared these with a bound. Then another of the events of this eventful afternoon happened. Instead of the hard turf, his foot struck something soft, something which sat up suddenly with a yell. Barrett rolled down the slope and halfway up the other side like a shot rabbit. Dimly he recognized that he had jumped on to a human being. The figure did not wear the official velveteens. Therefore he had no business in the Dingle. And close behind thundered the keeper, now on his feet once more, dust on his clothes and wrath in his heart in equal proportions. 'Look out, man!' shouted Barrett, as the injured person rose to his feet. 'Run! Cut, quick! Keeper!' There was no time to say more. He ran. Another second and he was at the top, over the railing, and in the good, honest, public high-road again, safe. A hoarse shout of 'Got yer!' from below told a harrowing tale of capture. The stranger had fallen into the hands of the enemy. Very cautiously Barrett left the road and crept to the railing again. It was a rash thing to do, but curiosity overcame him. He had to see, or, if that was impossible, to hear what had happened.

For a moment the only sound to be heard was the gasping of the keeper. After a few seconds a rapidly nearing series of crashes announced the arrival of the man from the right flank of the pursuing forces, while almost simultaneously his colleague on the left came up.

Barrett could see nothing, but it was easy to understand what was going on. Keeper number one was exhibiting his prisoner. His narrative, punctuated with gasps, was told mostly in hoarse whispers, and Barrett missed most of it.

'Foot (gasp) rabbit-'ole.' More gasps. 'Up agen . . . minute . . . (indistinct mutterings) . . . and (triumphantly) COTCHED 'IM!'

Exclamations of approval from the other two. 'I assure you,' said another voice. The prisoner was having his say. 'I assure you that I was doing no harm whatever in this wood. I . . .'

'Better tell that tale to Sir Alfred,' cut in one of his captors.

' 'E'll learn yer,' said the keeper previously referred to as number one, vindictively. He was feeling shaken up with his run and his heavy fall, and his temper was proportionately short.

'I swear I've heard that voice before somewhere,' thought Barrett. 'Wonder if it's a Coll. chap.'

Keeper number one added something here, which was inaudible to Barrett.

'I tell you I'm not a poacher,' said the prisoner, indignantly. 'And I object to your language. I tell you I was lying here doing nothing and some fool or other came and jumped on me. I . . .'

The rest was inaudible. But Barrett had heard enough.

'I knew I'd heard that voice before. Plunkett, by Jove! Golly, what *is* the world coming to, when heads of Houses and School-prefects go on the poach! Fancy! Plunkett of all people, too! This is a knock-out, I'm hanged if it isn't.'

From below came the sound of movement. The keepers were going down the hill again. To Barrett's guilty conscience it seemed that they were coming up. He turned and fled.

The hedge separating Sir Alfred Venner's land from the road was not a high one, though the drop the other side was considerable. Barrett had not reckoned on this. He leapt the hedge, and staggered across the road. At the same moment a grey-clad cyclist, who was pedalling in a leisurely manner in the direction of the School, arrived at the spot. A collision seemed imminent, but the stranger in a perfectly composed manner, as if he had suddenly made up his mind to take a sharp turning, rode his machine up the bank, whence he fell with easy grace to the road, just in time to act as a cushion for Barrett. The two lay there in a tangled heap. Barrett was the first to rise.

[9]

Enter the Sleuth-hound

'I'm awfully sorry,' he said, disentangling himself carefully from the heap. 'I hope you're not hurt.'

The man did not reply for a moment. He appeared to be laying the question before himself as an impartial judge, as who should say: 'Now tell me candidly, *are* you hurt? Speak freely and without bias.'

'No,' he said at last, feeling his left leg as if he were not absolutely easy in his mind about that, 'no, not hurt, thank you. Not much, that is,' he added with the air of one who thinks it best to qualify too positive a statement. 'Left leg. Shin. Slight bruise. Nothing to signify.'

'It was a rotten thing to do, jumping over into the road like that,' said Barrett. 'Didn't remember there'd be such a big drop.'

'My fault in a way,' said the man. 'Riding wrong side of road. Out for a run?'

'More or less.'

'Excellent thing.'

'Yes.'

It occurred to Barrett that it was only due to the man on whom he had been rolling to tell him the true facts of the case. Besides, it might do something towards removing the impression which must, he felt, be forming in the stranger's mind that he was mad.

'You see,' he said, in a burst of confidence, 'it was rather a close thing. There were some keepers after me.'

'Ah!' said the man. 'Thought so. Trespassing?'

'Yes.'

'Ah. Keepers don't like trespassers. Curious thing – don't know if it ever occurred to you – if there were no trespassers, there would be no need for keepers. To their interest, then, to encourage trespassers. But do they?'

Barrett admitted that they did not very conspicuously.

'No. Same with all professions. Not poaching, I suppose?'

'Rather not. I was after eggs. By Jove, that reminds me.' He felt in

63

his pocket for the pill-boxes. Could they have survived the stormy times through which they had been passing? He heaved a sigh of relief as he saw that the eggs were uninjured. He was so intent on examining them that he missed the stranger's next remark.

'Sorry. What? I didn't hear.'

'Asked if I was going right for St Austin's School.'

'College!' said Barrett with a convulsive shudder. The most deadly error mortal man can make, with the exception of calling a school a college, is to call a college a school.

'College!' said the man. 'Is this the road?'

'Yes. You can't miss it. I'm going there myself. It's only about a mile.'

'Ah,' said the man, with a touch of satisfaction in his voice. 'Going there yourself, are you? Perhaps you're one of the scholars?'

'Not much,' said Barrett, 'ask our form-beak if I'm a scholar. Oh. I see. Yes, I'm there all right.'

Barrett was a little puzzled as to how to class his companion. No old public school man would talk of scholars. And yet he was emphatically not a bargee. Barrett set him down as a sort of superior tourist, a Henry as opposed to an 'Arry.

'Been bit of a disturbance there, hasn't there? Cricket pavilion. Cups.'

'Rather. But how on earth –'

'How on earth did I get to hear of it, you were going to say. Well, no need to conceal anything. Fact is, down here to look into the matter. Detective. Name, Roberts, Scotland Yard. Now we know each other, and if you can tell me one or two things about this burglary, it would be a great help to me, and I should be very much obliged.'

Barrett had heard that a detective was coming down to look into the affair of the cups. His position was rather a difficult one. In a sense it was simple enough. He had found the cups. He could (keepers permitting) go and fetch them now, and there would – No. There would *not* be an end of the matter. It would be very pleasant, exceedingly pleasant, to go to the Headmaster and the detective, and present the cups to them with a 'Bless you, my children' air. The Headmaster would say, 'Barrett, you're a marvel. How can I thank you sufficiently?' while the detective would observe that he had been in the profession over twenty years, but never had he seen so remarkable an exhibition of sagacity and acumen as this. That, at least, was what ought to take place. But Barrett's experience of life, short as it was, had taught him the difference between the ideal and the real. The real, he suspected, would in this case be painful. Certain facts would come to light. When had he found the cups? About four in the afternoon? Oh. Roll-call took place at four in the afternoon. How came it that he was not at roll-call? Furthermore, how came it that he was marked on the list as having answered his name at that ceremony? Where had he found the cups? In a hollow tree? Just so. Where was the hollow tree? In Sir Alfred Venner's woods. Did he know that Sir Alfred Venner's woods were out of bounds? Did he know that, in consequence of complaints from Sir Alfred Venner, Sir Alfred Venner's woods were more out of bounds than any other out of bounds woods in the entire county that did *not* belong to Sir Alfred Venner? He did? Ah! No, the word for his guidance in this emergency, he felt instinctively, was 'mum'. Time might provide him with a solution. He might, for instance, abstract the cups secretly from their resting-place, place them in the middle of the football field, and find them there dramatically after morning school. Or he might reveal his secret from the carriage window as his train moved out of the station on the first day of the holidays. There was certain to be some way out of the difficulty. But for the present, silence.

He answered his companion's questions freely, however. Of the actual burglary he knew no more than any other member of the School, considerably less, indeed, than Jim Thomson, of Merevale's, at present staggering under the weight of a secret even more gigantic than Barrett's own. In return for his information he extracted sundry reminiscences. The scar on the detective's cheekbone, barely visible now, was the mark of a bullet, which a certain burglar, named, singularly enough, Roberts, had fired at him from a distance of five yards. The gentleman in question, who, the detective hastened to inform Barrett, was no relation of his, though owning the same name, happened to be a poor marksman and only scored a bad outer, assuming the detective's face to have been the bull. He also turned up his cuff to show a larger scar. This was another testimonial from the burglar world. A Kensington practitioner had had the bad taste to bite off a piece of that part of the detective. In short, Barrett enlarged his knowledge of the seamy side of things considerably in the mile of road which had to be traversed before St Austin's appeared in sight. The two parted at the big gates, Barrett going in the direction of Philpott's, the detective wheeling his machine towards the porter's lodge.

Barrett's condition when he turned in at Philpott's door was critical. He was so inflated with news that any attempt to keep it in might have serious results. Certainly he could not sleep that night in such a bomb-like state.

It was thus that he broke in upon Reade. Reade had passed an absurdly useless afternoon. He had not stirred from the study. For all that it would have mattered to him, it might have been raining hard the whole afternoon, instead of being, as it had been, the finest afternoon of the whole term. In a word, and not to put too fine a point on the matter, he had been frousting, and consequently was feeling dull and sleepy, and generally under-vitalized and futile. Barrett entered the study with a rush, and was carried away by excitement to such an extent that he addressed Reade as if the deadly feud between them not only did not exist, but never had existed.

'I say, Reade. Heave that beastly book away. My aunt, I have had an afternoon of it.'

'Oh?' said Reade, politely, 'where did you go?'

'After eggs in the Dingle.'

Reade was fairly startled out of his dignified reserve. For the first time since they had had their little difference, he addressed Barrett in a sensible manner.

'You idiot!' he said.

'Don't see it. The Dingle's just the place to spend a happy day. Like Rosherville. Jove, it's worth going there. You should see the birds. Place is black with 'em.'

'How about keepers? See any?'

'Did I not! Three of them chased me like good 'uns all over the place.'

'You got away all right, though.'

'Only just. I say, do you know what happened? You know that rotter Plunkett. Used to be a day boy. Head of Ward's now. Wears specs.'

'Yes?'

'Well, just as I was almost out of the wood, I jumped a bush and landed right on top of him. The man was asleep or something. Fancy choosing the Dingle of all places to sleep in, where you can't go a couple of yards without running into a keeper! He hadn't even the sense to run. I yelled to him to look out, and then I hooked it myself. And then the nearest keeper, who'd just come down a buster over a rabbit-hole, sailed in and had him. I couldn't do anything, of course.'

'Jove, there'll be a fair-sized row about this. The Old Man's on to trespassing like tar. I say, think Plunkett'll say anything about you being there too?'

'Shouldn't think so. For one thing I don't think he recognized me. Probably doesn't know me by sight, and he was fast asleep, too. No, I fancy I'm all right.'

'Well, it was a jolly narrow shave. Anything else happen?'

'Anything else! Just a bit. That's to say, no, nothing much else. No.'

'Now then,' said Reade, briskly. 'None of your beastly mysteries. Out with it.'

'Look here, swear you'll keep it dark?'

'Of course I will.'

'On your word of honour?'

'If you think –' began Reade in an offended voice.

'No, it's all right. Don't get shirty. The thing is, though, it's so frightfully important to keep it dark.'

'Well? Buck up.'

'Well, you needn't believe me, of course, but I've found the pots.'

Reade gasped.

'What!' he cried. 'The pot for the quarter?'

'And the one for the hundred yards. Both of them. It's a fact.'

'But where? How? What have you done with them?'

Barrett unfolded his tale concisely.

'You see,' he concluded, 'what a hole I'm in. I can't tell the Old Man anything about it, or I get booked for cutting roll-call, and going out of bounds. And then, while I'm waiting and wondering what to do, and all that, the thief, whoever he is, will most likely go off with the pots. What do you think I ought to do?'

Reade perpended.

'Well,' he said, 'all you can do is to lie low and trust to luck, as far as I can see. Besides, there's one consolation. This Plunkett business'll make every keeper in the Dingle twice as keen after trespassers. So the pot man won't get a chance of getting the things away.'

'Yes, there's something in that,' admitted Barrett.

'It's all you can do,' said Reade.

'Yes. Unless I wrote an anonymous letter to the Old Man explaining things. How would that do?'

'Do for you, probably. Anonymous letters always get traced to the person who wrote them. Or pretty nearly always. No, you simply lie low.'

'Right,' said Barrett, 'I will.'

The process of concealing one's superior knowledge is very irritating. So irritating, indeed, that very few people do it. Barrett, however, was obliged to by necessity. He had a good chance of displaying his abilities in that direction when he met Grey the next morning.

'Hullo,' said Grey, 'have a good time yesterday?'

'Not bad. I've got an egg for you.'

'Good man. What sort?'

'Hanged if I know. I know you haven't got it, though.'

'Thanks awfully. See anything of the million keepers?'

'Heard them oftener than I saw them.'

'They didn't book you?'

'Rather fancy one of them saw me, but I got away all right.'

'Find the place pretty lively?'

'Pretty fair.'

'Stay there long?'

'Not very.'

'No. Thought you wouldn't. What do you say to a small ice? There's time before school.'

'Thanks. Are you flush?'

'Flush isn't the word for it. I'm a plutocrat.'

'Uncle came out fairly strong then?'

'Rather. To the tune of one sovereign, cash. He's a jolly good sort, my uncle.'

'So it seems,' said Barrett.

The meeting then adjourned to the School shop, Barrett enjoying his ice all the more for the thought that his secret still was a secret. A thing which it would in all probability have ceased to be, had he been rash enough to confide it to K. St H. Grey, who, whatever his other merits, was very far from being the safest sort of confidant. His usual practice was to speak first, and to think, if at all, afterwards.

10

Mr Thompson Investigates

The Pavilion burglary was discussed in other places besides Charteris' study. In the Masters' Common Room the matter came in for its full share of comment. The masters were, as at most schools, divided into the athletic and non-athletic, and it was for the former class that the matter possessed most interest. If it had been that apple of the College Library's eye, the original MS. of St Austin's private diary, or even that lesser treasure, the black-letter Eucalyptides, that had disappeared, the elder portion of the staff would have had a great deal to say upon the subject. But, apart from the excitement caused by the strangeness of such an occurrence, the theft of a couple of Sports prizes had little interest for them.

On the border-line between these two castes came Mr Thompson, the Master of the Sixth Form, spelt with a *p* and no relation to the genial James or the amiable Allen, with the former of whom, indeed, he was on very indifferent terms of friendship. Mr Thompson, though an excellent classic, had no knowledge of the inwardness of the Human Boy. He expected every member of his form not only to be earnest – which very few members of a Sixth Form are – but also to communicate his innermost thoughts to him. His aim was to be their confidant, the wise friend to whom they were to bring their troubles and come for advice. He was, in fact, poor man, the good young master. Now, it is generally the case at school that troubles are things to be worried through alone, and any attempt at interference is usually resented. Mr Thompson had asked Jim to tea, and, while in the very act of passing him the muffins, had embarked on a sort of unofficial sermon, winding up by inviting confidences. Jim had naturally been first flippant, and then rude, and relations had been strained ever since.

'It must have been a professional,' alleged Perkins, the master of the Upper Fourth. 'If it hadn't been for the fact of the money having been stolen as well as the cups, I should have put it down to one of our fellows.'

'My dear Perkins,' expostulated Merevale.

'My dear Merevale, my entire form is capable of any crime except the theft of money. A boy might have taken the cups for a joke, or just for the excitement of the thing, meaning to return them in time for the Sports. But the two pounds knocks that on the head. It must have been a professional.'

'I always said that the Pavilion was a very unsafe place in which to keep anything of value,' said Mr Thompson.

'You were profoundly right, Thompson,' replied Perkins. 'You deserve a diploma.'

'This business is rather in your line, Thompson,' said Merevale. 'You must bring your powers to bear on the subject, and scent out the criminal.'

Mr Thompson took a keen pride in his powers of observation. He would frequently observe, like the lamented Sherlock Holmes, the vital necessity of taking notice of trifles. The daily life of a Sixth Form master at a big public school does not afford much scope for the practice of the detective art, but Mr Thompson had once detected a piece of cribbing, when correcting some Latin proses for the master of the Lower Third, solely by the exercise of his powers of observation, and he had never forgotten it. He burned to add another scalp to his collection, and this Pavilion burglary seemed peculiarly suited to his talents. He had given the matter his attention, and, as far as he could see, everything pointed to the fact that skilled hands had been at work.

From eleven until half-past twelve that day, the Sixth were doing an unseen examination under the eye of the Headmaster, and Mr Thompson was consequently off duty. He took advantage of this to stroll down to the Pavilion and make a personal inspection of the first room, from which what were left of the prizes had long been removed to a place of safety.

He was making his way to the place where the ground-man was usually to be found, with a view to obtaining the keys, when he noticed that the door was already open, and on going thither he came upon Biffen, the ground-man, in earnest conversation with a stranger.

'Morning, sir,' said the ground-man. He was on speaking terms with most of the masters and all the boys. Then, to his companion, 'This is Mr Thompson, one of our masters.'

'Morning, sir,' said the latter. 'Weather keeps up. I am Inspector Roberts, Scotland Yard. But I think we're in for rain soon. Yes. 'Fraid so. Been asked to look into this business, Mr Thompson. Queer business.'

'Very. Might I ask – I am very interested in this kind of thing – whether you have arrived at any conclusions yet?'

The detective eyed him thoughtfully, as if he were hunting for the answer to a riddle.

'No. Not yet. Nothing definite.'

'I presume you take it for granted it was the work of a professional burglar.'

'No. No. Take nothing for granted. Great mistake. Prejudices one way or other great mistake. But, I think, yes, I think it was probably – almost certainly – *not* done by a professional.'

Mr Thompson looked rather blank at this. It shook his confidence in his powers of deduction.

'But,' he expostulated. 'Surely no one but a practised burglar would have taken a pane of glass out so – ah – neatly?'

Inspector Roberts rubbed a finger thoughtfully round the place where the glass had been. Then he withdrew it, and showed a small cut from which the blood was beginning to drip.

'Do you notice anything peculiar about that cut?' he enquired.

Mr Thompson did not. Nor did the ground-man.

'Look carefully. Now do you see? No? Well, it's not a clean cut. Ragged. Very ragged. Now if a professional had cut that pane out he wouldn't have left it jagged like that. No. He would have used a diamond. Done the job neatly.'

This destroyed another of Mr Thompson's premises. He had taken it for granted that a diamond had been used.

'Oh!' he said, 'was that pane not cut by a diamond; what did the burglar use, then?'

'No. No diamond. Diamond would have left smooth surface. Smooth as a razor edge. This is like a saw. Amateurish work. Can't say for certain, but probably done with a chisel.'

'With a chisel? Surely not.'

'Yes. Probably with a chisel. Probably the man knocked the pane out with one blow, then removed all the glass so as to make it look like the work of an old hand. Very good idea, but amateurish. I am told that three cups have been taken. Could you tell me how long they had been in the Pavilion?'

Mr Thompson considered.

'Well,' he said. 'Of course it's difficult to remember exactly, but I think they were placed there soon after one o'clock the day before yesterday.'

'Ah! And the robbery took place yesterday in the early morning, or the night before?'

'Yes.'

'Is the Pavilion the usual place to keep the prizes for the Sports?'

'No, it is not. They were only put there temporarily. The Board Room, where they are usually kept, and which is in the main buildings of the School, happened to be needed until the next day. Most of us were very much against leaving them in the Pavilion, but it was thought that no harm could come to them if they were removed next day.'

'But they were removed that night, which made a great difference,' said Mr Roberts, chuckling at his mild joke. 'I see. Then I suppose none outside the School knew that they were not in their proper place?'

'I imagine not.'

'Just so. Knocks the idea of professional work on the head. None of the regular trade can have known this room held so much silver for one night. No regular would look twice at a cricket pavilion under ordinary circumstances. Therefore, it must have been somebody who had something to do with the School. One of the boys, perhaps.'

'Really, I do not think that probable.'

'You can't tell. Never does to form hasty conclusions. Boy might have done it for many reasons. Some boys would have done it for the sake of the excitement. That, perhaps, is the least possible explanation. But you get boy kleptomaniacs just as much in proportion as grown-up kleptomaniacs. I knew a man. Had a son. Couldn't keep him away from anything valuable. Had to take him away in a hurry from three schools, good schools, too.'

'Really? What became of him? He did not come to us, I suppose?'

'No. Somebody advised the father to send him to one of those North-Country schools where they flog. Great success. Stole some money. Got flogged, instead of expelled. Did it again with same result. Gradually got tired of it. Reformed character now . . . I don't say it is a boy, mind you. Most probably not. Only say it may be.'

All the while he was talking, his eyes were moving restlessly round the room. He came to the window through which Jim had effected his entrance, and paused before the broken pane.

'I suppose he tried that window first, before going round to the other?' hazarded Mr Thompson.

'Yes. Most probably. Broke it, and then remembered that anyone at the windows of the boarding Houses might see him, so left his job half done, and shifted his point of action. I think so. Yes.'

He moved on again till he came to the other window. Then he gave vent to an excited exclamation, and picked up a piece of caked mud from the sill as carefully as if it were some fragile treasure.

'Now, see this,' he said. 'This was wet when the robbery was done. The man brought it in with him. On his boot. Left it on the sill as he climbed in. Got out in a hurry, startled by something – you can see he was startled and left in a hurry from the different values of the cups he took – and as he was going, put his hand on this. Left a clear impression. Good as plaster of Paris very nearly.'

Mr Thompson looked at the piece of mud, and there, sure enough, was the distinct imprint of the palm of a hand. He could see the larger of the lines quite clearly, and under a magnifying-glass there was no doubt that more could be revealed.

He drew in a long breath of satisfaction and excitement.

'Yes,' said the detective. 'That piece of mud couldn't prove anything by itself, but bring it up at the end of a long string of evidence, and if it fits your man, it convicts him as much as a snap-shot photograph would. Morning, sir. I must be going.' And he retired, carrying the piece of mud in his hand, leaving Mr Thompson in the full grip of the detective-fever, hunting with might and main for more clues.

After some time, however, he was reluctantly compelled to give up the search, for the bell rang for dinner, and he always lunched, as did many of the masters, in the Great Hall. During the course of the meal he exercised his brains without pause in the effort to discover a fitting suspect. Did he know of any victim of kleptomania in the School? No, he was sorry to say he did not. Was anybody in urgent need of money? He could not say. Very probably yes, but he had no means of knowing.

After lunch he went back to the Common Room. There was a letter lying on the table. He picked it up. It was addressed to 'J. Thomson, St Austin's.' Now Mr Thompson's Christian name was John. He did not notice the omission of the *p* until he had opened the envelope and caught a glimpse of the contents. The letter was so short that only a glimpse was needed, and it was not till he had read the whole that he realized that it was somebody else's letter that he had opened.

This was the letter:

'Dear Jim – Frantic haste. Can you let me have that two pounds directly you come back? Beg, borrow, or steal it. I simply must have it. – Yours ever,

Allen.'

11

The Sports

Sports weather at St Austin's was as a rule a quaint but unpleasant solution of mud, hail, and iced rain. These were taken as a matter of course, and the School counted it as something gained when they were spared the usual cutting east wind.

This year, however, occurred that invaluable exception which is so useful in proving rules. There was no gale, only a gentle breeze. The sun was positively shining, and there was a general freshness in the air which would have made a cripple cast away his crutches, and, after backing himself heavily both ways, enter for the Strangers' Hundred Yards.

Jim had wandered off alone. He was feeling too nervous at the thought of the coming mile and all it meant to him to move in society for the present. Charteris, Welch, and Tony, going out shortly before lunch to inspect the track, found him already on the spot, and in a very low state of mind.

'Hullo, you chaps,' he said dejectedly, as they came up.

'Hullo.'

'Our James is preoccupied,' said Charteris. 'Why this jaundiced air, Jim? Look at our other Thompson over there.'

'Our other Thompson' was at that moment engaged in conversation with the Headmaster at the opposite side of the field.

'Look at him,' said Charteris, 'prattling away as merrily as a little che-ild to the Old Man. You should take a lesson from him.'

'Look here, I say,' said Jim, after a pause, 'I believe there's something jolly queer up between Thompson and the Old Man, and I believe it's about me.'

'What on earth makes you think that?' asked Welch.

'It's his evil conscience,' said Charteris. 'No one who hadn't committed the awful crime that Jim has, could pay the least attention to anything Thompson said. What does our friend Thucydides remark on the subject? –

' "*Conscia mens recti, nec si sinit esse dolorem
Sed revocare gradum.*"

Very well then.'

'But why should you think anything's up?' asked Tony.

'Perhaps nothing is, but it's jolly fishy. You see Thompson and the Old 'Un pacing along there? Well, they've been going like that for about twenty minutes. I've been watching them.'

'But you can't tell they're talking about you, you rotter,' said Tony. 'For all you know they may be discussing the exams.'

'Or why the sea is boiling hot, and whether pigs have wings,' put in Charteris.

'Or anything,' added Welch profoundly.

'Well, all I know is that Thompson's been doing all the talking, and the Old Man's been getting more and more riled.'

'Probably Thompson's been demanding a rise of screw or asking for a small loan or something,' said Charteris. 'How long have you been watching them?'

'About twenty minutes.'

'From here?'

'Yes.'

'Why didn't you go and join them? There's nothing like tact. If you were to go and ask the Old Man why the whale wailed or something after that style it 'ud buck him up like a tonic. I wish you would. And then you could tell him to tell you all about it and see if you couldn't do something to smooth the wrinkles from his careworn brow and let the sunshine of happiness into his heart. He'd like it awfully.'

'Would he!' said Jim grimly. 'Well, I got the chance just now. Thompson said something to him, and he spun round, saw me, and shouted "Thomson". I went up and capped him, and he was starting to say something when he seemed to change his mind, and instead of confessing everything, he took me by the arm, and said, "No, no, Thomson. Go away. It's nothing. I will send for you later." '

'And did you knock him down?' asked Charteris.

'What happened?' said Welch.

'He gave me a shove as if he were putting the weight, and said again, "It's no matter. Go away, Thomson, now." So I went.'

'And you've kept an eye on him ever since?' said Charteris. 'Didn't he seem at all restive?'

'I don't think he noticed me. Thompson had the floor and he was pretty well full up listening to him.'

'I suppose you don't know what it's all about?' asked Tony.

'Must be this Pavilion business.'

'Now, my dear, sweet cherub,' said Charteris, 'don't you go and make an utter idiot of yourself and think you're found out and all that sort of thing. Even if they suspect you they've got to prove it. There's no sense in your giving them a helping hand in the business. What you've got to do is to look normal. Don't overdo it or you'll look like a swashbuckler, and that'll be worse than underdoing it. Can't you make yourself look less like a convicted forger? For my sake?'

'You really do look a bit off it,' said Welch critically. 'As if you were sickening for the flu., or something. Doesn't he, Tony?'

'Rather!' said that expert in symptoms. 'You simply must buck up, Jim, or Drake'll walk away from you.'

'It's disappointing,' said Charteris, 'to find a chap who can crack a crib as neatly as you can doubling up like this. Think how Charles Peace would have behaved under the circs. Don't disgrace him, poor man.'

'Besides,' said Jim, with an attempt at optimism, 'it isn't as if I'd actually done anything, is it?'

'Just so,' said Charteris, 'that's what I've been trying to get you to see all along. Keep that fact steadily before you, and you'll be all right.'

'There goes the lunch-bell,' said Tony. 'You can always tell Merevale's bell in a crowd. William rings it as if he was doing it for his health.'

William, also known in criminal circles as the Moke, was the gentleman who served the House – in a perpetual grin and a suit of livery four sizes too large for him – as a sort of butler.

'He's an artist,' agreed Charteris, as he listened to the performance. 'Does it as if he enjoyed it, doesn't he? Well, if we don't want to spoil Merevale's appetite by coming in at half-time, we might be moving.' They moved accordingly.

The Sports were to begin at two o'clock with a series of hundred-yards races, which commenced with the 'under twelve' (Cameron of Prater's a warm man for this, said those who had means of knowing), and culminated at about a quarter past with the open event, for which Welch was a certainty. By a quarter to the hour the places round the ropes were filled, and more visitors were constantly streaming in at the two entrances to the School grounds, while in the centre of the ring the band of the local police force – the military being unavailable owing to exigencies of distance – were seating themselves with the grim determination of those who know that they are going to play the soldiers' chorus out of *Faust*. The band at the Sports had played the soldiers' chorus out of *Faust* every year for decades past, and will in all probability play it for decades to come.

The Sports at St Austin's were always looked forward to by everyone with the keenest interest, and when the day arrived, were as regularly voted slow. In all school sports there are too many foregone conclusions. In the present instance everybody knew, and none better than the competitors themselves, that Welch would win the quarter and hundred. The high jump was an equal certainty for a boy named Reece in Halliday's House. Jackson, unless he were quite out of form, would win the long jump, and the majority of the other events had already been decided. The gem of the afternoon would be the mile, for not even the shrewdest judge of form could say whether Jim would beat Drake, or Drake Jim. Both had done equally good times in practice, and both were known to be in the best of training. The adherents of Jim pointed to the fact that he had won the half off Drake – by a narrow margin, true, but still he had won it. The other side argued that a half-mile is no criterion for a mile, and that if Drake had timed his sprint better he would probably have won, for he had finished up far more strongly than his opponent. And so on the subject of the mile, public opinion was for once divided.

The field was nearly full by this time. The only clear space outside the ropes was where the Headmaster stood to greet and talk about the weather to such parents and guardians and other celebrities as might pass. This habit of his did not greatly affect the unattached members of the School, those whose parents lived in distant parts of the world and were not present on Sports Day, but to St Jones Brown (for instance) of the Lower Third, towing Mr Brown, senior, round the ring, it was a nervous ordeal to have to stand by while his father and the Head exchanged polite commonplaces. He could not help feeling that there was *just a chance* (horrible thought) that the Head, searching for something to say, might seize upon that little matter of broken bounds or shaky examination papers as a subject for discussion. He was generally obliged, when the interview was over, to conduct his parent to the shop by way of pulling his system together again, the latter, of course, paying.

At intervals round the ropes Old Austinian number one was meeting Old Austinian number two (whom he emphatically detested, and had hoped to avoid), and was conversing with him in a nervous manner, the clearness of his replies being greatly handicapped by a feeling, which grew with the minutes, that he would never be able to get rid of him and go in search of Old Austinian number three, his bosom friend.

At other intervals, present Austinians of tender years were manoeuvring half-companies of sisters, aunts, and mothers, and trying without much success to pretend that they did not belong to them. A pretence which came down heavily when one of the aunts addressed them as 'Willie' or 'Phil', and wanted to know audibly if 'that boy who had just passed' (*the* one person in the School whom they happened to hate and despise) was their best friend. It was a little trying, too, to have to explain in the middle of a crowd that the reason why you were not running in 'that race' (the 'under thirteen' hundred, by Jove, which ought to have been a gift to you, only, etc.) was because you had been ignominiously knocked out in the trial heats.

In short, the afternoon wore on. Welch won the hundred by two yards and the quarter by twenty, and the other events fell in nearly every case to the favourite. The hurdles created something of a surprise – Jackson, who ought to have won, coming down over the last hurdle but two, thereby enabling Dallas to pull off an unexpected victory by a couple of yards. Vaughan's enthusiastic watch made the time a little under sixteen seconds, but the official timekeeper had other views. There were no instances of the timid new boy, at whom previously the world had scoffed, walking away with the most important race of the day.

And then the spectators were roused from a state of coma by the sound of the bell ringing for the mile. Old Austinian number one gratefully seized the opportunity to escape from Old Austinian number two, and lose himself in the crowd. Young Pounceby-Green with equal gratitude left his father talking to the Head, and shot off without ceremony to get a good place at the ropes. In fact, there was a general stir of anticipation, and all round the ring paterfamilias was asking his son and heir which was Drake and which Thomson, and settling his glasses more firmly on the bridge of his nose.

The staff of *The Glow Worm* conducted Jim to the starting-place, and did their best to relieve his obvious nervousness with light conversation.

'Eh, old chap?' said Jim. He had been saying 'Eh?' to everything throughout the afternoon.

'I said, "Is my hat on straight, and does it suit the colour of my eyes?" ' said Charteris.

'Oh, yes. Yes, rather. Ripping,' in a far-off voice.

'And have you a theory of the Universe?'

'Eh, old chap?'

'I said, "Did you want your legs rubbed before you start?" I believe it's an excellent specific for the gout.'

'Gout? What? No, I don't think so, thanks.'

'And you'll write to us sometimes, Jim, and give my love to little Henry, and *always* wear flannel next your skin, my dear boy?' said Charteris.

This seemed to strike even Jim as irrelevant.

'Do shut up for goodness sake, Alderman,' he said irritably. 'Why can't you go and rag somebody else?'

'My place is by your side. Go, my son, or else they'll be starting without you. Give us your blazer. And take my tip, the tip of an old runner, and don't pocket your opponent's ball in your own twenty-five. And come back victorious, or on the shields of your soldiers. All right, sir (to the starter), he's just making his will. Good-bye Jim. Buck up, or I'll lynch you after the race.'

Jim answered by muffling him in his blazer, and walking to the line. There were six competitors in all, each of whom owned a name ranking alphabetically higher than Thomson. Jim, therefore, had the outside berth. Drake had the one next to the inside, which fell to Adamson, the victim of the lost two pounds episode.

Both Drake and Jim got off well at the sound of the pistol, and the pace was warm from the start. Jim evidently had his eye on the inside berth, and, after half a lap had been completed, he got it, Drake falling back. Jim continued to make the running, and led at the end of the first lap by about five yards. Then came Adamson, followed by a batch of three, and finally Drake, taking things exceedingly coolly, a couple of yards behind them. The distance separating him from Jim was little over a dozen yards. A roar of applause greeted the runners as they started on the second lap, and it was significant that while Jim's supporters shouted, 'Well run', those of Drake were fain to substitute advice for approval, and cry 'Go it'. Drake, however, had not the least intention of 'going it' in the generally accepted meaning of the phrase. A yard or two to the rear meant nothing in the first lap, and he was running quite well enough to satisfy himself, with a nice, springy stride, which he hoped would begin to tell soon.

With the end of the second lap the real business of the race began, for the survival of the fittest had resulted in eliminations and changes of order. Jim still led, but now by only eight or nine yards. Drake had come up to second, and Adamson had dropped to a bad third. Two of the runners had given the race up, and retired, and the last man was a long way behind, and, to all practical purposes, out of the running. There were only three laps, and, as the last lap began, the pace quickened, fast as it had been before. Jim was exerting every particle of his strength. He was not a runner who depended overmuch on his final dash. He hoped to gain so much ground before Drake made his sprint as to neutralize it when it came. Adamson he did not fear.

And now they were in the last two hundred yards, Jim by this time some thirty yards ahead, but in great straits. Drake had quickened his pace, and gained slowly on him. As they rounded the corner and came into the straight, the cheers were redoubled. It was a great race. Then, fifty yards from the tape, Drake began his final sprint. If he had saved himself before, he made up for it now. The gap dwindled and dwindled. Neither could improve his pace. It was a question whether there was enough of the race left for Drake to catch his man, or whether he had once more left his sprint till too late. Jim could hear the roars of the spectators, and the frenzied appeals of Merevale's House to him to sprint, but he was already doing his utmost. Everything seemed black to him, a black, surging mist, and in its centre a thin white line, the tape. Could he reach it before Drake? Or would he collapse before he reached it? There were only five more yards to go now, and still he led. Four. Three. Two. Then something white swept past him on the right, the white line quivered, snapped, and vanished, and he pitched blindly forward on to the turf at the track-side. Drake had won by a foot.

[12]

An Interesting Interview

For the rest of the afternoon Jim had a wretched time. To be beaten
after such a race by a foot, and to be beaten by a foot when victory
would have cut the Gordian knot of his difficulties once and for all,
was enough to embitter anybody's existence. He found it hard to
accept the well-meant condolences of casual acquaintances, and still
harder to do the right thing and congratulate Drake on his victory, a
refinement of self-torture which is by custom expected of the van-
quished in every branch of work or sport. But he managed it somehow,
and he also managed to appear reasonably gratified when he went up
to take his prize for the half-mile. Tony and the others, who knew
what his defeat meant to him, kept out of his way, for which he was
grateful. After lock-up, however, it was a different matter, but by that
time he was more ready for society. Even now there might be some
way out of the difficulty. He asked Tony's advice on the subject. Tony
was perplexed. The situation was beyond his grip.

'I don't see what you can do, Jim,' he said, 'unless the Rugby
chap'll be satisfied with a pound on account. It's a beastly business.
Do you think your pater will give you your money all the same as it
was such a close finish?'

Jim thought not. In fact, he was certain that he would not, and
Tony relapsed into silence as he tried to bring another idea to the
surface. He had not succeeded when Charteris came in.

'Jim,' he said 'you have my sympathy. It was an awfully near thing.
But I've got something more solid than sympathy. I will take a seat.'

'Don't rag, Charteris,' said Tony. 'It's much too serious.'

'Who's ragging, you rotter? I say I have something more solid than
sympathy, and instead of giving me an opening, as a decent individual
would, by saying, "What?" you accuse me of ragging. James, my son,
if you will postpone your suicide for two minutes, I will a tale unfold.
I have an idea.'

'Well?'

'That's more like it. Now you *are* talking. We will start at the beginning. First, you want a pound. So do I. Secondly, you want it before next Tuesday. Thirdly, you haven't it on you. How, therefore, are you to get it? As the song hath it, you don't know, they don't know, but – now we come to the point – I *do* know.'

'Yes?' said Jim and Tony together.

'It is a luminous idea. Why shouldn't we publish a special number of *The Glow Worm* before the end of term?'

Jim was silent at the brilliance of the scheme. Then doubts began to harass him.

'Is there time?'

'Time? Yards of it. This is Saturday. We start tonight, and keep at it all night, if necessary. We ought to manage it easily before tomorrow morning. On Sunday we jellygraph it – it'll have to be a jellygraphed number this time. On Monday and Tuesday we sell it, and there you are.'

'How are you going to sell it? In the ordinary way at the shop?'

'Yes, I've arranged all that. All we've got to do is to write the thing. As the penalty for your sins you shall take on most of it. I'll do the editorial, Welch is pegging away at the Sports account now, and I waylaid Jackson just before lock-up, and induced him by awful threats to knock off some verses. So we're practically published already.'

'It's grand,' said Jim. 'And it's awfully decent of you chaps to fag yourselves like this for me. I'll start on something now.'

'But can you raise a sovereign on one number?' asked Tony.

'Either that, or I've arranged with the shop to give us a quid down, and take all profits on this and the next number. They're as keen as anything on the taking-all-profits idea, but I've kept that back to be used only in case of necessity. But the point is that Jim gets his sovereign in any case. I must be off to my editorial. So long,' and he went.

'Grand man, Charteris,' said Tony, as he leant back in his chair in search of a subject. 'You'd better weigh in with an account of the burglary. It's a pity you can't give the realistic description you gave us. It would sell like anything.'

'Wouldn't do to risk it.'

At that moment the door swung violently open, with Merevale holding on to the handle, and following it in its course. Merevale very rarely knocked at a study door, a peculiarity of his which went far towards shattering the nervous systems of the various inmates, who never knew when it was safe to stop work and read fiction.

'Ah, Thomson,' he said, 'I was looking for you. The Headmaster wants to see you over at his House, if you are feeling well enough after your exertions. *Very* close thing, that mile. I don't know when I have seen a better-run race on the College grounds. I suppose you are feeling pretty tired, eh?'

'I am rather, sir, but I had better see the Head. Will he be in his study, sir?'

'Yes, I think so.'

Jim took his cap and went off, while Merevale settled down to spend the evening in Tony's study, as he often did when the term's work was over, and it was no longer necessary to keep up the pretence of preparation.

Parker, the Head's butler, conducted Jim into the presence.

'Sit down, Thomson,' said the Head.

Jim took a seat, and he had just time to notice that his namesake, Mr Thompson, was also present, and that, in spite of the fact that his tie had crept up to the top of his collar, he was looking quite unnecessarily satisfied with himself, when he became aware that the Head was speaking to him.

'I hope you are not feeling any bad effects from your race, Thomson?'

Jim was half inclined to say that his effects were *nil*, but he felt that the quip was too subtle, and would be lost on his present audience, so he merely said that he was not. There was a rather awkward silence for a minute. Then the Head coughed, and said:

'Thomson.'

'Yes, sir.'

'I think it would be fairest to you to come to the point at once, and to tell you the reason why I wished to see you.'

Jim ran over the sins which shot up in his mind like rockets as he heard these ominous words, and he knew that this must be the matter of the Pavilion. He was, therefore, in a measure prepared for the Head's next words.

'Thomson.'

'Yessir.'

'A very serious charge has been brought against you. You are accused of nothing less than this unfortunate burglary of the prizes for the Sports.'

'Yes, sir. Is my accuser Mr Thompson?'

The Headmaster hesitated for a moment, and Mr Thompson spoke. 'That is so,' he said.

'Yes,' said the Head, 'the accusation is brought by Mr Thompson.'

'Yes, sir,' said Jim again, and this time the observation was intended to convey the meaning, 'My dear, good sir, when you've known him as long as I have, you won't mind what Mr Thompson says or does. It's a kind of way he's got, and if he's not under treatment for it, he ought to be.'

'I should like to hear from your own lips that the charge is groundless.'

'Anything to oblige,' thought Jim. Then aloud, 'Yes, sir.'

'You say it is groundless?' This from Mr Thompson.

'Yes, sir.'

'I must warn you, Thomson, that the evidence against you is very strong indeed,' said the Head. 'Without suggesting that you are guilty of this thing, I think I ought to tell you that if you have any confession to make, it will be greatly, very greatly, to your own advantage to make it at once.'

'And give myself away, free, gratis and for nothing,' thought Jim. 'Not for me, thank you.'

'Might I hear Mr Thompson's evidence, sir?' he asked.

'Certainly, Thomson.' He effected a movement in Mr Thompson's direction, midway between a bow and a nod.

Mr Thompson coughed. Jim coughed, too, in the same key. This put Mr Thompson out, and he had to cough again.

'In the first place,' he began, 'it has been conclusively proved that the burglary was the work of an unskilful hand.'

'That certainly seems to point to me as the author,' said Jim flippantly.

'Silence, Thomson,' said the Head, and counsel for the prosecution resumed.

'In the second place, it has been proved that you were at the time of the burglary in great need of money.'

This woke Jim up. It destroyed that feeling of coolness with which he had started the interview. Awful thoughts flashed across his mind. Had he been seen at the time of his burglarious entry? At any rate, how did Mr Thompson come to know of his pecuniary troubles?

'Did you say it had been proved, sir?'

'Yes.'

'How, sir?'

He felt the question was a mistake as he was uttering it. Your really injured innocent would have called all the elements to witness that he was a millionaire. But it was too late to try that now. And, besides, he really did want to know how Mr Thompson had got to hear of this skeleton in his cupboard.

The Headmaster interrupted hurriedly. 'It is a very unfortunate affair altogether, and this is quite the most unfortunate part. A letter came to the College addressed to J. Thomson, and Mr Thompson opened and read it inadvertently. Quite inadvertently.'

'Yes, sir,' said Jim, in a tone which implied, 'I am no George Washington myself, but when you say he read it inadvertently, well –'

'This letter was signed "Allen" –'

'My brother, sir.'

'Exactly. And it asked for two pounds. Evidently in payment of a debt, and the tone of the letter certainly seemed to show that you were not then in possession of the money.'

'Could I have the letter, sir?' Then with respectful venom to Mr Thompson: 'If you have finished with it.' The letter was handed over, and pocketed, and Jim braced his moral pecker up for the next round of the contest.

'I take it, then, Thomson,' resumed the Head, 'that you owe your brother this money?'

'Yes, sir.'

'Two pounds is a great deal of money for one boy to lend another.'

'It was not lent, sir. It was a bet.'

'A bet!' in a nasty tone from the Head.

'A bet!' in a sepulchral echo from Mr Thompson.

There was a long pause.

'At any other time,' said the Head, 'I should feel it my duty to take serious notice of this, but beside this other matter with which you are charged, it becomes trivial. I can only repeat that the circumstances are exceedingly suspicious, and I think it would be in your interests to tell us all you know without further delay.'

'You take it for granted I am guilty, sir,' began Jim hotly.

'I say that the circumstances seems to point to it. In the first place, you were in need of money. You admit that?'

'Yes, sir.'

'In the second place,' said the Head slowly, 'in the second place, I am told that you were nowhere to be found in the House at half-past eight on the night of the burglary, when you ought certainly to have been in your study at your work.'

Bombshell number two, and a worse one than the first. For the moment Jim's head swam. If he had been asked just then in so many words where he had been at that time, it is likely that he would have admitted everything. By some miracle the Head did not press his point.

'You may go now, Thomson,' he said. 'I should like to see you after morning school on Monday. Good-night.'

'Good-night, sir,' said Jim, and went without another word. Coming so soon after the exertion and strain of the mile, this shock made him feel sick and dizzy.

When he had gone, the Head turned to Mr Thompson with a worried look on his face. 'I feel as certain as I do of anything,' he said thoughtfully, 'that that boy is telling the truth. If he had been guilty, he would not have behaved like that. I feel sure of it.'

Mr Thompson looked equally thoughtful. 'The circumstances are certainly very suspicious,' he said, echoing the Head's own words. 'I wish I could think he was innocent, but I am bound to say I do not. I regard the evidence as conclusive.'

'Circumstantial evidence is proverbially uncertain, Mr Thompson. That is principally the reason why I was so bent on making him confess if he had anything to confess. I can't expel a boy and ruin his whole career on mere suspicion. The matter must be proved, doubly proved, and even then I should feel uneasy until he owned himself guilty. It is a most unpleasant affair, a terrible affair.'

'Most,' agreed Mr Thompson.

And exactly the same thing was occurring at that moment to Jim, as he sat on his bed in his dormitory, and pondered hopelessly on this new complication that had presented itself so unexpectedly. He was getting very near to the end of his tether, was J. Thomson of Merevale's. It seemed to him, indeed, that he had reached it already. Possibly if he had had a clearer conscience and a larger experience, he might have recognized that the evidence which Mr Thompson had described as conclusive, was in reality not strong enough to hang a cat on. Unfortunately, he did not enjoy those advantages.

Sir Alfred Scores

Soon after Jim had taken his departure, Mr Thompson, after waiting a few minutes in case the Headmaster had anything more to say, drifted silently out of the room. The Head, like the gentleman in the ballad, continued to wear a worried look. The more he examined the matter, the less did he know what to make of it. He believed, as he had said to Mr Thompson, that Jim was entirely innocent. It was an incredible thing, he thought, that a public school boy, a School-prefect, too, into the bargain, should break out of his House and into a cricket pavilion, however great a crisis his finances might be undergoing. And then to steal two of the prizes for the Sports. Impossible. Against this, however, must be placed the theft of the two pounds. It might occur to a boy, as indeed Mr Thompson had suggested, to steal the cups in order to give the impression that a practised burglar had been at work. There was certainly something to be said in favour of this view. But he would never believe such a thing. He was a good judge of character – a headmaster generally is – and he thought he could tell when a boy was speaking the truth and when he was not.

His reflections were interrupted by a knock at the door. The butler entered with a card on a tray. 'Sir Alfred Venner, M.P., Badgwick Hall,' said – almost shouted – the card. He read the words without any apparent pleasure.

'Is Sir Alfred here himself, Parker?' he said.

'He is, sir.'

The Headmaster sighed inaudibly but very wearily. He was feeling worried already, and he knew from experience that a *tête-à-tête* with Sir Alfred Venner, M.P., of Badgwick Hall, would worry him still more.

The Head was a man who tried his very hardest to like each and all of his fellow-creatures, but he felt bound to admit that he liked most people a great, a very great, deal better than he liked the gentleman who had just sent in his card. Sir Alfred's manner always jarred upon him. It was so exactly the antithesis of his own. He was quiet and dignified, and addressed everybody alike, courteously. Sir Alfred was restless and fussy. His manner was always dictatorial and generally rude. When he had risen in the House to make his maiden speech, calling the attention of the Speaker to what he described as 'a thorough draught', he had addressed himself with such severity to that official, that a party of Siamese noblemen, who, though not knowing a word of English, had come to listen to the debate, had gone away with the impression that he was the prime minister. No wonder the Headmaster sighed.

'Show him in, Parker,' said he resignedly.

'Yessir.'

Parker retired, leaving the Head to wonder what his visitor's grievance might be this time. Sir Alfred rarely called without a grievance, generally connected with the trespassing of the School on his land.

'Good evening, Sir Alfred,' he said, as his visitor whirled into the room.

'O-o-o, this sort of thing won't do, you know, Mr Perceval,' said Sir Alfred fussily, adjusting a pair of gold pince-nez on his nose. The Head's name, which has not before been mentioned, was the Reverend Herbert Perceval, M.A. He had shivered at the sound of the 'O-o-o' which had preceded Sir Alfred's remark. He knew, as did other unfortunate people, that the great man was at his worst when he said 'O-o-o'. In moments of comparative calm he said 'Er'.

'I can't put up with it, you know, Mr Perceval. It's too much. A great deal too much.'

'You refer to – ?' suggested the Head, with a patience that did him credit.

'This eternal trespassing and tramping in and out of my grounds all day.'

'You have been misinformed, I fear, Sir Alfred. I have not trespassed in your grounds for – ah – a considerable time.' The Head could not resist this thrust. In his unregenerate 'Varsity days he had been a power at the Union, where many a foeman had exposed himself to a verbal counter from him with disastrous results. Now the fencing must be done with buttons on the foils.

'You – what – I don't follow you, Mr Perceval.'

'I understand you to reproach me for trespassing and – ah – tramping in and out of your grounds all day. Was that not your meaning?'

Sir Alfred almost danced with impatience.

'No, no, no. You misunderstand me. You don't follow my drift.'

'In that case, I beg your pardon. I gathered from the extreme severity of your attitude towards me that I was the person to whom you referred.'

'No, no, no. I've come here to complain of your boys.'

It occurred to the Head to ask if the complaint embraced the entire six hundred of them, or merely referred to one of them. But he reflected that the longer he fenced, the longer his visitor would stay. And he decided, in spite of the illicit pleasure to be derived from the exercise, that it was not worth while.

'Ah,' he said.

'Yes,' continued Sir Alfred, 'my keepers tell me the woods were full of them, sir.'

The Head suggested that possibly the keepers had exaggerated.

'Possibly. Possibly they may have exaggerated. But that is not the point. The nuisance is becoming intolerable, Mr Perceval, perfectly intolerable. It is time to take steps.'

'I have already done all that can be done. I have placed your land out of bounds, considerably out of bounds indeed. And I inflict the severest penalties when a breach of the rule is reported to me.'

'It's not enough. It's not nearly enough.'

'I can scarcely do more, I fear, Sir Alfred. There are more than six hundred boys at St Austin's, and it is not within my power to place them all under my personal supervision.'

Here the Head, who had an eye to the humorous, conjured up a picture of six hundred Austinians going for walks, two and two, the staff posted at intervals down the procession, and himself bringing up the rear. He made a mental mem. to laugh when his visitor had retired.

'H'm,' said the baffled M.P. thoughtfully, adjusting his pince-nez once more. ' 'M no. No, perhaps not. But' – here he brightened up – 'you can punish them when they do trespass.'

'That is so, Sir Alfred. I can and invariably do.'

'Then punish that what's-his-name, Plinkett, Plunkett – I've got the name down somewhere. Yes, Plunkett. I thought so. Punish Plunkett.'

'Plunkett!' said the Head, taken completely by surprise. He, in common with the rest of the world, had imagined Plunkett to be a perfect pattern of what should be. A headmaster, like other judges of character, has his failures.

'Plunkett. Yes, that is the name. Boy with spectacles. Good gracious, Mr Perceval, don't tell me the boy gave me a false name.'

'No. His name is Plunkett. Am I to understand that he was trespassing on your land? Surely there is some mistake? The boy's a School-prefect.'

Here it suddenly flashed upon his mind that he had used that expression before in the course of the day, on the occasion when Mr Thompson first told him of his suspicions in connection with Jim. 'Why, Mr Thompson, the boy's a School-prefect,' had been his exact words. School-prefects had been in his eyes above suspicion. It is a bad day for a school when they are not so. Had that day arrived for St Austin's? he asked himself.

'He may be a School-prefect, Mr Perceval, but the fact remains that he is a trespasser, and ought from your point of view to be punished for breaking bounds.'

The Head suddenly looked almost cheerful again.

'Of course,' he said, 'of course. I thought that there must be an explanation. The rules respecting bounds, Sir Alfred, do not apply to School-prefects, only to the rest of the School.'

'Indeed?' said Sir Alfred. His tone should have warned the Head that something more was coming, but it did not. He continued.

'Of course it was very wrong of him to trespass on your land, but I have no doubt that he did it quite unintentionally. I will speak to him, and I think I can guarantee that he will not do it again.'

'Oh,' said his visitor. 'That is very gratifying, I am sure. Might I ask, Mr Perceval, if School-prefects at St Austin's have any other privileges?'

The Head began to look puzzled. There was something in his visitor's manner which suggested unpleasant possibilities.

'A few,' he replied. 'They have a few technical privileges, which it would be a matter of some little time to explain.'

'It must be very pleasant to be a prefect at St Austin's,' said Sir Alfred nastily. 'Very pleasant indeed. Might I ask, Mr Perceval, if the technical privileges to which you refer include – smoking?'

The Head started as if, supposing such a thing possible, someone had pinched him. He did not know what to make of the question. From the expression on his face his visitor did not appear to be perpetrating a joke.

'No,' he said sharply, 'they do not include smoking.'

'I merely asked because this was found by my keeper on the boy when he caught him.'

He produced a small silver match-box. The Head breathed again.

The reputation of the School-prefect, though shaky, was still able to come up to the scratch.

'A match-box is scarcely a proof that a boy has been smoking, I think,' said he. 'Many boys carry matches for various purposes, I believe. I myself, though a non-smoker, frequently place a box in my pocket.'

For answer Sir Alfred laid a bloated and exceedingly vulgar-looking plush tobacco-pouch on the table beside the match-box.

'That also,' he observed, 'was found in his pocket by my keeper.'

He dived his hand once more into his coat. 'And also this,' he said.

And, with the air of a card-player who trumps his opponent's ace, he placed on the pouch a pipe. And, to make the matter, if possible, worse, the pipe was not a new pipe. It was caked within and coloured without, a pipe that had seen long service. The only mitigating circumstance that could possibly have been urged in favour of the accused, namely that of 'first offence', had vanished.

'It is pleasant,' said Sir Alfred with laborious sarcasm, 'to find a trespasser doing a thing which has caused the dismissal of several keepers. Smoking in my woods I – will – not – permit. I will not have my property burnt down while I can prevent it. Good evening, Mr Perceval.' With these words he made a dramatic exit.

For some minutes after he had gone the Head remained where he stood, thinking. Then he went across the room and touched the bell.

'Parker,' he said, when that invaluable officer appeared, 'go across to Mr Ward's House, and tell him I wish to see Plunkett. Say I wish to see him at once.'

'Yessir.'

After ten minutes had elapsed, Plunkett entered the room, looking nervous.

'Sit down, Plunkett.'

Plunkett collapsed into a seat. His eye had caught sight of the smoking apparatus on the table.

The Head paced the room, something after the fashion of the tiger at the Zoo, whose clock strikes lunch.

'Plunkett,' he said, suddenly, 'you are a School-prefect.'

'Yes, sir,' murmured Plunkett. The fact was undeniable.

'You know the duties of a School-prefect?'

'Yes, sir.'

'And yet you deliberately break one of the most important rules of the School. How long have you been in the habit of smoking?'

Plunkett evaded the question.

'My father lets me smoke, sir, when I'm at home.'

(A hasty word in the reader's ear. If ever you are accused of smoking, please – for my sake, if not for your own – try to refrain from saying that your father lets you do it at home. It is a fatal mistake.)

At this, to employ a metaphor, the champagne of the Head's wrath, which had been fermenting steadily during his late interview, got the better of the cork of self-control, and he exploded. If the Mutual Friend ever has grandchildren he will probably tell them with bated breath the story of how the Head paced the room, and the legend of the things he said. But it will be some time before he will be able to speak about it with any freedom. At last there was a lull in the storm.

'I am not going to expel you, Plunkett. But you cannot come back after the holidays. I will write to your father to withdraw you.' He pointed to the door. Plunkett departed in level time.

'What did the Old 'Un want you for?' asked Dallas, curiously, when he returned to the study.

Plunkett had recovered himself by this time sufficiently to be able to tell a lie.

'He wanted to tell me he'd heard from my father about my leaving.'

'About your leaving!' Dallas tried to keep his voice as free as possible from triumphant ecstasy.

'Are you leaving? When?'

'This term.'

'Oh!' said Dallas. It was an uncomfortable moment. He felt that at least some conventional expression of regret ought to proceed from him.

'Don't trouble to lie about being sorry,' said Plunkett with a sneer.

'Thanks,' said Dallas, gratefully, 'since you mention it, I rather think I won't.'

[14]

The Long Run

Vaughan came up soon afterwards, and Dallas told him the great news. They were neither of them naturally vindictive, but the Mutual Friend had been a heavy burden to them during his stay in the House, and they did not attempt to conceal from themselves their unfeigned pleasure at the news of his impending departure.

'I'll never say another word against Mr Plunkett, senior, in my life,' said Vaughan. 'He's a philanthropist. I wonder what the Mutual's going to do? Gentleman of leisure, possibly. Unless he's going to the 'Varsity.'

'Same thing, rather. I don't know a bit what he's going to do, and I can't say I care much. He's going, that's the main point.'

'I say,' said Vaughan. 'I believe the Old Man was holding a sort of reception tonight. I know he had Thomson over to his House. Do you think there's a row on?'

'Oh, I don't know. Probably only wanted to see if he was all right after the mile. By Jove, it was a bit of a race, wasn't it?' And the conversation drifted off into matters athletic.

There were two persons that night who slept badly. Jim lay awake until the College clock had struck three, going over in his mind the various points of his difficulties, on the chance of finding a solution of them. He fell asleep at a quarter past, without having made any progress. The Head, also, passed a bad night. He was annoyed for many reasons, principally, perhaps, because he had allowed Sir Alfred Venner to score so signal a victory over him. Besides that, he was not easy in his mind about Jim. He could not come to a decision. The evidence was all against him, but evidence is noted for its untrustworthiness. The Head would have preferred to judge the matter from his knowledge of Jim's character. But after the Plunkett episode he mistrusted his powers in that direction. He thought the matter over for a time, and then, finding himself unable to sleep, got up and wrote an article for a leading review on the subject of the Doxology. The article was subsequently rejected – which proves that Providence is not altogether incapable of a kindly action – but it served its purpose by sending its author to sleep.

Barrett, too, though he did not allow it to interfere with his slumbers, was considerably puzzled as to what he ought to do about the cups which he had stumbled upon in the wood. He scarcely felt equal to going to the Dingle again to fetch them, and yet every minute he delayed made the chances of their remaining there more remote. He rather hoped that Reade would think of some way out of it. He had a great respect for Reade's intellect, though he did not always show it. The next day was the day of the Inter-House cross-country race. It was always fixed for the afternoon after Sports Day, a most inconvenient time for it, as everybody who had exerted or over-exerted himself the afternoon before was unable to do himself justice. Today, contrary to general expectation, both Drake and Thomson had turned out. The knowing ones, however, were prepared to bet anything you liked (except cash), that both would drop out before the first mile was over. Merevale's pinned their hopes on Welch. At that time Welch had not done much long-distance running. He confined himself to the hundred yards and the quarter. But he had it in him to do great things, as he proved in the following year, when he won the half, and would have beaten the great Mitchell-Jones record for the mile, but for an accident, or rather an event, which prevented his running. The tale of which is told elsewhere.

The course for the race was a difficult one. There were hedges and brooks to be negotiated, and, worst of all, ploughed fields. The first ploughed field usually thinned the ranks of the competitors considerably. The distance was about ten miles.

The race started at three o'clock. Jim and Welch, Merevale's first string, set the pace from the beginning, and gradually drew away from the rest. Drake came third, and following him the rest of the Houses in a crowd.

Welch ran easily and springily; Jim with more effort. He felt from the start that he could not last. He resolved to do his best for the honour of the House, but just as the second mile was beginning, the first of the ploughed fields appeared in view, stretching, so it appeared to Jim, right up to the horizon. He groaned.

'Go on, Welch,' he gasped. 'I'm done.'

Welch stopped short in his stride, and eyed him critically.

'Yes,' he said, 'better get back to the House. You overdid it yesterday. Lie down somewhere. G'bye.' And he got into his stride again.

Jim watched his figure diminish, until at last it was a shapeless dot of white against the brown surface. Then he lay down on his back and panted.

It was in this attitude that Drake found him. For a moment an almost irresistible wish seized him to act in the same way. There was an unstudied comfort about Jim's pose which appealed to him strongly. His wind still held out, but his legs were beginning to feel as if they did not belong to him at all. He pulled up for an instant.

'Hullo,' he said, 'done up?'

For reply Jim merely grunted.

'Slacker,' said Drake. 'Where's Welch?'

'Miles ahead.'

'Oh Lord!' groaned Drake and, pulling himself together, set out painfully once more across the heavy surface of the field.

Jim lay where he was a little longer. The recollection of the other runners, who might be expected to arrive shortly, stirred him to action. He did not wish to interview everyone on the subject of his dropping out. He struck off at right angles towards the hedge on the left. As he did so, the first of the crowd entered the field. Simpson *major*, wearing the colours of Perkins's House on his manly bosom, was leading. Behind him came a group of four, two School House, Dallas of Ward's, and a representative of Prater's. A minute later they were followed by a larger group, consisting this time of twenty or more runners – all that was left of the fifty who had started. The rest had dropped out at the sight of the ploughed field.

Jim watched the procession vanish over the brow of the hill, and, as it passed out of sight, began to walk slowly back to the School again.

He reached it at last, only to find it almost entirely deserted. In Merevale's House there was nobody. He had hoped that Charteris and Tony might have been somewhere about. When he had changed into his ordinary clothes, he made a tour of the School grounds. The only sign of life, as far as he could see, was Biffen, who was superintending the cutting of the grass on the cricket-field. During the winter Biffen always disappeared, nobody knew where, returning at the beginning of Sports Week to begin preparations for the following cricket season. It had been stated that during the winter he shut himself up and lived on himself after the fashion of a bear. Others believed that he went and worked in some Welsh mine until he was needed again at the School. Biffen himself was not communicative on the subject, a fact which led a third party to put forward the awful theory that he was a professional association player and feared to mention his crime in a school which worshipped Rugby.

'Why, Mr Thomson,' he said, as Jim came up, 'I thought you was running. Whoa!' The last remark was addressed to a bored-looking horse attached to the mowing-machine. From the expression on its face, the animal evidently voted the whole process pure foolishness. He pulled up without hesitation, and Biffen turned to Jim again.

'Surely they ain't come back yet?' he said.

'I have,' said Jim. 'I did myself up rather in the mile yesterday, and couldn't keep up the pace. I dropped out at that awfully long ploughed field by Parker's Spinney.'

Biffen nodded.

'And 'oo was winning, sir?'

'Well, Welch was leading, the last I saw of it. Shouldn't wonder if he won either. He was going all right. I say, the place seems absolutely deserted. Isn't anybody about?'

'Just what Mr MacArthur was saying to me just this minute, sir. 'E went into the Pavilion.'

'Good. I'll go and hunt for him.'

Biffen 'clicked' the *blasé* horse into movement again. Jim went to the Pavilion and met the Babe coming down the steps.

'Hullo, Babe! I was looking for you.'

'Hullo! Why aren't you running?'

'Dropped out. Come and have tea in my study.'

'No, I'll tell you what. You come back with me. I've got rather a decent dog I want to show you. Only got him yesterday.'

Jim revelled in dogs, so he agreed instantly. The Babe lived with his parents in a big house about a mile from the College, and in so doing was the object of much envy amongst those who had to put up with life at the Houses. Jim had been to his home once or twice before, and had always had a very good time indeed there. The two strolled off. In another hour the place began to show signs of life again. The School began to return by ones and twos, most of them taking up a position near the big gates. This was where the race was to finish. There was a straight piece of road about two hundred yards in length before the high road was reached. It was a sight worth seeing when the runners, paced by their respective Houses on each side of the road, swept round the corner, and did their best to sprint with all that was left in them after ten miles of difficult country. Suddenly a distant shouting began to be heard. The leaders had been sighted. The noise increased, growing nearer and nearer, until at last it swelled into a roar, and a black mass of runners turned the corner. In the midst of the black was one white figure – Welch, as calm and unruffled as if he had been returning from a short trot to improve his wind. Merevale's surged round him in a cheering mob. Welch simply disregarded them. He knew where he wished to begin his sprint, and he would begin it at that spot and no other. The spot he had chosen was well within a hundred yards from the gates. When he reached it, he let himself go, and from the uproar, the crowd appeared to be satisfied. A long pause, and still none of the other runners appeared. Five minutes went by before they began to appear. First Jones, of the School House, and Simpson, who raced every yard of the way, and finished in the order named, and then three of Philpott's House in a body. The rest dropped in at intervals for the next quarter of an hour.

The Headmaster always made a point of watching the finish of the cross-country run. Indeed, he was generally one of the last to leave. With the majority of the spectators it was enough to see the first five safely in.

The last man and lock-up arrived almost simultaneously, and the Head went off to a well-earned dinner.

He had just finished this meal, and was congratulating himself on not being obliged to spend the evening in a series of painful interviews, as had happened the night before, when Parker, the butler, entered the room.

'Well, Parker, what is it?' asked he.

'Mr Roberts, sir, wishes to see you.'

For a moment the Head was at a loss. He could not recall any friend or acquaintance of that name. Then he remembered that Roberts was the name of the detective who had come down from London to look into the matter of the prizes.

'Very well,' he said, resignedly, 'show him into the study.'

Parker bowed, and retired. The Head, after an interval, followed him, and made his way to the study.

[15]

Mr Roberts Explains

Inspector Roberts was standing with his back to the door, examining a photograph of the College, when the Head entered. He spun round briskly. 'Good evening, Mr Roberts. Pray be seated. You wish to see me?'

The detective took a seat.

'This business of the cups, sir.'

'Ah!' said the Head, 'have you made any progress?'

'Considerable. Yes, very considerable progress. I've found out who stole them.'

'You have?' cried the Head. 'Excellent. I suppose it *was* Thomson, then? I was afraid so.'

'Thomson, sir? That was certainly not the name he gave me. Stokes he called himself.'

'Stokes? Stokes? This is curious. Perhaps if you were to describe his appearance? Was he a tall boy, of a rather slight build –'

The detective interrupted.

'Excuse me, sir, but I rather fancy we have different persons in our mind. Stokes is not a boy. Not at all. Well over thirty. Red moustache. Height, five foot seven, I should say. Not more. Works as a farmhand when required, and does odd jobs at times. That's the man.'

The Head's face expressed relief, as he heard this description. 'Then Thomson did not do it after all,' he said.

'Thomson?' queried Mr Roberts.

'Thomson,' explained the Head, 'is the name of one of the boys at the School. I am sorry to say that I strongly suspected him of this robbery.'

'A boy at the School. Curious. Unusual, I should have thought, for a boy to be mixed up in an affair like this. Though I have known cases.'

'I was very unwilling, I can assure you, to suspect him of such a thing, but really the evidence all seemed to point to it. I am afraid,

Mr Roberts, that I have been poaching on your preserves without much success.'

'Curious thing evidence,' murmured Mr Roberts, fixing with his eye a bust of Socrates on the writing-desk, as if he wished it to pay particular attention to his words. 'Very curious. Very seldom able to trust it. Case the other day. Man charged with robbery from the person. *With* violence. They gave the case to me. Worked up beautiful case against the man. Not a hitch anywhere. Whole thing practically proved. Man brings forward *alibi*. Proves it. Turned out that at time of robbery he had been serving seven days without the option for knocking down two porters and a guard on the District Railway. Yet the evidence seemed conclusive. Yes, curious thing evidence.' He nodded solemnly at Socrates, and resumed an interested study of the carpet.

The Head, who had made several spirited attempts at speaking during this recital, at last succeeded in getting in a word.

'You have the cups?'

'No. No, cups still missing. Only flaw in the affair. Perhaps I had better begin from the beginning?'

'Exactly. Pray let me hear the whole story. I am more glad than I can say that Thomson is innocent. There is no doubt of that, I hope?'

'Not the least, sir. Not the very least. Stokes is the man.'

'I am very glad to hear it.'

The inspector paused for a moment, coughed, and drifted into his narrative.

'. . . Saw at once it was not the work of a practised burglar. First place, how could regular professional know that the cups were in the Pavilion at all? Quite so. Second place, work very clumsily done. No neatness. Not the professional touch at all. Tell it in a minute. No mistaking it. Very good. Must, therefore, have been amateur – this night only – and connected with School. Next question, who? Helped a little there by luck. Capital thing luck, when it's not bad luck. Was passing by the village inn – you know the village inn, I dare say, sir?'

The Head, slightly scandalized, explained that he was seldom in the village. The detective bowed and resumed his tale.

'As I passed the door, I ran into a man coming out. In a very elevated, not to say intoxicated, state. As a matter of fact, barely able to stand. Reeled against wall, and dropped handful of money. I lent helping hand, and picked up his money for him. Not my place to arrest drunken men. Constable's! No constable there, of course. Noticed, as I picked the money up, that there was a good deal of it. For ordinary rustic, a *very* good deal. Sovereign and plenty of silver.' He paused, mused for a while, and went on again.

'Yes. Sovereign, and quite ten shillings' worth of silver. Now the nature of my profession makes me a suspicious man. It struck me as curious, not to say remarkable, that such a man should have thirty shillings or more about him so late in the week. And then there was another thing. I thought I'd seen this particular man somewhere on the School grounds. Couldn't recall his face exactly, but just had a sort of general recollection of having seen him before. I happened to have a camera with me. As a matter of fact I had been taking a few photographs of the place. Pretty place, sir.'

'Very,' agreed the Head.

'You photograph yourself, perhaps?'

'No. I – ah – do not.'

'Ah. Pity. Excellent hobby. However – I took a snap-shot of this man to show to somebody who might know him better than I did. This is the photograph. Drunk as a lord, is he not?'

He exhibited a small piece of paper. The Head examined it gravely, and admitted that the subject of the picture did not appear to be ostentatiously sober. The sunlight beat full on his face, which wore the intensely solemn expression of the man who, knowing his own condition, hopes, by means of exemplary conduct, to conceal it from the world. The Head handed the photograph back without further comment.

'I gave the man back his money,' went on Mr Roberts, 'and saw him safely started again, and then I set to work to shadow him. Not a difficult job. He walked very slowly, and for all he seemed to care, the whole of Scotland Yard might have been shadowing him. Went up the street, and after a time turned in at one of the cottages. I marked the place, and went home to develop the photograph. Took it to show the man who looks after the cricket-field.'

'Biffen?'

'Just so, Biffen. Very intelligent man. Given me a good deal of help in one way and another all along. Well, I showed it to him and he said he thought he knew the face. Was almost certain it was one of the men at work on the grounds at the time of the robbery. Showed it to friend of his, the other ground-man. He thought same. That made it as certain as I had any need for. Went off at once to the man's cottage, found him sober, and got the whole thing out of him. But not the cups. He had been meaning to sell them, but had not known where to go. Wanted combination of good price and complete safety. Very hard to find, so had kept cups hidden till further notice.'

Here the Head interrupted.

'And the cups? Where are they?'

'We-e-ll,' said the detective, slowly. 'It is this way. We have only got his word to go on as regards the cups. This man, Stokes, it seems is a notorious poacher. The night after the robbery he took the cups out with him on an expedition in some woods that lie in the direction of Badgwick. I think Badgwick is the name.'

'Badgwick! Not Sir Alfred Venner's woods?'

'Sir Alfred Venner it was, sir. That was the name he mentioned. Stokes appears to have been in the habit of visiting that gentleman's property pretty frequently. He had a regular hiding-place, a sort of store where he used to keep all the game he killed. He described the place to me. It is a big tree on the bank of the stream nearest the high road. The tree is hollow. One has to climb to find the opening to it. Inside are the cups, and, I should say, a good deal of mixed poultry. That is what he told me, sir. I should advise you, if I may say so, to write a note to Sir Alfred Venner, explaining the case, and ask him to search the tree, and send the cups on here.'

This idea did not appeal to the Head at all. Why, he thought bitterly, was this wretched M.P. always mixed up with his affairs? Left to himself, he could have existed in perfect comfort without either seeing, writing to, or hearing from the great man again for the rest of his life. 'I will think it over,' he said, 'though it seems the only thing to be done. As for Stokes, I suppose I must prosecute –'

The detective raised a hand in protest.

'Pardon my interruption, sir, but I really should advise you not to prosecute.'

'Indeed! Why?'

'It is this way. If you prosecute, you get the man his term of imprisonment. A year, probably. Well and good. But then what happens? After his sentence has run out, he comes out of prison an ex-convict. Tries to get work. No good. Nobody will look at him. Asks for a job. People lock up their spoons and shout for the police. What happens then? Not being able to get work, tries another burglary. Being a clumsy hand at the game, gets caught again and sent back to prison, and so is ruined and becomes a danger to society. Now, if he is let off this time, he will go straight for the rest of his life. Run a mile to avoid a silver cup. He's badly scared, and I took the opportunity of scaring him more. Told him nothing would happen this time, if the cups came back safely, but that he'd be watched ever afterwards to see he did not get into mischief. Of course he won't really be watched, you understand, but he thinks he will. Which is better, for it saves trouble. Besides, we know where the cups are – I feel sure he was speaking the truth about them, he was too frightened to invent a story – and here is most of the money. So it all ends well, if I may put it so. My advice, sir, and I think you will find it good advice – is not to prosecute.'

'Very well,' said the Head, 'I will not.'

'Very good, sir. Good morning, sir.' And he left the room.

The Head rang the bell.

'Parker,' said he, 'go across to Mr Merevale's, and ask him to send Thomson to me.'

It was with mixed feelings that he awaited Jim's arrival. The detective's story had shown how unjust had been his former suspicions, and he felt distinctly uncomfortable at the prospect of the apology which he felt bound to make to him. On the other hand, this feeling was more than equalled by his relief at finding that his faith in the virtue of the *genus* School-prefect, though at fault in the matter of Plunkett, was not altogether misplaced. It made up for a good deal. Then his thoughts drifted to Sir Alfred Venner. Struggle with his feelings as he might, the Head could *not* endure that local potentate. The recent interview between them had had no parallel in their previous acquaintance, but the Head had always felt vaguely irritated by his manner and speech, and he had always feared that matters would come to a head sooner or later. The prospect of opening communication with him once more was not alluring. In the meantime there was his more immediate duty to be performed, the apology to Thomson. But that reminded him. The apology must only be of a certain kind. It must not be grovelling. And this for a very excellent reason. After the apology must come an official lecture on the subject of betting. He had rather lost sight of that offence in the excitement of the greater crime of which Thomson had been accused, and very nearly convicted. Now the full heinousness of it came back to him. Betting! Scandalous!

'Come in,' he cried, as a knock at the door roused him from his thoughts. He turned. But instead of Thomson, there appeared Parker. Parker carried a note. It was from Mr Merevale.

The Head opened it.

'What!' he cried, as he read it. 'Impossible.' Parker made no comment. He stood in the doorway, trying to look as like a piece of furniture as possible – which is the duty of a good butler.

'Impossible!' said the Head again.

What Mr Merevale had said in his note was this, that Thomson was not in the House, and had not been in the House since lunch-time. He ought to have returned at six o'clock. It was now half-past eight, and still there were no signs of him. Mr Merevale expressed a written opinion that this was a remarkable thing, and the Head agreed with him unreservedly.

[16]

The Disappearance of J. Thomson

Certainly the Head was surprised.

He read the note again. No. There was no mistake. 'Thomson is not in the House.' There could be no two meanings about that.

'Go across to Mr Merevale's,' he said at last, 'and ask him if he would mind seeing me here for a moment.'

The butler bowed his head gently, but with more than a touch of pained astonishment. He thought the Headmaster might show more respect for persons. A butler is not an errand-boy.

'Sir?' he said, giving the Head a last chance, as it were, of realizing the situation.

'Ask Mr Merevale to step over here for a moment.'

The poor man bowed once more. The phantom of a half-smoked cigar floated reproachfully before his eyes. He had lit it a quarter of an hour ago in fond anticipation of a quiet evening. Unless a miracle had occurred, it must be out by this time. And he knew as well as anybody else that a relighted cigar is never at its best. But he went, and in a few minutes Mr Merevale entered the room.

'Sit down, Mr Merevale,' said the Head. 'Am I to understand from your note that Thomson is actually not in the House?'

Mr Merevale thought that if he had managed to understand anything else from the note he must possess a mind of no common order, but he did not say so.

'No,' he said. 'Thomson has not been in the House since lunch-time, as far as I know. It is a curious thing.'

'It is exceedingly serious. Exceedingly so. For many reasons. Have you any idea where he was seen last?'

'Harrison in my House says he saw him at about three o'clock.'

'Ah!'

'According to Harrison, he was walking in the direction of Stapleton.'

'Ah. Well, it is satisfactory to know even as little as that.'

'Just so. But Mace – he is in my House, too – declares that he saw Thomson at about the same time cycling in the direction of Badgwick. Both accounts can scarcely be correct.'

'But – dear me, are you certain, Mr Merevale?'

Merevale nodded to imply that he was. The Head drummed irritably with his fingers on the arm of his chair. This mystery, coming as it did after the series of worries through which he had been passing for the last few days, annoyed him as much as it is to be supposed the last straw annoyed the proverbial camel.

'As a matter of fact,' said Merevale, 'I know that Thomson started to run in the long race this afternoon. I met him going to the starting-place, and advised him to go and change again. He was not looking at all fit for such a long run. It seems to me that Welch might know where he is. Thomson and he got well ahead of the others after the start, so that if, as I expect, Thomson dropped out early in the race, Welch could probably tell us where it happened. That would give us some clue to his whereabouts, at any rate.'

'Have you questioned Welch?'

'Not yet. Welch came back very tired, quite tired out, in fact and went straight to bed. I hardly liked to wake him except as a last resource. Perhaps I had better do so now?'

'I think you should most certainly. Something serious must have happened to Thomson to keep him out of his House as late as this. Unless –'

He stopped. Merevale looked up enquiringly. The Head, after a moment's deliberation, proceeded to explain.

'I have made a very unfortunate mistake with regard to Thomson, Mr Merevale. A variety of reasons led me to think that he had had something to do with this theft of the Sports prizes.'

'Thomson!' broke in Merevale incredulously.

'There was a considerable weight of evidence against him, which I have since found to be perfectly untrustworthy, but which at the time seemed to me almost conclusive.'

'But surely,' put in Merevale again, 'surely Thomson would be the last boy to do such a thing. Why should he? What would he gain by it?'

'Precisely. I can understand that perfectly in the light of certain information which I have just received from the inspector. But at the time, as I say, I believed him guilty. I even went so far as to send for him and question him upon the subject. Now it has occurred to me,

Mr Merevale – you understand that I put it forward merely as a conjecture – it occurs to me –'

'That Thomson has run away,' said Merevale bluntly.

The Head, slightly discomposed by this Sherlock-Holmes-like reading of his thoughts, pulled himself together, and said, 'Ah – just so. I think it very possible.'

'I do not agree with you,' said Merevale. 'I know Thomson well, and I think he is the last boy to do such a thing. He is neither a fool nor a coward, to put it shortly, and he would need to have a great deal of both in him to run away.'

The Head looked slightly relieved at this.

'You – ah – think so?' he said.

'I certainly do. In the first place, where, unless he went home, would he run to? And as he would be going home in a couple of days in the ordinary course of things, he would hardly be foolish enough to risk expulsion in such a way.'

Mr Merevale always rather enjoyed his straight talks with the Headmaster. Unlike most of his colleagues he stood in no awe of him whatever. He always found him ready to listen to sound argument, and, what was better, willing to be convinced. It was so in this case.

'Then I think we may dismiss that idea,' said the Head with visible relief. The idea of such a scandal occurring at St Austin's had filled him with unfeigned horror. 'And now I think it would be as well to go across to your House and hear what Welch has to say about the matter. Unless Thomson returns soon – and it is already past nine o'clock – we shall have to send out search-parties.'

Five minutes later Welch, enjoying a sound beauty-sleep, began to be possessed of a vague idea that somebody was trying to murder him. His subsequent struggles for life partially woke him, and enabled him to see dimly that two figures were standing by his bed.

'Yes?' he murmured sleepily, turning over on to his side again, and preparing to doze off. The shaking continued. This was too much. 'Look here,' said he fiercely, sitting up. Then he recognized his visitors. As his eye fell on Merevale, he wondered whether anything had occurred to bring down his wrath upon him. Perhaps he had gone to bed without leave, and was being routed out to read at prayers or do some work? No, he remembered distinctly getting permission to turn in. What then could be the matter?

At this point he recognized the Headmaster, and the last mists of sleep left him.

'Yes, sir?' he said, wide-awake now.

Merevale put the case briefly and clearly to him. 'Sorry to disturb you, Welch. I know you are tired.'

'Not at all, sir,' said Welch, politely.

'But there is something we must ask you. You probably do not know that Thomson has not returned?'

'Not returned!'

'No. Nobody knows where he is. You were probably the last to see him. What happened when you and he started for the long run this afternoon? You lost sight of the rest, did you not?'

'Yes, sir.'

'Well?'

'And Thomson dropped out.'

'Ah.' This from the Headmaster.

'Yes, sir. He said he couldn't go any farther. He told me to go on. And, of course, I did, as it was a race. I advised him to go back to the House and change. He looked regularly done up. I think he ran too hard in the mile yesterday.'

The Head spoke.

'I thought that some such thing must have happened. Where was it that he dropped out, Welch?'

'It was just as we came to a long ploughed field, sir, by the side of a big wood.'

'Parker's Spinney, I expect,' put in Merevale.

'Yes, sir. About a mile from the College.'

'And you saw nothing more of him after that?' enquired the Headmaster.

'No, sir. He was lying on his back when I left him. I should think some of the others must have seen him after I did. He didn't look as if he was likely to get up for some time.'

'Well,' said the Head, as he and Merevale went out of the room, leaving Welch to his slumbers, 'we have gained little by seeing Welch. I had hoped for something more. I must send the prefects out to look for Thomson at once.'

'It will be a difficult business,' said Merevale, refraining – to his credit be it said – from a mention of needles and haystacks. 'We have nothing to go upon. He may be anywhere for all we know. I suppose it is hardly likely that he is still where Welch left him?'

The Head seemed to think this improbable. 'That would scarcely be the case unless he were very much exhausted. It is more than five hours since Welch saw him. I can hardly believe that the worst exhaustion would last so long. However, if you would kindly tell your House-prefects of this –'

'And send them out to search?'

'Yes. We must do all we can. Tell them to begin searching where Thomson was last seen. I will go round to the other Houses. Dear me, this is exceedingly annoying. Exceedingly so.'

Merevale admitted that it was, and, having seen his visitor out of the House, went to the studies to speak to his prefects. He found Charteris and Tony together in the former's sanctum.

'Has anything been heard about Thomson, sir?' said Tony, as he entered.

'That is just what I want to see you about. Graham, will you go and bring the rest of the prefects here?'

'Now,' he said, as Tony returned with Swift and Daintree, the two remaining House-prefects, 'you all know, of course, that Thomson is not in the House. The Headmaster wants you to go and look for him. Welch seems to have been the last to see him, and he left him lying in a ploughed field near Parker's Spinney. You all know Parker's Spinney, I suppose?'

'Yes, sir.'

'Then you had better begin searching from there. Go in twos if you like, or singly. Don't all go together. I want you all to be back by eleven. All got watches?'

'Yes, sir.'

'Good. You'd better take lanterns of some sort. I think I can raise a bicycle lamp each, and there is a good moon. Look everywhere, and shout as much as you like. I think he must have sprained an ankle or something. He is probably lying somewhere unable to move, and too far away from the road to make his voice heard to anyone. If you start now, you will have just an hour and a half. You should have found him by then. The prefects from the other Houses will help you.'

Daintree put in a pertinent question.

'How about trespassing, sir?'

'Oh, go where you like. In reason, you know. Don't go getting the School mixed up in any unpleasantness, of course, but remember that your main object is to find Thomson. You all understand?'

'Yes, sir.'

'Very good. Then start at once.'

'By Jove,' said Swift, when he had gone, 'what an unholy rag! This suits yours truly. Poor old Jim, though. I wonder what the deuce has happened to him?'

At that very moment the Headmaster, leaving Philpott's House to go to Prater's, was wondering the same thing. In spite of Mr Merevale's argument, he found himself drifting back to his former belief that Jim had run away. What else could keep him out of his House more than three hours after lock-up? And he had had some reason for running away, for the *conscia mens recti*, though an excellent institution in theory, is not nearly so useful an ally as it should be in practice. The Head knocked at Prater's door, pondering darkly within himself.

17

'We'll Proceed
to Search for Thomson
if He Be Above the Ground'

'How sweet the moonlight sleeps on yonder haystack,' observed Charteris poetically, as he and Tony, accompanied by Swift and Daintree, made their way across the fields to Parker's Spinney. Each carried a bicycle lamp, and at irregular intervals each broke into piercing yells, to the marked discomfort of certain birds roosting in the neighbourhood, who burst noisily from the trees, and made their way with visible disgust to quieter spots.

'There's one thing,' said Swift, 'we ought to hear him if he yells on a night like this. A yell ought to travel about a mile.'

'Suppose we try one now,' said Charteris. 'Now. A concerted piece, *andante* in six-eight time. Ready?'

The next moment the stillness of the lovely spring night was shattered by a hideous uproar.

'R.S.V.P.,' said Charteris to space in general, as the echoes died away. But there was no answer, though they waited several minutes on the chance of hearing some sound that would indicate Jim's whereabouts.

'If he didn't hear that,' observed Tony, 'he can't be within three miles, that's a cert. We'd better separate, I think.'

They were at the ploughed field by Parker's Spinney now.

'Anybody got a coin?' asked Daintree. 'Let's toss for directions.'

Charteris produced a shilling.

'My ewe lamb,' he said. 'Tails.'

Tails it was. Charteris expressed his intention of striking westward and drawing the Spinney. He and Tony made their way thither, Swift and Daintree moving off together in the opposite direction.

'This is jolly rum,' said Tony, as they entered the Spinney. 'I wonder where the deuce the man has got to?'

'Yes. It's beastly serious, really, but I'm hanged if I can help feeling as if I were out on a picnic. I suppose it's the night air.'

'I wonder if we shall find him?'

'Not the slightest chance in my opinion. There's not the least good in looking through this forsaken Spinney. Still, we'd better do it.'

'Yes. Don't make a row. We're trespassing.'

They moved on in silence. Half-way through the wood Charteris caught his foot in a hole and fell.

'Hurt?' said Tony.

'Only in spirit, thanks. The absolute dashed foolishness of this is being rapidly borne in upon me, Tony. What *is* the good of it? We shan't find him here.'

Tony put his foot down upon these opinions with exemplary promptitude.

'We must go on trying. Hang it all, if it comes to the worst, it's better than frousting indoors.'

'Tony, you're a philosopher. Lead on, Macduff.'

Tony was about to do so, when a form appeared in front of him, blocking the way. He flashed his lamp at the form, and the form, prefacing its remarks with a good, honest swearword – of a variety peculiar to that part of the country – requested him, without any affectation of ceremonious courtesy, to take his something-or-other lamp out of his (the form's) what's-its-named face, and state his business briefly.

'Surely I know that voice,' said Charteris. 'Archibald, my long-lost brother.'

The keeper failed to understand him, and said so tersely.

'Can you tell *me*,' went on Charteris, 'if you have seen such a thing as a boy in this Spinney lately? We happen to have lost one. An ordinary boy. No special markings. His name is Thomson, on the Grampian Hills –'

At this point the keeper felt that he had had enough. He made a dive for the speaker.

Charteris dodged behind Tony, and his assailant, not observing this, proceeded to lay violent hands upon the latter, who had been standing waiting during the conversation.

'Let go, you fool,' cried he. The keeper's hand had come smartly into contact with his left eye, and from there had taken up a position on his shoulder. In reply the keeper merely tightened his grip.

'I'll count three,' said Tony, 'and –'

The keeper's hand shifted to his collar.

'All right, then,' said Tony between his teeth. He hit up with his left at the keeper's wrist. The hand on his collar loosed its grip. Its owner rushed, and as he came, Tony hit him in the parts about the third waistcoat-button with his right. He staggered and fell. Tony hit very hard when the spirit moved him.

'Come on, man,' said Charteris quickly, 'before he gets his wind again. We mustn't be booked trespassing.'

Tony recognized the soundness of the advice. They were out of the Spinney in two minutes.

'Now,' said Charteris, 'let's do a steady double to the road. This is no place for us. Come on, you man of blood.'

When they reached the road they slowed down to a walk again. Charteris laughed.

'I feel just as if we'd done a murder, somehow. What an ass that fellow was to employ violence. He went down all right, didn't he?'

'Think there'll be a row?'

'No. Should think not. He didn't see us properly. Anyhow, he was interfering with an officer in the performance of his duty. So were we, I suppose. Well, let's hope for the best. Hullo!'

'What's up?'

'All right. It's only somebody coming down the road. Thought it might be the keeper at first. Why, it's Biffen.'

It was Biffen. He looked at them casually as he came up, but stopped short in surprise when he saw who they were.

'Mr Charteris!'

'The same,' said Charteris. 'Enjoying a moonlight stroll, Biffen?'

'But what are you doing out of the 'ouse at this time of night, Mr Charteris?'

'It's this way,' said Tony, 'all the House-prefects have been sent out to look for Thomson. He's not come back.'

'Not come back, sir!'

'No. Bit queer, isn't it? The last anybody saw of him was when he dropped out of the long race near Parker's Spinney.'

'I seen him later than that, Mr Graham. He come on to the grounds while I was mowing the cricket field.'

'Not really? When was that?'

'Four. 'Alf past four, nearly.'

'What became of him?'

' 'E went off with Mr MacArthur. Mr MacArthur took 'im off 'ome with 'im, I think, sir.'

'By Jove,' said Charteris with enthusiasm. 'Now we *are* on the track. Thanks awfully, Biffen, I'll remember you in my will. Come on, Tony.'

'Where are you going now?'

'Babe's place, of course. The Babe holds the clue to this business. We must get it out of him. 'Night, Biffen.'

'Good-night, sir.'

Arrived at the Babe's residence, they rang the bell, and, in the interval of waiting for the door to be opened, listened with envy to certain sounds of revelry which filtered through the windows of a room to the right of the porch.

'The Babe seems to be making a night of it,' said Charteris. 'Oh' – as the servant opened the door – 'can we see Mr MacArthur, please?'

The servant looked doubtful on the point.

'There's company tonight, sir.'

'I knew he was making a night of it,' said Charteris to Tony. 'It's not Mr MacArthur we want to see. It's – dash it, what's the Babe's name?'

'Robert, I believe. Wouldn't swear to it.'

'Mr Robert. Is he in?' It seemed to Charteris that the form of this question smacked of Ollendorf. He half expected the servant to say 'No, but he has the mackintosh of his brother's cousin'. It produced the desired effect, however, for after inviting them to step in, the servant disappeared, and the Babe came on the scene, wearing a singularly prosperous expression, as if he had dined well.

'Hullo, you chaps,' he said.

'Sir to you,' said Charteris. 'Look here, Babe, we want to know what you have done with Jim. He was seen by competent witnesses to go off with you, and he's not come back. If you've murdered him, you might let us have the body.'

'Not come back! Rot. Are you certain?'

'My dear chap, every House-prefect on the list has been sent out to look for him. When did he leave here?'

The Babe reflected.

'Six, I should think. Little after, perhaps. Why – oh Lord!'

He broke off suddenly.

'What's up?' asked Tony.

'Why I sent him by a short cut through some woods close by here, and I've only just remembered there's a sort of quarry in the middle of them. I'll bet he's in there.'

'Great Scott, man, what sort of a quarry? I like the calm way the Babe talks of sending unsuspecting friends into quarries. Deep?'

'Not very, thank goodness. Still, if he fell down he might not be able to get up again, especially if he'd hurt himself at all. Half a second. Let me get on some boots, and I'll come out and look. Shan't be long.'

When he came back, the three of them set out for the quarry.

'There you are,' cried the Babe, with an entirely improper pride in his voice, considering the circumstances. 'What did I tell you?' Out of the darkness in front of them came a shout. They recognized the voice at once as Jim's.

Tony uttered a yell of encouragement, and was darting forward to the spot from which the cry had come, when the Babe stopped him. 'Don't do that, man,' he said. 'You'll be over yourself, if you don't look out. It's quite close here.'

He flashed one of the lamps in front of him. The light fell on a black opening in the ground, and Jim's voice sounded once more from the bowels of the earth, this time quite close to where they stood.

'Jim,' shouted Charteris, 'where are you?'

'Hullo,' said the voice, 'who's that? You might lug me out of here.'

'Are you hurt?'

'Twisted my ankle.'

'How far down are you?'

'Not far. Ten feet, about. Can't you get me out?'

'Half a second,' said the Babe, 'I'll go and get help. You chaps had better stay here and talk to him.' He ran off.

'How many of you are there up there?' asked Jim.

'Only Tony and myself,' said Charteris.

'Thought I heard somebody else.'

'Oh, that was the Babe. He's gone off to get help.'

'Oh. When he comes back, wring his neck, and heave him down here,' said Jim. 'I want a word with him on the subject of short cuts. I say, is there much excitement about this?'

'Rather. All the House-prefects are out after you. We've been looking in Parker's Spinney, and Tony was reluctantly compelled to knock out a keeper who tried to stop us. You should have been there. It was a rag.'

'Wish I had been. Hullo, is that the Babe come back?'

It was. The Babe, with his father and a party of friends arrayed in evening dress. They carried a ladder amongst them.

The pungent remarks Jim had intended to address to the Babe had no opportunity of active service. It was not the Babe who carried him up the ladder, but two of the dinner-party. Nor did the Babe have a hand in the carrying of the stretcher. That was done by as many of the evening-dress brigade as could get near enough. They seemed to enjoy it. One of them remarked that it reminded him of South Africa. To which another replied that it was far more like a party of policemen gathering in an 'early drunk' in the Marylebone Road. The procession moved on its stately way to the Babe's father's house, and the last Tony and Charteris saw of Jim, he was the centre of attraction, and appeared to be enjoying himself very much.

Charteris envied him, and did not mind saying so.

'Why can't *I* smash my ankle?' he demanded indignantly of Tony.

He was nearing section five, sub-section three, of his discourse, when they reached Merevale's gates. It was after eleven, but they felt that the news they were bringing entitled them to be a little late. Charteris brought his arguments to a premature end, and Tony rang the bell. Merevale himself opened the door to them.

18

In Which the Affairs of
Various Persons Are Wound Up

'Well,' he said, 'you're rather late. Any luck?'

'We've found him, sir,' said Tony.

'Really? That's a good thing. Where was he?'

'He'd fallen down a sort of quarry place near where MacArthur lives. MacArthur took him home with him to tea, and sent him back by a short cut, forgetting all about the quarry, and Thomson fell in and couldn't get out again.'

'Is he hurt?'

'Only twisted his ankle, sir.'

'Then where is he now?'

'They carried him back to the house.'

'MacArthur's house?'

'Yes, sir.'

'Oh, well, I suppose he will be all right then. Graham, just go across and report to the Headmaster, will you? You'll find him in his study.'

The Head was immensely relieved to hear Tony's narrative. After much internal debate he had at last come to the conclusion that Jim must have run away, and he had been wondering how he should inform his father of the fact.

'You are certain that he is not badly hurt, Graham?' he said, when Tony had finished his story.

'Yes, sir. It's only his ankle.'

'Very good. Good-night, Graham.'

The Head retired to bed that night filled with a virtuous resolve to seek Jim out on the following day, and speak a word in season to him on the subject of crime in general and betting in particular. This plan he proceeded to carry out as soon as afternoon school was over. When, however, he had arrived at the Babe's house, he found that there was one small thing which he had left out of his calculations. He had counted on seeing the invalid alone. On entering the sick-room he found there Mrs MacArthur, looking as if she intended to remain where she sat for several hours – which, indeed, actually was her intention – and Miss MacArthur, whose face and attitude expressed the same, only, if anything, more so. The fact was that the Babe, a very monument of resource on occasions, had, as he told Jim, 'given them the tip not to let the Old Man get at him, unless he absolutely chucked them out, you know'. When he had seen the Headmaster approaching, he had gone hurriedly to Jim's room to mention the fact, with excellent results.

The Head took a seat by the bed, and asked, with a touch of nervousness, after the injured ankle. This induced Mrs MacArthur to embark on a disquisition concerning the ease with which ankles are twisted, from which she drifted easily into a discussion of Rugby football, its merits and demerits. The Head, after several vain attempts to jerk the conversation into other grooves, gave it up, and listened for some ten minutes to a series of anecdotes about various friends and acquaintances of Mrs MacArthur's who had either twisted their own ankles or known people who had twisted theirs. The Head began to forget what exactly he had come to say that afternoon. Jim lay and grinned covertly through it all. When the Head did speak, his first words roused him effectually.

'I suppose, Mrs MacArthur, your son has told you that we have had a burglary at the School?'

'Hang it,' thought Jim, 'this isn't playing the game at all. Why talk shop, especially that particular brand of shop, here?' He wondered if the Head intended to describe the burglary, and then spring to his feet with a dramatic wave of the hand towards him, and say, 'There, Mrs MacArthur, is the criminal! There lies the viper on whom you have lavished your hospitality, the snaky and systematic serpent you have been induced by underhand means to pity. Look upon him, and loathe him. *He* stole the cups!'

'Yes, indeed,' replied Mrs MacArthur, 'I have heard a great deal about it. I suppose you have never found out who it was that did it?'

Jim lay back resignedly. After all, he had not done it, and if the Head liked to say he had, well, let him. *He* didn't care.

'Yes, Mrs MacArthur, we have managed to discover him.'

'And who was it?' asked Mrs MacArthur, much interested.

'Now for it,' said Jim to himself.

'We found that it was a man living in the village, who had been doing some work on the School grounds. He had evidently noticed the value of the cups, and determined to try his hand at appropriating them. He is well known as a poacher in the village, it seems. I think that for the future he will confine himself to that – ah – industry, for he is hardly likely ever to – ah – shine as a professional house-breaker. No.'

'Oh, well, that must be a relief to you, I am sure, Mr Perceval. These poachers are a terrible nuisance. They do frighten the birds so.'

She spoke as if it were an unamiable eccentricity on the part of the poachers, which they might be argued out of, if the matter were put before them in a reasonable manner. The Head agreed with her and rose to go. Jim watched him out of the room and then breathed a deep, satisfying breath of relief. His troubles were at an end.

In the meantime Barrett, who, having no inkling as to the rate at which affairs had been progressing since his visit to the Dingle, still imagined that the secret of the hollow tree belonged exclusively to Reade, himself, and one other, was much exercised in his mind about it. Reade candidly confessed himself baffled by the problem. Give him something moderately straightforward, and he was all right. This secret society and dark lantern style of affair was, he acknowledged, beyond him. And so it came about that Barrett resolved to do the only thing he could think of, and go to the Head about it. But before he had come to this decision, the Head had received another visit from Mr Roberts, as a result of which the table where Sir Alfred Venner had placed Plunkett's pipe and other accessories so dramatically during a previous interview, now bore another burden – the missing cups.

Mr Roberts had gone to the Dingle in person, and, by adroit use of the divinity which hedges a detective, had persuaded a keeper to lead him to the tree where, as Mr Stokes had said, the cups had been deposited.

The Head's first act, on getting the cups, was to send for Welch, to whom by right of conquest they belonged. Welch arrived shortly before Barrett. The Head was just handing him his prizes when the latter came into the room. It speaks well for Barrett's presence of mind that he had grasped the situation and decided on his line of action before Welch went, and the Head turned his attention to him.

'Well, Barrett?' said the Head.

'If you please, sir,' said Barrett, blandly, 'may I have leave to go to Stapleton?'

'Certainly, Barrett. Why do you wish to go?'

This was something of a poser, but Barrett's brain worked quickly.

'I wanted to send a telegram, sir.'

'Very well. But' – with suspicion – 'why did you not ask Mr Philpott? Your House-master can give you leave to go to Stapleton.'

'I couldn't find him, sir.' This was true, for he had not looked.

'Ah. Very well.'

'Thank you, sir.'

And Barrett went off to tell Reade that in some mysterious manner the cups had come back on their own account.

When Jim had congratulated himself that everything had ended happily, at any rate as far as he himself was concerned, he had forgotten for the moment that at present he had only one pound to his credit instead of the two which he needed. Charteris, however, had not. The special number of *The Glow Worm* was due on the following day, and Jim's accident left a considerable amount of 'copy' to be accounted for. He questioned Tony on the subject.

'Look here, Tony, have you time to do any more stuff for *The Glow Worm*?'

'My dear chap,' said Tony, 'I've not half done my own bits. Ask Welch.'

'I asked him just now. He can't. Besides, he only writes at about the rate of one word a minute, and we must get it all in by tonight at bed-time. I'm going to sit up as it is to jellygraph it. What's up?'

Tony's face had assumed an expression of dismay.

'Why,' he said, 'Great Scott, I never thought of it before. If we jellygraph it, our handwriting'll be recognized, and that will give the whole show away.'

Charteris took a seat, and faced this difficulty in all its aspects. The idea had never occurred to him before. And yet it should have been obvious.

'I'll have to copy the whole thing out in copper-plate,' he said desperately at last. 'My aunt, what a job.'

'I'll help,' said Tony. 'Welch will, too, I should think, if you ask him. How many jelly machine things can you raise?'

'I've got three. One for each of us. Wait a bit, I'll go and ask Welch.'

Welch, having first ascertained that the matter really was a pressing one, agreed without hesitation. He had objections to spoiling his sleep without reason, but in moments of emergency he put comfort behind him.

'Good,' said Charteris, when this had been settled, 'be here as soon as you can after eleven. I tell you what, we'll do the thing in style, and brew. It oughtn't to take more than an hour or so. It'll be rather a rag than otherwise.'

'And how about Jim's stuff?' asked Welch.

'I shall have to do that, as you can't. I've done my own bits. I think

I'd better start now.' He did, and with success. When he went to bed at half-past ten, *The Glow Worm* was ready in manuscript. Only the copying and printing remained to be done.

Charteris was out of bed and in the study just as eleven struck. Tony and Welch, arriving half-an-hour later, found him hard at work copying out an article of topical interest in a fair, round hand, quite unrecognizable as his own.

It was an impressive scene. The gas had been cut off, as it always was when the House went to bed, and they worked by the light of candles. Occasionally Welch, breathing heavily in his efforts to make his handwriting look like that of a member of a board-school (second standard), blew one or more of the candles out, and the others grunted fiercely. That was all they could do, for, for evident reasons, a vow of silence had been imposed. Charteris was the first to finish. He leant back in his chair, and the chair, which at a reasonable hour of the day would have endured any treatment, collapsed now with a noise like a pistol-shot.

'Now you've done it,' said Tony, breaking all rules by speaking considerably above a whisper.

Welch went to the door, and listened. The House was still. They settled down once more to work. Charteris lit the spirit-lamp, and began to prepare the meal. The others toiled painfully on at their round-hand. They finished almost simultaneously.

'Not another stroke do I do,' said Tony, 'till I've had something to drink. Is that water boiling yet?'

It was at exactly a quarter past two that the work was finished.

'Never again,' said Charteris, looking with pride at the piles of *Glow Worm*s stacked on the table; 'this jelly business makes one beastly sticky. I think we'll keep to print in future.'

And they did. Out of the twenty or more numbers of *The Glow Worm* published during Charteris' stay at School, that was the only one that did not come from the press. Readers who have themselves tried jellygraphing will sympathize. It is a curious operation, but most people will find one trial quite sufficient. That special number, however, reached a record circulation. The School had got its journey-money by the time it appeared, and wanted something to read in the train. Jim's pound was raised with ease.

Charteris took it round to him at the Babe's house, together with a copy of the special number.

'By Jove,' said Jim. 'Thanks awfully. Do you know, I'd absolutely forgotten all about *The Glow Worm*. I was to have written something for this number, wasn't I?'

And, considering the circumstances, that remark, as Charteris was at some pains to explain to him at the time, contained – when you came to analyse it – more cynical immorality to the cubic foot than any other half-dozen remarks he (Charteris) had ever heard in his life.

'It passes out of the realm of the merely impudent,' he said, with a happy recollection of a certain favourite author of his, 'and soars into the boundless empyrean of pure cheek.'

A PREFECT'S UNCLE

TO W. TOWNEND

Contents

[1]

Term Begins

Marriott walked into the senior day-room, and, finding no one there, hurled his portmanteau down on the table with a bang. The noise brought William into the room. William was attached to Leicester's House, Beckford College, as a mixture of butler and bootboy. He carried a pail of water in his hand. He had been engaged in cleaning up the House against the conclusion of the summer holidays, of which this was the last evening, by the simple process of transferring all dust, dirt, and other foreign substances from the floor to his own person.

' 'Ullo, Mr Marriott,' he said.

'Hullo, William,' said Marriott. 'How are you? Still jogging along? That's a mercy. I say, look here, I want a quiet word in season with the authorities. They must have known I was coming back this evening. Of course they did. Why, they specially wrote and asked me. Well, where's the red carpet? Where's the awning? Where's the brass band that ought to have met me at the station? Where's anything? I tell you what it is, William, my old companion, there's a bad time coming for the Headmaster if he doesn't mind what he's doing. He must learn that life is stern and life is earnest, William. Has Gethryn come back yet?'

William, who had been gasping throughout this harangue, for the intellectual pressure of Marriott's conversation (of which there was always plenty) was generally too much for him, caught thankfully at the last remark as being the only intelligible one uttered up to present date, and made answer –

'Mr Gethryn 'e's gorn out on to the field, Mr Marriott. 'E come 'arf an hour ago.'

'Oh! Right. Thanks. Goodbye, William. Give my respects to the cook, and mind you don't work too hard. Think what it would be if you developed heart disease. Awful! You mustn't do it, William.'

Marriott vanished, and William, slightly dazed, went about his professional duties once more.

Marriott walked out into the grounds in search of Gethryn. Gethryn was the head of Leicester's this term, *vice* Reynolds departed, and Marriott, who was second man up, shared a study with him. Leicester's had not a good name at Beckford, in spite of the fact that it was generally in the running for the cricket and football cups. The fact of the matter was that, with the exception of Gethryn, Marriott, a boy named Reece, who kept wicket for the School Eleven, and perhaps two others, Leicester's seniors were not a good lot. To the School in general, who gauged a fellow's character principally by his abilities in the cricket and football fields, it seemed a very desirable thing to be in Leicester's. They had been runners-up for the House football cup that year, and this term might easily see the cricket cup fall to them. Amongst the few, however, it was known that the House was passing through an unpleasant stage in its career. A House is either good or bad. It is seldom that it can combine the advantages of both systems. Leicester's was bad.

This was due partly to a succession of bad Head-prefects, and partly to Leicester himself, who was well-meaning but weak. His spirit was willing, but his will was not spirited. When things went on that ought not to have gone on, he generally managed to avoid seeing them, and the things continued to go on. Altogether, unless Gethryn's rule should act as a tonic, Leicester's was in a bad way.

The Powers that Be, however, were relying on Gethryn to effect some improvement. He was in the Sixth, the First Fifteen, and the First Eleven. Also a backbone was included in his anatomy, and if he made up his mind to a thing, that thing generally happened.

The Rev. James Beckett, the Headmaster of Beckford, had formed a very fair estimate of Gethryn's capabilities, and at the moment when Marriott was drawing the field for the missing one, that worthy was sitting in the Headmaster's study with a cup in his right hand and a muffin (half-eaten) in his left, drinking in tea and wisdom simultaneously. The Head was doing most of the talking. He had led up to the subject skilfully, and, once reached, he did not leave it. The text of his discourse was the degeneracy of Leicester's.

'Now, you know, Gethryn – another muffin? Help yourself. You know, Reynolds – well, he was a capital boy in his way, capital, and I'm sure we shall all miss him very much – *but* he was not a good head of a House. He was weak. Much too weak. Too easy-going. You must avoid that, Gethryn. Reynolds . . .' And much more in the same vein. Gethryn left the room half an hour later full of muffins and good resolutions.

He met Marriott at the fives-courts.

'Where have you been to?' asked Marriott. 'I've been looking for you all over the shop.'

'I and my friend the Headmaster,' said Gethryn, 'have been having a quiet pot of tea between us.'

'Really? Was he affable?'

'Distinctly affable.'

'You know,' said Marriott confidentially, 'he asked me in, but I told him it wasn't good enough. I said that if he would consent to make his tea with water that wasn't two degrees below lukewarm, and bring on his muffins cooked instead of raw, and supply some butter to eat with them, I might look him up now and then. Otherwise it couldn't be done at the price. But what did he want you for, really?'

'He was ragging me about the House. Quite right, too. You know, there's no doubt about it, Leicester's does want bucking up.'

'We're going to get the cricket cup,' said Marriott, for the defence.

'We may. If it wasn't for the Houses in between. School House and Jephson's especially. And anyhow, that's not what I meant. The games are all right. It's –'

'The moral *je-ne-sais-quoi*, so to speak,' said Marriott. 'That'll be all right. Wait till we get at 'em. What I want you to turn your great brain to now is this letter.'

He produced a letter from his pocket. 'Don't you bar chaps who show you their letters?' he said. 'This was written by an aunt of mine. I don't want to inflict the whole lot on you. Just look at line four. You see what she says: "A boy is coming to Mr Leicester's House this term, whom I particularly wish you to befriend. He is the son of a great friend of a friend of mine, and is a nice, bright little fellow, very jolly and full of spirits." '

'That means,' interpolated Gethryn grimly, 'that he is up to the eyes in pure, undiluted cheek, and will want kicking after every meal and before retiring to rest. Go on.'

'His name is –'

'Well?'

'That's the point. At this point the manuscript becomes absolutely illegible. I have conjectured Percy for the first name. It may be Richard, but I'll plunge on Percy. It's the surname that stumps me. Personally, I think it's MacCow, though I trust it isn't, for the kid's sake. I showed the letter to my brother, the one who's at Oxford. He swore it was Watson, but, on being pressed, hedged with Sandys. You may as well contribute your little bit. What do you make of it?'

Gethryn scrutinized the document with care.

'She begins with a D. You can see that.'

'Well?'

'Next letter a or u. I see. Of course. It's Duncan.'

'Think so?' said Marriott doubtfully. 'Well, let's go and ask the matron if she knows anything about him.'

'Miss Jones,' he said, when they had reached the House, 'have you on your list of new boys a sportsman of the name of MacCow or Watson? I am also prepared to accept Sandys or Duncan. The Christian name is either Richard or Percy. There, that gives you a fairly wide field to choose from.'

'There's a P. V. Wilson on the list,' said the matron, after an inspection of that document.

'That must be the man,' said Marriott. 'Thanks very much. I suppose he hasn't arrived yet?'

'No, not yet. You two are the only ones so far.'

'Oh! Well, I suppose I shall have to see him when he does come. I'll come down for him later on.'

They strolled out on to the field again.

'In *re* the proposed bucking-up of the House,' said Marriott, 'it'll be rather a big job.'

'Rather. I should think so. We ought to have a most fearfully sporting time. It's got to be done. The Old Man talked to me like several fathers.'

'What did he say?'

'Oh, heaps of things.'

'I know. Did he mention amongst other things that Reynolds was the worst idiot on the face of this so-called world?'

'Something of the sort.'

'So I should think. The late Reynolds was a perfect specimen of the gelatine-backboned worm. That's not my own, but it's the only description of him that really suits. Monk and Danvers and the mob in general used to do what they liked with him. Talking of Monk, when you embark on your tour of moral agitation, I should advise you to start with him.'

'Yes. And Danvers. There isn't much to choose between them. It's a pity they're both such good bats. When you see a chap putting them through the slips like Monk does, you can't help thinking there must be something in him.'

'So there is,' said Marriott, 'and it's all bad. I bar the man. He's slimy. It's the only word for him. And he uses scent by the gallon. Thank goodness this is his last term.'

'Is it really? I never heard that.'

'Yes. He and Danvers are both leaving. Monk's going to Heidelberg to study German, and Danvers is going into his pater's business in the City. I got that from Waterford.'

'Waterford is another beast,' said Gethryn thoughtfully. 'I suppose he's not leaving by any chance?'

'Not that I know of. But he'll be nothing without Monk and Danvers. He's simply a sort of bottle-washer to the firm. When they go he'll collapse. Let's be strolling towards the House now, shall we? Hullo! Our only Reece! Hullo, Reece!'

'Hullo!' said the new arrival. Reece was a weird, silent individual, whom everybody in the School knew up to a certain point, but very few beyond that point. His manner was exactly the same when talking to the smallest fag as when addressing the Headmaster. He rather gave one the impression that he was thinking of something a fortnight ahead, or trying to solve a chess problem without the aid of the board. In appearance he was on the short side, and thin. He was in the Sixth, and a conscientious worker. Indeed, he was only saved from being considered a swot, to use the vernacular, by the fact that from childhood's earliest hour he had been in the habit of keeping wicket like an angel. To a good wicket-keeper much may be forgiven.

He handed Gethryn an envelope.

'Letter, Bishop,' he said. Gethryn was commonly known as the Bishop, owing to a certain sermon preached in the College chapel some five years before, in aid of the Church Missionary Society, in which the preacher had alluded at frequent intervals to another Gethryn, a bishop, who, it appeared, had a see, and did much excellent work among the heathen at the back of beyond. Gethryn's friends and acquaintances, who had been alternating between 'Ginger' – Gethryn's hair being inclined to redness – and 'Sneg', a name which utterly baffles the philologist, had welcomed the new name warmly, and it had stuck ever since. And, after all, there are considerably worse names by which one might be called.

'What the dickens!' he said, as he finished reading the letter.

'Tell us the worst,' said Marriott. 'You must read it out now out of common decency, after rousing our expectations like that.'

'All right! It isn't private. It's from an aunt of mine.'

'Seems to be a perfect glut of aunts,' said Marriott. 'What views has your representative got to air? Is *she* springing any jolly little fellow full of spirits on this happy community?'

'No, it's not that. It's only an uncle of mine who's coming down here. He's coming tomorrow, and I'm to meet him. The uncanny part of it is that I've never heard of him before in my life.'

'That reminds me of a story I heard –' began Reece slowly. Reece's observations were not frequent, but when they came, did so for the most part in anecdotal shape. Somebody was constantly doing something which reminded him of something he had heard somewhere from somebody. The unfortunate part of it was that he exuded these reminiscences at such a leisurely rate of speed that he was rarely known to succeed in finishing any of them. He resembled those serial stories which appear in papers destined at a moderate price to fill an obvious void, and which break off abruptly at the third chapter, owing to the premature decease of the said periodicals. On this occasion Marriott cut in with a few sage remarks on the subject of uncles as a class. 'Uncles,' he said, 'are tricky. You never know where you've got 'em. You think they're going to come out strong with a sovereign, and they make it a shilling without a blush. An uncle of mine once gave me a threepenny bit. If it hadn't been that I didn't wish to hurt his feelings, I should have flung it at his feet. Also I particularly wanted threepence at the moment. Is your uncle likely to do his duty, Bishop?'

'I tell you I don't know the man. Never heard of him. I thought I knew every uncle on the list, but I can't place this one. However, I suppose I shall have to meet him.'

'Rather,' said Marriott, as they went into the House; 'we should always strive to be kind, even to the very humblest. On the off chance, you know. The unknown may have struck it rich in sheep or something out in Australia. Most uncles come from Australia. Or he may be the boss of some trust, and wallowing in dollars. He may be anything. Let's go and brew, Bishop. Come on, Reece.'

'I don't mind watching you two chaps eat,' said Gethryn, 'but I can't join in myself. I have assimilated three pounds odd of the Headmagisterial muffins already this afternoon. Don't mind me, though.'

They went upstairs to Marriott's study, which was also Gethryn's. Two in a study was the rule at Beckford, though there were recluses who lived alone, and seemed to enjoy it.

When the festive board had ceased to groan, and the cake, which Marriott's mother had expected to last a fortnight, had been reduced to a mere wreck of its former self, the thought of his aunt's friend's friend's son returned to Marriott, and he went down to investigate, returning shortly afterwards unaccompanied, but evidently full of news.

'Well?' said Gethryn. 'Hasn't he come?'

'A little,' said Marriott, 'just a little. I went down to the fags' room, and when I opened the door I noticed a certain weird stillness in the atmosphere. There is usually a row going on that you could cut with a knife. I looked about. The room was apparently empty. Then I observed a quaint object on the horizon. Do you know one Skinner by any chance?'

'My dear chap!' said Gethryn. Skinner was a sort of juvenile Professor Moriarty, a Napoleon of crime. He reeked of crime. He revelled in his wicked deeds. If a Dormitory-prefect was kept awake at night by some diabolically ingenious contrivance for combining the minimum of risk with the maximum of noise, then it was Skinner who had engineered the thing. Again, did a master, playing nervously forward on a bad pitch at the nets to Gosling, the School fast bowler, receive the ball gaspingly in the small ribs, and look round to see whose was that raucous laugh which had greeted the performance, he would observe a couple of yards away Skinner, deep in conversation with some friend of equally villainous aspect. In short, in a word, the only adequate word, he was Skinner.

'Well?' said Reece.

'Skinner,' proceeded Marriott, 'was seated in a chair, bleeding freely into a rather dirty pocket-handkerchief. His usual genial smile was hampered by a cut lip, and his right eye was blacked in the most graceful and pleasing manner. I made tender inquiries, but could get nothing from him except grunts. So I departed, and just outside the door I met young Lee, and got the facts out of him. It appears that P. V. Wilson, my aunt's friend's friend's son, entered the fags' room at four-fifteen. At four-fifteen-and-a-half, punctually, Skinner was observed to be trying to rag him. Apparently the great Percy has no sense of humour, for at four-seventeen he got tired of it, and hit Skinner crisply in the right eyeball, blacking the same as per illustration. The subsequent fight raged gorily for five minutes odd, and then Wilson, who seems to be a professional pugilist in disguise, landed what my informant describes as three corkers on his opponent's proboscis. Skinner's reply was to sit down heavily on the floor, and give him to understand that the fight was over, and that for the next day or two his face would be closed for alterations and repairs. Wilson thereupon harangued the company in well-chosen terms, tried to get Skinner to shake hands, but failed, and finally took the entire crew out to the shop, where they made pigs of themselves at his expense. I have spoken.'

'And that's the kid you've got to look after,' said Reece, after a pause.

'Yes,' said Marriott. 'What I maintain is that I require a kid built on those lines to look after me. But you ought to go down and see Skinner's eye sometime. It's a beautiful bit of work.'

[2]

Introduces an Unusual Uncle

On the following day, at nine o'clock, the term formally began. There is nothing of Black Monday about the first day of term at a public school. Black Monday is essentially a private school institution.

At Beckford the first day of every term was a half holiday. During the morning a feeble pretence of work was kept up, but after lunch the school was free, to do as it pleased and to go where it liked. The nets were put up for the first time, and the School professional emerged at last from his winter retirement with his 'Coom *right* out to 'em, sir, right forward', which had helped so many Beckford cricketers to do their duty by the School in the field. There was one net for the elect, the remnants of last year's Eleven and the 'probables' for this season, and half a dozen more for lesser lights.

At the first net Norris was batting to the bowling of Gosling, a long, thin day boy, Gethryn, and the professional – as useful a trio as any school batsman could wish for. Norris was captain of the team this year, a sound, stylish bat, with a stroke after the manner of Tyldesley between cover and mid-off, which used to make Miles the professional almost weep with joy. But today he had evidently not quite got into form. Twice in successive balls Gosling knocked his leg stump out of the ground with yorkers, and the ball after that, Gethryn upset his middle with a beauty.

'Hat-trick, Norris,' shouted Gosling.

'Can't see 'em a bit today. Bowled, Bishop.'

A second teaser from Gethryn had almost got through his defence. The Bishop was undoubtedly a fine bowler. Without being quite so fast as Gosling, he nevertheless contrived to work up a very considerable speed when he wished to, and there was always something in every ball he bowled which made it necessary for the batsman to watch it all the way. In matches against other schools it was generally Gosling who took the wickets. The batsmen were bothered by his pace. But when the M.C.C. or the Incogniti came down, bringing seasoned county men who knew what fast bowling really was, and rather preferred it on the whole to slow, then Gethryn was called upon.

Most Beckfordians who did not play cricket on the first day of term went on the river. A few rode bicycles or strolled out into the country in couples, but the majority, amongst whom on this occasion was Marriott, sallied to the water and hired boats. Marriott was one of the six old cricket colours – the others were Norris, Gosling, Gethryn, Reece, and Pringle of the School House – who formed the foundation of this year's Eleven. He was not an ornamental bat, but stood quite alone in the matter of tall hitting. Twenty minutes of Marriott when in form would often completely alter the course of a match. He had been given his colours in the previous year for making exactly a hundred in sixty-one minutes against the Authentics when the rest of the team had contributed ninety-eight. The Authentics made a hundred and eighty-four, so that the School just won; and the story of how there were five men out in the deep for him, and how he put the slow bowler over their heads and over the ropes eight times in three overs, had passed into a school legend.

But today other things than cricket occupied his attention. He had run Wilson to earth, and was engaged in making his acquaintance, according to instructions received.

'Are you Wilson?' he asked. 'P.V. Wilson?'

Wilson confirmed the charge.

'My name's Marriott. Does that convey any significance to your young mind?'

'Oh, yes. My mater knows somebody who knows your aunt.'

'It is a true bill.'

'And she said you would look after me. I know you won't have time, of course.'

'I expect I shall have time to give you all the looking after you'll require. It won't be much, from all I've heard. Was all that true about you and young Skinner?'

Wilson grinned.

'I did have a bit of a row with a chap called Skinner,' he admitted.

'So Skinner seems to think,' said Marriott. 'What was it all about?'

'Oh, he made an ass of himself,' said Wilson vaguely.

Marriott nodded.

'He would. I know the man. I shouldn't think you'd have much trouble with Skinner in the future. By the way, I've got you for a fag this term. You don't have to do much in the summer. Just rot around, you know, and go to the shop for biscuits and things, that's all. And, within limits of course, you get the run of the study.'

'I see,' said Wilson gratefully. The prospect was pleasant.

'Oh yes, and it's your privilege to pipe-clay my cricket boots occasionally before First matches. You'll like that. Can you steer a boat?'

'I don't think so. I never tried.'

'It's easy enough. I'll tell you what to do. Anyhow, you probably won't steer any worse than I row, so let's go and get a boat out, and I'll try and think of a few more words of wisdom for your benefit.'

At the nets Norris had finished his innings, and Pringle was batting in his stead. Gethryn had given up his ball to Baynes, who bowled slow leg-breaks, and was the most probable of the probables abovementioned. He went to where Norris was taking off his pads, and began to talk to him. Norris was the head of Jephson's House, and he and the Bishop were very good friends, in a casual sort of way. If they did not see one another for a couple of days, neither of them broke his heart. Whenever, on the other hand, they did meet, they were always glad, and always had plenty to talk about. Most school friendships are of that description.

'You were sending down some rather hot stuff,' said Norris, as Gethryn sat down beside him, and began to inspect Pringle's performance with a critical eye.

'I did feel rather fit,' said he. 'But I don't think half those that got you would have taken wickets in a match. You aren't in form yet.'

'I tell you what it is, Bishop,' said Norris, 'I believe I'm going to be a rank failure this season. Being captain does put one off.'

'Don't be an idiot, man. How can you possibly tell after one day's play at the nets?'

'I don't know. I feel so beastly anxious somehow. I feel as if I was personally responsible for every match lost. It was all right last year when John Brown was captain. Good old John! Do you remember his running you out in the Charchester match?'

'Don't,' said Gethryn pathetically. 'The only time I've ever felt as if I really was going to make that century. By Jove, see that drive? Pringle seems all right.'

'Yes, you know, he'll simply walk into his Blue when he goes up to the 'Varsity. What do you think of Baynes?'

'Ought to be rather useful on his wicket. Jephson thinks he's good.'

Mr Jephson looked after the School cricket.

'Yes, I believe he rather fancies him,' said Norris. 'Says he ought to do some big things if we get any rain. Hullo, Pringle, are you coming out? You'd better go in, then, Bishop.'

'All right. Thanks. Oh, by Jove, though, I forgot. I can't. I've got to go down to the station to meet an uncle of mine.'

'What's he coming up today for? Why didn't he wait till we'd got a match of sorts on?'

'I don't know. The man's probably a lunatic. Anyhow, I shall have to go and meet him, and I shall just do it comfortably if I go and change now.'

'Oh! Right you are! Sammy, do you want a knock?'

Samuel Wilberforce Gosling, known to his friends and admirers as Sammy, replied that he did not. All he wanted now, he said, was a drink, or possibly two drinks, and a jolly good rest in the shade somewhere. Gosling was one of those rare individuals who cultivate bowling at the expense of batting, a habit the reverse of what usually obtains in schools.

Norris admitted the justice of his claims, and sent in a Second Eleven man, Baker, a member of his own House, in Pringle's place. Pringle and Gosling adjourned to the School shop for refreshment.

Gethryn walked with them as far as the gate which opened on to the road where most of the boarding Houses stood, and then branched off in the direction of Leicester's. To change into everyday costume took him a quarter of an hour, at the end of which period he left the House, and began to walk down the road in the direction of the station.

It was an hour's easy walking between Horton, the nearest station to Beckford, and the College. Gethryn, who was rather tired after his exertions at the nets, took it very easily, and when he arrived at his destination the church clock was striking four.

'Is the three-fifty-six in yet?' he asked of the solitary porter who ministered to the needs of the traveller at Horton station.

'Just a-coming in now, zur,' said the porter, adding, in a sort of inspired frenzy: ' 'Orton! 'Orton stertion! 'Orton!' and ringing a bell with immense enthusiasm and vigour.

Gethryn strolled to the gate, where the station-master's son stood at the receipt of custom to collect the tickets. His uncle was to arrive by this train, and if he did so arrive, must of necessity pass this way before leaving the platform. The train panted in, pulled up, whistled, and puffed out again, leaving three people behind it. One of these was a woman of sixty (approximately), the second a small girl of ten, the third a young gentleman in a top hat and Etons, who carried a bag, and looked as if he had seen the hollowness of things, for his face wore a bored, supercilious look. His uncle had evidently not arrived, unless he had come disguised as an old woman, an act of which Gethryn refused to believe him capable.

He enquired as to the next train that was expected to arrive from London. The station-master's son was not sure, but would ask the porter, whose name it appeared was Johnny. Johnny gave the correct answer without an effort. 'Seven-thirty it was, sir, except on Saturdays, when it was eight o'clock.'

'Thanks,' said the Bishop. 'Dash the man, he might at least have wired.'

He registered a silent wish concerning the uncle who had brought him a long three miles out of his way with nothing to show at the end of it, and was just turning to leave the station, when the top-hatted small boy, who had been hovering round the group during the conversation, addressed winged words to him. These were the winged words –

'I say, are you looking for somebody?' The Bishop stared at him as a naturalist stares at a novel species of insect.

'Yes,' he said. 'Why?'

'Is your name Gethryn?'

This affair, thought the Bishop, was beginning to assume an uncanny aspect.

'How the dickens did you know that?' he said.

'Oh, then you *are* Gethryn? That's all right. I was told you were going to be here to meet this train. Glad to make your acquaintance. My name's Farnie. I'm your uncle, you know.'

'My what?' gurgled the Bishop.

'Your uncle. U-n, un; c-l-e – kul. Uncle. Fact, I assure you.'

[3]

The Uncle Makes Himself at Home

'But, dash it,' said Gethryn, when he had finished gasping, 'that must be rot!'

'Not a bit,' said the self-possessed youth. 'Your mater was my elder sister. You'll find it works out all right. Look here. A, the daughter of B and C, marries. No, look here. I was born when you were four. See?'

Then the demoralized Bishop remembered. He had heard of his juvenile uncle, but the tales had made little impression upon him. Till now they had not crossed one another's tracks.

'Oh, all right,' said he, 'I'll take your word for it. You seem to have been getting up the subject.'

'Yes. Thought you might want to know about it. I say, how far is it to Beckford, and how do you get there?'

Up till now Gethryn had scarcely realized that his uncle was actually coming to the School for good. These words brought the fact home to him.

'Oh, Lord,' he said, 'are you coming to Beckford?'

The thought of having his footsteps perpetually dogged by an uncle four years younger than himself, and manifestly a youth with a fine taste in cheek, was not pleasant.

'Of course,' said his uncle. 'What did you think I was going to do? Camp out on the platform?'

'What House are you in?'

'Leicester's.'

The worst had happened. The bitter cup was full, the iron neatly inserted in Gethryn's soul. In his most pessimistic moments he had never looked forward to the coming term so gloomily as he did now. His uncle noted his lack of enthusiasm, and attributed it to anxiety on behalf of himself.

'What's up?' he asked. 'Isn't Leicester's all right? Is Leicester a beast?'

'No. He's a perfectly decent sort of man. It's a good enough House. At least it will be this term. I was only thinking of something.'

'I see. Well, how do you get to the place?'

'Walk. It isn't far.'

'How far?'

'Three miles.'

'The porter said four.'

'It may be four. I never measured it.'

'Well, how the dickens do you think I'm going to walk four miles with luggage? I wish you wouldn't rot.'

And before Gethryn could quite realize that he, the head of Leicester's, the second-best bowler in the School, and the best centre three-quarter the School had had for four seasons, had been requested in a peremptory manner by a youth of fourteen, a mere kid, not to rot, the offender was talking to a cabman out of the reach of retaliation. Gethryn became more convinced every minute that this was no ordinary kid.

'This man says,' observed Farnie, returning to Gethryn, 'that he'll drive me up to the College for seven bob. As it's a short four miles, and I've only got two boxes, it seems to me that he's doing himself fairly well. What do you think?'

'Nobody ever gives more than four bob,' said Gethryn.

'I told you so,' said Farnie to the cabman. 'You are a bally swindler,' he added admiringly.

'Look 'ere,' began the cabman, in a pained voice.

'Oh, dry up,' said Farnie. 'Want a lift, Gethryn?'

The words were spoken not so much as from equal to equal as in a tone of airy patronage which made the Bishop's blood boil. But as he intended to instil a few words of wisdom into his uncle's mind, he did not refuse the offer.

The cabman, apparently accepting the situation as one of those slings and arrows of outrageous fortune which no man can hope to escape, settled down on the box, clicked up his horse, and drove on towards the College.

'What sort of a hole is Beckford?' asked Farnie, after the silence had lasted some time.

'I find it good enough personally,' said Gethryn. 'If you'd let us know earlier that you were coming, we'd have had the place done up a bit for you.'

This, of course, was feeble, distinctly feeble. But the Bishop was not feeling himself. The essay in sarcasm left the would-be victim entirely uncrushed. He should have shrunk and withered up, or at the least have blushed. But he did nothing of the sort. He merely smiled in his supercilious way, until the Bishop felt very much inclined to spring upon him and throw him out of the cab.

There was another pause.

'Farnie,' began Gethryn at last.

'Um?'

'Doesn't it strike you that for a kid like you you've got a good deal of edge on?' asked Gethryn.

Farnie effected a masterly counter-stroke. He pretended not to be able to hear. He was sorry, but would the Bishop mind repeating his remark.

'Eh? What?' he said. 'Very sorry, but this cab's making such a row. I say, cabby, why don't you sign the pledge, and save your money up to buy a new cab? Eh? Oh, sorry! I wasn't listening.' Now, inasmuch as the whole virtue of the 'wretched-little-kid-like-you' argument lies in the crisp despatch with which it is delivered, Gethryn began to find, on repeating his observation for the third time, that there was not quite so much in it as he had thought. He prudently elected to change his style of attack.

'It doesn't matter,' he said wearily, as Farnie opened his mouth to demand a fourth encore, 'it wasn't anything important. Now, look here, I just want to give you a few tips about what to do when you get to the Coll. To start with, you'll have to take off that white tie you've got on. Black and dark blue are the only sorts allowed here.'

'How about yours then?' Gethryn was wearing a somewhat sweet thing in brown and yellow.

'Mine happens to be a First Eleven tie.'

'Oh! Well, as a matter of fact, you know, I was going to take off my tie. I always do, especially at night. It's a sort of habit I've got into.'

'Not quite so much of your beastly cheek, please,' said Gethryn.

'Right-ho!' said Farnie cheerfully, and silence, broken only by the shrieking of the cab wheels, brooded once more over the cab. Then Gethryn, feeling that perhaps it would be a shame to jump too severely on a new boy on his first day at a large public school, began to think of something conciliatory to say. 'Look here,' he said, 'you'll get on all right at Beckford, I expect. You'll find Leicester's a fairly decent sort of House. Anyhow, you needn't be afraid you'll get bullied. There's none of that sort of thing at School nowadays.'

'Really?'

'Yes, and there's another thing I ought to warn you about. Have you brought much money with you?'

' 'Bout fourteen pounds, I fancy,' said Farnie carelessly.

'Fourteen *what!*' said the amazed Bishop. '*Pounds!*'

'Or sovereigns,' said Farnie. 'Each worth twenty shillings, you know.'

For a moment Gethryn's only feeling was one of unmixed envy. Previously he had considered himself passing rich on thirty shillings a term. He had heard legends, of course, of individuals who come to School bursting with bullion, but never before had he set eyes upon such an one. But after a time it began to dawn upon him that for a new boy at a public school, and especially at such a House as Leicester's had become under the rule of the late Reynolds and his predecessors, there might be such a thing as having too much money.

'How the deuce did you get all that?' he asked.

'My pater gave it me. He's absolutely cracked on the subject of pocket-money. Sometimes he doesn't give me a sou, and sometimes he'll give me whatever I ask for.'

'But you don't mean to say you had the cheek to ask for fourteen quid?'

'I asked for fifteen. Got it, too. I've spent a pound of it. I said I wanted to buy a bike. You can get a jolly good bike for five quid about, so you see I scoop ten pounds. What?'

This ingenious, if slightly unscrupulous, feat gave Gethryn an insight into his uncle's character which up till now he had lacked. He began to see that the moral advice with which he had primed himself would be out of place. Evidently this youth could take quite good care of himself on his own account. Still, even a budding Professor Moriarty would be none the worse for being warned against Gethryn's *bête noire*, Monk, so the Bishop proceeded to deliver that warning.

'Well,' he said, 'you seem to be able to look out for yourself all right, I must say. But there's one tip I really can give you. When you get to Leicester's, and a beast with a green complexion and an oily smile comes up and calls you "Old Cha-a-p", and wants you to swear eternal friendship, tell him it's not good enough. Squash him!'

'Thanks,' said Farnie. 'Who is this genial merchant?'

'Chap called Monk. You'll recognize him by the smell of scent. When you find the place smelling like an Eau-de-Cologne factory, you'll know Monk's somewhere near. Don't you have anything to do with him.'

'You seem to dislike the gentleman.'

'I bar the man. But that isn't why I'm giving you the tip to steer clear of him. There are dozens of chaps I bar who haven't an ounce of vice in them. And there are one or two chaps who have got tons. Monk's one of them. A fellow called Danvers is another. Also a beast of the name of Waterford. There are some others as well, but those are the worst of the lot. By the way, I forgot to ask, have you ever been to school before?'

'Yes,' said Farnie, in the dreamy voice of one who recalls memories from the misty past, 'I was at Harrow before I came here, and at Wellington before I went to Harrow, and at Clifton before I went to Wellington.'

Gethryn gasped.

'Anywhere before you went to Clifton?' he enquired.

'Only private schools.'

The recollection of the platitudes which he had been delivering, under the impression that he was talking to an entirely raw beginner, made Gethryn feel slightly uncomfortable. What must this wanderer, who had seen men and cities, have thought of his harangue?

'Why did you leave Harrow?' asked he.

'Sacked,' was the laconic reply.

Have you ever, asks a modern philosopher, gone upstairs in the dark, and trodden on the last step when it wasn't there? That sensation and the one Gethryn felt at this unexpected revelation were identical. And the worst of it was that he felt the keenest desire to know why Harrow had seen fit to dispense with the presence of his uncle.

'Why?' he began. 'I mean,' he went on hurriedly, 'why did you leave Wellington?'

'Sacked,' said Farnie again, with the monotonous persistence of a Solomon Eagle.

Gethryn felt at this juncture much as the unfortunate gentleman in *Punch* must have felt, when, having finished a humorous story, the point of which turned upon squinting and red noses, he suddenly discovered that his host enjoyed both those peculiarities. He struggled manfully with his feelings for a time. Tact urged him to discontinue his investigations and talk about the weather. Curiosity insisted upon knowing further details. Just as the struggle was at its height, Farnie came unexpectedly to the rescue.

'It may interest you,' he said, 'to know that I was not sacked from Clifton.'

Gethryn with some difficulty refrained from thanking him for the information.

'I never stop at a school long,' said Farnie. 'If I don't get sacked my father takes me away after a couple of terms. I went to four private schools before I started on the public schools. My pater took me away from the first two because he thought the drains were bad, the third because they wouldn't teach me shorthand, and the fourth because he didn't like the headmaster's face. I worked off those schools in a year and a half.' Having finished this piece of autobiography, he relapsed into silence, leaving Gethryn to recollect various tales he had heard of his grandfather's eccentricity. The silence lasted until the College was reached, when the matron took charge of Farnie, and Gethryn went off to tell Marriott of these strange happenings.

Marriott was amused, nor did he attempt to conceal the fact. When he had finished laughing, which was not for some time, he favoured the Bishop with a very sound piece of advice. 'If I were you,' he said, 'I should try and hush this affair up. It's all fearfully funny, but I think you'd enjoy life more if nobody knew this kid was your uncle. To see the head of the House going about with a juvenile uncle in his wake might amuse the chaps rather, and you might find it harder to keep order; I won't let it out, and nobody else knows apparently. Go and square the kid. Oh, I say though, what's his name? If it's Gethryn, you're done. Unless you like to swear he's a cousin.'

'No; his name's Farnie, thank goodness.'

'That's all right then. Go and talk to him.'

Gethryn went to the junior study. Farnie was holding forth to a knot of fags at one end of the room. His audience appeared to be amused at something.

'I say, Farnie,' said the Bishop, 'half a second.'

Farnie came out, and Gethryn proceeded to inform him that, all things considered, and proud as he was of the relationship, it was not absolutely essential that he should tell everybody that he was his uncle. In fact, it would be rather better on the whole if he did not. Did he follow?

Farnie begged to observe that he did follow, but that, to his sorrow, the warning came too late.

'I'm very sorry,' he said, 'I hadn't the least idea you wanted the thing kept dark. How was I to know? I've just been telling it to some of the chaps in there. Awfully decent chaps. They seemed to think it rather funny. Anyhow, I'm not ashamed of the relationship. Not yet, at any rate.'

For a moment Gethryn seemed about to speak. He looked fixedly at his uncle as he stood framed in the doorway, a cheerful column of cool, calm, concentrated cheek. Then, as if realizing that no words that he knew could do justice to the situation, he raised his foot in silence, and 'booted' his own flesh and blood with marked emphasis. After which ceremony he went, still without a word, upstairs again.

As for Farnie, he returned to the junior day-room whistling 'Down South' in a soft but cheerful key, and solidified his growing popularity with doles of food from a hamper which he had brought with him. Finally, on retiring to bed and being pressed by the rest of his dormitory for a story, he embarked upon the history of a certain Pollock and an individual referred to throughout as the Porroh Man, the former of whom caused the latter to be decapitated, and was ever afterwards haunted by his head, which appeared to him all day and every day (not excepting Sundays and Bank Holidays) in an upside-down position and wearing a horrible grin. In the end Pollock very sensibly committed suicide (with ghastly details), and the dormitory thanked Farnie in a subdued and chastened manner, and tried, with small success, to go to sleep. In short, Farnie's first evening at Beckford had been quite a triumph.

[4]

Pringle Makes a Sporting Offer

Estimating it roughly, it takes a new boy at a public school about a
week to find his legs and shed his skin of newness. The period is, of
course, longer in the case of some and shorter in the case of others.
Both Farnie and Wilson had made themselves at home immediately.
In the case of the latter, directly the Skinner episode had been noised
abroad, and it was discovered in addition that he was a promising bat,
public opinion recognized that here was a youth out of the common
run of new boys, and the Lower Fourth – the form in which he had
been placed on arrival – took him to its bosom as an equal. Farnie's
case was exceptional. A career at Harrow, Clifton, and Wellington,
however short and abruptly terminated, gives one some sort of grip
on the way public school life is conducted. At an early date, moreover,
he gave signs of what almost amounted to genius in the Indoor Game
department. Now, success in the field is a good thing, and undoubtedly
makes for popularity. But if you desire to command the respect and
admiration of your fellow-beings to a degree stretched almost to the
point of idolatry, make yourself proficient in the art of whiling away
the hours of afternoon school. Before Farnie's arrival, his form, the
Upper Fourth, with the best intentions in the world, had not been
skilful 'raggers'. They had ragged in an intermittent, once-a-week
sort of way. When, however, he came on the scene, he introduced a
welcome element of science into the sport. As witness the following.
Mr Strudwick, the regular master of the form, happened on one
occasion to be away for a couple of days, and a stop-gap was put in in
his place. The name of the stop-gap was Mr Somerville Smith.
He and Farnie exchanged an unspoken declaration of war almost
immediately. The first round went in Mr Smith's favour. He contrived
to catch Farnie in the act of performing some ingenious breach of the
peace, and, it being a Wednesday and a half-holiday, sent him into
extra lesson. On the following morning, more by design than accident,
Farnie upset an inkpot. Mr Smith observed icily that unless the stain

was wiped away before the beginning of afternoon school, there would be trouble. Farnie observed (to himself) that there would be trouble in any case, for he had hit upon the central idea for the most colossal 'rag' that, in his opinion, ever was. After morning school he gathered the form around him, and disclosed his idea. The floor of the form-room, he pointed out, was some dozen inches below the level of the door. Would it not be a pleasant and profitable notion, he asked, to flood the floor with water to the depth of those dozen inches? On the wall outside the form-room hung a row of buckets, placed there in case of fire, and the lavatory was not too far off for practical purposes. Mr Smith had bidden him wash the floor. It was obviously his duty to do so. The form thought so too. For a solid hour, thirty weary but enthusiastic reprobates laboured without ceasing, and by the time the bell rang all was prepared. The floor was one still, silent pool. Two caps and a few notebooks floated sluggishly on the surface, relieving the picture of any tendency to monotony. The form crept silently to their places along the desks. As Mr Smith's footsteps were heard approaching, they began to beat vigorously upon the desks, with the result that Mr Smith, quickening his pace, dashed into the form-room at a hand gallop. The immediate results were absolutely satisfactory, and if matters subsequently (when Mr Smith, having changed his clothes, returned with the Headmaster) did get somewhat warm for the thirty criminals, they had the satisfying feeling that their duty had been done, and a hearty and unanimous vote of thanks was passed to Farnie. From which it will be seen that Master Reginald Farnie was managing to extract more or less enjoyment out of his life at Beckford.

Another person who was enjoying life was Pringle of the School House. The keynote of Pringle's character was superiority. At an early period of his life – he was still unable to speak at the time – his grandmother had died. This is probably the sole reason why he had never taught that relative to suck eggs. Had she lived, her education in that direction must have been taken in hand. Baffled in this, Pringle had turned his attention to the rest of the human race. He had a rooted conviction that he did everything a shade better than anybody else. This belief did not make him arrogant at all, and certainly not offensive, for he was exceedingly popular in the School. But still there were people who thought that he might occasionally draw the line some-where. Watson, the ground-man, for example, thought so when Pringle primed him with advice on the subject of preparing a wicket. And Langdale, who had been captain of the team five years before, had thought so most decidedly, and had not hesitated to say so when

Pringle, then in his first term and aged twelve, had stood behind the First Eleven net and requested him peremptorily to 'keep 'em down, sir, keep 'em down'. Indeed, the great man had very nearly had a fit on that occasion, and was wont afterwards to attribute to the effects of the shock so received a sequence of three 'ducks' which befell him in the next three matches.

In short, in every department of life, Pringle's advice was always (and generally unsought) at everybody's disposal. To round the position off neatly, it would be necessary to picture him as a total failure in the practical side of all the subjects in which he was so brilliant a theorist. Strangely enough, however, this was not the case. There were few better bats in the School than Pringle. Norris on his day was more stylish, and Marriott not infrequently made more runs, but for consistency Pringle was unrivalled.

That was partly the reason why at this time he was feeling pleased with life. The School had played three matches up to date, and had won them all. In the first, an Oxford college team, containing several Old Beckfordians, had been met and routed, Pringle contributing thirty-one to a total of three hundred odd. But Norris had made a century, which had rather diverted the public eye from this performance. Then the School had played the Emeriti, and had won again quite comfortably. This time his score had been forty-one, useful, but still not phenomenal. Then in the third match, *versus* Charchester, one of the big school matches of the season, he had found himself. He ran up a hundred and twenty-three without a chance, and felt that life had little more to offer. That had been only a week ago, and the glow of satisfaction was still pleasantly warm.

It was while he was gloating silently in his study over the bat with which a grateful Field Sports Committee had presented him as a reward for this feat, that he became aware that Lorimer, his study companion, appeared to be in an entirely different frame of mind to his own. Lorimer was in the Upper Fifth, Pringle in the Remove. Lorimer sat at the study table gnawing a pen in a feverish manner that told of an overwrought soul. Twice he uttered sounds that were obviously sounds of anguish, half groans and half grunts. Pringle laid down his bat and decided to investigate.

'What's up?' he asked.

'This bally poem thing,' said Lorimer.

'Poem? Oh, ah, I know.' Pringle had been in the Upper Fifth himself a year before, and he remembered that every summer term there descended upon that form a Bad Time in the shape of a poetry prize. A certain Indian potentate, the Rajah of Seltzerpore, had paid a visit to the school some years back, and had left behind him on his departure certain monies in the local bank, which were to be devoted to providing the Upper Fifth with an annual prize for the best poem on a subject to be selected by the Headmaster. Entrance was compulsory. The wily authorities knew very well that if it had not been, the entries for the prize would have been somewhat small. Why the Upper Fifth were so favoured in preference to the Sixth or Remove is doubtful. Possibly it was felt that, what with the Jones History, the Smith Latin Verse, the Robinson Latin Prose, and the De Vere Crespigny Greek Verse, and other trophies open only to members of the Remove and Sixth, those two forms had enough to keep them occupied as it was. At any rate, to the Upper Fifth the prize was given, and every year, three weeks after the commencement of the summer term, the Bad Time arrived.

'Can't you get on?' asked Pringle.

'No.'

'What's the subject?'

'Death of Dido.'

'Something to be got out of that, surely.'

'Wish you'd tell me what.'

'Heap of things.'

'Such as what? Can't see anything myself. I call it perfectly indecent dragging the good lady out of her well-earned tomb at this time of day. I've looked her up in the Dic. of Antiquities, and it appears that she committed suicide some years ago. Body-snatching, I call it. What do I want to know about her?'

'What's Hecuba to him or he to Hecuba?' murmured Pringle.

'Hecuba?' said Lorimer, looking puzzled, 'What's Hecuba got to do with it?'

'I was only quoting,' said Pringle, with gentle superiority.

'Well, I wish instead of quoting rot you'd devote your energies to helping me with these beastly verses. How on earth shall I begin?'

'You might adapt my quotation. "What's Dido got to do with me, or I to do with Dido?" I rather like that. Jam it down. Then you go on in a sort of rag-time metre. In the "Coon Drum-Major" style. Besides, you see, the beauty of it is that you administer a wholesome snub to the examiner right away. Makes him sit up at once. Put it down.'

Lorimer bit off another quarter of an inch of his pen. 'You needn't be an ass,' he said shortly.

'My dear chap,' said Pringle, enjoying himself immensely, 'what on earth is the good of my offering you suggestions if you won't take them?'

Lorimer said nothing. He bit off another mouthful of penholder.

'Well, anyway,' resumed Pringle. 'I can't see why you're so keen on the business. Put down anything. The beaks never make a fuss about these special exams.'

'It isn't the beaks I care about,' said Lorimer in an injured tone of voice, as if someone had been insinuating that he had committed some crime, 'only my people are rather keen on my doing well in this exam.'

'Why this exam, particularly?'

'Oh, I don't know. My grandfather or someone was a bit of a pro at verse in his day, I believe, and they think it ought to run in the family.'

Pringle examined the situation in all its aspects. 'Can't you get along?' he enquired at length.

'Not an inch.'

'Pity. I wish we could swop places.'

'So do I for some things. To start with, I shouldn't mind having made that century of yours against Charchester.'

Pringle beamed. The least hint that his fellow-man was taking him at his own valuation always made him happy.

'Thanks,' he said. 'No, but what I meant was that I wished I was in for this poetry prize. I bet I could turn out a rattling good screed. Why, last year I almost got the prize. I sent in fearfully hot stuff.'

'Think so?' said Lorimer doubtfully, in answer to the 'rattling good screed' passage of Pringle's speech. 'Well, I wish you'd have a shot. You might as well.'

'What, really? How about the prize?'

'Oh, hang the prize. We'll have to chance that.'

'I thought you were keen on getting it.'

'Oh, no. Second or third will do me all right, and satisfy my people. They only want to know for certain that I've got the poetic afflatus all right. Will you take it on?'

'All right.'

'Thanks, awfully.'

'I say, Lorimer,' said Pringle after a pause.

'Yes?'

'Are your people coming down for the O.B.s' match?'

The Old Beckfordians' match was the great function of the Beckford cricket season. The Headmaster gave a garden-party. The School band played; the School choir sang; and sisters, cousins, aunts, and parents flocked to the School in platoons.

'Yes, I think so,' said Lorimer. 'Why?'

'Is your sister coming?'

'Oh, I don't know.' A brother's utter lack of interest in his sister's actions is a weird and wonderful thing for an outsider to behold.

'Well, look here, I wish you'd get her to come. We could give them tea in here, and have rather a good time, don't you think?'

'All right. I'll make her come. Look here, Pringle, I believe you're rather gone on Mabel.'

This was Lorimer's vulgar way.

'Don't be an ass,' said Pringle, with a laugh which should have been careless, but was in reality merely feeble. 'She's quite a kid.'

Miss Mabel Lorimer's exact age was fifteen. She had brown hair, blue eyes, and a smile which disclosed to view a dimple. There are worse things than a dimple. Distinctly so, indeed. When ladies of fifteen possess dimples, mere man becomes but as a piece of damp blotting-paper. Pringle was seventeen and a half, and consequently too old to take note of such frivolous attributes; but all the same he had a sort of vague, sketchy impression that it would be pleasanter to run up a lively century against the O.B.s with Miss Lorimer as a spectator than in her absence. He felt pleased that she was coming.

'I say, about this poem,' said Lorimer, dismissing a subject which manifestly bored him, and returning to one which was of vital interest, 'you're sure you can write fairly decent stuff? It's no good sending in stuff that'll turn the examiner's hair grey. Can you turn out something really decent?'

Pringle said nothing. He smiled gently as who should observe, 'I and Shakespeare.'

Farnie Gets Into Trouble –

It was perhaps only natural that Farnie, having been warned so strongly of the inadvisability of having anything to do with Monk, should for that very reason be attracted to him. Nobody ever wants to do anything except what they are not allowed to do. Otherwise there is no explaining the friendship that arose between them. Jack Monk was not an attractive individual. He had a slack mouth and a shifty eye, and his complexion was the sort which friends would have described as olive, enemies (with more truth) as dirty green. These defects would have mattered little, of course, in themselves. There's many a bilious countenance, so to speak, covers a warm heart. With Monk, however, appearances were not deceptive. He looked a bad lot, and he was one.

It was on the second morning of term that the acquaintanceship began. Monk was coming downstairs from his study with Danvers, and Farnie was leaving the fags' day-room.

'See that kid?' said Danvers. 'That's the chap I was telling you about. Gethryn's uncle, you know.'

'Not really? Let's cultivate him. I say, old chap, don't walk so fast.'

Farnie, rightly concluding that the remark was addressed to him, turned and waited, and the three strolled over to the School buildings together.

They would have made an interesting study for the observer of human nature, the two seniors fancying that they had to deal with a small boy just arrived at his first school, and in the grip of that strange, lost feeling which attacks the best of new boys for a day or so after their arrival; and Farnie, on the other hand, watching every move, as perfectly composed and at home as a youth should be with the experience of three public schools to back him up.

When they arrived at the School gates, Monk and Danvers turned to go in the direction of their form-room, the Remove, leaving Farnie at the door of the Upper Fourth. At this point a small comedy took place. Monk, after feeling hastily in his pockets, requested Danvers to lend him five shillings until next Saturday. Danvers knew this request of old, and he knew the answer that was expected of him. By replying that he was sorry, but he had not got the money, he gave Farnie, who was still standing at the door, his cue to offer to supply the deficiency. Most new boys – they had grasped this fact from experience – would have felt it an honour to oblige a senior with a small loan. As Farnie made no signs of doing what was expected of him, Monk was obliged to resort to the somewhat cruder course of applying for the loan in person. He applied. Farnie with the utmost willingness brought to light a handful of money, mostly gold. Monk's eye gleamed approval, and he stretched forth an itching palm. Danvers began to think that it would be rash to let a chance like this slip. Ordinarily the tacit agreement between the pair was that only one should borrow at a time, lest confidence should be destroyed in the victim. But here was surely an exception, a special case. With a young gentleman so obviously a man of coin as Farnie, the rule might well be broken for once.

'While you're about it, Farnie, old man,' he said carelessly, 'you might let me have a bob or two if you don't mind. Five bob'll see me through to Saturday all right.'

'Do you mean tomorrow?' enquired Farnie, looking up from his heap of gold.

'No, Saturday week. Let you have it back by then at the latest. Make a point of it.'

'How would a quid do?'

'Ripping,' said Danvers ecstatically.

'Same here,' assented Monk.

'Then that's all right,' said Farnie briskly; 'I thought perhaps you mightn't have had enough. You've got a quid, I know, Monk, because I saw you haul one out at breakfast. And Danvers has got one too, because he offered to toss you for it in the study afterwards. And besides, I couldn't lend you anything in any case, because I've only got about fourteen quid myself.'

With which parting shot he retired, wrapped in gentle thought, into his form-room; and from the noise which ensued immediately upon his arrival, the shrewd listener would have deduced, quite correctly, that he had organized and taken the leading part in a general rag.

Monk and Danvers proceeded upon their way.

'You got rather left there, old chap,' said Monk at length.

'I like that,' replied the outraged Danvers. 'How about you, then? It seemed to me you got rather left, too.'

Monk compromised.

'Well, anyhow,' he said, 'we shan't get much out of that kid.'

'Little beast,' said Danvers complainingly. And they went on into their form-room in silence.

'I saw your young – er – relative in earnest conversation with friend Monk this morning,' said Marriott, later on in the day, to Gethryn; 'I thought you were going to give him the tip in that direction?'

'So I did,' said the Bishop wearily; 'but I can't always be looking after the little brute. He only does it out of sheer cussedness, because I've told him not to. It stands to reason that he can't *like* Monk.'

'You remind me of the psalmist and the wicked man, surname unknown,' said Marriott. 'You *can't* see the good side of Monk.'

'There isn't one.'

'No. He's only got two sides, a bad side and a worse side, which he sticks on on the strength of being fairly good at games. I wonder if he's going to get his First this season. He's not a bad bat.'

'I don't think he will. He is a good bat, but there are heaps better in the place. I say, I think I shall give young Farnie the tip once more, and let him take it or leave it. What do you think?'

'He'll leave it,' said Marriott, with conviction.

Nor was he mistaken. Farnie listened with enthusiasm to his nephew's second excursus on the Monk topic, and, though he said nothing, was apparently convinced. On the following afternoon Monk, Danvers, Waterford, and he hired a boat and went up the river together. Gethryn and Marriott, steered by Wilson, who was rapidly developing into a useful coxswain, got an excellent view of them moored under the shade of a willow, drinking ginger-beer, and apparently on the best of terms with one another and the world in general. In a brief but moving speech the Bishop finally excommunicated his erring relative. 'For all I care,' he concluded, 'he can do what he likes in future. I shan't stop him.'

'No,' said Marriott, 'I don't think you will.'

For the first month of his school life Farnie behaved, except in his choice of companions, much like an ordinary junior. He played cricket moderately well, did his share of compulsory fielding at the First Eleven net, and went for frequent river excursions with Monk, Danvers, and the rest of the Mob.

At first the other juniors of the House were inclined to resent this extending of the right hand of fellowship to owners of studies and Second Eleven men, and attempted to make Farnie see the sin and folly of his ways. But Nature had endowed that youth with a fund of vitriolic repartee. When Millett, one of Leicester's juniors, evolved some laborious sarcasm on the subject of Farnie's swell friends, Farnie, in a series of three remarks, reduced him, figuratively speaking, to a small and palpitating spot of grease. After that his actions came in for no further, or at any rate no outspoken comment.

Given sixpence a week and no more, Farnie might have survived an entire term without breaking any serious School rule. But when, after buying a bicycle from Smith of Markham's, he found himself with eight pounds to his name in solid cash, and the means of getting far enough away from the neighbourhood of the School to be able to spend it much as he liked, he began to do strange and risky things in his spare time.

The great obstacle to illicit enjoyment at Beckford was the four o'clock roll-call on half-holidays. There were other obstacles, such as half-holiday games and so forth, but these could be avoided by the exercise of a little judgement. The penalty for non-appearance at a half-holiday game was a fine of sixpence. Constant absence was likely in time to lead to a more or less thrilling interview with the captain of cricket, but a very occasional attendance was enough to stave off this disaster; and as for the sixpence, to a man of means like Farnie it was a mere nothing. It was a bad system, and it was a wonder, under the circumstances, how Beckford produced the elevens it did. But it was the system, and Farnie availed himself of it to the full.

The obstacle of roll-call he managed also to surmount. Some reckless and penniless friend was generally willing, for a consideration, to answer his name for him. And so most Saturday afternoons would find Farnie leaving behind him the flannelled fools at their various wickets, and speeding out into the country on his bicycle in the direction of the village of Biddlehampton, where mine host of the 'Cow and Cornflower', in addition to other refreshment for man and beast, advertised that ping-pong and billiards might be played on the premises. It was not the former of these games that attracted Farnie. He was no pinger. Nor was he a pongster. But for billiards he had a decided taste, a genuine taste, not the pumped-up affectation some-times displayed by boys of his age. Considering his age he was a remarkable player. Later on in life it appeared likely that he would have the choice of three professions open to him, namely, professional billard player, billiard marker, and billiard sharp. At each of the three he showed distinct promise. He was not 'lured to the green cloth' by Monk or Danvers. Indeed, if there had been any luring to be done, it is probable that he would have done it, and not they. Neither Monk nor Danvers was in his confidence in the matter. Billiards is not a cheap amusement. By the end of his sixth week Farnie was reduced to a single pound, a sum which, for one of his tastes, was practically poverty. And just at the moment when he was least able to bear up against it, Fate dealt him one of its nastiest blows. He was playing a fifty up against a friendly but unskilful farmer at the 'Cow and Cornflower'. 'Better look out,' he said, as his opponent effected a somewhat rustic stroke, 'you'll be cutting the cloth in a second.' The farmer grunted, missed by inches, and retired, leaving the red ball in the jaws of the pocket, and Farnie with three to make to win.

It was an absurdly easy stroke, and the Bishop's uncle took it with an absurd amount of conceit and carelessness. Hardly troubling to aim, he struck his ball. The cue slid off in one direction, the ball rolled sluggishly in another. And when the cue had finished its run, the smooth green surface of the table was marred by a jagged and unsightly cut. There was another young man gone wrong!

To say that the farmer laughed would be to express the matter feebly. That his young opponent, who had been irritating him unspeakably since the beginning of the game with advice and criticism, should have done exactly what he had cautioned him, the farmer, against a moment before, struck him as being the finest example of poetic justice he had ever heard of, and he signalized his appreciation of the same by nearly dying of apoplexy.

The marker expressed an opinion that Farnie had been and gone and done it.

' 'Ere,' he said, inserting a finger in the cut to display its dimensions. 'Look 'ere. This'll mean a noo cloth, young feller me lad. That's wot this'll mean. That'll be three pound we will trouble you for, if *you* please.'

Farnie produced his sole remaining sovereign.

'All I've got,' he said. 'I'll leave my name and address.'

'Don't you trouble, young feller me lad,' said the marker, who appeared to be a very aggressive and unpleasant sort of character altogether, with meaning, 'I know yer name and I knows yer address. Today fortnight at the very latest, if *you* please. You don't want me to 'ave to go to your master about it, now, do yer? What say? No. Ve' well then. Today fortnight is the time, and you remember it.'

What was left of Farnie then rode slowly back to Beckford. Why he went to Monk on his return probably he could not have explained himself. But he did go, and, having told his story in full, wound up by asking for a loan of two pounds. Monk's first impulse was to refer him back to a previous interview, when matters had been the other way about, that small affair of the pound on the second morning of the term. Then there flashed across his mind certain reasons against this move. At present Farnie's attitude towards him was unpleasantly independent. He made him understand that he went about with him from choice, and that there was to be nothing of the patron and dependant about their alliance. If he were to lend him the two pounds now, things would alter. And to have got a complete hold over Master Reginald Farnie, Monk would have paid more than two pounds. Farnie had the intelligence to carry through anything, however risky, and there were many things which Monk would have liked to do, but, owing to the risks involved, shirked doing for himself. Besides, he happened to be in funds just now.

'Well, look here, old chap,' he said, 'let's have strict business between friends. If you'll pay me back four quid at the end of term, you shall have the two pounds. How does that strike you?'

It struck Farnie, as it would have struck most people, that if this was Monk's idea of strict business, there were the makings of no ordinary financier in him. But to get his two pounds he would have agreed to anything. And the end of term seemed a long way off.

The awkward part of the billiard-playing episode was that the punishment for it, if detected, was not expulsion, but flogging. And Farnie resembled the lady in *The Ingoldsby Legends* who 'didn't mind death, but who couldn't stand pinching'. He didn't mind expulsion – he was used to it, but he could *not* stand flogging.

'That'll be all right,' he said. And the money changed hands.

[6]

– and Stays There

'I say,' said Baker of Jephson's excitedly some days later, reeling into the study which he shared with Norris, '*have* you seen the team the M.C.C.'s bringing down?'

At nearly every school there is a type of youth who asks this question on the morning of the M.C.C. match. Norris was engaged in putting the finishing touches to a snow-white pair of cricket boots.

'No. Hullo, where did you raise that Sporter? Let's have a look.'

But Baker proposed to conduct this business in person. It is ten times more pleasant to administer a series of shocks to a friend than to sit by and watch him administering them to himself. He retained *The Sportsman*, and began to read out the team.

'Thought Middlesex had a match,' said Norris, as Baker paused dramatically to let the name of a world-famed professional sink in.

'No. They don't play Surrey till Monday.'

'Well, if they've got an important match like Surrey on on Monday,' said Norris disgustedly, 'what on earth do they let their best man come down here today for, and fag himself out?'

Baker suggested gently that if anybody was going to be fagged out at the end of the day, it would in all probability be the Beckford bowlers, and not a man who, as he was careful to point out, had run up a century a mere three days ago against Yorkshire, and who was apparently at that moment at the very top of his form.

'Well,' said Norris, 'he might crock himself or anything. Rank bad policy, I call it. Anybody else?'

Baker resumed his reading. A string of unknowns ended in another celebrity.

'Blackwell?' said Norris. 'Not O. T. Blackwell?'

'It *says* A. T. But,' went on Baker, brightening up again, 'they always get the initials wrong in the papers. Certain to be O. T. By the way, I suppose you saw that he made eighty-three against Notts the other day?'

Norris tried to comfort himself by observing that Notts couldn't bowl for toffee.

'Last week, too,' said Baker, 'he made a hundred and forty-six not out against Malvern for the Gentlemen of Warwickshire. They couldn't get him out,' he concluded with unction. In spite of the fact that he himself was playing in the match today, and might under the circumstances reasonably look forward to a considerable dose of leather-hunting, the task of announcing the bad news to Norris appeared to have a most elevating effect on his spirits.

'That's nothing extra special,' said Norris, in answer to the last item of information, 'the Malvern wicket's like a billiard-table.'

'Our wickets aren't bad either at this time of year,' said Baker, 'and I heard rumours that they had got a record one ready for this match.'

'It seems to me,' said Norris, 'that what I'd better do if we want to bat at all today is to win the toss. Though Sammy and the Bishop and Baynes ought to be able to get any ordinary side out all right.'

'Only this isn't an ordinary side. It's a sort of improved county team.'

'They've got about four men who might come off, but the M.C.C. sometimes have a bit of a tail. We ought to have a look in if we win the toss.'

'Hope so,' said Baker. 'I doubt it, though.'

At a quarter to eleven the School always went out in a body to inspect the pitch. After the wicket had been described by experts in hushed whispers as looking pretty good, the bell rang, and all who were not playing for the team, with the exception of the lucky individual who had obtained for himself the post of scorer, strolled back towards the blocks. Monk had come out with Waterford, but seeing Farnie ahead and walking alone he quitted Waterford, and attached himself to the genial Reginald. He wanted to talk business. He had not found the speculation of the two pounds a very profitable one. He had advanced the money under the impression that Farnie, by accepting it, was practically selling his independence. And there were certain matters in which Monk was largely interested, connected with the breaking of bounds and the purchase of contraband goods, which he would have been exceedingly glad to have performed by deputy. He had fancied that Farnie would have taken over these jobs as part of his debt. But he had mistaken his man. On the very first occasion when he had attempted to put on the screw, Farnie had flatly refused to have anything to do with what he proposed. He said that he was not Monk's fag – a remark which had the merit of being absolutely true.

All this, combined with a slight sinking of his own funds, induced Monk to take steps towards recovering the loan.

'I say, Farnie, old chap.'

'Hullo!'

'I say, do you remember my lending you two quid some time ago?'

'You don't give me much chance of forgetting it,' said Farnie.

Monk smiled. He could afford to be generous towards such witticisms.

'I want it back,' he said.

'All right. You'll get it at the end of term.'

'I want it now.'

'Why?'

'Awfully hard up, old chap.'

'You aren't,' said Farnie. 'You've got three pounds twelve and sixpence half-penny. If you will keep counting your money in public, you can't blame a chap for knowing how much you've got.'

Monk, slightly disconcerted, changed his plan of action. He abandoned skirmishing tactics.

'Never mind that,' he said, 'the point is that I want that four pounds. I'm going to have it, too.'

'I know. At the end of term.'

'I'm going to have it now.'

'You can have a pound of it now.'

'Not enough.'

'I don't see how you expect me to raise any more. If I could, do you think I should have borrowed it? You might chuck rotting for a change.'

'Now, look here, old chap,' said Monk, 'I should think you'd rather raise that tin somehow than have it get about that you'd been playing pills at some pub out of bounds. What?'

Farnie, for one of the few occasions on record, was shaken out of his usual *sang-froid*. Even in his easy code of morality there had always been one crime which was an anathema, the sort of thing no fellow could think of doing. But it was obviously at this that Monk was hinting.

'Good Lord, man,' he cried, 'you don't mean to say you're thinking of sneaking? Why, the fellows would boot you round the field. You couldn't stay in the place a week.'

'There are heaps of ways,' said Monk, 'in which a thing can get about without anyone actually telling the beaks. At present I've not told a soul. But, you know, if I let it out to anyone they might tell someone else, and so on. And if everybody knows a thing, the beaks generally get hold of it sooner or later. You'd much better let me have that four quid, old chap.'

Farnie capitulated.

'All right,' he said, 'I'll get it somehow.'

'Thanks awfully, old chap,' said Monk, 'so long!'

In all Beckford there was only one person who was in the least degree likely to combine the two qualities necessary for the extraction of Farnie from his difficulties. These qualities were – in the first place ability, in the second place willingness to advance him, free of security, the four pounds he required. The person whom he had in his mind was Gethryn. He had reasoned the matter out step by step during the second half of morning school. Gethryn, though he had, as Farnie knew, no overwhelming amount of affection for his uncle, might in a case of great need prove blood to be thicker (as per advertisement) than water. But, he reflected, he must represent himself as in danger of expulsion rather than flogging. He had an uneasy idea that if the Bishop were to discover that all he stood to get was a flogging, he would remark with enthusiasm that, as far as he was concerned, the good work might go on. Expulsion was different. To save a member of his family from expulsion, he might think it worth while to pass round the hat amongst his wealthy acquaintances. If four plutocrats with four sovereigns were to combine, Farnie, by their united efforts, would be saved. And he rather liked the notion of being turned into a sort of limited liability company, like the Duke of Plaza Toro, at a pound a share. It seemed to add a certain dignity to his position.

To Gethryn's study, therefore, he went directly school was over. If he had reflected, he might have known that he would not have been there while the match was going on. But his brain, fatigued with his recent calculations, had not noted this point.

The study was empty.

Most people, on finding themselves in a strange and empty room, are seized with a desire to explore the same, and observe from internal evidence what manner of man is the owner. Nowhere does character come out so clearly as in the decoration of one's private den. Many a man, at present respected by his associates, would stand forth unmasked at his true worth, could the world but look into his room. For there they would see that he was so lost to every sense of shame as to cover his books with brown paper, or deck his walls with oleographs presented with the Christmas numbers, both of which habits argue a frame of mind fit for murderers, stratagems, and spoils. Let no such man be trusted.

The Bishop's study, which Farnie now proceeded to inspect, was not of this kind. It was a neat study, arranged with not a little taste. There were photographs of teams with the College arms on their plain oak frames, and photographs of relations in frames which tried to look, and for the most part succeeded in looking, as if they had not cost fourpence three farthings at a Christmas bargain sale. There were snap-shots of various moving incidents in the careers of the Bishop and his friends: Marriott, for example, as he appeared when carried to the Pavilion after that sensational century against the Authentics: Robertson of Blaker's winning the quarter mile: John Brown, Norris's predecessor in the captaincy, and one of the four best batsmen Beckford had ever had, batting at the nets: Norris taking a skier on the boundary in last year's M.C.C. match: the Bishop himself going out to bat in the Charchester match, and many more of the same sort.

All these Farnie observed with considerable interest, but as he moved towards the book-shelf his eye was caught by an object more interesting still. It was a cash-box, simple and unornamental, but undoubtedly a cash-box, and as he took it up it rattled.

The key was in the lock. In a boarding House at a public school it is not, as a general rule, absolutely necessary to keep one's valuables always hermetically sealed. The difference between *meum* and *tuum* is so very rarely confused by the occupants of such an establishment, that one is apt to grow careless, and every now and then accidents happen. An accident was about to happen now.

It was at first without any motive except curiosity that Farnie opened the cash-box. He merely wished to see how much there was inside, with a view to ascertaining what his prospects of negotiating a loan with his relative were likely to be. When, however, he did see, other feelings began to take the place of curiosity. He counted the money. There were ten sovereigns, one half-sovereign, and a good deal of silver. One of the institutions at Beckford was a mission. The School by (more or less) voluntary contributions supported a species of home somewhere in the wilds of Kennington. No one knew exactly what or where this home was, but all paid their subscriptions as soon as possible in the term, and tried to forget about it. Gethryn collected not only for Leicester's House, but also for the Sixth Form, and was consequently, if only by proxy, a man of large means. *Too* large, Farnie thought. Surely four pounds, to be paid back (probably) almost at once, would not be missed. Why shouldn't he –

'Hullo!'

Farnie spun round. Wilson was standing in the doorway.

'Hullo, Farnie,' said he, 'what are you playing at in here?'

'What are you?' retorted Farnie politely.

'Come to fetch a book. Marriott said I might. What are you up to?'

'Oh, shut up!' said Farnie. 'Why shouldn't I come here if I like? Matter of fact, I came to see Gethryn.'

'He isn't here,' said Wilson luminously.

'You don't mean to say you've noticed that already? You've got an eye like a hawk, Wilson. I was just taking a look round, if you really want to know.'

'Well, I shouldn't advise you to let Marriott catch you mucking his study up. Seen a book called *Round the Red Lamp*? Oh, here it is. Coming over to the field?'

'Not just yet. I want to have another look round. Don't you wait, though.'

'Oh, all right.' And Wilson retired with his book.

Now, though Wilson at present suspected nothing, not knowing of the existence of the cash-box, Farnie felt that when the money came to be missed, and inquiries were made as to who had been in the study, and when, he would recall the interview. Two courses, therefore, remained open to him. He could leave the money altogether, or he could take it and leave himself. In other words, run away.

In the first case there would, of course, remain the chance that he might induce Gethryn to lend him the four pounds, but this had never been more than a forlorn hope; and in the light of the possibilities opened out by the cash-box, he thought no more of it. The real problem was, should he or should he not take the money from the cash-box?

As he hesitated, the recollection of Monk's veiled threats came back to him, and he wavered no longer. He opened the box again, took out the contents, and dropped them into his pocket. While he was about it, he thought he might as well take all as only a part.

Then he wrote two notes. One – to the Bishop – he placed on top of the cash-box; the other he placed with four sovereigns on the table in Monk's study. Finally he left the room, shut the door carefully behind him, and went to the yard at the back of the House, where he kept his bicycle.

The workings of the human mind, and especially of the young human mind, are peculiar. It never occurred to Farnie that a result equally profitable to himself, and decidedly more convenient for all concerned – with the possible exception of Monk – might have been arrived at if he had simply left the money in the box, and run away without it.

However, as the poet says, you can't think of everything.

[7]

The Bishop Goes For a Ride

The M.C.C. match opened auspiciously. Norris, for the first time that season, won the toss. Tom Brown, we read, in a similar position, 'with the usual liberality of young hands', put his opponents in first. Norris was not so liberal. He may have been young, but he was not so young as that. The sun was shining on as true a wicket as was ever prepared when he cried 'Heads', and the coin, after rolling for some time in diminishing circles, came to a standstill with the dragon undermost. And Norris returned to the Pavilion and informed his gratified team that, all things considered, he rather thought that they would bat, and he would be obliged if Baker would get on his pads and come in first with him.

The M.C.C. men took the field – O. T. Blackwell, by the way, had shrunk into a mere brother of the century-making A. T. – and the two School House representatives followed them. An amateur of lengthy frame took the ball, a man of pace, to judge from the number of slips. Norris asked for 'two leg'. An obliging umpire informed him that he had got two leg. The long bowler requested short slip to stand finer, swung his arm as if to see that the machinery still worked, and dashed wildly towards the crease. The match had begun.

There are few pleasanter or more thrilling moments in one's school career than the first over of a big match. Pleasant, that is to say, if you are actually looking on. To have to listen to a match being started from the interior of a form-room is, of course, maddening. You hear the sound of bat meeting ball, followed by distant clapping. Somebody has scored. But who and what? It may be a four, or it may be a mere single. More important still, it may be the other side batting after all. Some miscreant has possibly lifted your best bowler into the road. The suspense is awful. It ought to be a School rule that the captain of the team should send a message round the form-rooms stating briefly and lucidly the result of the toss. Then one would know where one was. As it is, the entire form is dependent on the man sitting under the window. The form-master turns to write on the blackboard. The only hope of the form shoots up like a rocket, gazes earnestly in the direction of the Pavilion, and falls back with a thud into his seat. 'They haven't started yet,' he informs the rest in a stage whisper. 'Si-*lence*,' says the form-master, and the whole business must be gone through again, with the added disadvantage that the master now has his eye fixed coldly on the individual nearest the window, your only link with the outer world.

Various masters have various methods under such circumstances. One more than excellent man used to close his book and remark, 'I think we'll make up a little party to watch this match.' And the form, gasping its thanks, crowded to the windows. Another, the exact antithesis of this great and good gentleman, on seeing a boy taking fitful glances through the window, would observe acidly, 'You are at perfect liberty, Jones, to watch the match if you care to, *but* if you do you will come in in the afternoon and make up the time you waste.' And as all that could be seen from that particular window was one of the umpires and a couple of fieldsmen, Jones would reluctantly elect to reserve himself, and for the present to turn his attention to Euripides again.

If you are one of the team, and watch the match from the Pavilion, you escape these trials, but there are others. In the first few overs of a School match, every ball looks to the spectators like taking a wicket. The fiendish ingenuity of the slow bowler, and the lightning speed of the fast man at the other end, make one feel positively ill. When the first ten has gone up on the scoring-board matters begin to right themselves. Today ten went up quickly. The fast man's first ball was outside the off-stump and a half-volley, and Norris, whatever the state of his nerves at the time, never forgot his forward drive. Before the bowler had recovered his balance the ball was half-way to the ropes. The umpire waved a large hand towards the Pavilion. The bowler looked annoyed. And the School inside the form-rooms asked itself feverishly what had happened, and which side it was that was applauding.

Having bowled his first ball too far up, the M.C.C. man, on the principle of anything for a change, now put in a very short one. Norris, a new man after that drive, steered it through the slips, and again the umpire waved his hand.

The rest of the over was more quiet. The last ball went for four byes, and then it was Baker's turn to face the slow man. Baker was a steady, plodding bat. He played five balls gently to mid-on, and glanced the sixth for a single to leg. With the fast bowler, who had not yet got his length, he was more vigorous, and succeeded in cutting him twice for two.

With thirty up for no wickets the School began to feel more comfortable. But at forty-three Baker was shattered by the man of pace, and retired with twenty to his credit. Gethryn came in next, but it was not to be his day out with the bat.

The fast bowler, who was now bowling excellently, sent down one rather wide of the off-stump. The Bishop made most of his runs from off balls, and he had a go at this one. It was rising when he hit it, and it went off his bat like a flash. In a School match it would have been a boundary. But today there was unusual talent in the slips. The man from Middlesex darted forward and sideways. He took the ball one-handed two inches from the ground, and received the applause which followed the effort with a rather bored look, as if he were saying, 'My good sirs, *why* make a fuss over these trifles!' The Bishop walked slowly back to the Pavilion, feeling that his luck was out, and Pringle came in.

A boy of Pringle's character is exactly the right person to go in in an emergency like the present one. Two wickets had fallen in two balls, and the fast bowler was swelling visibly with determination to do the hat-trick. But Pringle never went in oppressed by the fear of getting out. He had a serene and boundless confidence in himself.

The fast man tried a yorker. Pringle came down hard on it, and forced the ball past the bowler for a single. Then he and Norris settled down to a lengthy stand.

'I do like seeing Pringle bat,' said Gosling. 'He always gives you the idea that he's doing you a personal favour by knocking your bowling about. Oh, well hit!'

Pringle had cut a full-pitch from the slow bowler to the ropes. Marriott, who had been silent and apparently in pain for some minutes, now gave out the following homemade effort:

> A dashing young sportsman named Pringle,
>   On breaking his duck (with a single),
>   Observed with a smile,
>   'Just notice my style,
>   How science with vigour I mingle.'

'Little thing of my own,' he added, quoting England's greatest librettist. 'I call it "Heart Foam". I shall not publish it. Oh, run it out!'

Both Pringle and Norris were evidently in form. Norris was now not far from his fifty, and Pringle looked as if he might make anything. The century went up, and a run later Norris off-drove the slow bowler's successor for three, reaching his fifty by the stroke.

'Must be fairly warm work fielding today,' said Reece.

'By Jove!' said Gethryn, 'I forgot. I left my white hat in the House. Any of you chaps like to fetch it?'

There were no offers. Gethryn got up.

'Marriott, you slacker, come over to the House.'

'My good sir, I'm in next. Why don't you wait till the fellows come out of school and send a kid for it?'

'He probably wouldn't know where to find it. I don't know where it is myself. No, I shall go, but there's no need to fag about it yet. Hullo! Norris is out.'

Norris had stopped a straight one with his leg. He had made fifty-one in his best manner, and the School, leaving the form-rooms at the exact moment when the fatal ball was being bowled, were just in time to applaud him and realize what they had missed.

Gethryn's desire for his hat was not so pressing as to make him deprive himself of the pleasure of seeing Marriott at the wickets. Marriott ought to do something special today. Unfortunately, after he had played out one over and hit two fours off it, the luncheon interval began.

It was, therefore, not for half an hour that the Bishop went at last in search of the missing headgear. As luck would have it, the hat was on the table, so that whatever chance he might have had of overlooking the note which his uncle had left for him on the empty cash-box disappeared. The two things caught his eye simultaneously. He opened the note and read it. It is not necessary to transcribe the note in detail. It was no masterpiece of literary skill. But it had this merit, that it was not vague. Reading it, one grasped its meaning immediately.

The Bishop's first feeling was that the bottom had dropped out of everything suddenly. Surprise was not the word. It was the arrival of the absolutely unexpected.

Then he began to consider the position.

Farnie must be brought back. That was plain. And he must be brought back at once, before anyone could get to hear of what had happened. Gethryn had the very strongest objections to his uncle, considered purely as a human being; but the fact remained that he *was* his uncle, and the Bishop had equally strong objections to any member of his family being mixed up in a business of this description.

Having settled that point, he went on to the next. How was he to be brought back? He could not have gone far, for he could not have been gone much more than half an hour. Again, from his knowledge of his uncle's character, he deduced that he had in all probability not gone to the nearest station, Horton. At Horton one had to wait hours at a time for a train. Farnie must have made his way – on his bicycle – straight for the junction, Anfield, fifteen miles off by a good road. A train left Anfield for London at three-thirty. It was now a little past two. On a bicycle he could do it easily, and get back with his prize by about five, if he rode hard. In that case all would be well. Only three of the School wickets had fallen, and the pitch was playing as true as concrete. Besides, there was Pringle still in at one end, well set, and surely Marriott and Jennings and the rest of them would manage to stay in till five. They couldn't help it. All they had to do was to play forward to everything, and they must stop in. He himself had got out, it was true, but that was simply a regrettable accident. Not one man in a hundred would have caught that catch. No, with luck he ought easily to be able to do the distance and get back in time to go out with the rest of the team to field.

He ran downstairs and out of the House. On his way to the bicycle-shed he stopped, and looked towards the field, part of which could be seen from where he stood. The match had begun again. The fast bowler was just commencing his run. He saw him tear up to the crease and deliver the ball. What happened then he could not see, owing to the trees which stood between him and the School grounds. But he heard the crack of ball meeting bat, and a great howl of applause went up from the invisible audience. A boundary, apparently. Yes, there was the umpire signalling it. Evidently a long stand was going to be made. He would have oceans of time for his ride. Norris wouldn't dream of declaring the innings closed before five o'clock at the earliest, and no bowler could take seven wickets in the time on such a pitch. He hauled his bicycle from the shed, and rode off at racing speed in the direction of Anfield.

[8]

The M.C.C. Match

But out in the field things were going badly with Beckford. The aspect of a game often changes considerably after lunch. For a while it looked as if Marriott and Pringle were in for their respective centuries. But Marriott was never a safe batsman.

A hundred and fifty went up on the board off a square leg hit for two, which completed Pringle's half-century, and then Marriott faced the slow bowler, who had been put on again after lunch. The first ball was a miss-hit. It went behind point for a couple. The next he got fairly hold of and drove to the boundary. The third was a very simple-looking ball. Its sole merit appeared to be the fact that it was straight. Also it was a trifle shorter than it looked. Marriott jumped out, and got too much under it. Up it soared, straight over the bowler's head. A trifle more weight behind the hit, and it would have cleared the ropes. As it was, the man in the deep-field never looked like missing it. The batsmen had time to cross over before the ball arrived, but they did it without enthusiasm. The run was not likely to count. Nor did it. Deep-field caught it like a bird. Marriott had made twenty-two.

And now occurred one of those rots which so often happen without any ostensible cause in the best regulated school elevens. Pringle played the three remaining balls of the over without mishap, but when it was the fast man's turn to bowl to Bruce, Marriott's successor, things began to happen. Bruce, temporarily insane, perhaps through nervousness, played back at a half-volley, and was clean bowled. Hill came in, and was caught two balls later at the wicket. And the last ball of the over sent Jennings's off-stump out of the ground, after that batsman had scored two.

'I can always bowl like blazes after lunch,' said the fast man to Pringle. 'It's the lobster salad that does it, I think.' Four for a hundred and fifty-seven had changed to seven for a hundred and fifty-nine in the course of a single over. Gethryn's calculations, if he had only known, could have done now with a little revision.

Gosling was the next man. He was followed, after a brief innings of three balls, which realized eight runs, by Baynes. Baynes, though abstaining from runs himself, helped Pringle to add three to the score, all in singles, and was then yorked by the slow man, who meanly and treacherously sent down, without the slightest warning, a very fast one on the leg stump. Then Reece came in for the last wicket, and the rot stopped. Reece always went in last for the School, and the School in consequence always felt that there were possibilities to the very end of the innings.

The lot of a last-wicket man is somewhat trying. As at any moment his best innings may be nipped in the bud by the other man getting out, he generally feels that it is hardly worth while to play himself in before endeavouring to make runs. He therefore tries to score off every ball, and thinks himself lucky if he gets half a dozen. Reece, however, took life more seriously. He had made quite an art of last-wicket batting. Once, against the Butterflies, he had run up sixty not out, and there was always the chance that he would do the same again. Today, with Pringle at the other end, he looked forward to a pleasant hour or two at the wicket.

No bowler ever looks on the last man quite in the same light as he does the other ten. He underrates him instinctively. The M.C.C. fast bowler was a man with an idea. His idea was that he could bowl a slow ball of diabolical ingenuity. As a rule, public feeling was against his trying the experiment. His captains were in the habit of enquiring rudely if he thought he was playing marbles. This was exactly what the M.C.C. captain asked on the present occasion, when the head ball sailed ponderously through the air, and was promptly hit by Reece into the Pavilion. The bowler grinned, and resumed his ordinary pace.

But everything came alike to Reece. Pringle, too, continued his career of triumph. Gradually the score rose from a hundred and seventy to two hundred. Pringle cut and drove in all directions, with the air of a prince of the blood royal distributing largesse. The second century went up to the accompaniment of cheers.

Then the slow bowler reaped his reward, for Pringle, after putting his first two balls over the screen, was caught on the boundary off the third. He had contributed eighty-one to a total of two hundred and thirteen.

So far Gethryn's absence had not been noticed. But when the

umpires had gone out, and the School were getting ready to take the field, inquiries were made.

'You might begin at the top end, Gosling,' said Norris.

'Right,' said Samuel. 'Who's going on at the other?'

'Baynes. Hullo, where's Gethryn?'

'Isn't he here? Perhaps he's in the Pavi –'

'Any of you chaps seen Gethryn?'

'He isn't in the Pav.,' said Baker. 'I've just come out of the First room myself, and he wasn't there. Shouldn't wonder if he's over at Leicester's.'

'Dash the man,' said Norris, 'he might have known we'd be going out to field soon. Anyhow, we can't wait for him. We shall have to field a sub. till he turns up.'

'Lorimer's in the Pav., changed,' said Pringle.

'All right. He'll do.'

And, reinforced by the gratified Lorimer, the team went on its way.

In the beginning the fortunes of the School prospered. Gosling opened, as was his custom, at a tremendous pace, and seemed to trouble the first few batsmen considerably. A worried-looking little person who had fielded with immense zeal during the School innings at cover-point took the first ball. It was very fast, and hit him just under the knee-cap. The pain, in spite of the pad, appeared to be acute. The little man danced vigorously for some time, and then, with much diffidence, prepared himself for the second instalment.

Now, when on the cricket field, the truculent Samuel was totally deficient in all the finer feelings, such as pity and charity. He could see that the batsman was in pain, and yet his second ball was faster than the first. It came in quickly from the off. The little batsman went forward in a hesitating, half-hearted manner, and played a clear two inches inside the ball. The off-stump shot out of the ground.

'Bowled, Sammy,' said Norris from his place in the slips.

The next man was a clergyman, a large man who suggested possibilities in the way of hitting. But Gosling was irresistible. For three balls the priest survived. But the last of the over, a fast yorker on the leg stump, was too much for him, and he retired.

Two for none. The critic in the deck chair felt that the match was as good as over.

But this idyllic state of things was not to last. The newcomer, a tall man with a light moustache, which he felt carefully after every ball, soon settled down. He proved to be a conversationalist. Until he had opened his account, which he did with a strong drive to the ropes, he was silent. When, however, he had seen the ball safely to the boundary, he turned to Reece and began.

'Rather a nice one, that. Eh, what? Yes. Got it just on the right place, you know. Not a bad bat this, is it? What? Yes. One of Slogbury and Whangham's Sussex Spankers, don't you know. Chose it myself. Had it in pickle all the winter. Yes.'

'Play, sir,' from the umpire.

'Eh, what? Oh, right. Yes, good make these Sussex – *Spankers*. Oh, well fielded.'

At the word spankers he had effected another drive, but Marriott at mid-off had stopped it prettily.

Soon it began to occur to Norris that it would be advisable to have a change of bowling. Gosling was getting tired, and Baynes apparently offered no difficulties to the batsman on the perfect wicket, the conversational man in particular being very severe upon him. It was at such a crisis that the Bishop should have come in. He was Gosling's understudy. But where was he? The innings had been in progress over half an hour now, and still there were no signs of him. A man, thought Norris, who could cut off during the M.C.C. match (of all matches!), probably on some rotten business of his own, was beyond the pale, and must, on reappearance, be fallen upon and rent. He – here something small and red whizzed at his face. He put up his hands to protect himself. The ball struck them and bounded out again. When a fast bowler is bowling a slip he should not indulge in absent-mindedness. The conversational man had received his first life, and, as he was careful to explain to Reece, it was a curious thing, but whenever he was let off early in his innings he always made fifty, and as a rule a century. Gosling's analysis was spoilt, and the match in all probability lost. And Norris put it all down to Gethryn. If he had been there, this would not have happened.

'Sorry, Gosling,' he said.

'All right,' said Gosling, though thinking quite the reverse. And he walked back to bowl his next ball, conjuring up a beautiful vision in his mind. J. Douglas and Braund were fielding slip to him in the vision, while in the background Norris appeared, in a cauldron of boiling oil.

'Tut, tut,' said Baker facetiously to the raging captain.

Baker's was essentially a flippant mind. Not even a moment of solemn agony, such as this, was sacred to him.

Norris was icy and severe.

'If you want to rot about, Baker,' he said, 'perhaps you'd better go and play stump-cricket with the juniors.'

'Well,' retorted Baker, with great politeness, 'I suppose seeing you miss a gaper like that right into your hands made me think I was playing stump-cricket with the juniors.'

At this point the conversation ceased, Baker suddenly remembering that he had not yet received his First Eleven colours, and that it would therefore be rash to goad the captain too freely, while Norris, for his part, recalled the fact that Baker had promised to do some Latin verse for him that evening, and might, if crushed with some scathing repartee, refuse to go through with that contract. So there was silence in the slips.

The partnership was broken at last by a lucky accident. The conversationalist called his partner for a short run, and when that unfortunate gentleman had sprinted some twenty yards, reconsidered the matter and sent him back. Reece had the bails off before the victim had completed a third of the return journey.

For some time after this matters began to favour the School again. With the score at a hundred and five, three men left in two overs, one bowled by Gosling, the others caught at point and in the deep off Jennings, who had deposed Baynes. Six wickets were now down, and the enemy still over a hundred behind.

But the M.C.C. in its school matches has this peculiarity. However badly it may seem to stand, there is always something up its sleeve. In this case it was a professional, a man indecently devoid of anything in the shape of nerves. He played the bowling with a stolid confidence, amounting almost to contempt, which struck a chill to the hearts of the School bowlers. It did worse. It induced them to bowl with the sole object of getting the conversationalist at the batting end, thus enabling the professional to pile up an unassuming but rapidly increasing score by means of threes and singles.

As for the conversationalist, he had made thirty or more, and wanted all the bowling he could get.

'It's a very curious thing,' he said to Reece, as he faced Gosling, after his partner had scored a three off the first ball of the over, 'but some fellows simply detest fast bowling. Now I –' He never finished the sentence. When he spoke again it was to begin a new one.

'How on earth did that happen?' he asked.

'I think it bowled you,' said Reece stolidly, picking up the two stumps which had been uprooted by Gosling's express.

'Yes. But how? Dash it! What? I can't underst –. Most curious thing I ever – dash it all, you know.'

He drifted off in the direction of the Pavilion, stopping on the way to ask short leg his opinion of the matter.

'Bowled, Sammy,' said Reece, putting on the bails.

'Well bowled, Gosling,' growled Norris from the slips.

'Sammy the marvel, by Jove,' said Marriott. 'Switch it on, Samuel, more and more.'

'I wish Norris would give me a rest. Where on earth is that man Gethryn?'

'Rum, isn't it? There's going to be something of a row about it. Norris seems to be getting rather shirty. Hullo! here comes the Deathless Author.'

The author referred to was the new batsman, a distinguished novelist, who played a good deal for the M.C.C. He broke his journey to the wicket to speak to the conversationalist, who was still engaged with short leg.

'Bates, old man,' he said, 'if you're going to the Pavilion you might wait for me. I shall be out in an hour or two.'

Upon which Bates, awaking suddenly to the position of affairs, went on his way.

With the arrival of the Deathless Author an unwelcome change came over the game. His cricket style resembled his literary style. Both were straightforward and vigorous. The first two balls he received from Gosling he drove hard past cover point to the ropes. Gosling, who had been bowling unchanged since the innings began, was naturally feeling a little tired. He was losing his length, and bowling more slowly than was his wont. Norris now gave him a rest for a few overs, Bruce going on with rather innocuous medium left-hand bowling. The professional continued to jog along slowly. The novelist hit. Everything seemed to come alike to him. Gosling resumed, but without effect, while at the other end bowler after bowler was tried. From a hundred and ten the score rose and rose, and still the two remained together. A hundred and ninety went up, and Norris in despair threw the ball to Marriott.

'Here you are, Marriott,' he said, 'I'm afraid we shall have to try you.'

'That's what I call really nicely expressed,' said Marriott to the umpire. 'Yes, over the wicket.'

Marriott was a slow, 'House-match' sort of bowler. That is to say, in a House match he was quite likely to get wickets, but in a First

Eleven match such an event was highly improbable. His bowling looked very subtle, and if the ball was allowed to touch the ground it occasionally broke quite a remarkable distance.

The forlorn hope succeeded. The professional for the first time in his innings took a risk. He slashed at a very mild ball almost a wide on the off side. The ball touched the corner of the bat, and soared up in the direction of cover-point, where Pringle held it comfortably.

'There you are,' said Marriott, 'when you put a really scientific bowler on you're bound to get a wicket. Why on earth didn't I go on before, Norris?'

'You wait,' said Norris, 'there are five more balls of the over to come.'

'Bad job for the batsman,' said Marriott.

There had been time for a run before the ball reached Pringle, so that the novelist was now at the batting end. Marriott's next ball was not unlike his first, but it was straighter, and consequently easier to get at. The novelist hit it into the road. When it had been brought back he hit it into the road again. Marriott suggested that he had better have a man there.

The fourth ball of the over was too wide to hit with any comfort, and the batsman let it alone. The fifth went for four to square leg, almost killing the umpire on its way, and the sixth soared in the old familiar manner into the road again. Marriott's over had yielded exactly twenty-two runs. Four to win and two wickets to fall.

'I'll never read another of that man's books as long as I live,' said Marriott to Gosling, giving him the ball. 'You're our only hope, Sammy. Do go in and win.'

The new batsman had the bowling. He snicked his first ball for a single, bringing the novelist to the fore again, and Samuel Wilberforce Gosling vowed a vow that he would dismiss that distinguished novelist.

But the best intentions go for nothing when one's arm is feeling like lead. Of all the miserable balls sent down that afternoon that one of Gosling's was the worst. It was worse than anything of Marriott's. It flew sluggishly down the pitch well outside the leg stump. The novelist watched it come, and his eye gleamed. It was about to bounce for the second time when, with a pleased smile, the batsman stepped out. There was a loud, musical report, the note of a bat when it strikes the ball fairly on the driving spot.

The man of letters shaded his eyes with his hand, and watched the ball diminish in the distance.

'I rather think,' said he cheerfully, as a crash of glass told of its arrival at the Pavilion, 'that that does it.'

He was perfectly right. It did.

[9]

The Bishop Finishes His Ride

Gethryn had started on his ride handicapped by two things. He did not know his way after the first two miles, and the hedges at the roadside had just been clipped, leaving the roads covered with small thorns.

It was the former of these circumstances that first made itself apparent. For two miles the road ran straight, but after that it was unexplored country. The Bishop, being in both cricket and football teams, had few opportunities for cycling. He always brought his machine to School, but he very seldom used it.

At the beginning of the unexplored country, an irresponsible person recommended him to go straight on. He couldn't miss the road, said he. It was straight all the way. Gethryn thanked him, rode on, and having gone a mile came upon three roads, each of which might quite well have been considered a continuation of the road on which he was already. One curved gently off to the right, the other two equally gently to the left. He dismounted and the feelings of gratitude which he had borne towards his informant for his lucid directions vanished suddenly. He gazed searchingly at the three roads, but to single out one of them as straighter than the other two was a task that baffled him completely. A sign-post informed him of three things. By following road one he might get to Brindleham, and ultimately, if he persevered, to Corden. Road number two would lead him to Old Inns, whatever they might be, with the further inducement of Little Benbury, while if he cast in his lot with road three he might hope sooner or later to arrive at Much Middlefold-on-the-Hill, and Lesser Middlefold-in-the-Vale. But on the subject of Anfield and Anfield Junction the board was silent.

Two courses lay open to him. Should he select a route at random, or wait for somebody to come and direct him? He waited. He went on waiting. He waited a considerable time, and at last, just as he was about to trust to luck, and make for Much Middlefold-on-the-Hill, a figure loomed in sight, a slow-moving man, who strolled down the Old Inns road at a pace which seemed to argue that he had plenty of time on his hands.

'I say, can you tell me the way to Anfield, please?' said the Bishop as he came up.

The man stopped, apparently rooted to the spot. He surveyed the Bishop with a glassy but determined stare from head to foot. Then he looked earnestly at the bicycle, and finally, in perfect silence, began to inspect the Bishop again.

'Eh?' he said at length.

'Can you tell me the way to Anfield?'

'Anfield?'

'Yes. How do I get there?'

The man perpended, and when he replied did so after the style of the late and great Ollendorf.

'Old Inns,' he said dreamily, waving a hand down the road by which he had come, 'be over there.'

'Yes, yes, I know,' said Gethryn.

'Was born at Old Inns, I was,' continued the man, warming to his subject. 'Lived there fifty-five years, I have. Yeou go straight down the road an' yeou cam t' Old Inns. Yes, that be the way t' Old Inns.'

Gethryn nobly refrained from rending the speaker limb from limb.

'I don't want to know the way to Old Inns,' he said desperately. 'Where I want to get is Anfield. Anfield, you know. Which way do I go?'

'Anfield?' said the man. Then a brilliant flash of intelligence illumined his countenance. 'Whoy, Anfield be same road as Old Inns. Yeou go straight down the road, an' –'

'Thanks very much,' said Gethryn, and without waiting for further revelations shot off in the direction indicated. A quarter of a mile farther he looked over his shoulder. The man was still there, gazing after him in a kind of trance.

The Bishop passed through Old Inns with some way on his machine. He had much lost time to make up. A signpost bearing the legend 'Anfield four miles' told him that he was nearing his destination. The notice had changed to three miles and again to two, when suddenly he felt that jarring sensation which every cyclist knows. His back tyre was punctured. It was impossible to ride on. He got off and walked. He was still in his cricket clothes, and the fact that he had on spiked boots did not make walking any the easier. His progress was not rapid.

Half an hour before his one wish had been to catch sight of a fellow-being. Now, when he would have preferred to have avoided his species, men seemed to spring up from nowhere, and every man of them had a remark to make or a question to ask about the punctured tyre. Reserve is not the leading characteristic of the average yokel.

Gethryn, however, refused to be drawn into conversation on the subject. At last one, more determined than the rest, brought him to bay.

'Hoy, mister, stop,' called a voice. Gethryn turned. A man was running up the road towards him.

He arrived panting.

'What's up?' said the Bishop.

'Yeou've got a puncture,' said the man, pointing an accusing finger at the flattened tyre.

It was not worth while killing the brute. Probably he was acting from the best motives.

'No,' said Gethryn wearily, 'it isn't a puncture. I always let the air out when I'm riding. It looks so much better, don't you think so? Why did they let *you* out? Good-bye.'

And feeling a little more comfortable after this outburst, he wheeled his bicycle on into Anfield High Street.

Minds in the village of Anfield worked with extraordinary rapidity. The first person of whom he asked the way to the Junction answered the riddle almost without thinking. He left his machine out in the road and went on to the platform. The first thing that caught his eye was the station clock with its hands pointing to five past four. And when he realized that, his uncle's train having left a clear half hour before, his labours had all been for nothing, the full bitterness of life came home to him.

He was turning away from the station when he stopped. Something else had caught his eye. On a bench at the extreme end of the platform sat a youth. And a further scrutiny convinced the Bishop of the fact that the youth was none other than Master Reginald Farnie, late of Beckford, and shortly, or he would know the reason why, to be once more of Beckford. Other people besides himself, it appeared, could miss trains.

Farnie was reading one of those halfpenny weeklies which – with a nerve which is the only creditable thing about them – call themselves comic. He did not see the Bishop until a shadow falling across his paper caused him to look up.

It was not often that he found himself unequal to a situation. Monk in a recent conversation had taken him aback somewhat, but his feelings on that occasion were not to be compared with what he felt on seeing the one person whom he least desired to meet standing at his side. His jaw dropped limply, *Comic Blitherings* fluttered to the ground.

The Bishop was the first to speak. Indeed, if he had waited for Farnie to break the silence, he would have waited long.

'Get up,' he said. Farnie got up.

'Come on.' Farnie came.

'Go and get your machine,' said Gethryn. 'Hurry up. And now you will jolly well come back to Beckford, you little beast.'

But before that could be done there was Gethryn's back wheel to be mended. This took time. It was nearly half past four before they started.

'Oh,' said Gethryn, as they were about to mount, 'there's that money. I was forgetting. Out with it.'

Ten pounds had been the sum Farnie had taken from the study. Six was all he was able to restore. Gethryn enquired after the deficit.

'I gave it to Monk,' said Farnie.

To Gethryn, in his present frame of mind, the mere mention of Monk was sufficient to uncork the vials of his wrath.

'What the blazes did you do that for? What's Monk got to do with it?'

'He said he'd get me sacked if I didn't pay him,' whined Farnie.

This was not strictly true. Monk had not said. He had hinted. And he had hinted at flogging, not expulsion.

'Why?' pursued the Bishop. 'What had you and Monk been up to?'

Farnie, using his out-of-bounds adventures as a foundation, worked up a highly artistic narrative of doings, which, if they had actually been performed, would certainly have entailed expulsion. He had judged Gethryn's character correctly. If the matter had been simply a case for a flogging, the Bishop would have stood aside and let the thing go on. Against the extreme penalty of School law he felt bound as a matter of family duty to shield his relative. And he saw a bad time coming for himself in the very near future. Either he must expose Farnie, which he had resolved not to do, or he must refuse to explain his absence from the M.C.C. match, for by now there was not the smallest chance of his being able to get back in time for the visitors' innings. As he rode on he tried to imagine what would happen in consequence of that desertion, and he could not do it. His crime was, so far as he knew, absolutely without precedent in the School history.

As they passed the cricket field he saw that it was empty. Stumps were usually drawn early in the M.C.C. match if the issue of the game was out of doubt, as the Marylebone men had trains to catch. Evidently this had happened today. It might mean that the School had won easily – they had looked like making a big score when he had left the ground – in which case public opinion would be more lenient towards him. After a victory a school feels that all's well that ends well. But it might, on the other hand, mean quite the reverse.

He put his machine up, and hurried to the study. Several boys, as he passed them, looked curiously at him, but none spoke to him.

Marriott was in the study, reading a book. He was still in flannels, and looked as if he had begun to change but had thought better of it. As was actually the case.

'Hullo,' he cried, as Gethryn appeared. 'Where the dickens have you been all the afternoon? What on earth did you go off like that for?'

'I'm sorry, old chap,' said the Bishop, 'I can't tell you. I shan't be able to tell anyone.'

'But, man! Try and realize what you've done. Do you grasp the fact that you've gone and got the School licked in the M.C.C. match, and that we haven't beaten the M.C.C. for about a dozen years, and that if you'd been there to bowl we should have walked over this time? Do try and grasp the thing.'

'Did they win?'

'Rather. By a wicket. Two wickets, I mean. We made 213. Your bowling would just have done it.'

Gethryn sat down.

'Oh Lord,' he said blankly, 'this is awful!'

'But, look here, Bishop,' continued Marriott, 'this is all rot. You can't do a thing like this, and then refuse to offer any explanation, and expect things to go on just as usual.'

'I don't,' said Gethryn. 'I know there's going to be a row, but I can't explain. You'll have to take me on trust.'

'Oh, as far as I am concerned, it's all right,' said Marriott. 'I know you wouldn't be ass enough to do a thing like that without a jolly good reason. It's the other chaps I'm thinking about. You'll find it jolly hard to put Norris off, I'm afraid. He's most awfully sick about the match. He fielded badly, which always makes him shirty. Jephson, too. You'll have a bad time with Jephson. His one wish after the match was to have your gore and plenty of it. Nothing else would have pleased him a bit. And think of the chaps in the House, too. Just consider what a pull this gives Monk and his mob over you. The House'll want some looking after now, I fancy.'

'And they'll get it,' said Gethryn. 'If Monk gives me any of his beastly cheek, I'll knock his head off.'

But in spite of the consolation which such a prospect afforded him, he did not look forward with pleasure to the next day, when he would have to meet Norris and the rest. It would have been bad in any case. He did not care to think what would happen when he refused to offer the slightest explanation.

10

In Which a Case is Fully Discussed

Gethryn was right in thinking that the interviews would be unpleasant.
They increased in unpleasantness in arithmetical progression, until
they culminated finally in a terrific encounter with the justly outraged
Norris.

Reece was the first person to institute inquiries, and if everybody
had resembled him, matters would not have been so bad for Gethryn.
Reece possessed a perfect genius for minding his own business. The
dialogue when they met was brief.

'Hullo,' said Reece.

'Hullo,' said the Bishop.

'Where did you get to yesterday?' said Reece.

'Oh, I had to go somewhere,' said the Bishop vaguely.

'Oh? Pity. Wasn't a bad match.' And that was all the comment
Reece made on the situation.

Gethryn went over to the chapel that morning with an empty sinking
feeling inside him. He was quite determined to offer no single word
of explanation, and he felt that that made the prospect all the worse.
There was a vast uncertainty in his mind as to what was going to
happen. Nobody could actually do anything to him, of course. It would
have been a decided relief to him if anybody had tried that line of
action, for moments occur when the only thing that can adequately
soothe the wounded spirit, is to hit straight from the shoulder at
someone. The punching-ball is often found useful under these circumstances. As he was passing Jephson's House he nearly ran into somebody who was coming out.

'Be firm, my moral pecker,' thought Gethryn, and braced himself
up for conflict.

'Well, Gethryn?' said Mr Jephson.

The question 'Well?' especially when addressed by a master to a
boy, is one of the few questions to which there is literally no answer.
You can look sheepish, you can look defiant, or you can look surprised

according to the state of your conscience. But anything in the way of verbal response is impossible.

Gethryn attempted no verbal response.

'Well, Gethryn,' went on Mr Jephson, 'was it pleasant up the river yesterday?'

Mr Jephson always preferred the rapier of sarcasm to the bludgeon of abuse.

'Yes, sir,' said Gethryn, 'very pleasant.' He did not mean to be massacred without a struggle.

'What!' cried Mr Jephson. 'You actually mean to say that you did go up the river?'

'No, sir.'

'Then what do you mean?'

'It is always pleasant up the river on a fine day,' said Gethryn.

His opponent, to use a metaphor suitable to a cricket master, changed his action. He abandoned sarcasm and condescended to direct inquiry.

'Where were you yesterday afternoon?' he said.

The Bishop, like Mr Hurry Bungsho Jabberjee, B.A., became at once the silent tomb.

'Did you hear what I said, Gethryn?' (icily). 'Where were you yesterday afternoon?'

'I can't say, sir.'

These words may convey two meanings. They may imply ignorance, in which case the speaker should be led gently off to the nearest asylum. Or they may imply obstinacy. Mr Jephson decided that in the present case obstinacy lay at the root of the matter. He became icier than ever.

'Very well, Gethryn,' he said, 'I shall report this to the Headmaster.'

And Gethryn, feeling that the conference was at an end, proceeded on his way.

After chapel there was Norris to be handled. Norris had been rather late for chapel that morning, and had no opportunity of speaking to the Bishop. But after the service was over, and the School streamed out of the building towards their respective houses, he waylaid him at the door, and demanded an explanation. The Bishop refused to give one. Norris, whose temper never had a chance of reaching its accustomed tranquillity until he had consumed some breakfast – he hated early morning chapel – raved. The Bishop was worried, but firm.

'Then you mean to say – you don't mean to say – I mean, you don't intend to explain?' said Norris finally, working round for the twentieth time to his original text.

'I can't explain.'

'You won't, you mean.'

'Yes. I'll apologize if you like, but I won't explain.'

Norris felt the strain was becoming too much for him.

'Apologize!' he moaned, addressing circumambient space. 'Apologize! A man cuts off in the middle of the M.C.C. match, loses us the game, and then comes back and offers to apologize.'

'The offer's withdrawn,' put in Gethryn. 'Apologies and explanations are both off.' It was hopeless to try and be conciliatory under the circumstances. They did not admit of it.

Norris glared.

'I suppose,' he said, 'you don't expect to go on playing for the First after this? We can't keep a place open for you in the team on the off chance of your not having a previous engagement, you know.'

'That's your affair,' said the Bishop, 'you're captain. Have you finished your address? Is there anything else you'd like to say?'

Norris considered, and, as he went in at Jephson's gate, wound up with this Parthian shaft –

'All I can say is that you're not fit to be at a public school. They ought to sack a chap for doing that sort of thing. If you'll take my advice, you'll leave.'

About two hours afterwards Gethryn discovered a suitable retort, but, coming to the conclusion that better late than never does not apply to repartees, refrained from speaking it.

It was Mr Jephson's usual custom to sally out after supper on Sunday evenings to smoke a pipe (or several pipes) with one of the other House-masters. On this particular evening he made for Robertson's, which was one of the four Houses on the opposite side of the School grounds. He could hardly have selected a better man to take his grievance to. Mr Robertson was a long, silent man with grizzled hair, and an eye that pierced like a gimlet. He had the enviable reputation of keeping the best order of any master in the School. He was also one of the most popular of the staff. This was all the more remarkable from the fact that he played no games.

To him came Mr Jephson, primed to bursting point with his grievance.

'Anything wrong, Jephson?' said Mr Robertson.

'Wrong? I should just think there was. Did you happen to be looking at the match yesterday, Robertson?'

Mr Robertson nodded.

'I always watch School matches. Good match. Norris missed a bad catch in the slips. He was asleep.'

Mr Jephson conceded the point. It was trivial.

'Yes,' he said, 'he should certainly have held it. But that's a mere detail. I want to talk about Gethryn. Do you know what he did yesterday? I never heard of such a thing in my life, never. Went off during the luncheon interval without a word, and never appeared again till lock-up. And now he refuses to offer any explanation whatever. I shall report the whole thing to Beckett. I told Gethryn so this morning.'

'I shouldn't,' said Mr Robertson; 'I really think I shouldn't. Beckett finds the ordinary duties of a Headmaster quite sufficient for his needs. This business is not in his province at all.'

'Not in his province? My dear sir, what is a headmaster for, if not to manage affairs of this sort?'

Mr Robertson smiled in a sphinx-like manner, and answered, after the fashion of Socrates, with a question.

'Let me ask you two things, Jephson. You must proceed gingerly. Now, firstly, it is a headmaster's business to punish any breach of school rules, is it not?'

'Well?'

'And school prefects do not attend roll-call, and have no restrictions placed upon them in the matter of bounds?'

'No. Well?'

'Then perhaps you'll tell me what School rule Gethryn has broken?' said Mr Robertson.

'You see you can't,' he went on. 'Of course you can't. He has not broken any School rule. He is a prefect, and may do anything he likes with his spare time. He chooses to play cricket. Then he changes his mind and goes off to some unknown locality for some reason at present unexplained. It is all perfectly legal. Extremely quaint behaviour on his part, I admit, but thoroughly legal.'

'Then nothing can be done,' exclaimed Mr Jephson blankly. 'But it's absurd. Something must be done. The thing can't be left as it is. It's preposterous!'

'I should imagine,' said Mr Robertson, 'from what small knowledge I possess of the Human Boy, that matters will be made decidedly unpleasant for the criminal.'

'Well, I know one thing; he won't play for the team again.'

'There is something very refreshing about your logic, Jephson. Because a boy does not play in one match, you will not let him play in any of the others, though you admit his absence weakens the team. However, I suppose that is unavoidable. Mind you, I think it is a pity. Of course Gethryn has some explanation, if he would only favour us with it. Personally I think rather highly of Gethryn. So does poor old Leicester. He is the only Head-prefect Leicester has had for the last half-dozen years who knows even the rudiments of his business. But it's no use my preaching his virtues to you. You wouldn't listen. Take another cigar, and let's talk about the weather.'

Mr Jephson took the proffered weed, and the conversation, though it did not turn upon the suggested topic, ceased to have anything to do with Gethryn.

The general opinion of the School was dead against the Bishop. One or two of his friends still clung to a hope that explanations might come out, while there were also a few who always made a point of thinking differently from everybody else. Of this class was Pringle. On the Monday after the match he spent the best part of an hour of his valuable time reasoning on the subject with Lorimer. Lorimer's vote went with the majority. Although he had fielded for the Bishop, he was not, of course, being merely a substitute, allowed to bowl, as the Bishop had had his innings, and it had been particularly galling to him to feel that he might have saved the match, if it had only been possible for him to have played a larger part.

'It's no good jawing about it,' he said, 'there isn't a word to say for the man. He hasn't a leg to stand on. Why, it would be bad enough in a House or form match even, but when it comes to first matches –!' Here words failed Lorimer.

'Not at all,' said Pringle, unmoved. 'There are heaps of reasons, jolly good reasons, why he might have gone away.'

'Such as?' said Lorimer.

'Well, he might have been called away by a telegram, for instance.'

'What rot! Why should he make such a mystery of it if that was all?'

'He'd have explained all right if somebody had asked him properly. You get a chap like Norris, who, when he loses his hair, has got just about as much tact as a rhinoceros, going and ballyragging the man, and no wonder he won't say anything. I shouldn't myself.'

'Well, go and talk to him decently, then. Let's see you do it, and I'll bet it won't make a bit of difference. What the chap has done is to go and get himself mixed up in some shady business somewhere. That's the only thing it can be.'

'Rot,' said Pringle, 'the Bishop isn't that sort of chap.'

'You can't tell. I say,' he broke off suddenly, 'have you done that poem yet?'

Pringle started. He had not so much as begun that promised epic.

'I – er – haven't quite finished it yet. I'm thinking it out, you know. Getting a sort of general grip of the thing.'

'Oh. Well, I wish you'd buck up with it. It's got to go in tomorrow week.'

'Tomorrow week. Tuesday the what? Twenty-second, isn't it? Right. I'll remember. Two days after the O.B.s' match. That'll fix it in my mind. By the way, your people are going to come down all right, aren't they? I mean, we shall have to be getting in supplies and so on.'

'Yes. They'll be coming. There's plenty of time, though, to think of that. What you've got to do for the present is to keep your mind glued on the death of Dido.'

'Rather,' said Pringle, 'I won't forget.'

This was at six twenty-two p.m. By the time six-thirty boomed from the College clock-tower Pringle was absorbing a thrilling work of fiction, and Dido, her death, and everything connected with her, had faded from his mind like a beautiful dream.

11

Poetry and Stump-cricket

The Old Beckfordians' match came off in due season, and Pringle enjoyed it thoroughly. Though he only contributed a dozen in the first innings, he made up for this afterwards in the second, when the School had a hundred and twenty to get in just two hours. He went in first with Marriott, and they pulled the thing off and gave the School a ten wickets victory with eight minutes to spare. Pringle was in rare form. He made fifty-three, mainly off the bowling of a certain J. R. Smith, whose fag he had been in the old days. When at School, Smith had always been singularly aggressive towards Pringle, and the latter found that much pleasure was to be derived from hitting fours off his bowling. Subsequently he ate more strawberries and cream than were, strictly speaking, good for him, and did the honours at the study tea-party with the grace of a born host. And, as he had hoped, Miss Mabel Lorimer *did* ask what that silver-plate was stuck on to that bat for.

It is not to be wondered at that in the midst of these festivities such trivialities as Lorimer's poem found no place in his thoughts. It was not until the following day that he was reminded of it.

That Sunday was a visiting Sunday. Visiting Sundays occurred three times a term, when everybody who had friends and relations in the neighbourhood was allowed to spend the day with them. Pringle on such occasions used to ride over to Biddlehampton, the scene of Farnie's adventures, on somebody else's bicycle, his destination being the residence of a certain Colonel Ashby, no relation, but a great friend of his father's.

The gallant Colonel had, besides his other merits – which were numerous – the pleasant characteristic of leaving his guests to them-selves. To be left to oneself under some circumstances is apt to be a drawback, but in this case there was never any lack of amusements. The only objection that Pringle ever found was that there was too much to do in the time. There was shooting, riding, fishing, and also stump-cricket. Given proper conditions, no game in existence yields to stump-cricket in the matter of excitement. A stable-yard makes the best pitch, for the walls stop all hits and you score solely by boundaries, one for every hit, two if it goes past the coach-room door, four to the end wall, and out if you send it over. It is perfect.

There were two junior Ashbys, twins, aged sixteen. They went to school at Charchester, returning to the ancestral home for the week-end. Sometimes when Pringle came they would bring a school friend, in which case Pringle and he would play the twins. But as a rule the programme consisted of a series of five test matches, Charchester *versus* Beckford; and as Pringle was almost exactly twice as good as each of the twins taken individually, when they combined it made the sides very even, and the test matches were fought out with the most deadly keenness.

After lunch the Colonel was in the habit of taking Pringle for a stroll in the grounds, to watch him smoke a cigar or two. On this Sunday the conversation during the walk, after beginning, as was right and proper, with cricket, turned to work.

'Let me see,' said the Colonel, as Pringle finished the description of how point had almost got to the square cut which had given him his century against Charchester, 'you're out of the Upper Fifth now, aren't you? I always used to think you were going to be a fixture there. You are like your father in that way. I remember him at Rugby spending years on end in the same form. Couldn't get out of it. But you did get your remove, if I remember?'

'Rather,' said Pringle, 'years ago. That's to say, last term. And I'm jolly glad I did, too.'

His errant memory had returned to the poetry prize once more.

'Oh,' said the Colonel, 'why is that?'

Pringle explained the peculiar disadvantages that attended membership of the Upper Fifth during the summer term.

'I don't think a man ought to be allowed to spend his money in these special prizes,' he concluded; 'at any rate they ought to be Sixth Form affairs. It's hard enough having to do the ordinary work and keep up your cricket at the same time.'

'They are compulsory then?'

'Yes. Swindle, I call it. The chap who shares my study at Beckford is in the Upper Fifth, and his hair's turning white under the strain. The worst of it is, too, that I've promised to help him, and I never seem to have any time to give to the thing. I could turn out a great poem if I had an hour or two to spare now and then.'

'What's the subject?'

'Death of Dido this year. They are always jolly keen on deaths. Last year it was Cato, and the year before Julius Caesar. They seem to have very morbid minds. I think they might try something cheerful for a change.'

'Dido,' said the Colonel dreamily. 'Death of Dido. Where have I heard either a story or a poem or a riddle or something in some way connected with the death of Dido? It was years ago, but I distinctly remember having heard somebody mention the occurrence. Oh, well, it will come back presently, I dare say.'

It did come back presently. The story was this. A friend of Colonel Ashby's – the one-time colonel of his regiment, to be exact – was an earnest student of everything in the literature of the country that dealt with Sport. This gentleman happened to read in a publisher's list one day that a limited edition of *The Dark Horse*, by a Mr Arthur James, was on sale, and might be purchased from the publisher by all who were willing to spend half a guinea to that end.

'Well, old Matthews,' said the Colonel, 'sent off for this book. Thought it must be a sporting novel, don't you know. I shall never forget his disappointment when he opened the parcel. It turned out to be a collection of poems. *The Dark Horse, and Other Studies in the Tragic*, was its full title.

'Matthews never had a soul for poetry, good or bad. *The Dark Horse* itself was about a knight in the Middle Ages, you know. Great nonsense it was, too. Matthews used to read me passages from time to time. When he gave up the regiment he left me the book as a farewell gift. He said I was the only man he knew who really sympathized with him in the affair. I've got it still. It's in the library somewhere, if you care to look at it. What recalled it to my mind was your mention of Dido. The second poem was about the death of Dido, as far as I can remember. I'm no judge of poetry, but it didn't strike me as being very good. At the same time, you might pick up a hint or two from it. It ought to be in one of the two lower shelves on the right of the door as you go in. Unless it has been taken away. That is not likely, though. We are not very enthusiastic poetry readers here.'

Pringle thanked him for his information, and went back to the stable-yard, where he lost the fourth test match by sixteen runs, owing to preoccupation. You can't play a yorker on the leg-stump with a thin walking-stick if your mind is occupied elsewhere. And the leg-stump yorkers of James, the elder (by a minute) of the two Ashbys, were achieving a growing reputation in Charchester cricket circles.

One ought never, thought Pringle, to despise the gifts which Fortune bestows on us. And this mention of an actual completed poem on the very subject which was in his mind was clearly a gift of Fortune. How much better it would be to read thoughtfully through this poem, and quarry out a set of verses from it suitable to Lorimer's needs, than to waste his brain-tissues in trying to evolve something original from his own inner consciousness. Pringle objected strongly to any unnecessary waste of his brain-tissues. Besides, the best poets borrowed. Virgil did it. Tennyson did it. Even Homer – we have it on the authority of Mr Kipling – when he smote his blooming lyre went and stole what he thought he might require. Why should Pringle of the School House refuse to follow in such illustrious footsteps?

It was at this point that the guileful James delivered his insidious yorker, and the dull thud of the tennis ball on the board which served as the wicket told a listening world that Charchester had won the fourth test match, and that the scores were now two all.

But Beckford's star was to ascend again. Pringle's mind was made up. He would read the printed poem that very night, and before retiring to rest he would have Lorimer's verses complete and ready to be sent in for judgement to the examiner. But for the present he would dismiss the matter from his mind, and devote himself to polishing off the Charchester champions in the fifth and final test match. And in this he was successful, for just as the bell rang, summoning the players in to a well-earned tea, a sweet forward drive from his walking-stick crashed against the end wall, and Beckford had won the rubber.

'As the young batsman, undefeated to the last, reached the pavilion,' said Pringle, getting into his coat, 'a prolonged and deafening salvo of cheers greeted him. His twenty-three not out, compiled as it was against the finest bowling Charchester could produce, and on a wicket that was always treacherous (there's a brick loose at the top end), was an effort unique in its heroism.'

'Oh, *come* on,' said the defeated team.

'If you have fluked a win,' said James, 'it's nothing much. Wait till next visiting Sunday.'

And the teams went in to tea.

In the programme which Pringle had mapped out for himself, he was to go to bed with his book at the highly respectable hour of ten, work till eleven, and then go to sleep. But programmes are notoriously subject to alterations. Pringle's was altered owing to a remark made immediately after dinner by John Ashby, who, desirous of retrieving the fallen fortunes of Charchester, offered to play Pringle a hundred up at billiards, giving him thirty. Now Pringle's ability in the realm of sport did not extend to billiards. But the human being who can hear unmoved a fellow human being offering him thirty start in a game of a hundred has yet to be born. He accepted the challenge, and permission to play having been granted by the powers that were, on the understanding that the cloth was not to be cut and as few cues broken as possible, the game began, James acting as marker.

There are doubtless ways by which a game of a hundred up can be got through in less than two hours, but with Pringle and his opponent desire outran performance. When the highest break on either side is six, and the average break two, matters progress with more stateliness than speed. At last, when the hands of the clock both pointed to the figure eleven, Pringle, whose score had been at ninety-eight since half-past ten, found himself within two inches of his opponent's ball, which was tottering on the very edge of the pocket. He administered the *coup de grâce* with the air of a John Roberts, and retired triumphant; while the Charchester representatives pointed out that as their score was at seventy-four, they had really won a moral victory by four points. To which specious and unsportsmanlike piece of sophistry Pringle turned a deaf ear.

It was now too late for any serious literary efforts. No bard can do without his sleep. Even Homer used to nod at times. So Pringle contented himself with reading through the poem, which consisted of some thirty lines, and copying the same down on a sheet of notepaper for future reference. After which he went to bed.

In order to arrive at Beckford in time for morning school, he had to start from the house at eight o'clock punctually. This left little time for poetical lights. The consequence was that when Lorimer, on the following afternoon, demanded the poem as per contract, all that Pringle had to show was the copy which he had made of the poem in the book. There was a moment's suspense while Conscience and Sheer Wickedness fought the matter out inside him, and then Conscience, which had started on the encounter without enthusiasm, being obviously flabby and out of condition, threw up the sponge.

'Here you are,' said Pringle, 'it's only a rough copy, but here it *is*.'

Lorimer perused it hastily.

'But, I say,' he observed in surprised and awestruck tones, 'this is rather good.'

It seemed to strike him as quite a novel idea.

'Yes, not bad, is it?'

'But it'll get the prize.'

'Oh, we shall have to prevent that somehow.'

He did not mention how, and Lorimer did not ask.

'Well, anyhow,' said Lorimer, 'thanks awfully. I hope you've not fagged about it too much.'

'Oh no,' said Pringle airily, 'rather not. It's been no trouble at all.'

He thus, it will be noticed, concluded a painful and immoral scene by speaking perfect truth. A most gratifying reflection.

[12]

'We, the Undersigned –'

Norris kept his word with regard to the Bishop's exclusion from the Eleven. The team which had beaten the O.B.s had not had the benefit of his assistance, Lorimer appearing in his stead. Lorimer was a fast right-hand bowler, deadly in House matches or on a very bad wicket. He was the mainstay of the Second Eleven attack, and in an ordinary year would have been certain of his First Eleven cap. This season, however, with Gosling, Baynes, and the Bishop, the School had been unusually strong, and Lorimer had had to wait.

The non-appearance of his name on the notice-board came as no surprise to Gethryn. He had had the advantage of listening to Norris's views on the subject. But when Marriott grasped the facts of the case, he went to Norris and raved. Norris, as is right and proper in the captain of a School team when the wisdom of his actions is called into question, treated him with no respect whatever.

'It's no good talking,' he said, when Marriott had finished a brisk opening speech, 'I know perfectly well what I'm doing.'

'Then there's no excuse for you at all,' said Marriott. 'If you were mad or delirious I could understand it.'

'Come and have an ice,' said Norris.

'Ice!' snorted Marriott. 'What's the good of standing there babbling about ices! Do you know we haven't beaten the O.B.s for four years?'

'We shall beat them this year.'

'Not without Gethryn.'

'We certainly shan't beat them with Gethryn, because he's not going to play. A chap who chooses the day of the M.C.C. match to go off for the afternoon, and then refuses to explain, can consider himself jolly well chucked until further notice. Feel ready for that ice yet?'

'Don't be an ass.'

'Well, if ever you do get any ice, take my tip and tie it carefully round your head in a handkerchief. Then perhaps you'll be able to see why Gethryn isn't playing against the O.B.s on Saturday.'

And Marriott went off raging, and did not recover until late in the afternoon, when he made eighty-three in an hour for Leicester's House in a scratch game.

There were only three of the eleven Houses whose occupants seriously expected to see the House cricket cup on the mantelpiece of their dining-room at the end of the season. These were the School House, Jephson's, and Leicester's. In view of Pringle's sensational feats throughout the term, the knowing ones thought that the cup would go to the School House, with Leicester's runners-up. The various members of the First Eleven were pretty evenly distributed throughout the three Houses. Leicester's had Gethryn, Reece, and Marriott. Jephson's relied on Norris, Bruce, and Baker. The School House trump card was Pringle, with Lorimer and Baynes to do the bowling, and Hill of the First Eleven and Kynaston and Langdale of the second to back him up in the batting department. Both the other First Eleven men were day boys.

The presence of Gosling in any of the House elevens, however weak on paper, would have lent additional interest to the fight for the cup; for in House matches, where every team has more or less of a tail, one really good fast bowler can make a surprising amount of difference to a side.

There was a great deal of interest in the School about the House cup. The keenest of all games at big schools are generally the House matches. When Beckford met Charchester or any of the four schools which it played at cricket and football, keenness reached its highest pitch. But next to these came the House matches.

Now that he no longer played for the Eleven, the Bishop was able to give his whole mind to training the House team in the way it should go. Exclusion from the First Eleven meant also that he could no longer, unless possessed of an amount of *sang-froid* so colossal as almost to amount to genius, put in an appearance at the First Eleven net. Under these circumstances Leicester's net summoned him. Like Mr Phil May's lady when she was ejected (with perfect justice) by a barman, he went somewhere where he would be respected. To the House, then, he devoted himself, and scratch games and before-breakfast field-outs became the order of the day.

House fielding before breakfast is one of the things which cannot be classed under the head of the Lighter Side of Cricket. You get up in the small hours, dragged from a comfortable bed by some sportsman who, you feel, carries enthusiasm to a point where it ceases to be a virtue and becomes a nuisance. You get into flannels, and, still half asleep, stagger off to the field, where a hired ruffian hits you up catches which bite like serpents and sting like adders. From time to time he adds insult to injury by shouting 'get to 'em!', 'get to 'em!' – a remark which finds but one parallel in the language, the 'keep moving' of the football captain. Altogether there are many more pleasant occupations than early morning field-outs, and it requires a considerable amount of keenness to carry the victim through them without hopelessly souring his nature and causing him to foster uncharitable thoughts towards his House captain.

J. Monk of Leicester's found this increased activity decidedly uncongenial. He had no real patriotism in him. He played cricket well, but he played entirely for himself.

If, for instance, he happened to make fifty in a match – and it happened fairly frequently – he vastly preferred that the rest of the side should make ten between them than that there should be any more half-centuries on the score sheet, even at the expense of losing the match. It was not likely, therefore, that he would take kindly to this mortification of the flesh, the sole object of which was to make everybody as conspicuous as everybody else. Besides, in the matter of fielding he considered that he had nothing to learn, which, as Euclid would say, was absurd. Fielding is one of the things which is never perfect.

Monk, moreover, had another reason for disliking the field-outs. Gethryn, as captain of the House team, was naturally master of the ceremonies, and Monk objected to Gethryn. For this dislike he had solid reasons. About a fortnight after the commencement of term, the Bishop, going downstairs from his study one afternoon, was aware of what appeared to be a species of free fight going on in the doorway of the senior day-room. The senior day-room was where the rowdy element of the House collected, the individuals who were too old to be fags, and too low down in the School to own studies.

Under ordinary circumstances the Bishop would probably have passed on without investigating the matter. A head of a house hates above all things to get a name for not minding his own business in unimportant matters. Such a reputation tells against him when he has to put his foot down over big things. To have invaded the senior day-room and stopped a conventional senior day-room 'rag' would have been interfering with the most cherished rights of the citizens, the freedom which is the birthright of every Englishman, so to speak.

But as he passed the door which had just shut with a bang behind the free fighters, he heard Monk's voice inside, and immediately afterwards the voice of Danvers, and he stopped. In the first place, he reasoned within himself, if Monk and Danvers were doing anything, it was probably something wrong, and ought to be stopped. Gethryn always had the feeling that it was his duty to go and see what Monk and Danvers were doing, and tell them they mustn't. He had a profound belief in their irreclaimable villainy. In the second place, having studies of their own, they had no business to be in the senior day-room at all. It was contrary to the etiquette of the House for a study man to enter the senior day-room, and as a rule the senior day-room resented it. As to all appearances they were not resenting it now, the obvious conclusion was that something was going on which ought to cease.

The Bishop opened the door. Etiquette did not compel the head of the House to knock, the rule being that you knocked only at the doors of those senior to you in the House. He was consequently enabled to witness a tableau which, if warning had been received of his coming, would possibly have broken up before he entered. In the centre of the group was Wilson, leaning over the study table, not so much as if he liked so leaning as because he was held in that position by Danvers. In the background stood Monk, armed with a walking-stick. Round the walls were various ornaments of the senior day-room in attitudes of expectant attention, being evidently content to play the part of 'friends and retainers', leaving the leading parts in the hands of Monk and his colleague.

'Hullo,' said the Bishop, 'what's going on?'

'It's all right, old chap,' said Monk, grinning genially, 'we're only having an execution.'

'What's the row?' said the Bishop. 'What's Wilson been doing?'

'Nothing,' broke in that youth, who had wriggled free from Danvers's clutches. 'I haven't done a thing, Gethryn. These beasts lugged me out of the junior day-room without saying what for or anything.'

The Bishop began to look dangerous. This had all the outward aspect of a case of bullying. Under Reynolds's leadership Leicester's had gone in rather extensively for bullying, and the Bishop had waited hungrily for a chance of catching somebody actively engaged in the sport, so that he might drop heavily on that person and make life unpleasant for him.

'Well?' he said, turning to Monk, 'let's have it. What was it all about, and what have you got to do with it?'

Monk began to shuffle.

'Oh, it was nothing much,' he said.

'Then what are you doing with the stick?' pursued the Bishop relentlessly.

'Young Wilson cheeked Perkins,' said Monk.

Murmurs of approval from the senior day-room. Perkins was one of the ornaments referred to above.

'How?' asked Gethryn.

Wilson dashed into the conversation again.

'Perkins told me to go and get him some grub from the shop. I was doing some work, so I couldn't. Besides, I'm not his fag. If Perkins wants to go for me, why doesn't he do it himself, and not get about a hundred fellows to help him?'

'Exactly,' said the Bishop. 'A very sensible suggestion. Perkins, fall upon Wilson and slay him. I'll see fair play. Go ahead.'

'Er – no,' said Perkins uneasily. He was a small, weedy-looking youth, not built for fighting except by proxy, and he remembered the episode of Wilson and Skinner.

'Then the thing's finished,' said Gethryn. 'Wilson walks over. We needn't detain you, Wilson.'

Wilson departed with all the honours of war, and the Bishop turned to Monk.

'Now perhaps you'll tell me,' he said, 'what the deuce you and Danvers are doing here?'

'Well, hang it all, old chap –'

The Bishop begged that Monk would not call him 'old chap'.

'I'll call you "sir", if you like,' said Monk.

A gleam of hope appeared in the Bishop's eye. Monk was going to give him the opportunity he had long sighed for. In cold blood he could attack no one, not even Monk, but if he was going to be rude, that altered matters.

'What business have you in the day-room?' he said. 'You've got studies of your own.'

'If it comes to that,' said Monk, 'so have you. We've got as much business here as you. What the deuce are you doing here?'

Taken by itself, taken neat, as it were, this repartee might have been insufficient to act as a *casus belli*, but by a merciful dispensation of Providence the senior day-room elected to laugh at the remark, and to laugh loudly. Monk also laughed. Not, however, for long. The next moment the Bishop had darted in, knocked his feet from under him, and dragged him to the door. Captain Kettle himself could not have done it more neatly.

'Now,' said the Bishop, 'we can discuss the point.'

Monk got up, looking greener than usual, and began to dust his clothes.

'Don't talk rot,' he said, 'I can't fight a prefect.'

This, of course, the Bishop had known all along. What he had intended to do if Monk had kept up his end he had not decided when he embarked upon the engagement. The head of a House cannot fight by-battles with his inferiors without the loss of a good deal of his painfully acquired dignity. But Gethryn knew Monk, and he had felt justified in risking it. He improved the shining hour with an excursus on the subject of bullying, dispensed a few general threats, and left the room.

Monk had – perhaps not unnaturally – not forgotten the incident, and now that public opinion ran strongly against Gethryn on account of his M.C.C. match manoeuvres, he acted. A mass meeting of the Mob was called in his study, and it was unanimously voted that field-outs in the morning were undesirable, and that it would be judicious if the team were to strike. Now, as the Mob included in their numbers eight of the House Eleven, their opinions on the subject carried weight.

'Look here,' said Waterford, struck with a brilliant idea, 'I tell you what we'll do. Let's sign a round-robin refusing to play in the House matches unless Gethryn resigns the captaincy and the field-outs stop.'

'We may as well sign in alphabetical order,' said Monk prudently. 'It'll make it safer.'

The idea took the Mob's fancy. The round-robin was drawn up and signed.

'Now, if we could only get Reece,' suggested Danvers. 'It's no good asking Marriott, but Reece might sign.'

'Let's have a shot at any rate,' said Monk.

And a deputation, consisting of Danvers, Waterford, and Monk, duly waited upon Reece in his study, and broached the project to him.

Leicester's House Team
Goes Into a Second Edition

Reece was working when the deputation entered. He looked up enquiringly, but if he was pleased to see his visitors he managed to conceal the fact.

'Oh, I say, Reece,' began Monk, who had constituted himself spokesman to the expedition, 'are you busy?'

'Yes,' said Reece simply, going on with his writing.

This might have discouraged some people, but Nature had equipped Monk with a tough skin, which hints never pierced. He dropped into a chair, crossed his legs, and coughed. Danvers and Waterford leaned in picturesque attitudes against the door and mantelpiece. There was a silence for a minute, during which Reece continued to write unmoved.

'Take a seat, Monk,' he said at last, without looking up.

'Oh, er, thanks, I have,' said Monk. 'I say, Reece, we wanted to speak to you.'

'Go ahead then,' said Reece. 'I can listen and write at the same time. I'm doing this prose against time.'

'It's about Gethryn.'

'What's Gethryn been doing?'

'Oh, I don't know. Nothing special. It's about his being captain of the House team. The chaps seem to think he ought to resign.'

'Which chaps?' enquired Reece, laying down his pen and turning round in his chair.

'The rest of the team, you know.'

'Why don't they think he ought to be captain? The head of the House is always captain of the House team unless he's too bad to be in it at all. Don't the chaps think Gethryn's good at cricket?'

'Oh, he's good enough,' said Monk. 'It's more about this M.C.C. match business, you know. His cutting off like that in the middle of the match. The chaps think the House ought to take some notice of it. Express its disapproval, and that sort of thing.'

'And what do the chaps think of doing about it?'

Monk inserted a hand in his breast-pocket, and drew forth the round-robin. He straightened it out, and passed it over to Reece.

'We've drawn up this notice,' he said, 'and we came to see if you'd sign it. Nearly all the other chaps in the team have.'

Reece perused the document gravely. Then he handed it back to its owner.

'What rot,' said he.

'I don't think so at all,' said Monk.

'Nor do I,' broke in Danvers, speaking for the first time. 'What else can we do? We can't let a chap like Gethryn stick to the captaincy.'

'Why not?'

'A cad like that!'

'That's a matter of opinion. I don't suppose everyone thinks him a cad. I don't, personally.'

'Well, anyway,' asked Waterford, 'are you going to sign?'

'My good man, of course I'm not. Do you mean to say you seriously intend to hand in that piffle to Gethryn?'

'Rather,' said Monk.

'Then you'll be making fools of yourselves. I'll tell you exactly what'll happen, if you care to know. Gethryn will read this rot, and simply cut everybody whose name appears on the list out of the House team. I don't know if you're aware of it, but there are several other fellows besides you in the House. And if you come to think of it, you aren't so awfully good. You three are in the Second. The other five haven't got colours at all.'

'Anyhow, we're all in the House team,' said Monk.

'Don't let that worry you,' said Reece, 'you won't be long, if you show Gethryn that interesting document. Anything else I can do for you?'

'No, thanks,' said Monk. And the deputation retired.

When they had gone, Reece made his way to the Bishop's study. It was not likely that the deputation would deliver their ultimatum until late at night, when the study would be empty. From what Reece knew of Monk, he judged that it would be pleasanter to him to leave the document where the Bishop could find it in the morning, rather than run the risks that might attend a personal interview. There was time, therefore, to let Gethryn know what was going to happen, so that he might not be surprised into doing anything rash, such as resigning the captaincy, for example. Not that Reece thought it likely that he would, but it was better to take no risks.

Both Marriott and Gethryn were in the study when he arrived.

'Hullo, Reece,' said Marriott, 'come in and take several seats. Have a biscuit? Have two. Have a good many.'

Reece helped himself, and gave them a brief description of the late interview.

'I'm not surprised,' said Gethryn, 'I thought Monk would be getting at me somehow soon. I shall *have* to slay that chap someday. What ought I to do, do you think?'

'My dear chap,' said Marriott, 'there's only one thing you can do. Cut the lot of them out of the team, and fill up with substitutes.'

Reece nodded approval.

'Of course. That's what you must do. As a matter of fact, I told them you would. I've given you a reputation. You must live up to it.'

'Besides,' continued Marriott, 'after all it isn't such a crusher, when you come to think of it. Only four of them are really certainties for their places, Monk, Danvers, Waterford, and Saunders. The rest are simply tail.'

Reece nodded again. 'Great minds think alike. Exactly what I told them, only they wouldn't listen.'

'Well, whom do you suggest instead of them? Some of the kids are jolly keen and all that, but they wouldn't be much good against Baynes and Lorimer, for instance.'

'If I were you,' said Marriott, 'I shouldn't think about their batting at all. I should go simply for fielding. With a good fielding side we ought to have quite a decent chance. There's no earthly reason why you and Reece shouldn't put on enough for the first wicket to win all the matches. It's been done before. Don't you remember the School House getting the cup four years ago when Twiss was captain? They had nobody who was any earthly good except Twiss and Birch, and those two used to make about a hundred and fifty between them in every match. Besides, some of the kids can bat rather well. Wilson for one. He can bowl, too.'

'Yes,' said the Bishop, 'all right. Stick down Wilson. Who else? Gregson isn't bad. He can field in the slips, which is more than a good many chaps can.'

'Gregson's good,' said Reece, 'put him down. That makes five. You might have young Lee in too. I've seen him play like a book at his form net once or twice.'

'Lee – six. Five more wanted. Where's a House list? Here we are. Now. Adams, Bond, Brown, Burgess. Burgess has his points. Shall I stick him down?'

'Not presume to dictate,' said Marriott, 'but Adams is streets better than Burgess as a field, and just as good a bat.'

'Why, when have you seen him?'

'In a scratch game between his form and another. He was carting all over the shop. Made thirty something.'

'We'll have both of them in, then. Plenty of room. This is the team so far. Wilson, Gregson, Lee, Adams, and Burgess, with Marriott, Reece, and Gethryn. Jolly hot stuff it is, too, by Jove. We'll simply walk that tankard. Now, for the last places. I vote we each select a man, and nobody's allowed to appeal against the other's decision. I lead off with Crowinshaw. Good name, Crowinshaw. Look well on a score sheet.'

'Heave us the list,' said Marriott. 'Thanks. My dear sir, there's only one man in the running at all, which his name's Chamberlain. Shove down Joseph, and don't let me hear anyone breathe a word against him. Come on, Reece, let's have your man. I bet Reece selects some weird rotter.'

Reece pondered.

'Carstairs,' he said.

'Oh, my very dear sir! Carstairs!'

'All criticism barred,' said the Bishop.

'Sorry. By the way, what House are we drawn against in the first round?'

'Webster's.'

'Ripping. We can smash Webster's. They've got nobody. It'll be rather a good thing having an easy time in our first game. We shall be able to get some idea about the team's play. I shouldn't think we could possibly get beaten by Webster's.'

There was a knock at the door. Wilson came in with a request that he might fetch a book that he had left in the study.

'Oh, Wilson, just the man I wanted to see,' said the Bishop. 'Wilson, you're playing against Webster's next week.'

'By Jove,' said Wilson, 'am I really?'

He had spent days in working out on little slips of paper during school his exact chances of getting a place in the House team. Recently, however, he had almost ceased to hope. He had reckoned on at least eight of the senior study being chosen before him.

'Yes,' said the Bishop, 'you must buck up. Practise fielding every minute of your spare time. Anybody'll hit you up catches if you ask them.'

'Right,' said Wilson, 'I will.'

'All right, then. Go, and tell Lee that I want to see him.'

'Lee,' said the Bishop, when that worthy appeared, 'I wanted to see you, to tell you you're playing for the House against Webster's. Thought you might like to know.'

'By Jove,' said Lee, 'am I really?'

'Yes. Buck up with your fielding.'

'Right,' said Lee.

'That's all. If you're going downstairs, you might tell Adams to come up.'

For a quarter of an hour the Bishop interviewed the junior members of his team, and impressed on each of them the absolute necessity of bucking up with his fielding. And each of them protested that the matter should receive his best consideration.

'Well, they're keen enough anyway,' said Marriott, as the door closed behind Carstairs, the last of the new recruits, 'and that's the great thing. Hullo, who's that? I thought you had worked through the lot. Come in!'

A small form appeared in the doorway, carrying in its right hand a neatly-folded note.

'Monk told me to give you this, Gethryn.'

'Half a second,' said the Bishop, as the youth made for the door. 'There may be an answer.'

'Monk said there wouldn't be one.'

'Oh. No, it's all right. There isn't an answer.'

The door closed. The Bishop laughed, and threw the note over to Reece.

'Recognize it?'

Reece examined the paper.

'It's a fair copy. The one Monk showed me was rather smudged. I suppose they thought you might be hurt if you got an inky round-robin. Considerate chap, Monk.'

'Let's have a look,' said Marriott. 'By Jove. I say, listen to this bit. Like Macaulay, isn't it?'

He read extracts from the ultimatum.

'Let's have it,' said Gethryn, stretching out a hand.

'Not much. I'm going to keep it, and have it framed.'

'All right. I'm going down now to put up the list.'

When he had returned to the study, Monk and Danvers came quietly downstairs to look at the notice-board. It was dark in the passage, and Monk had to strike a light before he could see to read.

'By George,' he said, as the match flared up, 'Reece was right. He has.'

'Well, there's one consolation,' commented Danvers viciously, 'they can't possibly get that cup now. They'll have to put us in again soon, you see if they don't.'

' 'M, yes,' said Monk doubtfully.

[14]

Norris Takes a Short Holiday

'It's all rot,' observed Pringle, 'to say that they haven't a chance, because they have.'

He and Lorimer were passing through the cricket-field on their way back from an early morning visit to the baths, and had stopped to look at Leicester's House team (revised version) taking its daily hour of fielding practice. They watched the performance keenly and critically, as spies in an enemy's camp.

'Who said they hadn't a chance?' said Lorimer. 'I didn't.'

'Oh, everybody. The chaps call them the Kindergarten and the Kids' Happy League, and things of that sort. Rot, I call it. They seem to forget that you only want two or three really good men in a team if the rest can field. Look at our crowd. They've all either got their colours, or else are just outside the teams, and I swear you can't rely on one of them to hold the merest sitter right into his hands.'

On the subject of fielding in general, and catching in particular, Pringle was feeling rather sore. In the match which his House had just won against Browning's, he had put himself on to bowl in the second innings. He was one of those bowlers who manage to capture from six to ten wickets in the course of a season, and the occasions on which he bowled really well were few. On this occasion he had bowled excellently, and it had annoyed him when five catches, five soft, gentle catches, were missed off him in the course of four overs. As he watched the crisp, clean fielding which was shown by the very smallest of Leicester's small 'tail', he felt that he would rather have any of that despised eight on his side than any of the School House lights except Baynes and Lorimer.

'Our lot's all right, really,' said Lorimer, in answer to Pringle's sweeping condemnation. 'Everybody has his off days. They'll be all right next match.'

'Doubt it,' replied Pringle. 'It's all very well for you. You bowl to hit the sticks. I don't. Now just watch these kids for a moment. Now! Look! No, he couldn't have got to that. Wait a second. Now!'

Gethryn had skied one into the deep. Wilson, Burgess, and Carstairs all started for it.

'Burgess,' called the Bishop.

The other two stopped dead. Burgess ran on and made the catch.

'Now, there you are,' said Pringle, pointing his moral, 'see how those two kids stopped when Gethryn called. If that had happened in one of our matches, you'd have had half a dozen men rotting about underneath the ball, and getting in one another's way, and then probably winding up by everybody leaving the catch to everybody else.'

'Oh, come on,' said Lorimer, 'you're getting morbid. Why the dickens didn't you think of having our fellows out for fielding practice, if you're so keen on it?'

'They wouldn't have come. When a chap gets colours, he seems to think he's bought the place. You can't drag a Second Eleven man out of his bed before breakfast to improve his fielding. He thinks it can't be improved. They're a heart-breaking crew.'

'Good,' said Lorimer, 'I suppose that includes me?'

'No. You're a model man. I have seen you hold a catch now and then.'

'Thanks. Oh, I say, I gave in the poem yesterday. I hope the deuce it won't get the prize. I hope they won't spot, either, that I didn't write the thing.'

'Not a chance,' said Pringle complacently, 'you're all right. Don't you worry yourself.'

Webster's, against whom Leicester's had been drawn in the opening round of the House matches, had three men in their team, and only three, who knew how to hold a bat. It was the slackest House in the School, and always had been. It did not cause any overwhelming surprise, accordingly, when Leicester's beat them without fatigue by an innings and a hundred and twenty-one runs. Webster's won the toss, and made thirty-five. For Leicester's, Reece and Gethryn scored fifty and sixty-two respectively, and Marriott fifty-three not out. They then, with two wickets down, declared, and rattled Webster's out for seventy. The public, which had had its eye on the team, in order to see how its tail was likely to shape, was disappointed. The only definite fact that could be gleaned from the match was that the junior members of the team were not to be despised in the field. The early morning field-outs had had their effect. Adams especially shone, while Wilson at cover and Burgess in the deep recalled Jessop and Tyldesley.

The School made a note of the fact. So did the Bishop. He summoned the eight juniors *seriatim* to his study, and administered much praise, coupled with the news that fielding before breakfast would go on as usual.

Leicester's had drawn against Jephson's in the second round. Norris's lot had beaten Cooke's by, curiously enough, almost exactly the same margin as that by which Leicester's had defeated Webster's. It was generally considered that this match would decide Leicester's chances for the cup. If they could beat a really hot team like Jephson's, it was reasonable to suppose that they would do the same to the rest of the Houses, though the School House would have to be reckoned with. But the School House, as Pringle had observed, was weak in the field. It was not a coherent team. Individually its members were good, but they did not play together as Leicester's did.

But the majority of the School did not think seriously of their chances. Except for Pringle, who, as has been mentioned before, always made a point of thinking differently from everyone else, no one really believed that they would win the cup, or even appear in the final. How could a team whose tail began at the fall of the second wicket defeat teams which, like the School House, had no real tail at all?

Norris supported this view. It was for this reason that when, at breakfast on the day on which Jephson's were due to play Leicester's, he received an invitation from one of his many uncles to spend a week-end at his house, he decided to accept it.

This uncle was a man of wealth. After winning two fortunes on the Stock Exchange and losing them both, he had at length amassed a third, with which he retired in triumph to the country, leaving Throgmorton Street to exist as best it could without him. He had bought a 'show-place' at a village which lay twenty miles by rail to the east of Beckford, and it had always been Norris's wish to see this show-place, a house which was said to combine the hoariest of antiquity with a variety of modern comforts.

Merely to pay a flying visit there would be good. But his uncle held out an additional attraction. If Norris could catch the one-forty from Horton, he would arrive just in time to take part in a cricket match, that day being the day of the annual encounter with the neighbouring village of Pudford. The rector of Pudford, the opposition captain, so wrote Norris's uncle, had by underhand means lured down three really decent players from Oxford – not Blues, but almost – who had come to the village ostensibly to read classics with him as their coach, but in reality for the sole purpose of snatching from Little Bindlebury (his own village) the laurels they had so nobly earned the year before. He had heard that Norris was captaining the Beckford team this year, and had an average of thirty-eight point nought three two, so would he come and make thirty-eight point nought three two for Little Bindlebury?

'This,' thought Norris, 'is Fame. This is where I spread myself. I must be in this at any price.'

He showed the letter to Baker.

'What a pity,' said Baker.

'What's a pity?'

'That you won't be able to go. It seems rather a catch.'

'Can't go?' said Norris; 'my dear sir, you're talking through your hat. Think I'm going to refuse an invitation like this? Not if I know it. I'm going to toddle off to Jephson, get an exeat, and catch that one-forty. And if I don't paralyse the Pudford bowling, I'll shoot myself.'

'But the House match! Leicester's! This afternoon!' gurgled the amazed Baker.

'Oh, hang Leicester's. Surely the rest of you can lick the Kids' Happy League without my help. If you can't, you ought to be ashamed of yourselves. I've chosen you a wicket with my own hands, fit to play a test match on.'

'Of course we ought to lick them. But you can never tell at cricket what's going to happen. We oughtn't to run any risks when we've got such a good chance of winning the pot. Why, it's centuries since we won the pot. Don't you go.'

'I must, man. It's the chance of a lifetime.'

Baker tried another method of attack.

'Besides,' he said, 'you don't suppose Jephson'll let you off to play in a beastly little village game when there's a House match on?'

'He must never know!' hissed Norris, after the manner of the Surrey-side villain.

'He's certain to ask why you want to get off so early.'

'I shall tell him my uncle particularly wishes me to come early.'

'Suppose he asks why?'

'I shall say I can't possibly imagine.'

'Oh, well, if you're going to tell lies –'

'Not at all. Merely a diplomatic evasion. I'm not bound to go and sob out my secrets on Jephson's waistcoat.'

Baker gave up the struggle with a sniff. Norris went to Mr Jephson and got leave to spend the week-end at his uncle's. The interview went without a hitch, as Norris had prophesied.

'You will miss the House match, Norris, then?' said Mr Jephson.

'I'm afraid so, sir. But Mr Leicester's are very weak.'

'H'm. Reece, Marriott, and Gethryn are a good beginning.'

'Yes, sir. But they've got nobody else. Their tail starts after those three.'

'Very well. But it seems a pity.'

'Thank you, sir,' said Norris, wisely refraining from discussing the matter. He had got his exeat, which was what he had come for.

In all the annals of Pudford and Little Bindlebury cricket there had never been such a match as that year's. The rector of Pudford and his three Oxford experts performed prodigies with the bat, prodigies, that is to say, judged from the standpoint of ordinary Pudford scoring, where double figures were the exception rather than the rule.

The rector, an elderly, benevolent-looking gentleman, played with astounding caution and still more remarkable luck for seventeen. Finally, after he had been in an hour and ten minutes, mid-on accepted the eighth easy chance offered to him, and the ecclesiastic had to retire. The three 'Varsity men knocked up a hundred between them, and the complete total was no less than a hundred and thirty-four.

Then came the sensation of the day. After three wickets had fallen for ten runs, Norris and the Little Bindlebury curate, an old Cantab, stayed together and knocked off the deficit.

Norris's contribution of seventy-eight not out was for many a day the sole topic of conversation over the evening pewter at the 'Little Bindlebury Arms'. A non-enthusiast, who tried on one occasion to introduce the topic of Farmer Giles's grey pig, found himself the most unpopular man in the village.

On the Monday morning Norris returned to Jephson's, with pride in his heart and a sovereign in his pocket, the latter the gift of his excellent uncle.

He had had, he freely admitted to himself, a good time. His uncle had done him well, exceedingly well, and he looked forward to going to the show-place again in the near future. In the meantime he felt a languid desire to know how the House match was going on. They must almost have finished the first innings, he thought – unless Jephson's had run up a very big score, and kept their opponents in the field all the afternoon.

'Hullo, Baker,' he said, tramping breezily into the study, 'I've had the time of a lifetime. Great, simply! No other word for it. How's the match getting on?'

Baker looked up from the book he was reading.

'What match?' he enquired coldly.

'House match, of course, you lunatic. What match did you think I meant? How's it going on?'

'It's not going on,' said Baker, 'it's stopped.'

'You needn't be a funny goat,' said Norris complainingly. 'You know what I mean. What happened on Saturday?'

'They won the toss,' began Baker slowly.

'Yes?'

'And went in and made a hundred and twenty.'

'Good. I told you they were no use. A hundred and twenty's rotten.'

'Then we went in, and made twenty-one.'

'Hundred and twenty-one.'

'No. Just a simple twenty-one without any trimmings of any sort.'

'But, man! How? Why? How on earth did it happen?'

'Gethryn took eight for nine. Does that seem to make it any clearer?'

'Eight for nine? Rot.'

'Show you the score-sheet if you care to see it. In the second innings –'

'Oh, you began a second innings?'

'Yes. We also finished it. We scored rather freely in the second innings. Ten was on the board before the fifth wicket fell. In the end we fairly collared the bowling, and ran up a total of forty-eight.'

Norris took a seat, and tried to grapple with the situation.

'Forty-eight! Look here, Baker, swear you're not ragging.'

Baker took a green scoring-book from the shelf and passed it to him.

'Look for yourself,' he said.

Norris looked. He looked long and earnestly. Then he handed the book back.

'Then they've won!' he said blankly.

'How do you guess these things?' observed Baker with some bitterness.

'Well, you are a crew,' said Norris. 'Getting out for twenty-one and forty-eight! I see Gethryn got nine for thirty in the second innings. He seems to have been on the spot. I suppose the wicket suited him.'

'If you can call it a wicket. Next time you specially select a pitch for the House to play on, I wish you'd hunt up something with some slight pretensions to decency.'

'Why, what was wrong with the pitch? It was a bit worn, that was all.'

'If,' said Baker, 'you call having holes three inches deep just where every ball pitches being a bit worn, I suppose it was. Anyhow, it would have been almost as well, don't you think, if you'd stopped and played for the House, instead of going off to your rotten village match? You were sick enough when Gethryn went off in the M.C.C. match.'

'Oh, curse,' said Norris.

For he had been hoping against hope that the parallel nature of the two incidents would be less apparent to other people than it was to himself.

And so it came about that Leicester's passed successfully through the first two rounds and soared into the dizzy heights of the semi-final.

Versus *Charchester*
(at Charchester)

From the fact that he had left his team so basely in the lurch on the day of an important match, a casual observer might have imagined that Norris did not really care very much whether his House won the cup or not. But this was not the case. In reality the success of Jephson's was a very important matter to him. A sudden whim had induced him to accept his uncle's invitation, but now that that acceptance had had such disastrous results, he felt inclined to hire a sturdy menial by the hour to kick him till he felt better. To a person in such a frame of mind there are three methods of consolation. He can commit suicide, he can take to drink, or he can occupy his mind with other matters, and cure himself by fixing his attention steadily on some object, and devoting his whole energies to the acquisition of the same.

Norris chose the last method. On the Saturday week following his performance for Little Bindlebury, the Beckford Eleven was due to journey to Charchester, to play the return match against that school on their opponents' ground, and Norris resolved that that match should be won. For the next week the team practised assiduously, those members of it who were not playing in House matches spending every afternoon at the nets. The treatment was not without its effect. The team had been a good one before. Now every one of the eleven seemed to be at the very summit of his powers. New and hitherto unsuspected strokes began to be developed, leg glances which recalled the Hove and Ranjitsinhji, late cuts of Palairetical brilliance. In short, all Nature may be said to have smiled, and by the end of the week Norris was beginning to be almost cheerful once more. And then, on the Monday before the match, Samuel Wilberforce Gosling came to school with his right arm in a sling. Norris met him at the School gates, rubbed his eyes to see whether it was not after all some horrid optical illusion, and finally, when the stern truth came home to him, almost swooned with anguish.

'What? How? Why?' he enquired lucidly.

The injured Samuel smiled feebly.

'I'm fearfully sorry, Norris,' he said.

'Don't say you can't play on Saturday,' moaned Norris.

'Frightfully sorry. I know it's a bit of a sickener. But I don't see how I can, really. The doctor says I shan't be able to play for a couple of weeks.'

Now that the blow had definitely fallen, Norris was sufficiently himself again to be able to enquire into the matter.

'How on earth did you do it? How did it happen?'

Gosling looked guiltier than ever.

'It was on Saturday evening,' he said. 'We were ragging about at home a bit, you know, and my young sister wanted me to send her down a few balls. Somebody had given her a composition bean and a bat, and she's been awfully keen on the game ever since she got them.'

'I think it's simply sickening the way girls want to do everything we do,' said Norris disgustedly.

Gosling spoke for the defence.

'Well, she's only thirteen. You can't blame the kid. Seemed to me a jolly healthy symptom. Laudable ambition and that sort of thing.'

'Well?'

'Well, I sent down one or two. She played 'em like a book. Bit inclined to pull. All girls are. So I put in a long hop on the off, and she let go at it like Jessop. She's got a rattling stroke in mid-on's direction. Well, the bean came whizzing back rather wide on the right. I doubled across to bring off a beefy c-and-b, and the bally thing took me right on the tips of the fingers. Those composition balls hurt like blazes, I can tell you. Smashed my second finger simply into hash, and I couldn't grip a ball now to save my life. Much less bowl. I'm awfully sorry. It's a shocking nuisance.'

Norris agreed with him. It was more than a nuisance. It was a staggerer. Now that Gethryn no longer figured for the First Eleven, Gosling was the School's one hope. Baynes was good on his wicket, but the wickets he liked were the sea-of-mud variety, and this summer fine weather had set in early and continued. Lorimer was also useful, but not to be mentioned in the same breath as the great Samuel. The former was good, the latter would be good in a year or so. His proper sphere of action was the tail. If the first pair of bowlers could dismiss five good batsmen, Lorimer's fast, straight deliveries usually accounted for the rest. But there had to be somebody to pave the way for him. He was essentially a change bowler. It is hardly to be wondered at that Norris very soon began to think wistfully of the Bishop, who was just now doing such great things with the ball, wasting his sweetness on the desert air of the House matches. Would it be consistent with his dignity to invite him back into the team? It was a nice point. With some persons there might be a risk. But Gethryn, as he knew perfectly well, was not the sort of fellow to rub in the undeniable fact that the School team could not get along without him. He had half decided to ask him to play against Charchester, when Gosling suggested the very same thing.

'Why don't you have Gethryn in again?' he said. 'You've stood him out against the O.B.s and the Masters. Surely that's enough. Especially as he's miles the best bowler in the School.'

'Bar yourself.'

'Not a bit. He can give me points. You take my tip and put him in again.'

'Think he'd play if I put him down? Because, you know, I'm dashed if I'm going to do any grovelling and that sort of thing.'

'Certain to, I should think. Anyhow, it's worth trying.'

Pringle, on being consulted, gave the same opinion, and Norris was convinced. The list went up that afternoon, and for the first time since the M.C.C. match Gethryn's name appeared in its usual place.

'Norris is learning wisdom in his old age,' said Marriott to the Bishop, as they walked over to the House that evening.

Leicester's were in the middle of their semi-final, and looked like winning it.

'I was just wondering what to do about it,' said Gethryn. 'What would you do? Play, do you think?'

'Play! My dear man, what else did you propose to do? You weren't thinking of refusing?'

'I was.'

'But, man! That's rank treason. If you're put down to play for the School you must play. There's no question about it. If Norris knocked you down with one hand and put you up on the board with the other, you'd have to play all the same. You mustn't have any feelings where the School is concerned. Nobody's ever refused to play in a first match. It's one of the things you can't do. Norris hasn't given you much of a time lately, I admit. Still, you must lump that. Excuse sermon. I hope it's done you good.'

'Very well. I'll play. It's rather rot, though.'

'No, it's all right, really. It's only that you've got into a groove. You're so used to doing the heavy martyr, that the sudden change has knocked you out rather. Come and have an ice before the shop shuts.'

So Gethryn came once more into the team, and travelled down to Charchester with the others. And at this point a painful alternative faces me. I have to choose between truth and inclination. I should like to say that the Bishop eclipsed himself, and broke all previous records in the Charchester match. By the rules of the dramatic, nothing else is possible. But truth, though it crush me, and truth compels me to admit that his performance was in reality distinctly mediocre. One of his weak points as a bowler was that he was at sea when opposed to a left-hander. Many bowlers have this failing. Some strange power seems to compel them to bowl solely on the leg side, and nothing but long hops and full pitches. It was so in the case of Gethryn. Charchester won the toss, and batted first on a perfect wicket. The first pair of batsmen were the captain, a great bat, who had scored seventy-three not out against Beckford in the previous match, and a left-handed fiend. Baynes's leg-breaks were useless on a wicket which, from the hardness of it, might have been constructed of asphalt, and the rubbish the Bishop rolled up to the left-handed artiste was painful to witness. At four o'clock – the match had started at half-past eleven – the Charchester captain reached his century, and was almost immediately stumped off Baynes. The Bishop bowled the next man first ball, the one bright spot in his afternoon's performance. Then came another long stand, against which the Beckford bowling raged in vain. At five o'clock, Charchester by that time having made two hundred and forty-one for two wickets, the left-hander ran into three figures, and the captain promptly declared the innings closed. Beckford's only chance was to play for a draw, and in this they succeeded. When stumps were drawn at a quarter to seven, the score was a hundred and three, and five wickets were down. The Bishop had the satisfaction of being not out with twenty-eight to his credit, but nothing less than a century would have been sufficient to soothe him after his shocking bowling performance. Pringle, who during the luncheon interval had encountered his young friends the Ashbys, and had been duly taunted by them on the subject of leather-hunting, was top scorer with forty-one. Norris, I regret to say, only made three, running himself out in his second over. As the misfortune could not, by any stretch of imagination, be laid at anybody else's door but his own, he was decidedly savage. The team returned to Beckford rather footsore, very disgusted, and abnormally silent. Norris sulked by himself at one end of the saloon carriage, and the Bishop sulked by himself at the other end, and even Marriott forbore to treat the situation lightly. It was a mournful home-coming. No cheering wildly as the brake drove to the

College from Horton, no shouting of the School song in various keys as they passed through the big gates. Simply silence. And except when putting him on to bowl, or taking him off, or moving him in the field, Norris had not spoken a word to the Bishop the whole afternoon.

It was shortly after this disaster that Mr Mortimer Wells came to stay with the Headmaster. Mr Mortimer Wells was a brilliant and superior young man, who was at some pains to be a cynic. He was an old pupil of the Head's in the days before he had succeeded to the rule of Beckford. He had the reputation of being a 'ripe' scholar, and to him had been deputed the task of judging the poetical outbursts of the bards of the Upper Fifth, with the object of awarding to the most deserving – or, perhaps, to the least undeserving – the handsome prize bequeathed by his open-handed highness, the Rajah of Seltzerpore.

This gentleman sat with his legs stretched beneath the Headmaster's generous table. Dinner had come to an end, and a cup of coffee, acting in co-operation with several glasses of port and an excellent cigar, had inspired him to hold forth on the subject of poetry prizes. He held forth.

'The poetry prize system,' said he – it is astonishing what nonsense a man, ordinarily intelligent, will talk after dinner – 'is on exactly the same principle as those penny-in-the-slot machines that you see at stations. You insert your penny. You set your prize subject. In the former case you hope for wax vestas, and you get butterscotch. In the latter, you hope for something at least readable, and you get the most complete, terrible, uninspired twaddle that was ever written on paper. The boy mind' – here the ash of his cigar fell off on to his waistcoat – 'the merely boy mind is incapable of poetry.'

From which speech the shrewd reader will infer that Mr Mortimer Wells was something of a prig. And perhaps, altogether shrewd reader, you're right.

Mr Lawrie, the master of the Sixth, who had been asked to dinner to meet the great man, disagreed as a matter of principle. He was one of those men who will take up a cause from pure love of argument.

'I think you're wrong, sir. I'm perfectly convinced you're wrong.'

Mr Wells smiled in his superior way, as if to say that it was a pity that Mr Lawrie was so foolish, but that perhaps he could not help it.

'Ah,' he said, 'but you have not had to wade through over thirty of these gems in a single week. I have. I can assure you your views would undergo a change if you could go through what I have. Let me read you a selection. If that does not convert you, nothing will. If you will excuse me for a moment, Beckett, I will leave the groaning board, and fetch the manuscripts.'

He left the room, and returned with a pile of paper, which he deposited in front of him on the table.

'Now,' he said, selecting the topmost manuscript, 'I will take no unfair advantage. I will read you the very pick of the bunch. None of the other – er – poems come within a long way of this. It is a case of Eclipse first and the rest nowhere. The author, the gifted author, is a boy of the name of Lorimer, whom I congratulate on taking the Rajah's prize. I drain this cup of coffee to him. Are you ready? Now, then.'

He cleared his throat.

[16]

A Disputed Authorship

'One moment,' said Mr Lawrie, 'might I ask what is the subject of the poem?'

'Death of Dido,' said the Headmaster. 'Good, hackneyed, evergreen subject, mellow with years. Go on, Wells.'

Mr Wells began.

> Queen of Tyre, ancient Tyre,
> Whilom mistress of the wave.

Mr Lawrie, who had sunk back into the recesses of his chair in an attitude of attentive repose, sat up suddenly with a start.

'What!' he cried.

'Hullo,' said Mr Wells, 'has the beauty of the work come home to you already?'

'You notice,' he said, as he repeated the couplet, 'that flaws begin to appear in the gem right from the start. It was rash of Master Lorimer to attempt such a difficult metre. Plucky, but rash. He should have stuck to blank verse. Tyre, you notice, two syllables to rhyme with "deny her" in line three. "What did fortune e'er deny her? Were not all her warriors brave?" That last line seems to me distinctly weak. I don't know how it strikes you.'

'You're hypercritical, Wells,' said the Head. 'Now, for a boy I consider that a very good beginning. What do you say, Lawrie?'

'I – er. Oh, I think I am hardly a judge.'

'To resume,' said Mr Mortimer Wells. He resumed, and ran through the remaining verses of the poem with comments. When he had finished, he remarked that, in his opinion a whiff of fresh air would not hurt him. If the Headmaster would excuse him, he would select another of those excellent cigars, and smoke it out of doors.

'By all means,' said the Head; 'I think I won't join you myself, but perhaps Lawrie will.'

'No, thank you. I think I will remain. Yes, I think I will remain.'

Mr Wells walked jauntily out of the room. When the door had shut, Mr Lawrie coughed nervously.

'Another cigar, Lawrie?'

'I – er – no, thank you. I want to ask you a question. What is your candid opinion of those verses Mr Wells was reading just now?'

The Headmaster laughed.

'I don't think Wells treated them quite fairly. In my opinion they were distinctly promising. For a boy in the Upper Fifth, you understand. Yes, on the whole they showed distinct promise.'

'They were mine,' said Mr Lawrie.

'Yours! I don't understand. How were they yours?'

'I wrote them. Every word of them.'

'You wrote them! But, my dear Lawrie –'

'I don't wonder that you are surprised. For my own part I am amazed, simply amazed. How the boy – I don't even remember his name – contrived to get hold of them, I have not the slightest conception. But that he did so contrive is certain. The poem is word for word, literally word for word, the same as one which I wrote when I was at Cambridge.'

'You don't say so!'

'Yes. It can hardly be a coincidence.'

'Hardly,' said the Head. 'Are you certain of this?'

'Perfectly certain. I am not eager to claim the authorship, I can assure you, especially after Mr Wells's very outspoken criticisms, but there is nothing else to be done. The poem appeared more than a dozen years ago, in a small book called *The Dark Horse.*'

'Ah! Something in the Whyte Melville style, I suppose?'

'No,' said Mr Lawrie sharply. 'No. Certainly not. They were serious poems, tragical most of them. I had them collected, and published them at my own expense. Very much at my own expense. I used a pseudonym, I am thankful to say. As far as I could ascertain, the total sale amounted to eight copies. I have never felt the very slightest inclination to repeat the performance. But how this boy managed to see the book is more than I can explain. He can hardly have bought it. The price was half-a-guinea. And there is certainly no copy in the School library. The thing is a mystery.'

'A mystery that must be solved,' said the Headmaster. 'The fact remains that he did see the book, and it is very serious. Wholesale plagiarism of this description should be kept for the School magazine. It should not be allowed to spread to poetry prizes. I must see Lorimer about this tomorrow. Perhaps he can throw some light upon the matter.'

When, in the course of morning school next day, the School porter entered the Upper Fifth form-room and informed Mr Sims, who was engaged in trying to drive the beauties of Plautus' colloquial style into the Upper Fifth brain, that the Headmaster wished to see Lorimer, Lorimer's conscience was so abnormally good that for the life of him he could not think why he had been sent for. As far as he could remember, there was no possible way in which the authorities could get at him. If he had been in the habit of smoking out of bounds in lonely fields and deserted barns, he might have felt uneasy. But whatever his failings, that was not one of them. It could not be anything about bounds, because he had been so busy with cricket that he had had no time to break them this term. He walked into the presence, glowing with conscious rectitude. And no sooner was he inside than the Headmaster, with three simple words, took every particle of starch out of his anatomy.

'Sit down, Lorimer,' he said.

There are many ways of inviting a person to seat himself. The genial 'take a pew' of one's equal inspires confidence. The raucous 'sit down in front' of the frenzied pit, when you stand up to get a better view of the stage, is not so pleasant. But worst of all is the icy 'sit down' of the annoyed headmaster. In his mouth the words take to themselves new and sinister meanings. They seem to accuse you of nameless crimes, and to warn you that anything you may say will be used against you as evidence.

'Why have I sent for you, Lorimer?'

A nasty question that, and a very favourite one of the Rev. Mr Beckett, Headmaster of Beckford. In nine cases out of ten, the person addressed, paralysed with nervousness, would give himself away upon the instant, and confess everything. Lorimer, however, was saved by the fact that he had nothing to confess. He stifled an inclination to reply 'because the woodpecker would peck her', or words to that effect, and maintained a pallid silence.

'Have you ever heard of a book called *The Dark Horse*, Lorimer?'

Lorimer began to feel that the conversation was too deep for him. After opening in the conventional 'judge-then-placed-the-black-cap-on-his-head' manner, his assailant had suddenly begun to babble lightly of sporting literature. He began to entertain doubts of the Headmaster's sanity. It would not have added greatly to his mystific-

ation if the Head had gone on to insist that he was the Emperor of
Peru, and worked solely by electricity.

The Headmaster, for his part, was also surprised. He had worked
for dismay, conscious guilt, confessions, and the like, instead of blank
amazement. He, too, began to have his doubts. Had Mr Lawrie been
mistaken? It was not likely, but it was barely possible. In which case
the interview had better be brought to an abrupt stop until he had
made inquiries. The situation was at a deadlock.

Fortunately at this point half-past twelve struck, and the bell rang
for the end of morning school. The situation was saved, and the tension
relaxed.

'You may go, Lorimer,' said the Head, 'I will send for you later.'

He swept out of the room, and Lorimer raced over to the House to
inform Pringle that the Headmaster had run suddenly mad, and should
by rights be equipped with a strait-waistcoat.

'You never saw such a man,' he said, 'hauled me out of school in
the middle of a Plautus lesson, dumps me down in a chair, and then
asks me if I've read some weird sporting novel or other.'

'Sporting novel! My dear man!'

'Well, it sounded like it from the title.'

'The title. Oh!'

'What's up?'

Pringle had leaped to his feet as if he had suddenly discovered that
he was sitting on something red-hot. His normal air of superior calm
had vanished. He was breathless with excitement. A sudden idea had
struck him with the force of a bullet.

'What was the title he asked you if you'd read the book of?' he
demanded incoherently.

'*The Derby Winner*.'

Pringle sat down again, relieved.

'Oh. Are you certain?'

'No, of course it wasn't that. I was only ragging. The real title was
The Dark Horse. Hullo, what's up now? Have you got 'em too?'

'What's up? I'll tell you. We're done for. Absolutely pipped. That's
what's the matter.'

'Hang it, man, do give us a chance. Why can't you explain, instead
of sitting there talking like that? Why are we done? What have we
done, anyway?'

'The poem, of course, the prize poem. I forgot, I never told you. I
hadn't time to write anything of my own, so I cribbed it straight out
of a book called *The Dark Horse*. Now do you see?'

Lorimer saw. He grasped the whole unpainted beauty of the situation in a flash, and for some moments it rendered him totally unfit for intellectual conversation. When he did speak his observation was brief, but it teemed with condensed meaning. It was the conversational parallel to the ox in the tea-cup.

'My aunt!' he said.

'There'll be a row about this,' said Pringle.

'What am I to say when he has me in this afternoon? He said he would.'

'Let the whole thing out. No good trying to hush it up. He may let us down easy if you're honest about it.'

It relieved Lorimer to hear Pringle talk about 'us'. It meant that he was not to be left to bear the assault alone. Which, considering that the whole trouble was, strictly speaking, Pringle's fault, was only just.

'But how am I to explain? I can't reel off a long yarn all about how you did it all, and so on. It would be too low.'

'I know,' said Pringle, 'I've got it. Look here, on your way to the Old Man's room you pass the Remove door. Well, when you pass, drop some money. I'll be certain to hear it, as I sit next the door. And then I'll ask to leave the room, and we'll go up together.'

'Good man, Pringle, you're a genius. Thanks, awfully.'

But as it happened, this crafty scheme was not found necessary. The blow did not fall till after lock-up.

Lorimer being in the Headmaster's House, it was possible to interview him without the fuss and advertisement inseparable from a 'sending for during school'. Just as he was beginning his night-work, the butler came with a message that he was wanted in the Headmaster's part of the House.

'It was only Mr Lorimer as the master wished to see,' said the butler, as Pringle rose to accompany his companion in crime.

'That's all right,' said Pringle, 'the Headmaster's always glad to see me. I've got a standing invitation. He'll understand.'

At first, when he saw two where he had only sent for one, the Headmaster did not understand at all, and said so. He had prepared to annihilate Lorimer hip and thigh, for he was now convinced that his blank astonishment at the mention of *The Dark Horse* during their previous interview had been, in the words of the bard, a mere veneer, a wile of guile. Since the morning he had seen Mr Lawrie again, and had with his own eyes compared the two poems, the printed and the written, the author by special request having hunted up a copy of that valuable work, *The Dark Horse*, from the depths of a cupboard in his rooms.

His astonishment melted before Pringle's explanation, which was brief and clear, and gave way to righteous wrath. In well-chosen terms he harangued the two criminals. Finally he perorated.

'There is only one point which tells in your favour. You have not attempted concealment.' (Pringle nudged Lorimer surreptitiously at this.) 'And I may add that I believe that, as you say, you did not desire actually to win the prize by underhand means. But I cannot overlook such an offence. It is serious. Most serious. You will, both of you, go into extra lesson for the remaining Saturdays of the term.'

Extra lesson meant that instead of taking a half-holiday on Saturday like an ordinary law-abiding individual, you treated the day as if it were a full-school day, and worked from two till four under the eye of the Headmaster. Taking into consideration everything, the punishment was not an extraordinarily severe one, for there were only two more Saturdays to the end of term, and the sentence made no mention of the Wednesday half-holidays.

But in effect it was serious indeed. It meant that neither Pringle nor Lorimer would be able to play in the final House match against Leicester's, which was fixed to begin on the next Saturday at two o'clock. Among the rules governing the House matches was one to the effect that no House might start a match with less than eleven men, nor might the Eleven be changed during the progress of the match – a rule framed by the Headmaster, not wholly without an eye to emergencies like the present.

'Thank goodness,' said Pringle, 'that there aren't any more First matches. It's bad enough, though, by Jove, as it is. I suppose it's occurred to you that this cuts us out of playing in the final?'

Lorimer said the point had not escaped his notice.

'I wish,' he observed, with simple pathos, 'that I'd got the Rajah of Seltzerpore here now. I'd strangle him. I wonder if the Old Man realizes that he's done his own House out of the cup?'

'Wouldn't care if he did. Still, it's a sickening nuisance. Leicester's are a cert now.'

'Absolute cert,' said Lorimer; 'Baynes can't do all the bowling, especially on a hard wicket, and there's nobody else. As for our batting and fielding –'

'Don't,' said Pringle gloomily, 'it's too awful.'

On the following Saturday, Leicester's ran up a total in their first innings which put the issue out of doubt, and finished off the game on the Monday by beating the School House by six wickets.

17

The Winter Term

It was the first day of the winter term.

The Bishop, as he came back by express, could not help feeling that, after all, life considered as an institution had its points. Things had mended steadily during the last weeks of the term. He had kept up his end as head of the House perfectly. The internal affairs of Leicester's were going as smoothly as oil. And there was the cricket cup to live up to. Nothing pulls a House together more than beating all comers in the field, especially against odds, as Leicester's had done. And then Monk and Danvers had left. That had set the finishing touch to a good term's work. The Mob were no longer a power in the land. Waterford remained, but a subdued, benevolent Waterford, with a wonderful respect for law and order. Yes, as far as the House was concerned, Gethryn felt no apprehensions. As regarded the School at large, things were bound to come right in time. A school has very little memory. And in the present case the Bishop, being second man in the Fifteen, had unusual opportunities of righting himself in the eyes of the multitude. In the winter term cricket is forgotten. Football is the only game that counts.

And to round off the whole thing, when he entered his study he found a letter on the table. It was from Farnie, and revealed two curious and interesting facts. Firstly he had left, and Beckford was to know him no more. Secondly – this was even more remarkable – he possessed a conscience.

'Dear Gethryn,' ran the letter, 'I am writing to tell you my father is sending me to a school in France, so I shall not come back to Beckford. I am sorry about the M.C.C. match, and I enclose the four pounds you lent me. I utterly bar the idea of going to France. It's beastly, yours truly, R. Farnie.'

The money mentioned was in the shape of a cheque, signed by Farnie senior.

Gethryn was distinctly surprised. That all this time remorse like a worm i' the bud should have been feeding upon his uncle's damask cheek, as it were, he had never suspected. His relative's demeanour since the M.C.C. match had, it is true, been considerably toned down, but this he had attributed to natural causes, not unnatural ones like conscience. As for the four pounds, he had set it down as a bad debt. To get it back was like coming suddenly into an unexpected fortune. He began to think that there must have been some good in Farnie after all, though he was fain to admit that without the aid of a microscope the human eye might well have been excused for failing to detect it.

His next thought was that there was nothing now to prevent him telling the whole story to Reece and Marriott. Reece, if anybody, deserved to have his curiosity satisfied. The way in which he had abstained from questions at the time of the episode had been nothing short of magnificent. Reece must certainly be told.

Neither Reece nor Marriott had arrived at the moment. Both were in the habit of returning at the latest possible hour, except at the beginning of the summer term. The Bishop determined to reserve his story until the following evening.

Accordingly, when the study kettle was hissing on the Etna, and Wilson was crouching in front of the fire, making toast in his own inimitable style, he embarked upon his narrative.

'I say, Marriott.'

'Hullo.'

'Do you notice a subtle change in me this term? Does my expressive purple eye gleam more brightly than of yore? It does. Exactly so. I feel awfully bucked up. You know that kid Farnie has left?'

'I thought I missed his merry prattle. What's happened to him?'

'Gone to a school in France somewhere.'

'Jolly for France.'

'Awfully. But the point is that now he's gone I can tell you about that M.C.C. match affair. I know you want to hear what really did happen that afternoon.'

Marriott pointed significantly at Wilson, whose back was turned.

'Oh, that's all right,' said Gethryn. 'Wilson.'

'Yes?'

'You mustn't listen. Try and think you're a piece of furniture. See? And if you do happen to overhear anything, you needn't go gassing about it. Follow?'

'All right,' said Wilson, and Gethryn told his tale.

'Jove,' he said, as he finished, 'that's a relief. It's something to have got that off my chest. I do bar keeping a secret.'

'But, I say,' said Marriott.

'Well?'

'Well, it was beastly good of you to do it, and that sort of thing, I suppose. I see that all right. But, my dear man, what a rotten thing to do. A kid like that. A little beast who simply cried out for sacking.'

'Well, at any rate, it's over now. You needn't jump on me. I acted from the best motives. That's what my grandfather, Farnie's *pater*, you know, always used to say when he got at me for anything in the happy days of my childhood. Don't sit there looking like a beastly churchwarden, you ass. Buck up, and take an intelligent interest in things.'

'No, but really, Bishop,' said Marriott, 'you must treat this seriously. You'll have to let the other chaps know about it.'

'How? Put it up on the notice-board? This is to certify that Mr Allan Gethryn, of Leicester's House, Beckford, is dismissed without a stain on his character. You ass, how can I let them know? I seem to see myself doing the boy-hero style of things. My friends, you wronged me, you wronged me very grievously. But I forgive you. I put up with your cruel scorn. I endured it. I steeled myself against it. And now I forgive you profusely, every one of you. Let us embrace. It wouldn't do. You must see that much. Don't be a goat. Is that toast done yet, Wilson?'

Wilson exhibited several pounds of the article in question.

'Good,' said the Bishop. 'You're a great man, Wilson. You can make a small selection of those biscuits, and if you bag all the sugar ones I'll slay you, and then you can go quietly downstairs, and rejoin your sorrowing friends. And don't you go telling them what I've been saying.'

'Rather not,' said Wilson.

He made his small selection, and retired. The Bishop turned to Marriott again.

'I shall tell Reece, because he deserves it, and I rather think I shall tell Gosling and Pringle. Nobody else, though. What's the good of it? Everybody'll forget the whole thing by next season.'

'How about Norris?' asked Marriott.

'Now there you have touched the spot. I can't possibly tell Norris myself. My natural pride is too enormous. Descended from a primordial atomic globule, you know, like Pooh Bah. And I shook hands with a duke once. The man Norris and I, I regret to say, had something of a row on the subject last term. We parted with mutual expressions of hate, and haven't spoken since. What I should like would be for somebody else to tell him all about it. Not you. It would look too much like a put-up job. So don't you go saying anything. Swear.'

'Why not?'

'Because you mustn't. Swear. Let me hear you swear by the bones of your ancestors.'

'All right. I call it awful rot, though.'

'Can't be helped. Painful but necessary. Now I'm going to tell Reece, though I don't expect he'll remember anything about it. Reece never remembers anything beyond his last meal.'

'Idiot,' said Marriott after him as the door closed. 'I don't know, though,' he added to himself.

And, pouring himself out another cup of tea, he pondered deeply over the matter.

Reece heard the news without emotion.

'You're a good sort, Bishop,' he said, 'I knew something of the kind must have happened. It reminds me of a thing that happened to –'

'Yes, it is rather like it, isn't it?' said the Bishop. 'By the way, talking about stories, a chap I met in the holidays told me a ripper. You see, this chap and his brother –'

He discoursed fluently for some twenty minutes. Reece sighed softly, but made no attempt to resume his broken narrative. He was used to this sort of thing.

It was a fortnight later, and Marriott and the Bishop were once more seated in their study waiting for Wilson to get tea ready. Wilson made toast in the foreground. Marriott was in football clothes, rubbing his shin gently where somebody had kicked it in the scratch game that afternoon. After rubbing for a few moments in silence, he spoke suddenly.

'You must tell Norris,' he said. 'It's all rot.'

'I can't.'

'Then I shall.'

'No, don't. You swore you wouldn't.'

'Well, but look here. I just want to ask you one question. What sort of a time did you have in that scratch game tonight?'

'Beastly. I touched the ball exactly four times. If I wasn't so awfully ornamental, I don't see what would be the use of my turning out at all. I'm no practical good to the team.'

'Exactly. That's just what I wanted to get at. I don't mean your remark about your being ornamental, but about your never touching the ball. Until you explain matters to Norris, you never will get a decent pass. Norris and you are a rattling good pair of centre threes, but if he never gives you a pass, I don't see how we can expect to have any combination in the First. It's no good my slinging out the ball if the centres stick to it like glue directly they get it, and refuse to give it up. It's simply sickening.'

Marriott played half for the First Fifteen, and his soul was in the business.

'But, my dear chap,' said Gethryn, 'you don't mean to tell me that a man like Norris would purposely rot up the First's combination because he happened to have had a row with the other centre. He's much too decent a fellow.'

'No. I don't mean that exactly. What he does is this. I've watched him. He gets the ball. He runs with it till his man is on him, and then he thinks of passing. You're backing him up. He sees you, and says to himself, "I can't pass to that cad" –'

'Meaning me?'

'Meaning you.'

'Thanks awfully.'

'Don't mention it. I'm merely quoting his thoughts, as deduced by me. He says, "I can't pass to that – well, individual, if you prefer it. Where's somebody else?" So he hesitates, and gets tackled, or else slings the ball wildly out to somebody who can't possibly get to it. It's simply infernal. And we play the Nomads tomorrow, too. Something must be done.'

'Somebody ought to tell him. Why doesn't our genial skipper assert his authority?'

'Hill's a forward, you see, and doesn't get an opportunity of noticing it. I can't tell him, of course. I've not got my colours –'

'You're a cert. for them.'

'Hope so. Anyway, I've not got them yet, and Norris has, so I can't very well go slanging him to Hill. Sort of thing rude people would call side.'

'Well, I'll look out tomorrow, and if it's as bad as you think, I'll speak to Hill. It's a beastly thing to have to do.'

'Beastly,' agreed Marriott. 'It's got to be done, though. We can't go through the season without any combination in the three-quarter line, just to spare Norris's feelings.'

'It's a pity, though,' said the Bishop, 'because Norris is a ripping good sort of chap, really. I wish we hadn't had that bust-up last term.'

18

The Bishop Scores

At this point Wilson finished the toast, and went out. As he went he thought over what he had just heard. Marriott and Gethryn frequently talked the most important School politics before him, for they had discovered at an early date that he was a youth of discretion, who could be trusted not to reveal state secrets. But matters now seemed to demand such a revelation. It was a serious thing to do, but there was nobody else to do it, and it obviously must be done, so, by a simple process of reasoning, he ought to do it. Half an hour had to elapse before the bell rang for lock-up. There was plenty of time to do the whole thing and get back to the House before the door was closed. He took his cap, and trotted off to Jephson's.

Norris was alone in his study when Wilson knocked at the door. He seemed surprised to see his visitor. He knew Wilson well by sight, he being captain of the First Eleven and Wilson a distinctly promising junior bat, but this was the first time he had ever exchanged a word of conversation with him.

'Hullo,' he said, putting down his book.

'Oh, I say, Norris,' began Wilson nervously, 'can I speak to you for a minute?'

'All right. Go ahead.'

After two false starts, Wilson at last managed to get the thread of his story. He did not mention Marriott's remarks on football subjects, but confined himself to the story of Farnie and the bicycle ride, as he had heard it from Gethryn on the second evening of the term.

'So that's how it was, you see,' he concluded.

There was a long silence. Wilson sat nervously on the edge of his chair, and Norris stared thoughtfully into the fire.

'So shall I tell him it's all right?' asked Wilson at last.

'Tell who what's all right?' asked Norris politely.

'Oh, er, Gethryn, you know,' replied Wilson, slightly disconcerted. He had had a sort of idea that Norris would have rushed out of the room, sprinted over to Leicester's, and flung himself on the Bishop's bosom in an agony of remorse. He appeared to be taking things altogether too coolly.

'No,' said Norris, 'don't tell him anything. I shall have lots of chances of speaking to him myself if I want to. It isn't as if we were never going to meet again. You'd better cut now. There's the bell just going. Good night.'

'Good night, Norris.'

'Oh, and, I say,' said Norris, as Wilson opened the door, 'I meant to tell you some time ago. If you buck up next cricket season, it's quite possible that you'll get colours of some sort. You might bear that in mind.'

'I will,' said Wilson fervently. 'Good night, Norris. Thanks awfully.'

The Nomads brought down a reasonably hot team against Beckford as a general rule, for the School had a reputation in the football world. They were a big lot this year. Their forwards looked capable, and when, after the School full-back had returned the ball into touch on the half-way line, the line-out had resulted in a hand-ball and a scrum, they proved that appearances were not deceptive. They broke through in a solid mass – the Beckford forwards never somehow seemed to get together properly in the first scrum of a big match – and rushed the ball down the field. Norris fell on it. Another hastily-formed scrum, and the Nomads' front rank was off again. Ten yards nearer the School line there was another halt. Grainger, the Beckford full-back, whose speciality was the stopping of rushes, had curled himself neatly round the ball. Then the School forwards awoke to a sense of their responsibilities. It was time they did, for Beckford was now penned up well within its own twenty-five line, and the Nomad halves were appealing pathetically to their forwards to let that ball out, for goodness' *sake*. But the forwards fancied a combined rush was the thing to play. For a full minute they pushed the School pack towards their line, and then some rash enthusiast kicked a shade too hard. The ball dribbled out of the scrum on the School side, and Marriott punted into touch.

'You *must* let it out, you men,' said the aggrieved half-backs.

Marriott's kick had not brought much relief. The visitors were still inside the Beckford twenty-five line, and now that their forwards had realized the sin and folly of trying to rush the ball through, matters became decidedly warm for the School outsides. Norris and Gethryn in the centre and Grainger at back performed prodigies of tackling.

The wing three-quarter hovered nervously about, feeling that their time might come at any moment.

The Nomad attack was concentrated on the extreme right.

Philips, the International, was officiating for them as wing-three-quarters on that side, and they played to him. If he once got the ball he would take a considerable amount of stopping. But the ball never managed to arrive. Norris and Gethryn stuck to their men closer than brothers.

A prolonged struggle on the goal-line is a great spectacle. That is why (purely in the opinion of the present scribe) Rugby is such a much better game than Association. You don't get that sort of thing in Soccer. But such struggles generally end in the same way. The Nomads were now within a couple of yards of the School line. It was a question of time. In three minutes the whistle would blow for half-time, and the School would be saved.

But in those three minutes the thing happened. For the first time in the match the Nomad forwards heeled absolutely cleanly. Hitherto, the ball had always remained long enough in the scrum to give Marriott and Wogan, the School halves, time to get round and on to their men before they could become dangerous. But this time the ball was in and out again in a moment. The Nomad half who was taking the scrum picked it up, and was over the line before Marriott realized that the ball was out at all. The school lining the ropes along the touch-line applauded politely but feebly, as was their custom when the enemy scored.

The kick was a difficult one – the man had got over in the corner – and failed. The referee blew his whistle for half-time. The teams sucked lemons, and the Beckford forwards tried to explain to Hill, the captain, why they never got that ball in the scrums. Hill having observed bitterly, as he did in every match when the School did not get thirty points in the first half, that he 'would chuck the whole lot of them out next Saturday', the game recommenced.

Beckford started on the second half with three points against them, but with both wind, what there was of it, and slope in their favour. Three points, especially in a club match, where one's opponents may reasonably be expected to suffer from lack of training and combination, is not an overwhelming score.

Beckford was hopeful and determined.

To record all the fluctuations of the game for the next thirty-five minutes is unnecessary. Copies of *The Beckfordian* containing a full report, crammed with details, and written in the most polished English, may still be had from the editor at the modest price of sixpence. Suffice it to say that two minutes from the kick-off the Nomads increased their score with a goal from a mark, and almost immediately afterwards Marriott gave the School their first score with a neat drop-kick. It was about five minutes from the end of the game, and the Nomads still led, when the event of the afternoon took place. The Nomad forwards had brought the ball down the ground with one of their combined dribbles, and a scrum had been formed on the Beckford twenty-five line. The visitors heeled as usual. The half who was taking the scrum whipped the ball out in the direction of his colleague. But before it could reach him, Wogan had intercepted the pass, and was off down the field, through the enemy's three-quarter line, with only the back in front of him, and with Norris in close attendance, followed by Gethryn.

There is nothing like an intercepted pass for adding a dramatic touch to a close game. A second before it had seemed as though the School must be beaten, for though they would probably have kept the enemy out for the few minutes that remained, they could never have worked the ball down the field by ordinary give-and-take play. And now, unless Wogan shamefully bungled what he had begun so well, victory was certain.

There was a danger, though. Wogan might in the excitement of the moment try to get past the back and score himself, instead of waiting until the back was on him and then passing to Norris. The School on the touch-line shrieked their applause, but there was a note of anxiety as well. A slight reputation which Wogan had earned for playing a selfish game sprang up before their eyes. Would he pass? Or would he run himself? If the latter, the odds were anything against his succeeding.

But everything went right. Wogan arrived at the back, drew that gentleman's undivided attention to himself, and then slung the ball out to Norris, the model of what a pass ought to be. Norris made no mistake about it.

Then the remarkable thing happened. The Bishop, having backed Norris up for fifty yards at full speed, could not stop himself at once. His impetus carried him on when all need for expenditure of energy had come to an end. He was just slowing down, leaving Norris to complete the thing alone, when to his utter amazement he found the ball in his hands. Norris had passed to him. With a clear run in, and the nearest foeman yards to the rear, Norris had passed. It was certainly weird, but his first duty was to score. There must be no mistake about the scoring. Afterwards he could do any thinking that might be required. He shot at express speed over the line, and placed the ball in the exact centre of the white line which joined the posts. Then he walked back to where Norris was waiting for him.

'Good man,' said Norris, 'that was awfully good.'

His tone was friendly. He spoke as he had been accustomed to speak before the M.C.C. match. Gethryn took his cue from him. It was evident that, for reasons at present unexplained, Norris wished for peace, and such being the case, the Bishop was only too glad to oblige him.

'No,' he said, 'it was jolly good of you to let me in like that. Why, you'd only got to walk over.'

'Oh, I don't know. I might have slipped or something. Anyhow I thought I'd better pass. What price Beckford combination? The home-made article, eh?'

'Rather,' said the Bishop.

'Oh, by the way,' said Norris, 'I was talking to young Wilson yesterday evening. Or rather he was talking to me. Decent kid, isn't he? He was telling me about Farnie. The M.C.C. match, you know, and so on.'

'Oh!' said the Bishop. He began to see how things had happened.

'Yes,' said Norris. 'Hullo, that gives us the game.'

A roar of applause from the touch-line greeted the successful attempt of Hill to convert Gethryn's try into the necessary goal. The referee performed a solo on the whistle, and immediately afterwards another, as if as an encore.

'No side,' he said pensively. The School had won by two points.

'That's all right,' said Norris. 'I say, can you come and have tea in my study when you've changed? Some of the fellows are coming. I've asked Reece and Marriott, and Pringle said he'd turn up too. It'll be rather a tight fit, but we'll manage somehow.'

'Right,' said the Bishop. 'Thanks very much.'

Norris was correct. It was a tight fit. But then a study brew loses half its charm if there is room to breathe. It was a most enjoyable ceremony in every way. After the serious part of the meal was over, and the time had arrived when it was found pleasanter to eat wafer biscuits than muffins, the Bishop obliged once more with a recital of his adventures on that distant day in the summer term.

There were several comments when he had finished. The only one worth recording is Reece's.

Reece said it distinctly reminded him of a thing which had happened to a friend of a chap his brother had known at Sandhurst.

TALES OF ST AUSTIN'S

Preface

Most of these stories originally appeared in *The Captain*. I am indebted to the Editor of that magazine for allowing me to republish. The rest are from the *Public School Magazine*. The story entitled 'A Shocking Affair' appears in print for the first time. 'This was one of our failures.'

P. G. Wodehouse

AD MATREM

Contents

[1]

How Pillingshot Scored

Pillingshot was annoyed. He was disgusted, mortified; no other word for it. He had no objection, of course, to Mr Mellish saying that his work during the term, and especially his Livy, had been disgraceful. A master has the right to say that sort of thing if he likes. It is one of the perquisites of the position. But when he went on to observe, without a touch of shame, that there would be an examination in the Livy as far as they had gone in it on the following Saturday, Pillingshot felt that he exceeded. It was not playing the game. There were the examinations at the end of term. Those were fair enough. You knew exactly when they were coming, and could make your arrangements accordingly. But to spring an examination on you in the middle of the term out of a blue sky, as it were, was underhand and unsportsmanlike, and would not do at all. Pillingshot wished that he could put his foot down. He would have liked to have stalked up to Mr Mellish's desk, fixed him with a blazing eye, and remarked, 'Sir, withdraw that remark. Cancel that statement instantly, or –!' or words to that effect.

What he did say was: 'Oo, si-i-r!!'

'Yes,' said Mr Mellish, not troubling to conceal his triumph at Pillingshot's reception of the news, 'there will be a Livy examination next Saturday. And –' (he almost intoned this last observation) – 'anybody who does not get fifty per cent, Pillingshot, fifty per cent, will be severely punished. Very severely punished, Pillingshot.'

After which the lesson had proceeded on its course.

'Yes, it is rather low, isn't it?' said Pillingshot's friend, Parker, as Pillingshot came to the end of a stirring excursus on the rights of the citizen, with special reference to mid-term Livy examinations. 'That's the worst of Mellish. He always has you somehow.'

'But what am I to *do*?' raved Pillingshot.

'I should advise you to swot it up before Saturday,' said Parker.

'Oh, don't be an ass,' said Pillingshot, irritably.

What was the good of friends if they could only make idiotic suggestions like that?

He retired, brooding, to his house.

The day was Wednesday. There were only two more days, therefore, in which to prepare a quarter of a book of Livy. It couldn't be done. The thing was not possible.

In the house he met Smythe.

'What are you going to do about it?' he inquired. Smythe was top of the form, and if he didn't know how to grapple with a crisis of this sort, who *could* know?

'If you'll kindly explain,' said Smythe, 'what the dickens you are talking about, I might be able to tell you.'

Pillingshot explained, with unwonted politeness, that 'it' meant the Livy examination.

'Oh,' said Smythe, airily, 'that! I'm just going to skim through it in case I've forgotten any of it. Then I shall read up the notes carefully. And then, if I have time, I shall have a look at the history of the period. I should advise you to do that, too.'

'Oh, don't be a goat,' said Pillingshot.

And he retired, brooding, as before.

That afternoon he spent industriously, copying out the fourth book of *The Aeneid*. At the beginning of the week he had had a slight disagreement with M. Gerard, the French master.

Pillingshot's views on behaviour and deportment during French lessons did not coincide with those of M. Gerard. Pillingshot's idea of a French lesson was something between a pantomime rally and a scrum at football. To him there was something wonderfully entertaining in the process of 'barging' the end man off the edge of the form into space, and upsetting his books over him. M. Gerard, however, had a very undeveloped sense of humour. He warned the humorist twice, and on the thing happening a third time, suggested that he should go into extra lesson on the ensuing Wednesday.

So Pillingshot went, and copied out Virgil.

He emerged from the room of detention at a quarter past four. As he came out into the grounds he espied in the middle distance somebody being carried on a stretcher in the direction of the School House. At the same moment Parker loomed in sight, walking swiftly towards the School shop, his mobile features shining with the rapt expression of one who sees much ginger-beer in the near future.

'Hullo, Parker,' said Pillingshot, 'who's the corpse?'

'What, haven't you heard?' said Parker. 'Oh, no, of course, you were in extra. It's young Brown. He's stunned or something.'

'How did it happen?'

'That rotter, Babington, in Dacre's. Simply slamming about, you know, getting his eye in before going in, and Brown walked slap into one of his drives. Got him on the side of the head.'

'Much hurt?'

'Oh, no, I don't think so. Keep him out of school for about a week.'

'Lucky beast. Wish somebody would come and hit me on the head. Come and hit me on the head, Parker.'

'Come and have an ice,' said Parker.

'Right-ho,' said Pillingshot. It was one of his peculiarities, that whatever the hour or the state of the weather, he was always equal to consuming an ice. This was probably due to genius. He had an infinite capacity for taking pains. Scarcely was he outside the promised ice when another misfortune came upon him. Scott, of the First Eleven, entered the shop. Pillingshot liked Scott, but he was not blind to certain flaws in the latter's character. For one thing, he was too energetic. For another, he could not keep his energy to himself. He was always making Pillingshot do things. And Pillingshot's notion of the ideal life was complete *dolce far niente*.

'Ginger-beer, please,' said Scott, with parched lips. He had been bowling at the nets, and the day was hot. 'Hullo! Pillingshot, you young slacker, why aren't you changed? Been bunking half-holiday games? You'd better reform, young man.'

'I've been in extra,' said Pillingshot, with dignity.

'How many times does that make this term? You're going for the record, aren't you? Jolly sporting of you. Bit slow in there, wasn't it? 'Nother ginger-beer, please.'

'Just a bit,' said Pillingshot.

'I thought so. And now you're dying for some excitement. Of course you are. Well, cut over to the House and change, and then come back and field at the nets. The man Yorke is going to bowl me some of his celebrated slow tosh, and I'm going to show him exactly how Jessop does it when he's in form.'

Scott was the biggest hitter in the School. Mr Yorke was one of the masters. He bowled slow leg-breaks, mostly half-volleys and long hops. Pillingshot had a sort of instinctive idea that fielding out in the deep with Mr Yorke bowling and Scott batting would not contribute largely to the gaiety of his afternoon. Fielding deep at the nets meant that you stood in the middle of the football field, where there was no telling what a ball would do if it came at you along the ground. If you were lucky you escaped without injury. Generally, however, the ball bumped and deprived you of wind or teeth, according to the height to which it rose. He began politely, but firmly, to excuse himself.

'Don't talk rot,' said Scott, complainingly, 'you must have some exercise or you'll go getting fat. Think what a blow it would be to your family, Pillingshot, if you lost your figure. Buck up. If you're back here in a quarter of an hour you shall have another ice. A large ice, Pillingshot, price sixpence. Think of it.'

The word ice, as has been remarked before, touched chords in Pillingshot's nature to which he never turned a deaf ear. Within the prescribed quarter of an hour he was back again, changed.

'Here's the ice,' said Scott, 'I've been keeping it warm for you. Shovel it down. I want to be starting for the nets. Quicker, man, quicker! Don't roll it round your tongue as if it was port. Go for it. Finished? That's right. Come on.'

Pillingshot had not finished, but Scott so evidently believed that he had, that it would have been unkind to have mentioned the fact. He followed the smiter to the nets.

If Pillingshot had passed the earlier part of the afternoon in a sedentary fashion, he made up for it now. Scott was in rare form, and Pillingshot noticed with no small interest that, while he invariably hit Mr Yorke's deliveries a quarter of a mile or so, he never hit two balls in succession in the same direction. As soon as the panting fieldsman had sprinted to one side of the football ground and returned the ball, there was a beautiful, musical *plonk*, and the ball soared to the very opposite quarter of the field. It was a fine exhibition of hitting, but Pillingshot felt that he would have enjoyed it more if he could have watched it from a deck-chair.

'You're coming on as a deep field, young Pillingshot,' said Scott, as he took off his pads. 'You've got a knack of stopping them with your stomach, which the best first-class fields never have. You ought to give lessons at it. Now we'll go and have some tea.'

If Pillingshot had had a more intimate acquaintance with the classics, he would have observed at this point, '*Timeo Danaos*', and made a last dash for liberty in the direction of the shop. But he was deceived by the specious nature of Scott's remark. Visions rose before his eyes of sitting back in one of Scott's armchairs, watching a fag toasting muffins, which he would eventually dispatch with languid enjoyment. So he followed Scott to his study. The classical parallel to his situation is the well-known case of the oysters. They, too, were eager for the treat.

They had reached the study, and Pillingshot was about to fling himself, with a sigh of relief, into the most comfortable chair, when Scott unmasked his batteries.

'Oh, by the way,' he said, with a coolness which to Pillingshot appeared simply brazen, 'I'm afraid my fag won't be here today. The young crock's gone and got mumps, or the plague, or something. So would you mind just lighting that stove? It'll be rather warm, but that won't matter. There are some muffins in the cupboard. You might weigh in with them. You'll find the toasting-fork on the wall somewhere. It's hanging up. Got it? Good man. Fire away.'

And Scott collected five cushions, two chairs, and a tin of mixed biscuits, and made himself comfortable. Pillingshot, with feelings too deep for words (in the then limited state of his vocabulary), did as he was requested. There was something remarkable about the way Scott could always get people to do things for him. He seemed to take everything for granted. If he had had occasion to hire an assassin to make away with the German Emperor, he would have said, 'Oh, I say, you might run over to Germany and kill the Kaiser, will you, there's a good chap? Don't be long.' And he would have taken a seat and waited, without the least doubt in his mind that the thing would be carried through as desired.

Pillingshot had just finished toasting the muffins, when the door opened, and Venables, of Merevale's, came in.

'I thought I heard you say something about tea this afternoon, Scott,' said Venables. 'I just looked in on the chance. Good Heavens, man! Fancy muffins at this time of year! Do you happen to know what the thermometer is in the shade?'

'Take a seat,' said Scott. 'I attribute my entire success in life to the fact that I never find it too hot to eat muffins. Do you know Pillingshot? One of the hottest fieldsmen in the School. At least, he was just now. He's probably cooled off since then. Venables – Pillingshot, and *vice versa*. Buck up with the tea, Pillingshot. What, ready? Good man. Now we might almost begin.'

'Beastly thing that accident of young Brown's, wasn't it?' said Scott. 'Chaps oughtn't to go slamming about like that with the field full of fellows. I suppose he won't be right by next Saturday?'

'Not a chance. Why? Oh, yes, I forgot. He was to have scored for the team at Windybury, wasn't he?'

'Who are you going to get now?'

Venables was captain of the St Austin's team. The match next Saturday was at Windybury, on the latter's ground.

'I haven't settled,' said Venables. 'But it's easy to get somebody. Scoring isn't one of those things which only one chap in a hundred understands.'

Then Pillingshot had an idea – a great, luminous idea.

'May I score?' he asked, and waited trembling with apprehension lest the request be refused.

'All right,' said Venables, 'I don't see any reason why you shouldn't. We have to catch the 8.14 at the station. Don't you go missing it or anything.'

'Rather *not*,' said Pillingshot. 'Not much.'

On Saturday morning, at exactly 9.15, Mr Mellish distributed the Livy papers. When he arrived at Pillingshot's seat and found it empty, an expression passed over his face like unto that of the baffled villain in transpontine melodrama.

'Where is Pillingshot?' he demanded tragically. 'Where is he?'

'He's gone with the team to Windybury, sir,' said Parker, struggling to conceal a large size in grins. 'He's going to score.'

'No,' said Mr Mellish sadly to himself, 'he *has* scored.'

[2]

The Odd Trick

The attitude of Philip St H. Harrison, of Merevale's House, towards his fellow-man was outwardly one of genial and even sympathetic toleration. Did his form-master intimate that his conduct was not *his* idea of what Young England's conduct should be, P. St H. Harrison agreed cheerfully with every word he said, warmly approved his intention of laying the matter before the Headmaster, and accepted his punishment with the air of a waiter booking an order for a chump chop and fried potatoes. But the next day there would be a squeaking desk in the form-room, just to show the master that he had not been forgotten. Or, again, did the captain of his side at football speak rudely to him on the subject of kicking the ball through in the scrum, Harrison would smile gently, and at the earliest opportunity tread heavily on the captain's toe. In short, he was a youth who made a practice of taking very good care of himself. Yet he had his failures. The affair of Graham's mackintosh was one of them, and it affords an excellent example of the truth of the proverb that a cobbler should stick to his last. Harrison's *forte* was diplomacy. When he forsook the arts of the diplomatist for those of the brigand, he naturally went wrong. And the manner of these things was thus.

Tony Graham was a prefect in Merevale's, and part of his duties was to look after the dormitory of which Harrison was one of the ornaments. It was a dormitory that required a good deal of keeping in order. Such choice spirits as Braithwaite of the Upper Fourth, and Mace, who was rapidly driving the master of the Lower Fifth into a premature grave, needed a firm hand. Indeed, they generally needed not only a firm hand, but a firm hand grasping a serviceable walking-stick. Add to these Harrison himself, and others of a similar calibre, and it will be seen that Graham's post was no sinecure. It was Harrison's custom to throw off his mask at night with his other garments, and appear in his true character of an abandoned villain, willing to stick at nothing as long as he could do it strictly incog. In

255

this capacity he had come into constant contact with Graham. Even in the dark it is occasionally possible for a prefect to tell where a noise comes from. And if the said prefect has been harassed six days in the week by a noise, and locates it suddenly on the seventh, it is wont to be bad for the producer and patentee of same.

And so it came about that Harrison, enjoying himself one night, after the manner of his kind, was suddenly dropped upon with violence. He had constructed an ingenious machine, consisting of a biscuit tin, some pebbles, and some string. He put the pebbles in the tin, tied the string to it, and placed it under a chest of drawers. Then he took the other end of the string to bed with him, and settled down to make a night of it. At first all went well. Repeated inquiries from Tony failed to produce the author of the disturbance, and when finally the questions ceased, and the prefect appeared to have given the matter up as a bad job, P. St H. Harrison began to feel that under certain circumstances life was worth living. It was while he was in this happy frame of mind that the string, with which he had just produced a triumphant rattle from beneath the chest of drawers, was seized, and the next instant its owner was enjoying the warmest minute of a chequered career. Tony, like Brer Rabbit, had laid low until he was certain of the direction from which the sound proceeded. He had then slipped out of bed, crawled across the floor in a snake-like manner which would have done credit to a Red Indian, found the tin, and traced the string to its owner. Harrison emerged from the encounter feeling sore and unfit for any further recreation. This deed of the night left its impression on Harrison. The account had to be squared somehow, and in a few days his chance came. Merevale's were playing a 'friendly' with the School House, and in default of anybody better, Harrison had been pressed into service as umpire. This in itself had annoyed him. Cricket was not in his line – he was not one of your flannelled fools – and of all things in connection with the game he loathed umpiring most.

When, however, Tony came on to bowl at his end, *vice* Charteris, who had been hit for three fours in an over by Scott, the School slogger, he recognized that even umpiring had its advantages, and resolved to make the most of the situation.

Scott had the bowling, and he lashed out at Tony's first ball in his usual reckless style. There was an audible click, and what the sporting papers call confident appeals came simultaneously from Welch, Merevale's captain, who was keeping wicket, and Tony himself. Even Scott seemed to know that his time had come. He moved a step or two away from the wicket, but stopped before going farther to look at the umpire, on the off-chance of a miracle happening to turn his decision in the batsman's favour.

The miracle happened.

'Not out,' said Harrison.

'Awfully curious,' he added genially to Tony, 'how like a bat those bits of grass sound! You have to be jolly smart to know where a noise comes from, don't you!'

Tony grunted disgustedly, and walked back again to the beginning of his run.

If ever, in the whole history of cricket, a man was out leg-before-wicket, Scott was so out to Tony's second ball. It was hardly worth appealing for such a certainty. Still, the formality had to be gone through.

'How was *that*?' inquired Tony.

'Not out. It's an awful pity, don't you think, that they don't bring in that new leg-before rule?'

'Seems to me,' said Tony bitterly, 'the old rule holds pretty good when a man's leg's bang in front.'

'Rather. But you see the ball didn't pitch straight, and the rule says –'

'Oh, all right,' said Tony.

The next ball Scott hit for four, and the next after that for a couple. The fifth was a yorker, and just grazed the leg stump. The sixth was a beauty. You could see it was going to beat the batsman from the moment it left Tony's hand. Harrison saw it perfectly.

'No ball,' he shouted. And just as he spoke Scott's off-stump ricocheted towards the wicket-keeper.

'Heavens, man,' said Tony, fairly roused out of his cricket manners, a very unusual thing for him. 'I'll swear my foot never went over the crease. Look, there's the mark.'

'Rather not. Only, you see, it seemed to me you chucked that time. Of course, I know you didn't mean to, and all that sort of thing, but still, the rules –'

Tony would probably have liked to have said something very forcible about the rules at this point, but it occurred to him that after all Harrison was only within his rights, and that it was bad form to dispute the umpire's decision. Harrison walked off towards square-leg with a holy joy.

But he was too much of an artist to overdo the thing. Tony's next over passed off without interference. Possibly, however, this was because it was a very bad one. After the third over he asked Welch if he could get somebody else to umpire, as he had work to do. Welch heaved a sigh of relief, and agreed readily.

'Conscientious sort of chap that umpire of yours,' said Scott to Tony, after the match. Scott had made a hundred and four, and was feeling pleased. 'Considering he's in your House, he's awfully fair.'

'You mean that we generally swindle, I suppose?'

'Of course not, you rotter. You know what I mean. But, I say, that catch Welch and you appealed for must have been a near thing. I could have sworn I hit it.'

'Of course you did. It was clean out. So was the lbw. I say, did you think that ball that bowled you was a chuck? That one in my first over, you know.'

'Chuck! My dear Tony, you don't mean to say that man pulled you up for chucking? I thought your foot must have gone over the crease.'

'I believe the chap's mad,' said Tony.

'Perhaps he's taking it out of you this way for treading on his corns somehow. Have you been milling with this gentle youth lately?'

'By Jove,' said Tony, 'you're right. I gave him beans only the other night for ragging in the dormitory.'

Scott laughed.

'Well, he seems to have been getting a bit of his own back today. Lucky the game was only a friendly. Why will you let your angry passions rise, Tony? You've wrecked your analysis by it, though it's improved my average considerably. I don't know if that's any solid satisfaction to you.'

'It isn't.'

'You don't say so! Well, so long. If I were you, I should keep an eye on that conscientious umpire.'

'I will,' said Tony. 'Good-night.'

The process of keeping an eye on Harrison brought no results. When he wished to behave himself well, he could. On such occasions Sandford and Merton were literally not in it with him, and the hero of a Sunday-school story would simply have refused to compete. But Nemesis, as the poets tell us, though no sprinter, manages, like the celebrated Maisie, to get right there in time. Give her time, and she will arrive. She arrived in the case of Harrison. One morning, about a fortnight after the House-match incident, Harrison awoke with a new sensation. At first he could not tell what exactly this sensation was, and being too sleepy to discuss nice points of internal emotion with himself, was just turning over with the intention of going to sleep again, when the truth flashed upon him. The sensation he felt was loneliness, and the reason he felt lonely was because he was the only occupant of the dormitory. To right and left and all around were empty beds.

As he mused drowsily on these portents, the distant sound of a bell came to his ears and completed the cure. It was the bell for chapel. He dragged his watch from under his pillow, and looked at it with consternation. Four minutes to seven. And chapel was at seven. Now Harrison had been late for chapel before. It was not the thought of missing the service that worried him. What really was serious was that he had been late so many times before that Merevale had hinted at serious steps to be taken if he were late again, or, at any rate, until a considerable interval of punctuality had elapsed.

That threat had been uttered only yesterday, and here he was in all probability late once more.

There was no time to dress. He sprang out of bed, passed a sponge over his face as a concession to the decencies, and looked round for something to cover his night-shirt, which, however suitable for dormitory use, was, he felt instinctively, scarcely the garment to wear in public.

Fate seemed to fight for him. On one of the pegs in the wall hung a mackintosh, a large, blessed mackintosh. He was inside it in a moment.

Four minutes later he rushed into his place in chapel.

The short service gave him some time for recovering himself. He left the building feeling a new man. His costume, though quaint, would not call for comment. Chapel at St Austin's was never a full-dress ceremony. Mackintoshes covering night-shirts were the rule rather than the exception.

But between his costume and that of the rest there was this subtle distinction. They wore their own mackintoshes. He wore somebody else's.

The bulk of the School had split up into sections, each section making for its own House, and Merevale's was already in sight, when Harrison felt himself grasped from behind. He turned, to see Graham.

'Might I ask,' enquired Tony with great politeness, 'who said you might wear my mackintosh?'

Harrison gasped.

'I suppose you didn't know it was mine?'

'No, no, rather not. I didn't know.'

'And if you had known it was mine, you wouldn't have taken it, I suppose?'

'Oh no, of course not,' said Harrison. Graham seemed to be taking an unexpectedly sensible view of the situation.

'Well,' said Tony, 'now that you know that it is mine, suppose you give it up.'

'Give it up!'

'Yes; buck up. It looks like rain, and I mustn't catch cold.'

'But, Graham, I've only got on –'

'Spare us these delicate details. Back up, please, I want it.'

Finally, Harrison appearing to be difficult in the matter, Tony took the garment off for him, and went on his way.

Harrison watched him go with mixed feelings. Righteous indignation struggled with the gravest apprehension regarding his own future. If Merevale should see him! Horrible thought. He ran. He had just reached the House, and was congratulating himself on having escaped, when the worst happened. At the private entrance stood Merevale, and with him the Headmaster himself. They both eyed him with considerable interest as he shot in at the boys' entrance.

'Harrison,' said Merevale after breakfast.

'Yes, sir?'

'The Headmaster wishes to see you – again.'

'Yes, sir,' said Harrison.

There was a curious lack of enthusiasm in his voice.

L'Affaire Uncle John

(A Story in Letters)

I

From Richard Venables, of St Austin's School, to his brother Archibald Venables, of King's College, Cambridge:

Dear Archie – I take up my pen to write to you, not as one hoping for an answer, but rather in order that (you notice the Thucydidean construction) I may tell you of an event the most important of those that have gone before. You may or may not have heard far-off echoes of my adventure with Uncle John, who has just come back from the diamond-mines – and looks it. It happened thusly:

Last Wednesday evening I was going through the cricket field to meet Uncle John, at the station, as per esteemed favour from the governor, telling me to. Just as I got on the scene, to my horror, amazement, and disgust, I saw a middle-aged bounder, in loud checks, who, from his looks, might have been anything from a retired pawnbroker to a second-hand butler, sacked from his last place for stealing the sherry, standing in the middle of the field, on the very wicket the Rugborough match is to be played on next Saturday (tomorrow), and digging – *digging* – I'll trouble you. Excavating great chunks of our best turf with a walking-stick. I was so unnerved, I nearly fainted. It's bad enough being captain of a School team under any circs., as far as putting you off your game goes, but when you see the wicket you've been rolling by day, and dreaming about by night, being mangled by an utter stranger – well! They say a cow is slightly irritated when her calf is taken away from her, but I don't suppose the most maternal cow that ever lived came anywhere near the frenzy that surged up in my bosom at that moment. I flew up to him, foaming at the mouth. 'My dear sir,' I shrieked, '*are* you aware that you're spoiling the best wicket that has ever been prepared since cricket began?' He looked at me, in a dazed sort of way, and said, 'What?' I said: 'How on earth do you think we're going to play Rugborough on a ploughed field?' 'I don't follow, mister,' he replied. A man who calls you 'mister' is beyond the pale. You are justified in being a little rude to him. So I said: 'Then you must be either drunk or mad, and I trust it's the latter.' I believe that's from some book, though I don't remember which. This did seem to wake him up a bit, but before he could frame his opinion in words, up came Biffen, the ground-man, to have a last look at his wicket before retiring for the night. When he saw the holes – they were about a foot deep, and scattered promiscuously, just where two balls out of three pitch – he almost had hysterics. I gently explained the situation to him, and left him to settle with my friend of the check suit. Biffen was just settling down to a sort of Philippic when I went, and I knew that I had left the man in competent hands. Then I went to the station. The train I had been told to meet was the 5.30. By the way, of course, I didn't know in the least what Uncle John was like, not having seen him since I was about one-and-a-half, but I had been told to look out for a tall, rather good-looking man. Well, the 5.30 came in all right, but none of the passengers seemed to answer to the description. The ones who were tall were not good looking, and the only man who was good looking stood five feet nothing in his boots. I did ask him if he was Mr John Dalgliesh; but, his name happening to be Robinson, he could not oblige. I sat out a couple more trains, and then went back to the field. The man had gone, but Biffen was still there. 'Was you expecting anyone today, sir?' he asked, as I came up. 'Yes. Why?' I said. 'That was 'im,' said Biffen. By skilful questioning, I elicited the whole thing. It seems that the fearsome bargee, in checks, was the governor's 'tall, good-looking man'; in other words, Uncle John himself. He had come by the 4.30, I suppose. Anyway, there he was, and I had insulted him badly. Biffen told me that he had asked who I was, and that he (Biffen) had given the information, while he was thinking of something else to say to him about his digging. By the way, I suppose he dug from force of habit. Thought he'd find diamonds, perhaps. When Biffen told him this, he said in a nasty voice: 'Then, when he comes back will you have the goodness to tell him that my name is John Dalgliesh, and that he will hear more of this.' And I'm uncommonly afraid I shall. The governor bars Uncle John awfully, I know, but he wanted me to be particularly civil to him, because he was to get me a place in some beastly firm when I leave. I haven't heard from home yet, but I expect to soon. Still, I'd like to know how I could stand and watch him ruining the wicket for our spot match of the season. As it is, it won't be as good as it would have been. The Rugborough slow man will be unplayable if he can find one of these spots. Altogether, it's a beastly business. Write soon, though I know you won't – Yours ever,   *Dick*

II

Telegram from Major-General Sir Everard Venables, v.c., k.c.m.g., to his son Richard Venables:

Venables, St Austin's. What all this about Uncle John. Says were grossly rude. Write explanation next post – *Venables*.

III

Letter from Mrs James Anthony (née Miss Dorothy Venables) to her brother Richard Venables:

Dear Dick – What *have* you been doing to Uncle John? Jim and I are stopping for a fortnight with father, and have just come in for the whole thing. Uncle John – *isn't* he a horrible man? – says you were grossly insolent to him when he went down to see you. *Do* write and tell me all about it. I have heard no details as yet. Father refuses to give them, and gets simply *furious* when the matter is mentioned. Jim said at dinner last night that a conscientious boy would probably feel bound to be rude to Uncle John. Father said 'Conscience be –'; I forget the rest, but it was awful. Jim says if he gets any worse we shall have to sit on his head, and cut the traces. He is getting so dreadfully *horsey*. Do write the very minute you get this. I want to know all about it. – Your affectionate sister,   *Dorothy*

IV

Part of Letter from Richard Venables, of St Austin's, to his father Major-General Sir Everard Venables, V.C., K.C.M.G.:

. . . So you see it was really his fault. The Emperor of Germany has no right to come and dig holes in our best wicket. Take a parallel case. Suppose some idiot of a fellow (not that Uncle John's that, of course, but you know what I mean) came and began rooting up your azaleas. Wouldn't you want to say something cutting? I will apologize to Uncle John, if you like; but still, I do think he might have gone somewhere else if he really wanted to dig. So you see, etc., etc.

V

Letter from Richard Venables, of St Austin's, to his sister Mrs James Anthony:

Dear Dolly – Thanks awfully for your letter, and thank Jim for his message. He's a ripper. I'm awfully glad you married him and not that rotter, Thompson, who used to hang on so. I hope the most marvellous infant on earth is flourishing. And now about Uncle John. Really, I am jolly glad I did say all that to him. We played Rugborough yesterday, and the wicket was simply vile.

They won the toss, and made two hundred and ten. Of course, the wicket was all right at one end, and that's where they made most of their runs. I was wicket-keeping as usual, and I felt awfully ashamed of the beastly pitch when their captain asked me if it was the football-field. Of course, he wouldn't have said that if he hadn't been a pal of mine, but it was probably what the rest of the team thought, only they were too polite to say so. When we came to bat it was worse than ever. I went in first with Welch – that's the fellow who stopped a week at home a few years ago; I don't know whether you remember him. He got out in the first over, caught off a ball that pitched where Uncle John had been prospecting, and jumped up. It was rotten luck, of course, and worse was to follow, for by half-past five we had eight wickets down for just over the hundred, and only young Scott, who's simply a slogger, and another fellow to come in. Well, Scott came in. I had made about sixty then, and was fairly well set – and he started simply mopping up the bowling. He gave a chance every over as regular as clockwork, and it was always missed, and then he would make up for it with two or three tremendous whangs – a safe four every time. It wasn't batting. It was more like golf. Well, this went on for some time, and we began to get hopeful again, having got a hundred and eighty odd. I just kept up my wicket, while Scott hit. Then he got caught, and the last man, a fellow called Moore, came in. I'd put him in the team as a bowler, but he could bat a little, too, on occasions, and luckily this was one of them. There were only eleven to win, and I had the bowling. I was feeling awfully fit, and put their slow man clean over the screen twice running, which left us only three to get. Then it was over, and Moore played the fast man in grand style, though he didn't score. Well, I got the bowling again, and half-way through the over I carted a half-volley into the Pav., and that gave us the match. Moore hung on for a bit and made about ten, and then got bowled. We made 223 altogether, of which I had managed to get seventy-eight, not out. It pulls my average up a good bit. Rather decent, isn't it? The fellows rotted about a good deal, and chaired me into the Pav., but it was Scott who won us the match, I think. He made ninety-four. But Uncle John nearly did for us with his beastly walking-stick. On a good wicket we might have made any number. I don't know how the affair will end. Keep me posted up in the governor's symptoms, and write again soon. – Your affectionate brother,   *Dick*

PS. – On looking over this letter, I find I have taken it for granted that you know all about the Uncle John affair. Probably you do, but, in case you don't, it was this way. You see, I was going, etc., etc.

VI

From Archibald Venables, of King's College, Cambridge, to Richard Venables, of St Austin's:

Dear Dick – Just a line to thank you for your letter, and to tell you that since I got it I have had a visit from the great Uncle John, too. He *is* an outsider, if you like. I gave him the best lunch I could in my rooms, and the man started a long lecture on extravagance. He doesn't seem to understand the difference between the 'Varsity and a private school. He kept on asking leading questions about pocket-money and holidays, and wanted to know if my master allowed me to walk in the streets in that waistcoat – a remark which cut me to the quick, 'that waistcoat' being quite the most posh thing of the sort in Cambridge. He then enquired after my studies; and, finally, when I saw him off at the station, said that he had decided not to tip me, because he was afraid that I was inclined to be extravagant. I was quite kind to him, however, in spite of everything; but I was glad you had spoken to him like a father. The recollection of it soothed me, though it seemed to worry him. He talked a good deal about it. Glad you came off against Rugborough. – Yours ever, *A. Venables*

VII

From Mr John Dalgliesh to Mr Philip Mortimer, of Penge:

Dear Sir – In reply to your letter of the 18th inst., I shall be happy to recommend your son, Reginald, for the vacant post in the firm of Messrs Van Nugget, Diomonde, and Mynes, African merchants. I have written them to that effect, and you will, doubtless, receive a communication from them shortly. – I am, my dear sir, yours faithfully, *J. Dalgliesh*

VIII

From Richard Venables, of St Austin's, to his father Major-General Sir Everard Venables, V.C., K.C.M.G.:

Dear Father – Uncle John writes, in answer to my apology, to say that no apologies will meet the case; and that he has given his nomination in that rotten City firm of his to a fellow called Mortimer. But rather a decent thing has happened. There is a chap here I know pretty well, who is the son of Lord Marmaduke Twistleton, and it appears that the dook himself was down watching the Rugborough match, and liked my batting. He came and talked to me after the match, and asked me what I was going to do when I left, and I said I wasn't certain, and he said that, if I hadn't anything better on, he could give me a place on his estate up in Scotland, as a sort of land-agent, as he wanted a chap who could play cricket, because he was keen on the game himself, and always had a lot going on in the summer up there. So he says that, if I go up to the 'Varsity for three years, he can guarantee me the place when I come down, with a jolly good screw and a ripping open-air life, with lots of riding, and so on, which is just what I've always wanted. So, can I? It's the sort of opportunity that won't occur again, and you know you always said the only reason I couldn't go up to the 'Varsity was, that it would be a waste of time. But in this case, you see, it won't, because he wants me to go, and guarantees me the place when I come down. It'll be awfully fine, if I may. I hope you'll see it. – Your affectionate son, *Dick*

PS. – I think he's writing to you. He asked your address. I think Uncle John's a rotter. I sent him a rattling fine apology, and this is how he treats it. But it'll be all right if you like this land-agent idea. If you like, you might wire your answer.

IX

Telegram from Major-General Sir Everard Venables, V.C., K.C.M.G., to his son Richard Venables, of St Austin's:

Venables, St Austin's. Very well. – *Venables*

X

Extract from Letter from Richard Venables, of St Austin's, to his father Major-General Sir Everard Venables, V.C., K.C.M.G.:

. . . Thanks, awfully –

Extract from *The Austinian* of October:

The following O.A.s have gone into residence this year: At Oxford, J. Scrymgeour, Corpus Christi; R. Venables, Trinity; K. Crespigny-Brown, Balliol.

Extract from the *Daily Mail*'s account of the 'Varsity match of the following summer:

   ... The St Austin's freshman, Venables, fully justified his inclusion by scoring a stylish fifty-seven. He hit eight fours, and except for a miss-hit in the slips, at 51, which Smith might possibly have secured had he started sooner, gave nothing like a chance. Venables, it will be remembered, played several good innings for Oxford in the earlier matches, notably, his not out contribution of 103 against Sussex –

[4]

Harrison's Slight Error

The one o'clock down express was just on the point of starting. The engine-driver, with his hand on the lever, whiled away the moments, like the watchman in *The Agamemnon*, by whistling. The guard endeavoured to talk to three people at once. Porters flitted to and fro, cleaving a path for themselves with trucks of luggage. The Usual Old Lady was asking if she was right for some place nobody had ever heard of. Everybody was saying good-bye to everybody else, and last, but not least, P. St H. Harrison, of St Austin's, was strolling at a leisurely pace towards the rear of the train. There was no need for him to hurry. For had not his friend, Mace, promised to keep a corner-seat for him while he went to the refreshment-room to lay in supplies? Undoubtedly he had, and Harrison, as he watched the struggling crowd, congratulated himself that he was not as other men. A corner seat in a carriage full of his own particular friends, with plenty of provisions, and something to read in case he got tired of talking – it would be perfect.

So engrossed was he in these reflections, that he did not notice that from the opposite end of the platform a youth of about his own age was also making for the compartment in question. The first intimation he had of his presence was when the latter, arriving first at the door by a short head, hurled a bag on to the rack, and sank gracefully into the identical corner seat which Harrison had long regarded as his own personal property. And to make matters worse, there was no other vacant seat in the compartment. Harrison was about to protest, when the guard blew his whistle. There was nothing for it but to jump in and argue the matter out *en route*. Harrison jumped in, to be greeted instantly by a chorus of nine male voices. 'Outside there! No room! Turn him out!' said the chorus. Then the chorus broke up into its component parts, and began to address him one by one.

'You rotter, Harrison,' said Babington, of Dacre's, 'what do you come barging in here for? Can't you see we're five aside already?'

'Hope you've brought a sardine-opener with you, old chap,' said Barrett, the peerless pride of Philpott's, ' 'cos we shall jolly well need one when we get to the good old Junct-i-on. Get up into the rack, Harrison, you're stopping the ventilation.'

The youth who had commandeered Harrison's seat so neatly took another unpardonable liberty at this point. He grinned. Not the timid, deprecating smile of one who wishes to ingratiate himself with strangers, but a good, six-inch grin right across his face. Harrison turned on him savagely.

'Look here,' he said, 'just you get out of that. What do you mean by bagging my seat?'

'Are you a director of this line?' enquired the youth politely. Roars of applause from the interested audience. Harrison began to feel hot and uncomfortable.

'Or only the Emperor of Germany?' pursued his antagonist.

More applause, during which Harrison dropped his bag of provisions, which were instantly seized and divided on the share and share alike system, among the gratified Austinians.

'Look here, none of your cheek,' was the shockingly feeble retort which alone occurred to him. The other said nothing. Harrison returned to the attack.

'Look here,' he said, 'are you going to get out, or have I got to make you?'

Not a word did his opponent utter. To quote the bard: 'The stripling smiled.' To tell the truth, the stripling smiled inanely.

The other occupants of the carriage were far from imitating his reserve. These treacherous friends, realizing that, for those who were themselves comfortably seated, the spectacle of Harrison standing up with aching limbs for a journey of some thirty miles would be both grateful and comforting, espoused the cause of the unknown with all the vigour of which they were capable.

'Beastly bully, Harrison,' said Barrett. 'Trying to turn the kid out of his seat! Why can't you leave the chap alone? Don't you move, kid.'

'Thanks,' said the unknown, 'I wasn't going to.'

'Now you see what comes of slacking,' said Grey. 'If you'd bucked up and got here in time you might have bagged this seat I've got. By Jove, Harrison, you've no idea how comfortable it is in this corner.'

'Punctuality,' said Babington, 'is the politeness of princes.'

And again the unknown maddened Harrison with a 'best-on-record' grin.

'But, I say, you chaps,' said he, determined as a last resource to appeal to their better feelings (if any), 'Mace was keeping this seat for me, while I went to get some grub. Weren't you, Mace?' He turned to Mace for corroboration. To his surprise, Mace was nowhere to be seen.

His sympathetic school-fellows grasped the full humour of the situation as one man, and gave tongue once more in chorus.

'You weed,' they yelled joyfully, 'you've got into the wrong carriage. Mace is next door.'

And then, with the sound of unquenchable laughter ringing in his ears, Harrison gave the thing up, and relapsed into a disgusted silence. No single word did he speak until the journey was done, and the carriage emptied itself of its occupants at the Junction. The local train was in readiness to take them on to St Austin's, and this time Harrison managed to find a seat without much difficulty. But it was a bitter moment when Mace, meeting him on the platform, addressed him as a rotter, for that he had not come to claim the corner seat which he had been reserving for him. They had had, said Mace, a rattling good time coming down. What sort of a time had Harrison had in *his* carriage? Harrison's reply was not remarkable for its clearness.

The unknown had also entered the local train. It was plain, therefore, that he was coming to the School as a new boy. Harrison began to wonder if, under these circumstances, something might not be done in the matter by way of levelling up things. He pondered. When St Austin's station was reached, and the travellers began to stream up the road towards the College, he discovered that the newcomer was a member of his own House. He was standing close beside him, and heard Babington explaining to him the way to Merevale's. Merevale was Harrison's House-master.

It was two minutes after he had found out this fact that the Grand Idea came to Harrison. He saw his way now to a revenge so artistic, so beautifully simple, that it was with some difficulty that he restrained himself from bursting into song. For two pins, he felt, he could have done a cake-walk.

He checked his emotion. He beat it steadily back, and quenched it. When he arrived at Merevale's, he went first to the matron's room. 'Has Venables come back yet?' he asked.

Venables was the head of Merevale's House, captain of the School cricket, wing three-quarter of the School Fifteen, and a great man altogether.

'Yes,' said the matron, 'he came back early this afternoon.'

Harrison knew it. Venables always came back early on the last day of the holidays.

'He was upstairs a short while ago,' continued the matron. 'He was putting his study tidy.'

Harrison knew it. Venables always put his study tidy on the last day of the holidays. He took a keen and perfectly justifiable pride in his study, which was the most luxurious in the House.

'Is he there now?' asked Harrison.

'No. He has gone over to see the Headmaster.'

'Thanks,' said Harrison, 'it doesn't matter. It wasn't anything important.'

He retired triumphant. Things were going excellently well for his scheme.

His next act was to go to the fags' room, where, as he had expected, he found his friend of the train. Luck continued to be with him. The unknown was alone.

'Hullo!' said Harrison.

'Hullo!' said the fellow-traveller. He had resolved to follow Harrison's lead. If Harrison was bringing war, then war let it be. If, however, his intentions were friendly, he would be friendly too.

'I didn't know you were coming to Merevale's. It's the best House in the School.'

'Oh!'

'Yes, for one thing, everybody except the kids has a study.'

'What? Not really? Why, I thought we had to keep to this room. One of the chaps told me so.'

'Trying to green you, probably. You must look out for that sort of thing. I'll show you the way to your study, if you like. Come along upstairs.'

'Thanks, awfully. It's awfully good of you,' said the gratified unknown, and they went upstairs together.

One of the doors which they passed on their way was open, disclosing to view a room which, though bare at present, looked as if it might be made exceedingly comfortable.

'That's my den,' said Harrison. It was perhaps lucky that Graham, to whom the room belonged, in fact, as opposed to fiction, did not hear the remark. Graham and Harrison were old and tried foes. 'This is yours.' Harrison pushed open another door at the end of the passage.

His companion stared blankly at the Oriental luxury which met his eye. 'But, I say,' he said, 'are you sure? This seems to be occupied already.'

'Oh, no, that's all right,' said Harrison, airily. 'The chap who used to be here left last term. He didn't know he was going to leave till it was too late to pack up all his things, so he left his study as it was. All you've got to do is to cart the things out into the passage and leave them there. The Moke'll take 'em away.'

The Moke was the official who combined in a single body the duties of butler and bootboy at Merevale's House.

'Oh, right-ho!' said the unknown, and Harrison left him.

Harrison's idea was that when Venables returned and found an absolute stranger placidly engaged in wrecking his carefully-tidied study, he would at once, and without making inquiries, fall upon that absolute stranger and blot him off the face of the earth. Afterwards it might possibly come out that he, Harrison, had been not altogether unconnected with the business, and then, he was fain to admit, there might be trouble. But he was a youth who never took overmuch heed for the morrow. Sufficient unto the day was his motto. And, besides, it was distinctly worth risking. The main point, and the one with which alone the House would concern itself, was that he had completely taken in, scored off, and overwhelmed the youth who had done as much by him in the train, and his reputation as one not to be lightly trifled with would be restored to its former brilliance. Anything that might happen between himself and Venables subsequently would be regarded as a purely private matter between man and man, affecting the main point not at all.

About an hour later a small Merevalian informed Harrison that Venables wished to see him in his study. He went. Experience had taught him that when the Head of the House sent for him, it was as a rule as well to humour his whim and go. He was prepared for a good deal, for he had come to the conclusion that it was impossible for him to preserve his incognito in the matter, but he was certainly not prepared for what he saw.

Venables and the stranger were seated in two armchairs, apparently on the very best of terms with one another. And this, in spite of the fact that these two armchairs were the only furniture left in the study. The rest, as he had noted with a grin before he had knocked at the door, was picturesquely scattered about the passage.

'Hullo, Harrison,' said Venables, 'I wanted to see you. There seems to have been a slight mistake somewhere. Did you tell my brother to shift all the furniture out of the study?'

Harrison turned a delicate shade of green.

'Your – er – brother?' he gurgled.

'Yes. I ought to have told you my brother was coming to the Coll. this term. I told the Old Man and Merevale and the rest of the authorities. Can't make out why I forgot you. Slipped my mind somehow. However, you seem to have been doing the square thing by him, showing him round and so on. Very good of you.'

Harrison smiled feebly. Venables junior grinned. What seemed to Harrison a mystery was how the brothers had managed to arrive at the School at different times. The explanation of which was in reality very simple. The elder Venables had been spending the last week of the holidays with MacArthur, the captain of the St Austin's Fifteen, the same being a day boy, suspended within a mile of the School.

'But what I can't make out,' went on Venables, relentlessly, 'is this furniture business. To the best of my knowledge I didn't leave suddenly at the end of last term. I'll ask if you like, to make sure, but I fancy you'll find you've been mistaken. Must have been thinking of someone else. Anyhow, we thought you must know best, so we lugged all the furniture out into the passage, and now it appears there's been a mistake of sorts, and the stuff ought to be inside all the time. So would you mind putting it back again? We'd help you, only we're going out to the shop to get some tea. You might have it done by the time we get back. Thanks, awfully.'

Harrison coughed nervously, and rose to a point of order.

'I was going out to tea, too,' he said.

'I'm sorry, but I think you'll have to scratch the engagement,' said Venables.

Harrison made a last effort.

'I'm fagging for Welch this term,' he protested.

It was the rule at St Austin's that every fag had the right to refuse to serve two masters. Otherwise there would have been no peace for that down-trodden race.

'That,' said Venables, 'ought to be awfully jolly for Welch, don't you know, but as a matter of fact term hasn't begun yet. It doesn't start till tomorrow. Weigh in.'

Various feelings began to wage war beneath Harrison's Eton waistcoat. A profound disinclination to undertake the suggested task battled briskly with a feeling that, if he refused the commission, things might – nay, would – happen.

'Harrison,' said Venables gently, but with meaning, as he hesitated, 'do you know what it is to wish you had never been born?'

And Harrison, with a thoughtful expression on his face, picked up a photograph from the floor, and hung it neatly in its place over the mantelpiece.

[5]

Bradshaw's Little Story

The qualities which in later years rendered Frederick Wackerbath Bradshaw so conspicuous a figure in connection with the now celebrated affair of the European, African, and Asiatic Pork Pie and Ham Sandwich Supply Company frauds, were sufficiently in evidence during his school career to make his masters prophesy gloomily concerning his future. The boy was in every detail the father of the man. There was the same genial unscrupulousness, upon which the judge commented so bitterly during the trial, the same readiness to seize an opportunity and make the most of it, the same brilliance of tactics. Only once during those years can I remember an occasion on which Justice scored a point against him. I can remember it, because I was in a sense responsible for his failure. And he can remember it, I should be inclined to think, for other reasons. Our then Headmaster was a man with a straight eye and a good deal of muscular energy, and it is probable that the talented Frederick, in spite of the passage of years, has a tender recollection of these facts.

It was the eve of the Euripides examination in the Upper Fourth. Euripides is not difficult compared to some other authors, but he does demand a certain amount of preparation. Bradshaw was a youth who did less preparation than anybody I have ever seen, heard of, or read of, partly because he preferred to peruse a novel under the table during prep., but chiefly, I think, because he had reduced cribbing in form to such an exact science that he loved it for its own sake, and would no sooner have come tamely into school with a prepared lesson than a sportsman would shoot a sitting bird. It was not the marks that he cared for. He despised them. What he enjoyed was the refined pleasure of swindling under a master's very eye. At the trial the judge, who had, so ran report, been himself rather badly bitten by the Ham Sandwich Company, put the case briefly and neatly in the words, 'You appear to revel in villainy for villainy's sake,' and I am almost certain that I saw the beginnings of a gratified smile on Frederick's

275

expressive face as he heard the remark. The rest of our study – the juniors at St Austin's pigged in quartettes – were in a state of considerable mental activity on account of this Euripides examination. There had been House-matches during the preceding fortnight, and House-matches are not a help to study, especially if you are on the very fringe of the cock-house team, as I was. By dint of practising every minute of spare time, I had got the eleventh place for my fielding. And, better still, I had caught two catches in the second innings, one of them a regular gallery affair, and both off the captain's bowling. It was magnificent, but it was not Euripides, and I wished now that it had been. Mellish, our form-master, had an unpleasant habit of coming down with both feet, as it were, on members of his form who failed in the book-papers.

We were working, therefore, under forced draught, and it was distinctly annoying to see the wretched Bradshaw lounging in our only armchair with one of Rider Haggard's best, seemingly quite unmoved at the prospect of Euripides examinations. For all he appeared to care, Euripides might never have written a line in his life.

Kendal voiced the opinion of the meeting.

'Bradshaw, you worm,' he said. 'Aren't you going to do *any* work?'

'Think not. What's the good? Can't get up a whole play of Euripides in two hours.'

'Mellish'll give you beans.'

'Let him.'

'You'll get a jolly bad report.'

'Shan't get a report at all. I always intercept it before my guardian can get it. He never says anything.'

'Mellish'll probably run you in to the Old Man,' said White, the fourth occupant of the study.

Bradshaw turned on us with a wearied air.

'Oh, do give us a rest,' he said. 'Here you are just going to do a most important exam., and you sit jawing away as if you were paid for it. Oh, I say, by the way, who's setting the paper tomorrow?'

'Mellish, of course,' said White.

'No, he isn't,' I said. 'Shows what a lot you know about it. Mellish is setting the Livy paper.'

'Then, who's doing this one?' asked Bradshaw.

'Yorke.'

Yorke was the master of the Upper Fifth. He generally set one of the upper fourth book-papers.

'Certain?' said Bradshaw.

'Absolutely.'

'Thanks. That's all I wanted to know. By Jove, I advise you chaps to read this. It's grand. Shall I read out this bit about a fight?'

'No!' we shouted virtuously, all together, though we were dying to hear it, and we turned once more to the loathsome inanities of the second chorus. If we had been doing Homer, we should have felt more in touch with Bradshaw. There's a good deal of similarity, when you come to compare them, between Homer and Haggard. They both deal largely in bloodshed, for instance. As events proved, the Euripides paper, like many things which seem formidable at a distance, was not nearly so bad as I had expected. I did a fair-to-moderate paper, and Kendal and White both seemed satisfied with themselves. Bradshaw confessed without emotion that he had only attempted the last half of the last question, and on being pressed for further information, merely laughed mysteriously, and said vaguely that it would be all right.

It now became plain that he had something up his sleeve. We expressed a unanimous desire to know what it was.

'You might tell a chap,' I said.

'Out with it, Bradshaw, or we'll lynch you,' added Kendal.

Bradshaw, however, was not to be drawn. Much of his success in the paths of crime, both at school and afterwards, was due to his secretive habits. He never permitted accomplices.

On the following Wednesday the marks were read out. Out of a possible hundred I had obtained sixty – which pleased me very much indeed – White, fifty-five, Kendal, sixty-one. The unspeakable Bradshaw's net total was four.

Mellish always read out bad marks in a hushed voice, expressive of disgust and horror, but four per cent was too much for him. He shouted it, and the form yelled applause, until Ponsonby came in from the Upper Fifth next door with Mr Yorke's compliments, 'and would we recollect that his form were trying to do an examination'.

When order had been restored, Mellish settled his glasses and glared through them at Bradshaw, who, it may be remarked, had not turned a hair.

'Bradshaw,' he said, 'how do you explain this?'

It was merely a sighting shot, so to speak. Nobody was ever expected to answer the question. Bradshaw, however, proved himself the exception to the rule.

'I can explain, sir,' he said, 'if I may speak to you privately afterwards.'

I have seldom seen anyone so astonished as Mellish was at these words. In the whole course of his professional experience, he had never met with a parallel case. It was hard on the poor man not to be allowed to speak his mind about a matter of four per cent in a book-paper, but what could he do? He could not proceed with his denunciation, for if Bradshaw's explanation turned out a sufficient excuse, he would have to withdraw it all again, and vast stores of golden eloquence would be wasted. But, then, if he bottled up what he wished to say altogether, it might do him a serious internal injury. At last he hit on a compromise. He said, 'Very well, Bradshaw, I will hear what you have to say,' and then sprang, like the cat in the poem, 'all claws', upon an unfortunate individual who had scored twenty-nine, and who had been congratulating himself that Bradshaw's failings would act as a sort of lightning-conductor to him. Bradshaw worked off his explanation in under five minutes. I tried to stay behind to listen, on the pretext of wanting to tidy up my desk, but was ejected by request. Bradshaw explained that his statement was private.

After a time they came out together like long-lost brothers, Mellish with his hand on Bradshaw's shoulder. It was some small comfort to me to remember that Bradshaw had the greatest dislike to this sort of thing.

It was evident that Bradshaw, able exponent of the art of fiction that he was, must have excelled himself on this occasion. I tried to get the story out of him in the study that evening. White and Kendal assisted. We tried persuasion first. That having failed, we tried taunts. Then we tried kindness. Kendal sat on his legs, and I sat on his head, and White twisted his arm. I think that we should have extracted something soon, either his arm from its socket or a full confession, but we were interrupted. The door flew open, and Prater (the same being our House-master, and rather a good sort) appeared.

'Now then, now then,' he said. Prater's manner is always abrupt.

'What's this? I can't have this. I can't have this. Get up at once. Where's Bradshaw?'

I rose gracefully to my feet, thereby disclosing the classic features of the lost one.

'The Headmaster wants to see you at once, Bradshaw, at the School House. You others had better find something to do, or you will be getting into trouble.'

He and Bradshaw left together, while we speculated on the cause of the summons.

We were not left very long in suspense. In a quarter of an hour Bradshaw returned, walking painfully, and bearing what, to the expert's eye, are the unmistakable signs of a 'touching up', which, being interpreted, is corporal punishment.

'Hullo,' said White, as he appeared, 'what's all this?'

'How many?' enquired the statistically-minded Kendal. 'You'll be thankful for this when you're a man, Bradshaw.'

'That's what I always say to myself when I'm touched up,' added Kendal.

I said nothing, but it was to me that the wounded one addressed himself.

'You utter ass,' he said, in tones of concentrated venom.

'Look here, Bradshaw –' I began, protestingly.

'It's all through you – you idiot,' he snarled. 'I got twelve.'

'Twelve isn't so dusty,' said White, critically. 'Most I ever got was six.'

'But why was it?' asked Kendal. 'That's what we want to know. What have you been and gone and done?'

'It's about that Euripides paper,' said Bradshaw.

'Ah!' said Kendal.

'Yes, I don't mind telling you about it now. When Mellish had me up after school today, I'd got my yarn all ready. There wasn't a flaw in it anywhere as far as I could see. My idea was this. I told him I'd been to Yorke's room the day before the exam. to ask him if he had any marks for us. That was all right. Yorke was doing the two Unseen papers, and it was just the sort of thing a fellow would do to go and ask him about the marks.'

'Well?'

'Then when I got there he was out, and I looked about for the marks, and on the table I saw the Euripides paper.'

'By Jove!' said Kendal. We began to understand, and to realize that here was a master-mind.

'Well, of course, I read it, not knowing what it was, and then, as the only way of not taking an unfair advantage, I did as badly as I could in the exam. That was what I told Mellish. Any beak would have swallowed it.'

'Well, didn't he?'

'Mellish did all right, but the rotter couldn't keep it to himself. Went and told the Old Man. The Old Man sent for me. He was as decent as anything at first. That was just his guile. He made me describe exactly where I had seen the paper, and so on. That was rather risky, of course, but I put it as vaguely as I could. When I had finished, he suddenly whipped round, and said, "Bradshaw, why are you telling me all these lies?" That's the sort of thing that makes you feel rather a wreck. I was too surprised to say anything.'

'I can guess the rest,' said Kendal. 'But how on earth did he know it was all lies? Why didn't you stick to your yarn?'

'And, besides,' I put in, 'where do I come in? I don't see what I've got to do with it.'

Bradshaw eyed me fiercely. 'Why, the whole thing was your fault,' he said. 'You told me Yorke was setting the paper.'

'Well, so he did, didn't he?'

'No, he didn't. The Old Man set it himself,' said Bradshaw, gloomily.

[6]

A Shocking Affair

The Bradshaw who appears in the following tale is the same youth
who figures as the hero – or villain, label him as you like – of the
preceding equally veracious narrative. I mention this because I should
not care for you to go away with the idea that a waistcoat marked with
the name of Bradshaw must of necessity cover a scheming heart. It
may, however, be noticed that a good many members of the Bradshaw
family possess a keen and rather sinister sense of the humorous,
inherited doubtless from their great ancestor, the dry wag who wrote
that monument of quiet drollery, *Bradshaw's Railway Guide*. So with
the hero of my story.

Frederick Wackerbath Bradshaw was, as I have pointed out, my
contemporary at St Austin's. We were in the same House, and together
we sported on the green – and elsewhere – and did our best to turn
the majority of the staff of masters into confirmed pessimists, they in
the meantime endeavouring to do the same by us with every weapon
that lay to their hand. And the worst of these weapons were the end-
of-term examination papers. Mellish was our form-master, and once
a term a demon entered into Mellish. He brooded silently apart from
the madding crowd. He wandered through dry places seeking rest,
and at intervals he would smile evilly, and jot down a note on the back
of an envelope. These notes, collected and printed closely on the vilest
paper, made up the examination questions.

Our form read two authors a term, one Latin and one Greek. It was
the Greek that we feared most. Mellish had a sort of genius for picking
out absolutely untranslatable passages, and desiring us (in print) to
render the same with full notes. This term the book had been Thucydides, Book II, with regard to which I may echo the words of a certain
critic when called upon to give his candid opinion of a friend's first
novel, 'I dare not say what I think about that book.'

About a week before the commencement of the examinations, the
ordinary night-work used to cease, and we were supposed, during that

week, to be steadily going over the old ground and arming ourselves for the approaching struggle. There were, I suppose, people who actually did do this, but for my own part I always used to regard those seven days as a blessed period of rest, set apart specially to enable me to keep abreast of the light fiction of the day. And most of the form, so far as I know, thought the same. It was only on the night before the examination that one began to revise in real earnest. One's methods on that night resolved themselves into sitting in a chair and wondering where to begin. Just as one came to a decision, it was bedtime.

'Bradshaw,' I said, as I reached page 103 without having read a line, 'do you know any likely bits?'

Bradshaw looked up from his book. He was attempting to get a general idea of Thucydides' style by reading *Pickwick*.

'What?' he said.

I obliged with a repetition of my remark.

'Likely bits? Oh, you mean for the Thucydides. I don't know. Mellish never sets the bits any decent ordinary individual would set. I should take my chance if I were you.'

'What are you going to do?'

'I'm going to read *Pickwick*. Thicksides doesn't come within a mile of it.'

I thought so too.

'But how about tomorrow?'

'Oh, I shan't be there,' he said, as if it were the most ordinary of statements.

'Not there! Why, have you been sacked?'

This really seemed the only possible explanation. Such an event would not have come as a surprise. It was always a matter for wonder to me *why* the authorities never sacked Bradshaw, or at the least requested him to leave. Possibly it was another case of the ass and the bundles of hay. They could not make up their minds which special misdemeanour of his to attack first.

'No, I've not been sacked,' said Bradshaw.

A light dawned upon me.

'Oh,' I said, 'you're going to slumber in.' For the benefit of the uninitiated, I may mention that to slumber in is to stay in the House during school on a pretence of illness.

'That,' replied the man of mystery, with considerable asperity, 'is exactly the silly rotten kid's idea that would come naturally to a complete idiot like you.'

As a rule, I resent being called a complete idiot, but this was not the time for asserting one's personal dignity. I had to know what Bradshaw's scheme for evading the examination was. Perhaps there might be room for two in it; in which case I should have been exceedingly glad to have lent my moral support to it. I pressed for an explanation.

'You may jaw,' said Bradshaw at last, 'as much as you jolly well please, but I'm not going to give this away. All you're going to know is that I shan't be there tomorrow.'

'I bet you are, and I bet you do a jolly rank paper too,' I said, remembering that the sceptic is sometimes vouchsafed revelations to which the most devout believer may not aspire. It is, for instance, always the young man who scoffs at ghosts that the family spectre chooses as his audience. But it required more than a mere sneer or an empty gibe to pump information out of Bradshaw. He took me up at once.

'What'll you bet?' he said.

Now I was prepared to wager imaginary sums to any extent he might have cared to name, but as my actual worldly wealth at that moment consisted of one penny, and my expectations were limited to the shilling pocket-money which I should receive on the following Saturday – half of which was already mortgaged – it behoved me to avoid doing anything rash with my ready money. But, since a refusal would have meant the downfall of my arguments, I was obliged to name a figure. I named an even sixpence. After all, I felt, I must win. By what means, other than illness, could Bradshaw possibly avoid putting in an appearance at the Thucydides examination?

'All right,' said Bradshaw, 'an even sixpence. You'll lose.'

'Slumbering in barred.'

'Of course.'

'Real illness barred too,' I said. Bradshaw is a man of resource, and has been known to make himself genuinely ill in similar emergencies.

'Right you are. Slumbering in and real illness both barred. Anything else you'd like to bar?'

I thought.

'No. Unless –' an idea struck me – 'You're not going to run away?'

Bradshaw scorned to answer the question.

'Now you'd better buck up with your work,' he said, opening his book again. 'You've got about as long odds as anyone ever got. But you'll lose all the same.'

It scarcely seemed possible. And yet – Bradshaw was generally right. If he said he had a scheme for doing – though it was generally for not doing – something, it rarely failed to come off. I thought of my sixpence, my only sixpence, and felt a distinct pang of remorse. After all, only the other day the chaplain had said how wrong it was to bet. By Jove, so he had. Decent man the chaplain. Pity to do anything he would disapprove of. I was on the point of recalling my wager, when before my mind's eye rose a vision of Bradshaw rampant and sneering, and myself writhing in my chair a crushed and scored-off wreck. I drew the line at that. I valued my self-respect at more than sixpence. If it had been a shilling now –. So I set my teeth and turned once more to my Thucydides. Bradshaw, having picked up the thread of his story again, emitted hoarse chuckles like minute guns, until I very nearly rose and fell upon him. It is maddening to listen to a person laughing and not to know the joke.

'You will be allowed two hours for this paper,' said Mellish on the following afternoon, as he returned to his desk after distributing the Thucydides questions. 'At five minutes to four I shall begin to collect your papers, but those who wish may go on till ten past. Write only on one side of the paper, and put your names in the top right-hand corner. Marks will be given for neatness. Any boy whom I see looking at his neighbour's – *where's Bradshaw?*'

It was already five minutes past the hour. The latest of the late always had the decency to appear at least by three minutes past.

'Has anybody seen Bradshaw?' repeated Mellish. 'You, what's-your-name –' (I am what's-your-name, very much at your service) '– you are in his House. Have you seen him?'

I could have pointed out with some pleasure at this juncture that if Cain expressed indignation at being asked where his brother was, I, by a simple sum in proportion, might with even greater justice feel annoyed at having to locate a person who was no relative of mine at all. Did Mr Mellish expect me to keep an eye on every member of my House? Did Mr Mellish – in short, what did he mean by it?

This was what I thought. I said, 'No, sir.'

'This is extraordinary,' said Mellish, 'most extraordinary. Why, the boy was in school this morning.'

This was true. The boy had been in school that morning to some purpose, having beaten all records (his own records) in the gentle sport of Mellish-baiting. This evidently occurred to Mellish at the time, for he dropped the subject at once, and told us to begin our papers.

Now I have remarked already that I dare not say what I think of Thucydides, Book II. How then shall I frame my opinion of that

examination paper? It was Thucydides, Book II, with the few easy
parts left out. It was Thucydides, Book II, with special home-made
difficulties added. It was – well, in its way it was a masterpiece.
Without going into details – I dislike sensational and realistic writing –
I may say that I personally was not one of those who required an extra
ten minutes to finish their papers. I finished mine at half-past two,
and amused myself for the remaining hour and a half by writing neatly
on several sheets of foolscap exactly what I thought of Mr Mellish,
and precisely what I hoped would happen to him some day. It was
grateful and comforting.

At intervals I wondered what had become of Bradshaw. I was not
surprised at his absence. At first I had feared that he would keep his
word in that matter. As time went on I knew that he would. At more
frequent intervals I wondered how I should enjoy being a bankrupt.

Four o'clock came round, and found me so engrossed in putting the
finishing touches to my excursus of Mr Mellish's character, that I
stayed on in the form-room till ten past. Two other members of the
form stayed too, writing with the despairing energy of those who had
five minutes to say what they would like to spread over five hours. At
last Mellish collected the papers. He seemed a trifle surprised when I
gave up my modest three sheets. Brown and Morrison, who had their
eye on the form prize, each gave up reams. Brown told me subsequently
that he had only had time to do sixteen sheets, and wanted to know
whether I had adopted Rutherford's emendation in preference to the
old reading in Question II. My prolonged stay had made him regard
me as a possible rival.

I dwell upon this part of my story, because it has an important
bearing on subsequent events. If I had not waited in the form-room
I should not have gone downstairs just behind Mellish. And if I had
not gone downstairs just behind Mellish, I should not have been in at
the death, that is to say the discovery of Bradshaw, and this story
would have been all beginning and middle, and no ending, for I am
certain that Bradshaw would never have told me a word. He was a
most secretive animal.

I went downstairs, as I say, just behind Mellish. St Austin's, you
must know, is composed of three blocks of buildings, the senior, the
middle, and the junior, joined by cloisters. We left the senior block
by the door. To the captious critic this information may seem superfluous, but let me tell him that I have left the block in my time, and
entered it, too, though never, it is true, in the company of a master,
in other ways. There are windows.

Our procession of two, Mellish leading by a couple of yards, passed through the cloisters, and came to the middle block, where the Masters' Common Room is. I had no particular reason for going to that block, but it was all on my way to the House, and I knew that Mellish hated having his footsteps dogged. That Thucydides paper rankled slightly.

In the middle block, at the top of the building, far from the haunts of men, is the Science Museum, containing – so I have heard, I have never been near the place myself – two stuffed rats, a case of mouldering butterflies, and other objects of acute interest. The room has a staircase all to itself, and this was the reason why, directly I heard shouts proceeding from that staircase, I deduced that they came from the Museum. I am like Sherlock Holmes, I don't mind explaining my methods.

'Help!' shouted the voice. 'Help!'

The voice was Bradshaw's.

Mellish was talking to M. Gerard, the French master, at the moment. He had evidently been telling him of Bradshaw's non-appearance, for at the sound of his voice they both spun round, and stood looking at the staircase like a couple of pointers.

'Help,' cried the voice again.

Mellish and Gerard bounded up the stairs. I had never seen a French master run before. It was a pleasant sight. I followed. As we reached the door of the Museum, which was shut, renewed shouts filtered through it. Mellish gave tongue.

'Bradshaw!'

'Yes, sir,' from within.

'Are you there?' This I thought, and still think, quite a superfluous question.

'Yes, sir,' said Bradshaw.

'What are you doing in there, Bradshaw? Why were you not in school this afternoon? Come out at once.' This in deep and thrilling tones.

'Please, sir,' said Bradshaw complainingly, 'I can't open the door.' Now, the immediate effect of telling a person that you are unable to open a door is to make him try his hand at it. Someone observes that there are three things which everyone thinks he can do better than anyone else, namely poking a fire, writing a novel, and opening a door.

Gerard was no exception to the rule.

'Can't open the door?' he said. 'Nonsense, nonsense.' And, swooping at the handle, he grasped it firmly, and turned it.

At this point he made an attempt, a very spirited attempt, to lower the world's record for the standing high jump. I have spoken above of the pleasure it gave me to see a French master run. But for good, square enjoyment, warranted free from all injurious chemicals, give me a French master jumping.

'My dear Gerard,' said the amazed Mellish.

'I have received a shock. Dear me, I have received a most terrible shock.'

So had I, only of another kind. I really thought I should have expired in my tracks with the effort of keeping my enjoyment strictly to myself. I saw what had happened. The Museum is lit by electric light. To turn it on one has to shoot the bolt of the door, which, like the handle, is made of metal. It is on the killing two birds with one stone principle. You lock yourself in and light yourself up with one movement. It was plain that the current had gone wrong somehow, run amock, as it were. Mellish meanwhile, instead of being warned by Gerard's fate, had followed his example, and tried to turn the handle. His jump, though quite a creditable effort, fell short of Gerard's by some six inches. I began to feel as if some sort of round game were going on. I hoped that they would not want me to take a hand. I also hoped that the thing would continue for a good while longer. The success of the piece certainly warranted the prolongation of its run. But here I was disappointed. The disturbance had attracted another spectator, Blaize, the science and chemistry master. The matter was hastily explained to him in all its bearings. There was Bradshaw entombed within the Museum, with every prospect of death by star-vation, unless he could support life for the next few years on the two stuffed rats and the case of butterflies. The authorities did not see their way to adding a human specimen (youth's size) to the treasures in the Museum, *so* – how was he to be got out?

The scientific mind is equal to every emergency.

'Bradshaw,' shouted Blaize through the keyhole.

'Sir?'

'Are you there?'

I should imagine that Bradshaw was growing tired of this question by this time. Besides, it cast aspersions on the veracity of Gerard and Mellish. Bradshaw, with perfect politeness, hastened to inform the gentleman that he was there.

'Have you a piece of paper?'

'Will an envelope do, sir?'

'Bless the boy, anything will do so long as it is paper.'

Dear me, I thought, is it as bad as all that? Is Blaize, in despair of ever rescuing the unfortunate prisoner, going to ask him to draw up a 'last dying words' document, to be pushed under the door and despatched to his sorrowing guardian?

'Put it over your hand, and then shoot back the bolt.'

'But, sir, the electricity.'

'Pooh, boy!'

The scientific mind is always intolerant of lay ignorance.

'Pooh, boy, paper is a non-conductor. You won't get hurt.'

Bradshaw apparently acted on his instructions. From the other side of the door came the sharp sound of the bolt as it was shot back, and at the same time the light ceased to shine through the keyhole. A moment later the handle turned, and Bradshaw stepped forth – free!

'Dear me,' said Mellish. 'Now I never knew that before, Blaize. Remarkable. But this ought to be seen to. In the meantime, I had better ask the Headmaster to give out that the Museum is closed until further notice, I think.'

And closed the Museum has been ever since. That further notice has never been given. And yet nobody seems to feel as if an essential part of their life had ceased to be, so to speak. Curious. Bradshaw, after a short explanation, was allowed to go away without a stain – that is to say, without any additional stain – on his character. We left the authorities discussing the matter, and went downstairs.

'Sixpence isn't enough,' I said, 'take this penny. It's all I've got. You shall have the sixpence on Saturday.'

'Thanks,' said Bradshaw. 'Was the Thucydides paper pretty warm?'

'Warmish. But, I say, didn't you get a beastly shock when you locked the door?'

'I did the week before last, the first time I ever went to the place. This time I was more or less prepared for it. Blaize seems to think that paper dodge a special invention of his own. He'll be taking out a patent for it one of these days. Why, every kid knows that paper doesn't conduct electricity.'

'I didn't,' I said honestly.

'You don't know much,' said Bradshaw, with equal honesty.

'I don't,' I replied. 'Bradshaw, you're a great man, but you missed the best part of it all.'

'What, the Thucydides paper?' asked he with a grin.

'No, you missed seeing Gerard jump quite six feet.'

Bradshaw's face expressed keen disappointment.

'No, did he really? Oh, I say, I wish I'd seen it.'

The moral of which is that the wicked do not always prosper. If

Bradshaw had not been in the Museum, he might have seen Gerard jump six feet, which would have made him happy for weeks. On second thoughts, though, that does not work out quite right, for if Bradshaw had *not* been in the Museum, Gerard would not have jumped at all. No, better put it this way. I was virtuous, and I had the pleasure of witnessing the sight I have referred to. But then there was the Thucydides paper, which Bradshaw missed but which I did not. No. On consideration, the moral of this story shall be withdrawn and submitted to a committee of experts. Perhaps they will be able to say what it is.

[7]

The Babe and the Dragon

The annual inter-house football cup at St Austin's lay between Dacre's, who were the holders, and Merevale's, who had been runner-up in the previous year, and had won it altogether three times out of the last five. The cup was something of a tradition in Merevale's, but of late Dacre's had become serious rivals, and, as has been said before, were the present holders.

This year there was not much to choose between the two teams. Dacre's had three of the First Fifteen and two of the Second; Merevale's two of the First and four of the Second. St Austin's being not altogether a boarding-school, many of the brightest stars of the teams were day boys, and there was, of course, always the chance that one of these would suddenly see the folly of his ways, reform, and become a member of a House.

This frequently happened, and this year it was almost certain to happen again, for no less a celebrity than MacArthur, commonly known as the Babe, had been heard to state that he was negotiating with his parents to that end. Which House he would go to was at present uncertain. He did not know himself, but it would, he said, probably be one of the two favourites for the cup. This lent an added interest to the competition, for the presence of the Babe would almost certainly turn the scale. The Babe's nationality was Scots, and, like most Scotsmen, he could play football more than a little. He was the safest, coolest centre three-quarter the School had, or had had for some time. He shone in all branches of the game, but especially in tackling. To see the Babe spring apparently from nowhere, in the middle of an inter-school match, and bring down with violence a man who had passed the back, was an intellectual treat. Both Dacre's and Merevale's, therefore, yearned for his advent exceedingly. The reasons which finally decided his choice were rather curious. They arose in the following manner:

The Babe's sister was at Girton. A certain Miss Florence Beezley was also at Girton. When the Babe's sister revisited the ancestral home at the end of the term, she brought Miss Beezley with her to spend a week. What she saw in Miss Beezley was to the Babe a matter for wonder, but she must have liked her, or she would not have gone out of her way to seek her company. Be that as it may, the Babe would have gone a very long way out of his way to avoid her company. He led a fine, healthy, out-of-doors life during that week, and doubtless did himself a lot of good. But times will occur when it is imperative that a man shall be under the family roof. Meal-times, for instance. The Babe could not subsist without food, and he was obliged, Miss Beezley or no Miss Beezley, to present himself on these occasions. This, by the way, was in the Easter holidays, so that there was no school to give him an excuse for absence.

Breakfast was a nightmare, lunch was rather worse, and as for dinner, it was quite unspeakable. Miss Beezley seemed to gather force during the day. It was not the actual presence of the lady that revolted the Babe, for that was passable enough. It was her conversation that killed. She refused to let the Babe alone. She was intensely learned herself, and seemed to take a morbid delight in dissecting his ignorance, and showing everybody the pieces. Also, she persisted in calling him Mr MacArthur in a way that seemed somehow to point out and emphasize his youthfulness. She added it to her remarks as a sort of after-thought or echo.

'Do you read Browning, Mr MacArthur?' she would say suddenly, having apparently waited carefully until she saw that his mouth was full.

The Babe would swallow convulsively, choke, blush, and finally say –

'No, not much.'

'Ah!' This in a tone of pity not untinged with scorn.

'When you say "not much", Mr MacArthur, what exactly do you mean? Have you read any of his poems?'

'Oh, yes, one or two.'

'Ah! Have you read "Pippa Passes"?'

'No, I think not.'

'Surely you must know, Mr MacArthur, whether you have or not. Have you read "Fifine at the Fair"?'

'No.'

'Have you read "Sordello"?'

'No.'

'What *have* you read, Mr MacArthur?'

Brought to bay in this fashion, he would have to admit that he had read 'The Pied Piper of Hamelin', and not a syllable more, and Miss Beezley would look at him for a moment and sigh softly. The Babe's subsequent share in the conversation, provided the Dragon made no further onslaught, was not large.

One never-to-be-forgotten day, shortly before the end of her visit, a series of horrible accidents resulted in their being left to lunch together alone. The Babe had received no previous warning, and when he was suddenly confronted with this terrible state of affairs he almost swooned. The lady's steady and critical inspection of his style of carving a chicken completed his downfall. His previous experience of carving had been limited to those entertainments which went by the name of 'study-gorges', where, if you wanted to help a chicken, you took hold of one leg, invited an accomplice to attach himself to the other, and pulled.

But, though unskilful, he was plucky and energetic. He lofted the bird out of the dish on to the tablecloth twice in the first minute. Stifling a mad inclination to call out 'Fore!' or something to that effect, he laughed a hollow, mirthless laugh, and replaced the errant fowl. When a third attack ended in the same way, Miss Beezley asked permission to try what she could do. She tried, and in two minutes the chicken was neatly dismembered. The Babe re-seated himself in an over-wrought state.

'Tell me about St Austin's, Mr MacArthur,' said Miss Beezley, as the Babe was trying to think of something to say – not about the weather. 'Do you play football?'

'Yes.'

'Ah!'

A prolonged silence.

'Do you –' began the Babe at last.

'Tell me –' began Miss Beezley, simultaneously.

'I beg your pardon,' said the Babe; 'you were saying –?'

'Not at all, Mr MacArthur. *You* were saying –?'

'I was only going to ask you if you played croquet?'

'Yes; do you?'

'No.'

'Ah!'

'If this is going to continue,' thought the Babe, 'I shall be reluctantly compelled to commit suicide.'

There was another long pause.

'Tell me the names of some of the masters at St Austin's, Mr

MacArthur,' said Miss Beezley. She habitually spoke as if she were an examination paper, and her manner might have seemed to some to verge upon the autocratic, but the Babe was too thankful that the question was not on Browning or the higher algebra to notice this. He reeled off a list of names.

'. . . Then there's Merevale – rather a decent sort – and Dacre.'

'What sort of a man is Mr Dacre?'

'Rather a rotter, I think.'

'What is a rotter, Mr MacArthur?'

'Well, I don't know how to describe it exactly. He doesn't play cricket or anything. He's generally considered rather a crock.'

'Really! This is very interesting, Mr MacArthur. And what is a crock? I suppose what it comes to,' she added, as the Babe did his best to find a definition, 'is this, that you yourself dislike him.' The Babe admitted the impeachment. Mr Dacre had a finished gift of sarcasm which had made him writhe on several occasions, and sarcastic masters are rarely very popular.

'Ah!' said Miss Beezley. She made frequent use of that monosyllable. It generally gave the Babe the same sort of feeling as he had been accustomed to experience in the happy days of his childhood when he had been caught stealing jam.

Miss Beezley went at last, and the Babe felt like a convict who has just received a free pardon.

One afternoon in the following term he was playing fives with Charteris, a prefect in Merevale's House. Charteris was remarkable from the fact that he edited and published at his own expense an unofficial and highly personal paper, called *The Glow Worm*, which was a great deal more in demand than the recognized School magazine, *The Austinian*, and always paid its expenses handsomely.

Charteris had the journalistic taint very badly. He was always the first to get wind of any piece of School news. On this occasion he was in possession of an exclusive item. The Babe was the first person to whom he communicated it.

'Have you heard the latest romance in high life, Babe?' he observed, as they were leaving the court. 'But of course you haven't. You never do hear anything.'

'Well?' asked the Babe, patiently.

'You know Dacre?'

'I seem to have heard the name somewhere.'

'He's going to be married.'

'Yes. Don't trouble to try and look interested. You're one of those offensive people who mind their own business and nobody else's. Only I thought I'd tell you. Then you'll have a remote chance of understanding my quips on the subject in next week's *Glow Worm*. You laddies frae the north have to be carefully prepared for the subtler flights of wit.'

'Thanks,' said the Babe, placidly. 'Good-night.'

The Headmaster intercepted the Babe a few days after he was going home after a scratch game of football. 'MacArthur,' said he, 'you pass Mr Dacre's House, do you not, on your way home? Then would you mind asking him from me to take preparation tonight? I find I shall be unable to be there.' It was the custom at St Austin's for the Head to preside at preparation once a week; but he performed this duty, like the celebrated Irishman, as often as he could avoid it.

The Babe accepted the commission. He was shown into the drawing-room. To his consternation, for he was not a society man, there appeared to be a species of tea-party going on. As the door opened, somebody was just finishing a remark.

'. . . faculty which he displayed in such poems as "Sordello",' said the voice.

The Babe knew that voice.

He would have fled if he had been able, but the servant was already announcing him. Mr Dacre began to do the honours.

'Mr MacArthur and I have met before,' said Miss Beezley, for it was she. 'Curiously enough, the subject which we have just been discussing is one in which he takes, I think, a great interest. I was saying, Mr MacArthur, when you came in, that few of Tennyson's works show the poetic faculty which Browning displays in "Sordello".'

The Babe looked helplessly at Mr Dacre.

'I think you are taking MacArthur out of his depth there,' said Mr Dacre. 'Was there something you wanted to see me about, MacArthur?'

The Babe delivered his message.

'Oh, yes, certainly,' said Mr Dacre. 'Shall you be passing the School House tonight? If so, you might give the Headmaster my compliments, and say I shall be delighted.'

The Babe had had no intention of going out of his way to that extent, but the chance of escape offered by the suggestion was too good to be missed. He went.

On his way he called at Merevale's, and asked to see Charteris.

'Look here, Charteris,' he said, 'you remember telling me that Dacre was going to be married?'

'Yes.'

'Well, do you know her name by any chance?'

'I ken it weel, ma braw Hielander. She is a Miss Beezley.'

'Great Scott!' said the Babe.

'Hullo! Why, was your young heart set in that direction? You amaze and pain me, Babe. I think we'd better have a story on the subject in *The Glow Worm*, with you as hero and Dacre as villain. It shall end happily, of course. I'll write it myself.'

'You'd better,' said the Babe, grimly. 'Oh, I say, Charteris.'

'Well?'

'When I come as a boarder, I shall be a House-prefect, shan't I, as I'm in the Sixth?'

'Yes.'

'And prefects have to go to breakfast and supper, and that sort of thing, pretty often with the House-beak, don't they?'

'Such are the facts of the case.'

'Thanks. That's all. Go away and do some work. Good-night.'

The cup went to Merevale's that year. The Babe played a singularly brilliant game for them.

[8]

The Manoeuvres of Charteris

Chapter 1

'Might I observe, sir –'

'You may observe whatever you like,' said the referee kindly. 'Twenty-five.'

'The rules say –'

'I have given my decision. Twenty-*five*!' A spot of red appeared on the official cheek. The referee, who had been heckled since the kick-off, was beginning to be annoyed.

'The ball went behind without bouncing, and the rules say –'

'Twenty-FIVE!!' shouted the referee. 'I am perfectly well aware what the rules say.' And he blew his whistle with an air of finality. The secretary of the Bargees' F.C. subsided reluctantly, and the game was restarted.

The Bargees' match was a curious institution. Their real name was the Old Crockfordians. When, a few years before, the St Austin's secretary had received a challenge from them, dated from Stapleton, where their secretary happened to reside, he had argued within himself as follows: 'This sounds all right. Old Crockfordians? Never heard of Crockford. Probably some large private school somewhere. Anyhow, they're certain to be decent fellows.' And he arranged the fixture. It then transpired that Old Crockford was a village, and, from the appearance of the team on the day of battle, the Old Crockfordians seemed to be composed exclusively of the riff-raff of same. They wore green shirts with a bright yellow leopard over the heart, and C.F.C. woven in large letters about the chest. One or two of the outsides played in caps, and the team to a man criticized the referee's decisions with point and pungency. Unluckily, the first year saw a weak team of Austinians rather badly beaten, with the result that it became a point of honour to wipe this off the slate before the fixture could be cut out of the card. The next year was also unlucky. The Bargees managed to score a penalty goal in the first half, and won on that. The match resulted in a draw in the following season, and by this time the thing had become an annual event.

Now, however, the School was getting some of its own back. The Bargees had brought down a player of some reputation from the North, and were as strong as ever in the scrum. But St Austin's had a great team, and were carrying all before them. Charteris and Graham at half had the ball out to their centres in a way which made Merevale, who looked after the football of the School, feel that life was worth living. And when once it was out, things happened rapidly. MacArthur, the captain of the team, with Thomson as his fellow-centre, and Welch and Bannister on the wings, did what they liked with the Bargees' three-quarters. All the School outsides had scored, even the back, who dropped a neat goal. The player from the North had scarcely touched the ball during the whole game, and altogether the Bargees were becoming restless and excited.

The kick-off from the twenty-five line which followed upon the small discussion alluded to above, reached Graham. Under ordinary circumstances he would have kicked, but in a winning game original methods often pay. He dodged a furious sportsman in green and yellow, and went away down the touch-line. He was almost through when he stumbled. He recovered himself, but too late. Before he could pass, someone was on him. Graham was not heavy, and his opponent was muscular. He was swung off his feet, and the next moment the two came down together, Graham underneath. A sharp pain shot through his shoulder.

A doctor emerged from the crowd – there is always a doctor in a crowd – and made an examination.

'Anything bad?' asked the referee.

'Collar-bone,' said the doctor. 'The usual, you know. Rather badly smashed. Nothing dangerous, of course. Be all right in a month or so. Stop his playing. Rather a pity. Much longer before half-time?'

'No. I was just going to blow the whistle when this happened.'

The injured warrior was carried off, and the referee blew his whistle for half-time.

'I say, Charteris,' said MacArthur, 'who the deuce am I to put half instead of Graham?'

'Rogers used to play half in his childhood, I believe. But, I say, did you ever see such a scrag? Can't you protest, or something?'

'My dear chap, how can I? It's on our own ground. These Bargee beasts are visitors, if you come to think of it. I'd like to wring the chap's neck who did it. I didn't spot who it was. Did you see?'

'Rather. Their secretary. That man with the beard. I'll get Prescott to mark him this half.'

Prescott was the hardest tackler in the School. He accepted the commission cheerfully, and promised to do his best by the bearded one.

Charteris certainly gave him every opportunity. When he threw the ball out of touch, he threw it neatly to the criminal with the beard, and Prescott, who stuck to him closer than a brother, had generally tackled him before he knew what had happened. After a time he began to grow thoughtful, and when there was a line-out went and stood among the three-quarters. In this way much of Charteris's righteous retribution miscarried, but once or twice he had the pleasure and privilege of putting in a piece of tackling on his own account. The match ended with the enemy still intact, but considerably shaken. He was also rather annoyed. He spoke to Charteris on the subject as they were leaving the field.

'I was watching you,' he said, *apropos* of nothing apparently.

'That must have been nice for you,' said Charteris.

'You wait.'

'Certainly. Any time you're passing, I'm sure –'

'You ain't 'eard the last of me yet.'

'That's something of a blow,' said Charteris cheerfully, and they parted.

Charteris, having got into his blazer, ran after Welch and MacArthur, and walked back with them to the House. All three of them were at Merevale's.

'Poor old Tony,' said MacArthur. 'Where have they taken him to? The House?'

'Yes,' said Welch. 'I say, Babe, you ought to scratch this match next year. Tell 'em the card's full up or something.'

'Oh, I don't know. One expects fairly rough play in this sort of game. After all, we tackle pretty hard ourselves. I know I always try and go my hardest. If the man happens to be brittle, that's his lookout,' concluded the bloodthirsty Babe.

'My dear man,' said Charteris, 'there's all the difference between a decent tackle and a bally scrag like the one that doubled Tony up. You can't break a chap's collar-bone without trying to.'

'Well, if you come to think of it, I suppose the man must have been fairly riled. You can't expect a man to be in an angelic temper when his side's been licked by thirty points.'

The Babe was one of those thoroughly excellent persons who always try, when possible, to make allowances for everybody.

'Well, dash it,' said Charteris indignantly, 'if he had lost his hair he might have drawn the line at falling on Tony like that. It wasn't the tackling part of it that crocked him. The beast simply jumped on him like a Hooligan. Anyhow, I made him sit up a bit before we finished. I gave Prescott the tip to mark him out of touch. Have you ever been collared by Prescott? It's a liberal education. Now, there you are, you see. Take Prescott. He's never crocked a man seriously in his life. I don't count being winded. That's absolutely an accident. Well, there you are, then. Prescott weighs thirteen-ten, and he's all muscle, and he goes like a battering-ram. You'll own that. He goes as hard as he jolly well knows how, and yet the worst he has ever done is to lay a man out for a couple of minutes while he gets his wind back. Well, compare him with this Bargee man. The Bargee weighs a stone less and isn't nearly as strong, and yet he smashes Tony's collar-bone. It's all very well, Babe, but you can't get away from it. Prescott tackles fairly and the Bargee scrags.'

'Yes,' said MacArthur, 'I suppose you're right.'

'Rather,' said Charteris. 'I wish I'd broken his neck.'

'By the way,' said Welch, 'you were talking to him after the match. What was he saying?'

Charteris laughed.

'By Jove, I'd forgotten; he said I hadn't heard the last of him, and that I was to wait.'

'What did you say?'

'Oh, I behaved beautifully. I asked him to be sure and look in any time he was passing, and after a few chatty remarks we parted.'

'I wonder if he meant anything.'

'I believe he means to waylay me with a buckled belt. I shan't stir out except with the Old Man or some other competent bodyguard. " 'Orrible outrage, shocking death of a St Austin's schoolboy." It would look rather well on the posters.'

Welch stuck strenuously to the point.

'No, but, look here, Charteris,' he said seriously, 'I'm not rotting. You see, the man lives in Stapleton, and if he knows anything of School rules –'

'Which he doesn't probably. Why should he? Well?' – 'If he knows anything of the rules, he'll know that Stapleton's out of bounds, and he may book you there and run you in to Merevale.'

'Yes,' said MacArthur. 'I tell you what, you'd do well to knock off a few of your expeditions to Stapleton. You know you wouldn't go there once a month if it wasn't out of bounds. You'll be a prefect next term. I should wait till then, if I were you.'

'My dear chap, what does it matter? The worst that can happen to you for breaking bounds is a couple of hundred lines, and I've got a capital of four hundred already in stock. Besides, things would be so slow if you always kept in bounds. I always feel like a cross between Dick Turpin and Machiavelli when I go to Stapleton. It's an awfully jolly feeling. Like warm treacle running down your back. It's cheap at two hundred lines.'

'You're an awful fool,' said Welch, rudely but correctly.

Welch was a youth who treated the affairs of other people rather too seriously. He worried over them. This is not a particularly common trait in the character of either boy or man, but Welch had it highly developed. He could not probably have explained exactly why he was worried, but he undoubtedly was. Welch had a very grave and serious mind. He shared a study with Charteris – for Charteris, though not yet a School-prefect, was part owner of a study – and close observation had convinced him that the latter was not responsible for his actions, and that he wanted somebody to look after him. He had therefore elected himself to the post of a species of modified and unofficial guardian angel to him. The duties were heavy, and the remuneration exceedingly light.

'Really, you know,' said MacArthur, 'I don't see what the point of all your lunacy is. I don't know if you're aware of it, but the Old Man's getting jolly sick with you.'

'I didn't know,' said Charteris, 'but I'm very glad to hear it. For hist! I have a ger-rudge against the person. Beneath my ban that mystic man shall suffer, *coûte que coûte*, Matilda. He sat upon me – publicly, and the resultant blot on my scutcheon can only be wiped out with blood, or broken rules,' he added.

This was true. To listen to Charteris on the subject, one might have thought that he considered the matter rather amusing than otherwise. This, however, was simply due to the fact that he treated everything flippantly in conversation. But, like the parrot, he thought the more. The actual *casus belli* had been trivial. At least the mere spectator would have considered it trivial. It had happened after this fashion. Charteris was a member of the School corps. The orderly-room of the

School corps was in the junior part of the School buildings. Charteris had been to replace his rifle in that shrine of Mars after a mid-day drill, and on coming out into the passage had found himself in the middle of a junior school 'rag' of the conventional type. Somebody's cap had fallen off, and two hastily picked teams were playing football with it (Association rules). Now, Charteris was not a prefect (that, it may be observed in passing, was another source of bitterness in him towards the Powers, for he was fairly high up in the Sixth, and others of his set, Welch, Thomson, and Tony Graham, who were also in the Sixth – the two last below him in form order – had already received their prefects' caps). Not being a prefect, it would have been officious in him to have stopped the game. So he was passing on with what Mr Hurry Bungsho Jabberjee, B.A., would have termed a beaming simper of indescribable suavity, when a member of one of the opposing teams, in effecting a G. O. Smithian dribble, cannoned into him. To preserve his balance – this will probably seem a very thin line of defence, but 'I state but the facts' – he grabbed at the disciple of Smith amidst applause, and at that precise moment a new actor appeared on the scene – the Headmaster. Now, of all the things that lay in his province, the Headmaster most disliked to see a senior 'ragging' with a junior. He had a great idea of the dignity of the senior school, and did all that in him lay to see that it was kept up. The greater number of the juniors with whom the senior was found ragging, the more heinous the offence. Circumstantial evidence was dead against Charteris. To all outward appearances he was one of the players in the impromptu football match. The soft and fascinating beams of the simper, to quote Mr Jabberjee once more, had not yet faded from the act. A well-chosen word or two from the Headmagisterial lips put a premature end to the football match, and Charteris was proceeding on his way when the Headmaster called him. He stopped. The Headmaster was angry. So angry, indeed, that he did what in a more lucid interval he would not have done. He hauled a senior over the coals in the hearing of a number of juniors, one of whom (unidentified) giggled loudly. As Charteris had on previous occasions observed, the Old Man, when he did start to take a person's measure, didn't leave out much. The address was not long, but it covered a great deal of ground. The section of it which chiefly rankled in Charteris's mind, and which had continued to rankle ever since, was that in which the use of the word 'buffoon' had occurred. Everybody who has a gift of humour and (very naturally) enjoys exercising it, hates to be called a buffoon. It was Charteris's one weak spot. Every other abusive epithet in the language slid off him without penetrating or causing him the least discomfort. The word 'buffoon' went home, right up to the hilt. And, to borrow from Mr Jabberjee for positively the very last time, he had observed (mentally): 'Henceforward I will perpetrate heaps of the lowest dregs of vice.' He had, in fact, started a perfect bout of breaking rules, simply because they were rules. The injustice of the thing rankled. No one so dislikes being punished unjustly as the person who might have been punished justly on scores of previous occasions, if he had only been found out. To a certain extent, Charteris ran amok. He broke bounds and did little work, and – he was beginning gradually to find this out – got thoroughly tired of it all. Offended dignity, however, still kept him at it, and much as he would have preferred to have resumed a less feverish type of existence, he did not do so.

'I have a ger-rudge against the man,' he said.

'You *are* an idiot, really,' said Welch.

'Welch,' said Charteris, by way of explanation to MacArthur, 'is a lad of coarse fibre. He doesn't understand the finer feelings. He can't see that I am doing this simply for the Old Man's good. Spare the rod, spile the choild. Let's go and have a look at Tony when we're changed. He'll be in the sick-room if he's anywhere.'

'All right,' said the Babe, as he went into his study. 'Buck up. I'll toss you for first bath in a second.'

Charteris walked on with Welch to their sanctum.

'You know,' said Welch seriously, stooping to unlace his boots, 'rotting apart, you really are a most awful ass. I wish I could get you to see it.'

'Never you mind, ducky,' said Charteris, 'I'm all right. I'll look after myself.'

Chapter 2

It was about a week after the Bargees' match that the rules respecting bounds were made stricter, much to the popular indignation. The penalty for visiting Stapleton without leave was increased from two hundred lines to two extra lessons. The venomous characteristic of extra lesson was that it cut into one's football, for the criminal was turned into a form-room from two till four on half-holidays, and so had to scratch all athletic engagements for the day, unless he chose to go for a solitary run afterwards. In the cricket term the effect of this was not so deadly. It was just possible that you might get an innings somewhere after four o'clock, even if only at the nets. But during the football season – it was now February – to be in extra lesson meant a total loss of everything that makes life endurable, and the School protested (to one another, in the privacy of their studies) with no uncertain voice against this barbarous innovation.

The reason for the change had been simple. At the corner of the High Street at Stapleton was a tobacconist's shop, and Mr Prater, strolling in one evening to renew his stock of Pioneer, was interested to observe P. St H. Harrison, of Merevale's, purchasing a consignment of 'Girl of my Heart' cigarettes (at twopence-halfpenny the packet of twenty, including a coloured picture of Lord Kitchener). Now, Mr Prater was one of the most sportsmanlike of masters. If he had merely met Harrison out of bounds, and it had been possible to have overlooked him, he would have done so. But such a proceeding in the interior of a small shop was impossible. There was nothing to palliate the crime. The tobacconist also kept the wolf from the door, and lured the juvenile population of the neighbourhood to it, by selling various weird brands of sweets, but it was only too obvious that Harrison was not after these. Guilt was in his eye, and the packet of cigarettes in his hand. Also Harrison's House cap was fixed firmly at the back of his head. Mr Prater finished buying his Pioneer, and went out without a word. That night it was announced to Harrison that the Headmaster wished to see him. The Headmaster saw him, though for a certain period of the interview he did not see the Headmaster, having turned his back on him by request. On the following day Stapleton was placed doubly out of bounds.

Tony, who was still in bed, had not heard the news when Charteris came to see him on the evening of the day on which the edict had gone forth.

'How are you getting on?' asked Charteris.

'Oh, fairly well. It's rather slow.'

'The grub seems all right.' Charteris absently reached out for a slice of cake.

'Not bad.'

'And you don't have to do any work.'

'No.'

'Well, then, it seems to me you're having a jolly good time. What don't you like about it?'

'It's so slow, being alone all day.'

'Makes you appreciate intellectual conversation all the more when you get it. Mine, for instance.'

'I want something to read.'

'I'll bring you a Sidgwick's *Greek Prose Composition*, if you like. Full of racy stories.'

'I've read 'em, thanks.'

'How about Jebb's *Homer*? You'd like that. Awfully interesting. Proves that there never was such a man as Homer, you know, and that the *Iliad* and the *Odyssey* were produced by evolution. General style, quietly funny. Make you roar.'

'Don't be an idiot. I'm simply starving for something to read. Haven't you got anything?'

'You've read all mine.'

'Hasn't Welch got any books?'

'Not one. He bags mine when he wants to read. I'll tell you what I will do if you like.'

'What?'

'Go into Stapleton, and borrow something from Adamson.' Adamson was the College doctor.

'By Jove, that's not a bad idea.'

'It's a dashed good idea, which wouldn't have occurred to anybody but a genius. I've been quite a pal of Adamson's ever since I had the flu. I go to tea with him occasionally, and we talk medical shop. Have you ever tried talking medical shop during tea? Nothing like it for giving you an appetite.'

'Has he got anything readable?'

'Rather. Have you ever tried anything of James Payn's?'

'I've read *Terminations*, or something,' said Tony doubtfully, 'but he's so obscure.'

'Don't,' said Charteris sadly, 'please don't. *Terminations* is by one Henry James, and there is a substantial difference between him and James Payn. Anyhow, if you want a short biography of James Payn, he wrote a hundred books, and they're all simply ripping, and Adamson has got a good many of them, and I'm hoping to borrow a couple – any two will do – and you're going to read them. I know one always bars a book that's recommended to one, but you've got no choice. You're not going to get anything else till you've finished those two.'

'All right,' said Tony. 'But Stapleton's out of bounds. I suppose Merevale'll give you leave to go in.'

'He won't,' said Charteris. 'I shan't ask him. On principle. So long.'

On the following afternoon Charteris went into Stapleton. The distance by road was almost exactly one mile. If you went by the fields it was longer, because you probably lost your way.

Dr Adamson's house was in the High Street. Charteris knocked at the door. The servant was sorry, but the doctor was out. Her tone seemed to suggest that, if she had had any say in the matter, he would have remained in. Would Charteris come in and wait? Charteris rather thought he would. He waited for half an hour, and then, as the absent medico did not appear to be coming, took two books from the shelf, wrote a succinct note explaining what he had done, and why he had done it, hoping the doctor would not mind, and went out with his literary trophies into the High Street again.

The time was now close on five o'clock. Lock-up was not till a quarter past six – six o'clock nominally, but the doors were always left open till a quarter past. It would take him about fifteen minutes to get back, less if he trotted. Obviously, the thing to do here was to spend a thoughtful quarter of an hour or so inspecting the sights of the town. These were ordinarily not numerous, but this particular day happened to be market day, and there was a good deal going on. The High Street was full of farmers, cows, and other animals, the majority of the former well on the road to intoxication. It is, of course, extremely painful to see a man in such a condition, but when such a person is endeavouring to count a perpetually moving drove of pigs, the onlooker's pain is sensibly diminished. Charteris strolled along the High Street observing these and other phenomena with an attentive eye. Opposite the Town Hall he was button-holed by a perfect stranger, whom, by his conversation, he soon recognized as the Stapleton 'character'. There is a 'character' in every small country town. He is not a bad character; still less is he a good character. He is just a 'character' pure and simple. This particular man – or rather, this man, for he was anything but particular – apparently took a great fancy to Charteris at first sight. He backed him gently against a wall, and insisted on telling him an interminable anecdote of his shady past, when, it seemed, he had been a 'super' in some travelling company. The plot of the story, as far as Charteris could follow it, dealt with a theatrical tour in Dublin, where some person or persons unknown had, with malice prepense, scattered several pounds of snuff on the stage previous to a performance of *Hamlet*; and, according to the 'character', when the ghost of Hamlet's father sneezed steadily throughout his great scene, there was not a dry eye in the house. The 'character' had concluded that anecdote, and was half-way through another, when Charteris, looking at his watch, found that it was almost six o'clock. He interrupted one of the 'character's' periods by diving past him and moving rapidly down the street. The historian did not seem to object. Charteris looked round and saw that he had button-holed a fresh victim. He was still gazing in one direction and walking in another, when he ran into somebody.

'Sorry,' said Charteris hastily. 'Hullo!'

It was the secretary of the Old Crockfordians, and, to judge from the scowl on that gentleman's face, the recognition was mutual.

'It's you, is it?' said the secretary in his polished way.

'I believe so,' said Charteris.

'Out of bounds,' observed the man.

Charteris was surprised. This grasp of technical lore on the part of a total outsider was as unexpected as it was gratifying.

'What do you know about bounds?' said Charteris.

'I know you ain't allowed to come 'ere, and you'll get it 'ot from your master for coming.'

'Ah, but he won't know. I shan't tell him, and I'm sure you will respect my secret.'

Charteris smiled in a winning manner.

'Ho!' said the man. 'Ho indeed!'

There is something very clinching about the word 'Ho'. It seems definitely to apply the closure to any argument. At least, I have never yet met anyone who could tell me the suitable repartee.

'Well,' said Charteris affably, 'don't let me keep you. I must be going on.'

'Ho!' observed the man once more. 'Ho indeed!'

'That's a wonderfully shrewd remark,' said Charteris. 'I can see that, but I wish you'd tell me exactly what it means.'

'You're out of bounds.'

'Your mind seems to run in a groove. You can't get off that bounds business. How do you know Stapleton's out of bounds?'

'I have made enquiries,' said the man darkly.

'By Jove,' said Charteris delightedly, 'this is splendid. You're a regular sleuth-hound. I dare say you've found out my name and House too?'

'I may 'ave,' said the man, 'or I may not 'ave.'

'Well, now you mention it, I suppose one of the two contingencies is probable. Well, I'm awfully glad to have met you. Good-bye. I must be going.'

'You're goin' with me.'

'Arm in arm?'

'I don't want to 'ave to take you.'

'No,' said Charteris, 'I should jolly well advise you not to try. This is my way.'

He walked on till he came to the road that led to St Austin's. The secretary of the Old Crockfordians stalked beside him with determined stride.

'Now,' said Charteris, when they were on the road, 'you mustn't mind if I walk rather fast. I'm in a hurry.'

Charteris's idea of walking rather fast was to dash off down the road at quarter-mile pace. The move took the man by surprise, but, after a moment, he followed with much panting. It was evident that he was not in training. Charteris began to feel that the walk home might be amusing in its way. After they had raced some three hundred yards he slowed down to a walk again. It was at this point that his companion evinced a desire to do the rest of the journey with a hand on the collar of his coat.

'If you touch me,' observed Charteris with a surprising knowledge of legal *minutiae*, 'it'll be a technical assault, and you'll get run in; and you'll get beans anyway if you try it on.'

The man reconsidered matters, and elected not to try it on.

Half a mile from the College Charteris began to walk rather fast again. He was a good half-miler, and his companion was bad at every distance. After a game struggle he dropped to the rear, and finished a hundred yards behind in considerable straits. Charteris shot in at Merevale's door with five minutes to spare, and went up to his study to worry Welch by telling him about it.

'Welch, you remember the Bargee who scragged Tony? Well, there have been all sorts of fresh developments. He's just been pacing me all the way from Stapleton.'

'Stapleton! Have you been to Stapleton? Did Merevale give you leave?'

'No. I didn't ask him.'

'You *are* an idiot. And now this Bargee man will go straight to the Old Man and run you in. I wonder you didn't think of that.'

'Curious I didn't.'

'I suppose he saw you come in here?'

'Rather. He couldn't have had a better view if he'd paid for a seat. Half a second; I must just run up with these volumes to Tony.'

When he came back he found Welch more serious than ever.

'I told you so,' said Welch. 'You're to go to the Old Man at once. He's just sent over for you. I say, look here, if it's only lines I don't mind doing some of them, if you like.'

Charteris was quite touched by this sporting offer.

'It's awfully good of you,' he said, 'but it doesn't matter, really. I shall be all right.'

Ten minutes later he returned, beaming.

'Well,' said Welch, 'what's he given you?'

'Only his love, to give to you. It was this way. He first asked me if I wasn't perfectly aware that Stapleton was out of bounds. "Sir," says I, "I've known it from childhood's earliest hour." "Ah," says he to me, "did Mr Merevale give you leave to go in this afternoon?" "No," says I, "I never consulted the gent you mention." '

'Well?'

'Then he ragged me for ten minutes, and finally told me I must go into extra the next two Saturdays.'

'I thought so.'

'Ah, but mark the sequel. When he had finished, I said that I was sorry I had mistaken the rules, but I had thought that a chap was allowed to go into Stapleton if he got leave from a master. "But you said that Mr Merevale did not give you leave," said he. "Friend of my youth," I replied courteously, "you are perfectly correct. As always. Mr Merevale did not give me leave, but," I added suavely, "Mr Dacre did." And I came away, chanting hymns of triumph in a mellow baritone, and leaving him in a dead faint on the sofa. And the Bargee, who was present during the conflict, swiftly and silently vanished away, his morale considerably shattered. And that, my gentle Welch,' concluded Charteris cheerfully, 'put me one up. So pass the biscuits, and let us rejoice if we never rejoice again.'

Chapter 3

The Easter term was nearing its end. Football, with the exception of the final House-match, which had still to come off, was over, and life was in consequence a trifle less exhilarating than it might have been. In some ways the last few weeks before the Easter holidays are quite pleasant. You can put on running shorts and a blazer and potter about the grounds, feeling strong and athletic, and delude yourself into the notion that you are training for the sports. Ten minutes at the broad jump, five with the weight, a few sprints on the track – it is all very amusing and harmless, but it is apt to become monotonous after a time. And if the weather is at all inclined to be chilly, such an occupation becomes impossible.

Charteris found things particularly dull. He was a fair average runner, but there were others far better at every distance, so that he saw no use in mortifying the flesh with strict training. On the other hand, in view of the fact that the final House-match had yet to be played, and that Merevale's was one of the two teams that were going to play it, it behoved him to keep himself at least moderately fit. The genial muffin and the cheery crumpet were still things to be avoided. He thus found himself in a position where, apparently, the few things which it was possible for him to do were barred, and the net result was that he felt slightly dull.

To make matters worse, all the rest of his set were working full time at their various employments, and had no leisure for amusing him. Welch practised hundred-yard sprints daily, and imagined that it would be quite a treat for Charteris to be allowed to time him. So he gave him the stopwatch, saw him safely to the end of the track, and at a given signal dashed off in the approved American style. By the time he reached the tape, dutifully held by two sporting Merevalian juniors, Charteris's attention had generally been attracted elsewhere. 'What time?' Welch would pant. 'By Jove,' Charteris would observe blandly, 'I forgot to look. About a minute and a quarter, I fancy.' At which Welch, who always had a notion that he had done it in ten and a fifth *that* time, at any rate, would dissemble his joy, and mildly suggest that somebody else should hold the watch. Then there was Jim Thomson, generally a perfect mine of elevating conversation. He was in for the mile and also the half, and refused to talk about anything except those distances, and the best methods for running them in the minimum of time. Charteris began to feel a blue melancholy stealing over him. The Babe, again. He might have helped to while away the long hours, but unfortunately the Babe had been taken very bad with a notion that he was going to win the 'cross-country run, and when, in addition to this, he was seized with a panic with regard to the prospects of the House team in the final, and began to throw out hints concerning strict training, Charteris regarded him as a person to be avoided. If he fled to the Babe for sympathy now, the Babe would be just as likely as not to suggest that he should come for a ten-mile spin with him, to get him into condition for the final Houser. The very thought of a ten-mile spin made Charteris feel faint. Lastly, there was Tony. But Tony's company was worse than none at all. He went about with his arm in a sling, and declined to be comforted. But for his injury, he would by now have been training hard for the Aldershot Boxing Competition, and the fact that he was now definitely out of it had a very depressing effect upon him. He lounged moodily about the gymnasium, watching Menzies, who was to take his place, sparring with the instructor, and refused consolation. Altogether, Charteris found life a distinct bore.

He was reduced to such straits for amusement, that one Wednesday afternoon, finding himself with nothing else to do, he was working at a burlesque and remarkably scurrilous article on 'The Staff, by one who has suffered', which he was going to insert in *The Glow Worm*, an unofficial periodical which he had started for the amusement of the School and his own and his contributors' profit. He was just warming to his work, and beginning to enjoy himself, when the door opened without a preliminary knock. Charteris deftly slid a piece of blotting-paper over his MS., for Merevale occasionally entered a study in this manner. And though there was nothing about Merevale himself in the article, it would be better perhaps, thought Charteris, if he did not see it. But it was not Merevale. It was somebody far worse. The Babe.

The Babe was clothed as to his body in football clothes, and as to face, in a look of holy enthusiasm. Charteris knew what that look meant. It meant that the Babe was going to try and drag him out for a run.

'Go away, Babe,' he said, 'I'm busy.'

'Why on earth are you slacking in here on this ripping afternoon?'

'Slacking!' said Charteris. 'I like that. I'm doing berrain work, Babe. I'm writing an article on masters and their customs, which will cause a profound sensation in the Common Room. At least it would, if they ever saw it, but they won't. Or I hope they won't for their sake *and* mine. So run away, my precious Babe, and don't disturb your uncle when he's busy.'

'Rot,' said the Babe firmly, 'you haven't taken any exercise for a week.'

Charteris replied proudly that he had wound up his watch only last night. The Babe refused to accept the remark as relevant to the matter in hand.

'Look here, Alderman,' he said, sitting down on the table, and gazing sternly at his victim, 'it's all very well, you know, but the final comes on in a few days, and you know you aren't in any too good training.'

'I am,' said Charteris, 'I'm as fit as a prize fighter. Simply full of beans. Feel my ribs.'

The Babe declined the offer.

'No, but I say,' he said plaintively, 'I wish you'd treat it seriously. It's getting jolly serious, really. If Dacre's win that cup again this year, that'll make four years running.'

'Not so,' said Charteris, like the mariner of infinite-resource-and-sagacity; 'not so, but far otherwise. It'll only make three.'

'Well, three's bad enough.'

'True, oh king, three is quite bad enough.'

'Well, then, there you are. Now you see.'

Charteris looked puzzled.

'Would you mind explaining that remark?' he said. 'Slowly.'

But the Babe had got off the table, and was prowling round the room, opening cupboards and boxes.

'What are you playing at?' enquired Charteris.

'Where do you keep your footer things?'

'What do you want with my footer things, if you don't mind my asking?'

'I'm going to help you put them on, and then you're coming for a run.'

'Ah,' said Charteris.

'Yes. Just a gentle spin to keep you in training. Hullo, this looks like them.'

He plunged both hands into a box near the window and flung out a mass of football clothes. It reminded Charteris of a terrier digging at a rabbit-hole.

He protested.

'Don't, Babe. Treat 'em tenderly. You'll be spoiling the crease in those bags if you heave 'em about like that. I'm very particular about how I look on the football field. *I* was always taught to dress myself like a little gentleman, so to speak. Well, now you've seen them, put 'em away.'

'Put 'em on,' said the Babe firmly.

'You are a beast, Babe. I don't want to go for a run. I'm getting too old for violent exercise.'

'Buck up,' said the Babe. 'We mustn't chuck any chances away. Now that Tony can't play, we shall have to do all we know if we want to win.'

'I don't see what need there is to get nervous about it. Considering we've got three of the First three-quarter line, and the Second Fifteen back, we ought to do pretty well.'

'But look at Dacre's scrum. There's Prescott, to start with. He's worth any two of our men put together. Then they've got Carter, Smith, and Hemming out of the first, and Reeve-Jones out of the second. And their outsides aren't so very bad, if you come to think of it. Bannister's in the first, and the other three-quarters are all good. And they've got both the second halves. You'll have practically to look after both of them now that Tony's crocked. And Baddeley has come on a lot this term.'

'Babe,' said Charteris, 'you have reason. I will turn over a new leaf. I *will* be good. Give me my things and I'll come for a run. Only please don't let it be anything over twenty miles.'

'Good man,' said the gratified Babe. 'We won't go far, and will take it quite easy.'

'I tell you what,' said Charteris. 'Do you know a place called Worbury? I thought you wouldn't, probably. It's only a sort of hamlet, two cottages, three public-houses, and a duck-pond, and that sort of thing. I only know it because Welch and I ran there once last year. It's in the Badgwick direction, about three miles by road, mostly along the level. I vote we muffle up fairly well, blazers and sweaters and so on, run to Worbury, tea at one of the cottages, and back in time for lock-up. How does that strike you?'

'It sounds all right. How about tea though? Are you certain you can get it?'

'Rather. The Oldest Inhabitant is quite a pal of mine.'

Charteris's circle of acquaintances was a standing wonder to the Babe and other Merevalians. He seemed to know everybody in the county.

When once he was fairly started on any business, physical or mental, Charteris generally shaped well. It was the starting that he found the difficulty. Now that he was actually in motion, he was enjoying himself thoroughly. He wondered why on earth he had been so reluctant to come for this run. The knowledge that there were three miles to go, and that he was equal to them, made him feel a new man. He felt fit. And there is nothing like feeling fit for dispelling boredom. He swung along with the Babe at a steady pace.

'There's the cottage,' he said, as they turned a bend of the road, and Worbury appeared a couple of hundred yards away. 'Let's sprint.' They sprinted, and arrived at the door of the cottage with scarcely a yard between them, much to the admiration of the Oldest Inhabitant, who was smoking a thoughtful pipe in his front garden. Mrs Oldest Inhabitant came out of the cottage at the sound of voices, and Charteris broached the subject of tea. The menu was sumptuous and varied, and even the Babe, in spite of his devotion to strict training, could scarce forbear to smile happily at the mention of hot cakes.

During the *mauvais quart d'heure* before the meal, Charteris kept up an animated conversation with the Oldest Inhabitant, the Babe joining in from time to time when he could think of anything to say. Charteris appeared to be quite a friend of the family. He enquired after the Oldest Inhabitant's rheumatics. It was gratifying to find that they were distinctly better. How had Mrs O. I. been since his last visit? Prarper hearty? Excellent. How was the O. I.'s nevvy?

At the mention of his nevvy the O. I. became discursive. He told his audience everything that had happened in connection with the said nevvy for years back. After which he started to describe what he would probably do in the future. Amongst other things, there were going to be some sports at Rutton today week, and his nevvy was going to try and win the cup for what the Oldest Inhabitant vaguely described as 'a race'. He had won it last year. Yes, prarper good runner, his nevvy. Where was Rutton? the Babe wanted to know. About eight miles out of Stapleton, said Charteris, who was well up in local geography. You got there by train. It was the next station.

Mrs O. I. came out to say that tea was ready, and, being drawn into the conversation on the subject of the Rutton sports, produced a programme of the same, which her nevvy had sent them. From this it seemed that the nevvy's 'spot' event was the egg and spoon race. An asterisk against his name pointed him out as the last year's winner.

'Hullo,' said Charteris, 'I see there's a strangers' mile. I'm a demon at the mile when I'm roused. I think I shall go in for it.'

He handed the programme back and began his tea.

'You know, Babe,' he said, as they were going back that evening, 'I really think I shall go in for that race. It would be a most awful rag. It's the day before the House-match, so it'll just get me fit.'

'Don't be a fool,' said the Babe. 'There would be a fearful row about it if you were found out. You'd get extras for the rest of your life.'

'Well, the final Houser comes off on a Thursday, so it won't affect that.'

'Yes, but still –'

'I shall think about it,' said Charteris. 'You needn't go telling anyone.'

'If you'll take my advice, you'll drop it.'

'Your suggestion has been noted, and will receive due attention,' said Charteris. 'Put on the pace a bit.'

They lengthened their stride, and conversation came to an abrupt end.

Chapter 4

'I shall go, Babe,' said Charteris on the following night.

The Sixth Form had a slack day before them on the morrow, there being a temporary lull in the form-work which occurred about once a week, when there was no composition of any kind to be done. The Sixth did four compositions a week, two Greek and two Latin, and except for these did not bother themselves very much about overnight preparation. The Latin authors which the form were doing were Livy and Virgil, and when either of these were on the next day's programme, most of the Sixth considered that they were justified in taking a night off. They relied on their ability to translate both authors at sight and without previous acquaintance. The popular notion that Virgil is hard rarely appeals to a member of a public school. There are two ways of translating Virgil, the conscientious and the other. He prefers the other.

On this particular night, therefore, work was 'off'. Merevale was over at the Great Hall, taking preparation, and the Sixth-Form Merevalians had assembled in Charteris's study to talk about things in general. It was after a pause of some moments, that had followed upon a lively discussion of the House's prospects in the forthcoming final, that Charteris had spoken.

'I shall go, Babe,' said he.

'Go where?' asked Tony, from the depths of a deck-chair.

'Babe knows.'

The Babe turned to the company and explained.

'The lunatic's going in for the strangers' mile at some sports at Rutton next week. He'll get booked for a cert. He can't see that. I never saw such a man.'

'Rally round,' said Charteris, 'and reason with me. I'll listen. Tony, what do you think about it?'

Tony expressed his opinion tersely, and Charteris thanked him. Welch, who had been reading, now awoke to the fact that a discussion was in progress, and asked for details. The Babe explained once more, and Welch heartily corroborated Tony's remarks. Charteris thanked him too.

'You aren't really going, are you?' asked Welch.

'Rather,' said Charteris.

'The Old Man won't give you leave.'

'Shan't worry the poor man with such trifles.'

'But it's miles out of bounds. Stapleton station is out of bounds to start with. It's against rules to go in a train, and Rutton's even more out of bounds than Stapleton.'

'And as there are sports there,' said Tony, 'the Old Man is certain to put Rutton specially out of bounds for that day. He always bars a St Austin's chap going to a place when there's anything going on there.'

'I don't care. What have I to do with the Old Man's petty prejudices? Now, let me get at my time-table. Here we are. Now then.'

'Don't be a fool,' said Tony,

'Certainly not. Look here, there's a train starts from Stapleton at three. I can catch that all right. Gets to Rutton at three-twenty. Sports begin at three-fifteen. At least, they are supposed to. Over before five, I should think. At least, my race will be, though I must stop to see the Oldest Inhabitant's nevvy win the egg and spoon canter. But that ought to come on before the strangers' race. Train back at a quarter past five. Arrives at a quarter to six. Lock up six-fifteen. That gives me half an hour to get here from Stapleton. What more do you want? I shall do it easily, and . . . the odds against my being booked are about twenty-five to one. At which price if any gent present cares to deposit his money, I am willing to take him. Now I'll treat you to a tune, if you're good.'

He went to the cupboard and produced his gramophone. Charteris's musical instruments had at one time been strictly suppressed by the authorities, and, in consequence, he had laid in a considerable stock of them. At last, when he discovered that there was no rule against the use of musical instruments in the House, Merevale had yielded. The stipulation that Charteris should play only before prep. was rigidly observed, except when Merevale was over at the Hall, and the Sixth had no work. On such occasions Charteris felt justified in breaking through the rule. He had a gramophone, a banjo, a penny whistle, and a mouth organ. The banjo, which he played really well, was the most in request, but the gramophone was also popular.

'Turn on "Whistling Rufus",' observed Thomson.

'Whistling Rufus' was duly turned on, giving way after an encore to 'Bluebells'.

'I always weep when I hear this,' said Tony.

'It *is* beautiful, isn't it?' said Charteris.

> I'll be your sweetheart, if you – will be – mine,
> All my life, I'll be your valentine.
> Bluebells I've gathered – grrhhrh.

The needle of the gramophone, after the manner of its kind, slipped raspingly over the surface of the wax, and the rest of the ballad was lost.

'That,' said Charteris, 'is how I feel with regard to the Old Man. I'd be his sweetheart, if he'd be mine. But he makes no advances, and the stain on my scutcheon is not yet wiped out. I must say I haven't tried gathering bluebells for him yet, nor have I offered my services as a perpetual valentine, but I've been very kind to him in other ways.'

'Is he still down on you?' asked the Babe.

'He hasn't done much lately. We're in a state of truce at present. Did I tell you how I scored about Stapleton?'

'You've only told us about a hundred times,' said the Babe brutally. 'I tell you what, though, he'll score off you if he finds you going to Rutton.'

'Let's hope he won't.'

'He won't,' said Welch suddenly.

'Why?'

'Because you won't go. I'll bet you anything you like that you won't go.'

That settled Charteris. It was the sort of remark that always acted on him like a tonic. He had been intending to go all the time, but it was this speech of Welch's that definitely clinched the matter. One of his mottoes for everyday use was 'Let not thyself be scored off by Welch.'

'That's all right,' he said. 'Of course I shall go. What's the next item you'd like on this machine?'

The day of the sports arrived, and the Babe, meeting Charteris at Merevale's gate, made a last attempt to head him off from his purpose.

'How are you going to take your things?' he asked. 'You can't carry a bag. The first beak you met would ask questions.'

If he had hoped that this would be a crushing argument, he was disappointed.

Charteris patted a bloated coat pocket.

'Bags,' he said laconically. 'Vest,' he added, doing the same to his other pocket. 'Shoes,' he concluded, 'you will observe I am carrying in a handy brown paper parcel, and if anybody wants to know what's in it, I shall tell them it's acid drops. Sure you won't come, too?'

'Quite, thanks.'

'All right. So long then. Be good while I'm gone.'

And he passed on down the road that led to Stapleton.

The Rutton Recreation Ground presented, as the *Stapleton Herald* justly remarked in its next week's issue, 'a gay and animated appearance'. There was a larger crowd than Charteris had expected. He made his way through them, resisting without difficulty the entreaties of a hoarse gentleman in a check suit to have three to two on 'Enery something for the hundred yards, and came at last to the dressing-tent.

At this point it occurred to him that it would be judicious to find out when his race was to start. It was rather a chilly day, and the less time he spent in the undress uniform of shorts the better. He bought a correct card for twopence, and scanned it. The strangers' mile was down for four-fifty. There was no need to change for an hour yet. He wished the authorities could have managed to date the event earlier.

Four-fifty was running it rather fine. The race would be over by about five to five, and it was a walk of some ten minutes to the station, less if he hurried. That would give him ten minutes for recovering from the effects of the race, and changing back into his ordinary clothes again. It would be quick work. But, having come so far, he was not inclined to go back without running in the race. He would never be able to hold his head up again if he did that. He left the dressing-tent, and started on a tour of the field.

The scene was quite different from anything he had ever witnessed before in the way of sports. The sports at St Austin's were decorous to a degree. These leaned more to the rollickingly convivial. It was like an ordinary race-meeting, except that men were running instead of horses. Rutton was a quiet little place for the majority of the year, but it woke up on this day, and was evidently out to enjoy itself. The Rural Hooligan was a good deal in evidence, and though he was comparatively quiet just at present, the frequency with which he visited the various refreshment stalls that dotted the ground gave promise of livelier times in the future. Charteris felt that the afternoon would not be dull.

The hour soon passed, and Charteris, having first seen the Oldest Inhabitant's nevvy romp home in the egg and spoon event, took himself off to the dressing-tent, and began to get into his running clothes. The bell for his race was just ringing when he left the tent. He trotted over to the starting place.

Apparently there was not a very large 'field'. Two weedy-looking youths of about Charteris's age, dressed in blushing pink, put in an appearance, and a very tall, thin man came up almost immediately afterwards. Charteris had just removed his coat, and was about to get to his place on the line, when another competitor arrived, and, to judge by the applause that greeted his appearance, he was evidently a favourite in the locality. It was with shock that Charteris recognized his old acquaintance, the Bargees' secretary.

He was clad in running clothes of a bright orange and a smile of conscious superiority, and when somebody in the crowd called out 'Go it, Jarge!' he accepted the tribute as his due, and waved a condescending hand in the speaker's direction.

Some moments elapsed before he recognized Charteris, and the latter had time to decide upon his line of action. If he attempted concealment in any way, the man would recognize that on this occasion, at any rate, he had, to use an adequate if unclassical expression, got the bulge, and then there would be trouble. By brazening things out, however, there was just a chance that he might make him imagine that there was more in the matter than met the eye, and that, in some mysterious way, he had actually obtained leave to visit Rutton that day. After all, the man didn't know very much about School rules, and the recollection of the recent fiasco in which he had taken part would make him think twice about playing the amateur policeman again, especially in connection with Charteris.

So he smiled genially, and expressed a hope that the man enjoyed robust health.

The man replied by glaring in a simple and unaffected manner.

'Looked up the Headmaster lately?' asked Charteris.

'What are you doing here?'

'I'm going to run. Hope you don't mind.'

'You're out of bounds.'

'That's what you said before. You'd better enquire a bit before you make rash statements. Otherwise, there's no knowing what may happen. Perhaps Mr Dacre has given me leave.'

The man said something objurgatory under his breath, but forbore to continue the discussion. He was wondering, as Charteris had expected that he would, whether the latter had really got leave or not. It was a difficult problem.

Whether such a result was due to his mental struggles, or whether it was simply to be attributed to his poor running, is open to question, but the fact remains that the secretary of the Old Crockfordians did not shine in the strangers' mile. He came in last but one, vanquishing the pink sportsman by a foot. Charteris, after a hot finish, was beaten on the tape by one of the weedy youths, who exhibited astounding sprinting powers in the last two hundred yards, overhauling Charteris, who had led all the time, in fine style, and scoring what the *Stapleton Herald* described as a 'highly popular victory'.

As soon as he had recovered his normal stock of wind – which was not immediately – it was borne in upon Charteris that if he wanted to catch the five-fifteen back to Stapleton, he had better be beginning to change. He went to the dressing-tent, and on examining his watch was horrified to find that he had just ten minutes in which to do everything, and the walk to the station, he reflected, was a long five minutes. He literally hurled himself into his clothes, and, disregarding the Bargee, who had entered the tent and seemed to wish to continue the discussion at the point where they had left off, shot off towards the gate nearest the station. He had exactly four minutes and twenty-five seconds in which to complete the journey, and he had just run a mile.

Chapter 5

Fortunately the road was mainly level. On the other hand, he was hampered by an overcoat. After the first hundred yards he took this off, and carried it in an unwieldy parcel. This, he found, answered admirably. Running became easier. He had worked the stiffness out of his legs by this time, and was going well. Three hundred yards from the station it was anybody's race. The exact position of the other competitor, the train, could not be defined. It was at any rate not yet within earshot, which meant that it still had at least a quarter of a mile to go. Charteris considered that he had earned a rest. He slowed down to a walk, but after proceeding at this pace for a few yards, thought that he heard a distant whistle, and dashed on again. Suddenly a raucous bellow of laughter greeted his ears from a spot in front of him, hidden from his sight by a bend in the road.

'Somebody slightly tight,' thought Charteris, rapidly diagnosing the case. 'By Jove, if he comes rotting about with me I'll kill him.' Having to do anything in a desperate hurry always made Charteris's temper slightly villainous. He turned the corner at a sharp trot, and came upon two youths who seemed to be engaged in the harmless occupation of trying to ride a bicycle. They were of the type which he held in especial aversion, the Rural Hooligan type, and one at least of the two had evidently been present at a recent circulation of the festive bowl. He was wheeling the bicycle about the road in an aimless manner, and looked as if he wondered what was the matter with it that it would not stay in the same place for two consecutive seconds. The other youth was apparently of the 'Charles-his-friend' variety, content to look on and applaud, and generally to play chorus to his companion's 'lead'. He was standing at the side of the road, smiling broadly in a way that argued feebleness of mind. Charteris was not quite sure which of the two types he loathed the more. He was inclined to call it a tie.

However, there seemed to be nothing particularly lawless in what they were doing now. If they were content to let him pass without hindrance, he, for his part, was content generously to overlook the insult they offered him in daring to exist, and to maintain a state of truce. But, as he drew nearer, he saw that there was more in this business than the casual spectator might at first have supposed. A second and keener inspection of the reptiles revealed fresh phenomena. In the first place, the bicycle which Hooligan number one was playing with was a lady's bicycle, and a small one at that. Now, up to the age of fourteen and the weight of ten stone, a beginner at cycling often finds it more convenient to learn to ride on a lady's machine than on a gentleman's. The former offers greater facilities for rapid dismounting, a quality not to be despised in the earlier stages of initiation. But, though this is undoubtedly the case, and though Charteris knew that it was so, yet he felt instinctively that there was something wrong here. Hooligans of twenty years and twelve stone do not learn to ride on small ladies' machines, or, if they do, it is probably without the permission of the small lady who owns the same. Valuable as his time was, Charteris felt that it behoved him to spend a thoughtful minute or so examining into this affair. He slowed down once again to a walk, and, as he did so, his eye fell upon the character in the drama whose absence had puzzled him, the owner of the bicycle. And from that moment he felt that life would be a hollow mockery if he failed to fall upon those revellers and slay them. She stood by the hedge on the right, a forlorn little figure in grey, and she gazed sadly and helplessly at the manoeuvres that were going on in the middle of the road. Her age Charteris put down at a venture at twelve – a correct guess. Her state of mind he also conjectured. She was letting 'I dare not' wait upon 'I would', like the late Macbeth, the cat i' the adage, and numerous other celebrities. She evidently had plenty of remarks to make on the subject in hand, but refrained from motives of prudence.

Charteris had no such scruples. The feeling of fatigue that had been upon him had vanished, and his temper, which had been growing steadily worse for some twenty minutes, now boiled over gleefully at the prospect of something solid to work itself off upon. Even without a cause Charteris detested the Rural Hooligan. Now that a real, copper-bottomed motive for this dislike had been supplied to him, he felt himself capable of dealing with a whole regiment of the breed. The criminal with the bicycle had just let it fall with a crash to the ground when Charteris went for him low, in the style which the Babe always insisted on seeing in members of the First Fifteen on the football field, and hove him without comment into a damp ditch. 'Charles his friend' uttered a shout of disapproval and rushed into the fray. Charteris gave him the straight left, of the type to which the great John Jackson is reported to have owed so much in the days of the old Prize Ring, and Charles, taking it between the eyes, stopped in a discouraged and discontented manner, and began to rub the place. Whereupon Charteris dashed in, and, to use an expression suitable to the deed, 'swung his right at the mark'. The 'mark', it may be explained for the benefit of the non-pugilistic, is that portion of the anatomy which lies hid behind the third button of the human waistcoat. It covers – in a most inadequate way – the wind, and even a gentle tap in the locality is apt to produce a fleeting sense of discomfort. A genuine flush hit on the spot, shrewdly administered by a muscular arm with the weight of the body behind it, causes the passive agent in the transaction to wish fervently, as far as he is at the moment physically capable of wishing anything, that he had never been born. 'Charles his friend' collapsed like an empty sack, and Charteris, getting a grip of the outlying portions of his costume, dragged him to the ditch and rolled him in on top of his friend, who had just recovered sufficiently to be thinking about getting out again. The pair of them lay there in a tangled heap. Charteris picked up the bicycle and gave it a cursory examination. The enamel was a good deal scratched, but no material damage had been done. He wheeled it across to its owner.

'It isn't much hurt,' he said, as they walked on slowly together. 'Bit scratched, that's all.'

'Thanks *awfully*,' said the small lady.

'Oh, not at all,' replied Charteris. 'I enjoyed it.' (He felt he had said the right thing there. Your real hero always 'enjoys it'.) 'I'm sorry those bargees frightened you.'

'They did rather. But' – she added triumphantly after a pause – 'I didn't cry.'

'Rather not,' said Charteris. 'You were awfully plucky. I noticed. But hadn't you better ride on? Which way were you going?'

'I wanted to get to Stapleton.'

'Oh. That's simple enough. You've merely got to go straight on down this road, as straight as ever you can go. But, look here, you know, you shouldn't be out alone like this. It isn't safe. Why did they let you?'

The lady avoided his eye. She bent down and inspected the left pedal.

'They shouldn't have sent you out alone,' said Charteris, 'why did they?'

'They – they didn't. I came.'

There was a world of meaning in the phrase. Charteris felt that he was in the same case. They had not let *him*. He had come. Here was a kindred spirit, another revolutionary soul, scorning the fetters of convention and the so-called authority of self-constituted rules, aha! Bureaucrats!

'Shake hands,' he said, 'I'm in just the same way.'

They shook hands gravely.

'You know,' said the lady, 'I'm awfully sorry I did it now. It was very naughty.'

'I'm not sorry yet,' said Charteris, 'I'm rather glad than otherwise. But I expect I shall be sorry before long.'

'Will you be sent to bed?'

'I don't think so.'

'Will you have to learn beastly poetry?'

'Probably not.'

She looked at him curiously, as if to enquire, 'then if you won't have to learn poetry and you won't get sent to bed, what on earth is there for you to worry about?'

She would probably have gone on to investigate the problem further, but at that moment there came the sound of a whistle. Then another, closer this time. Then a faint rumbling, which increased in volume steadily. Charteris looked back. The railway line ran by the side of the road. He could see the smoke of a train through the trees. It was quite close now, and coming closer every minute, and he was still quite a hundred and fifty yards from the station gates.

'I say,' he cried. 'Great Scott, here comes my train. I must rush. Good-bye. You keep straight on.'

His legs had had time to grow stiff again. For the first few strides running was painful. But his joints soon adapted themselves to the strain, and in ten seconds he was sprinting as fast as he had ever sprinted off the running-track. When he had travelled a quarter of the distance the small cyclist overtook him.

'Be quick,' she said, 'it's just in sight.'

Charteris quickened his stride, and, paced by the bicycle, spun along in fine style. Forty yards from the station the train passed him. He saw it roll into the station. There were still twenty yards to go, exclusive of the station's steps, and he was already running as fast as it lay in him to run. Now there were only ten. Now five. And at last, with a hurried farewell to his companion, he bounded up the steps and on to the platform. At the end of the platform the line took a sharp curve to the left. Round that curve the tail end of the guard's van was just disappearing.

'Missed it, sir,' said the solitary porter, who managed things at Rutton, cheerfully. He spoke as if he was congratulating Charteris on having done something remarkably clever.

'When's the next?' panted Charteris.

'Eight-thirty,' was the porter's appalling reply.

For a moment Charteris felt quite ill. No train till eight-thirty! Then was he indeed lost. But it couldn't be true. There must be some sort of a train between now and then.

'Are you certain?' he said. 'Surely there's a train before that?'

'Why, yes, sir,' said the porter gleefully, 'but they be all exprusses. Eight-thirty be the only 'un what starps at Rootton.'

'Thanks,' said Charteris with marked gloom, 'I don't think that'll be much good to me. My aunt, what a hole I'm in.'

The porter made a sympathetic and interrogative noise at the back of his throat, as if inviting him to explain everything. But Charteris felt unequal to conversation. There are moments when one wants to be alone. He went down the steps again. When he got out into the road, his small cycling friend had vanished. Charteris was conscious of a feeling of envy towards her. She was doing the journey comfortably on a bicycle. He would have to walk it. Walk it! He didn't believe he could. The strangers' mile, followed by the Homeric combat with the two Hooligans and that ghastly sprint to wind up with, had left him decidedly unfit for further feats of pedestrianism. And it was eight miles to Stapleton, if it was a yard, and another mile from Stapleton to St Austin's. Charteris, having once more invoked the name of his aunt, pulled himself together with an effort, and limped gallantly on in the direction of Stapleton. But fate, so long hostile to him, at last relented. A rattle of wheels approached him from behind. A thrill of hope shot through him at the sound. There was the prospect of a lift. He stopped, and waited for the dog-cart – it sounded like a dog-cart – to arrive. Then he uttered a shout of rapture, and began to wave his arms like a semaphore. The man in the dog-cart was Dr Adamson.

'Hullo, Charteris,' said the Doctor, pulling up his horse, 'what are you doing here?'

'Give me a lift,' said Charteris, 'and I'll tell you. It's a long yarn. Can I get in?'

'Come along. Plenty of room.'

Charteris climbed up, and sank on to the cushioned seat with a sigh of pleasure. What glorious comfort. He had never enjoyed anything more in his life.

'I'm nearly dead,' he said, as the dog-cart went on again. 'This is how it all happened. You see, it was this way –'

And he embarked forthwith upon his narrative.

Chapter 6

By special request the Doctor dropped Charteris within a hundred yards of Merevale's door.

'Good-night,' he said. 'I don't suppose you will value my advice at all, but you may have it for what it is worth. I recommend you stop this sort of game. Next time something will happen.'

'By Jove, yes,' said Charteris, climbing painfully down from the dog-cart, 'I'll take that advice. I'm a reformed character from this day onwards. This sort of thing isn't good enough. Hullo, there's the bell for lock-up. Good-night, Doctor, and thanks most awfully for the lift. It was frightfully kind of you.'

'Don't mention it,' said Dr Adamson, 'it is always a privilege to be in your company. When are you coming to tea with me again?'

'Whenever you'll have me. I must get leave, though, this time.'

'Yes. By the way, how's Graham? It is Graham, isn't it? The fellow who broke his collar-bone?'

'Oh, he's getting on splendidly. Still in a sling, but it's almost well again now. But I must be off. Good-night.'

'Good-night. Come to tea next Monday.'

'Right,' said Charteris; 'thanks awfully.'

He hobbled in at Merevale's gate, and went up to his study. The Babe was in there talking to Welch.

'Hullo,' said the Babe, 'here's Charteris.'

'What's left of him,' said Charteris.

'How did it go off?'

'Don't, please.'

'Did you win?' asked Welch.

'No. Second. By a yard. Oh, Lord, I am dead.'

'Hot race?'

'Rather. It wasn't that, though. I had to sprint all the way to the station, and missed my train by ten seconds at the end of it all.'

'Then how did you get here?'

'That was the one stroke of luck I've had this afternoon. I started to walk back, and after I'd gone about a quarter of a mile, Adamson caught me up in his dog-cart. I suggested that it would be a Christian act on his part to give me a lift, and he did. I shall remember Adamson in my will.'

'Tell us what happened.'

'I'll tell thee everything I can,' said Charteris. 'There's little to relate. I saw an aged, aged man a-sitting on a gate. Where do you want me to begin?'

'At the beginning. Don't rot.'

'I was born,' began Charteris, 'of poor but honest parents, who sent me to school at an early age in order that I might acquire a grasp of the Greek and Latin languages, now obsolete. I –'

'How did you lose?' enquired the Babe.

'The other man beat me. If he hadn't, I should have won hands down. Oh, I say, guess who I met at Rutton.'

'Not a beak?'

'No. Almost as bad, though. The Bargee man who paced me from Stapleton. Man who crocked Tony.'

'Great *Scott*!' cried the Babe. 'Did he recognize you?'

'Rather. We had a very pleasant conversation.'

'If he reports you,' began the Babe.

'Who's that?'

Charteris looked up. Tony Graham had entered the study.

'Hullo, Tony! Adamson told me to remember him to you.'

'So you've got back?'

Charteris confirmed the hasty guess.

'But what are you talking about, Babe?' said Tony. 'Who's going to be reported, and who's going to report?'

The Babe briefly explained the situation.

'If the man,' he said, 'reports Charteris, he may get run in tomorrow, and then we shall have both our halves away against Dacre's. Charteris, you are a fool to go rotting about out of bounds like this.'

'Nay, dry the starting tear,' said Charteris cheerfully. 'In the first place, I shouldn't get kept in on a Thursday anyhow. I should be shoved into extra on Saturday. Also, I shrewdly conveyed to the Bargee the impression that I was at Rutton by special permission.'

'He's bound to know that that can't be true,' said Tony.

'Well, I told him to think it over. You see, he got so badly left last time he tried to compass my downfall, that I shouldn't be a bit surprised if he let the job alone this journey.'

'Let's hope so,' said the Babe gloomily.

'That's right, Babby,' remarked Charteris encouragingly, nodding at the pessimist.

'You buck up and keep looking on the bright side. It'll be all right. You see if it won't. If there's any running in to be done, I shall do it. I shall be frightfully fit tomorrow after all this dashing about today. I haven't an ounce of superfluous flesh on me. I'm a fine, strapping specimen of sturdy young English manhood. And I'm going to play a *very* selfish game tomorrow, Babe.'

'Oh, my dear chap, you mustn't.' The Babe's face wore an expression of horror. The success of the House-team in the final was very near to his heart. He could not understand anyone jesting on the subject. Charteris respected his anguish, and relieved it speedily.

'I was only ragging,' he said. 'Considering that our three-quarter line is our one strong point, I'm not likely to keep the ball from it, if I get a chance of getting it out. Make your mind easy, Babe.'

The final House-match was always a warmish game. The rivalry between the various Houses was great, and the football cup especially was fought for with immense keenness. Also, the match was the last fixture of the season, and there was a certain feeling in the teams that if they *did* happen to disable a man or two, it would not matter much. The injured sportsman would not be needed for School-match purposes for another six months. As a result of which philosophical reflection, the tackling was ruled slightly energetic, and the handing-off was done with vigour.

This year, to add a sort of finishing touch, there was just a little ill-feeling between Dacre's and Merevale's. The cause of it was the Babe.

Until the beginning of the term he had been a day boy. Then the news began to circulate that he was going to become a boarder, either at Dacre's or at Merevale's. He chose the latter, and Dacre's felt slightly aggrieved. Some of the less sportsmanlike members of the House had proposed that a protest should be made against his being allowed to play, but, fortunately for the credit of Dacre's, Prescott, the captain of the House Fifteen, had put his foot down with an emphatic bang at the suggestion. As he sagely pointed out, there were some things which were bad form, and this was one of them. If the team wanted to express their disapproval, said he, let them do it on the field by tackling their very hardest. He personally was going to do his best, and he advised them to do the same.

The rumour of this bad blood had got about the School in some mysterious manner, and when Swift, Merevale's only First Fifteen forward, kicked off up the hill, a large crowd was lining the ropes. It was evident from the outset that it would be a good game.

Dacre's were the better side – as a team. They had no really weak spot. But Merevale's extraordinarily strong three-quarter line somewhat made up for an inferior scrum. And the fact that the Babe was in the centre was worth much.

At first Dacre's pressed. Their pack was unusually heavy for a House-team, and they made full use of it. They took the ball down the field in short rushes till they were in Merevale's twenty-five. Then they began to heel, and, if things had been more or less exciting for the Merevalians before, they became doubly so now. The ground was dry, and so was the ball, and the game consequently waxed fast. Time after time the ball went along Dacre's three-quarter line, only to end by finding itself hurled, with the wing who was carrying it, into touch. Occasionally the centres, instead of feeding their wings, would try to dodge through themselves. And that was where the Babe came in. He was admittedly the best tackler in the School, but on this occasion he excelled himself. His man never had a chance of getting past. At last a lofty kick into touch over the heads of the spectators gave the players a few seconds' rest.

The Babe went up to Charteris.

'Look here,' he said, 'it's risky, but I think we'll try having the ball out a bit.'

'In our own twenty-five?' said Charteris.

'Wherever we are. I believe it will come off all right. Anyway, we'll try it. Tell the forwards.'

For forwards playing against a pack much heavier than themselves, it is easier to talk about letting the ball out than to do it. The first half dozen times that Merevale's scrum tried to heel they were shoved off their feet, and it was on the enemy's side that the ball went out. But the seventh attempt succeeded. Out it came, cleanly and speedily. Daintree, who was playing instead of Tony, switched it across to Charteris. Charteris dodged the half who was marking him, and ran. Heeling and passing in one's own twenty-five is like smoking – an excellent practice if indulged in in moderation. On this occasion it answered perfectly. Charteris ran to the half-way line, and handed the ball on to the Babe. The Babe was tackled from behind, and passed to Thomson. Thomson dodged his man, and passed to Welch on the wing. Welch was the fastest sprinter in the School. It was a pleasure – if you did not happen to be one of the opposing side – to see him race down the touch-line. He was off like an arrow. Dacre's back made a futile attempt to get at him. Welch could have given the back fifteen yards in a hundred. He ran round him, and, amidst terrific applause from the Merevale's-supporting section of the audience, scored between the posts. The Babe took the kick and converted without difficulty. Five minutes afterwards the whistle blew for half-time.

The remainder of the game does not call for detailed description. Dacre's pressed nearly the whole of the last half hour, but twice more the ball came out and went down Merevale's three-quarter line. Once it was the Babe who scored with a run from his own goal-line, and once Charteris, who got in from half-way, dodging through the whole team. The last ten minutes of the game was marked by a slight excess of energy on both sides. Dacre's forwards were in a decidedly bad temper, and fought like tigers to break through, and Merevale's played up to them with spirit. The Babe seemed continually to be precipitating himself at the feet of rushing forwards, and Charteris felt as if at least a dozen bones were broken in various portions of his anatomy. The game ended on Merevale's line, but they had won the match and the cup by two goals and a try to nothing.

Charteris limped off the field, cheerful but damaged. He ached all over, and there was a large bruise on his left cheek-bone. He and Babe were going to the House, when they were aware that the Headmaster was beckoning to them.

'Well, MacArthur, and what was the result of the match?'

'We won, sir,' boomed the Babe. 'Two goals and a try to *nil*.'

'You have hurt your cheek, Charteris?'

'Yes, sir.'

'How did you do that?'

'I got a kick, sir, in one of the rushes.'

'Ah. I should bathe it, Charteris. Bathe it well. I hope it will not be very painful. Bathe it well in warm water.'

He walked on.

'You know,' said Charteris to the Babe, as they went into the House, 'the Old Man isn't such a bad sort after all. He has his points, don't you think?'

The Babe said that he did.

'I'm going to reform, you know,' continued Charteris confidentially.

'It's about time,' said the Babe. 'You can have the bath first if you like. Only buck up.'

Charteris boiled himself for ten minutes, and then dragged his weary limbs to his study. It was while he was sitting in a deck-chair eating mixed biscuits, and wondering if he would ever be able to summon up sufficient energy to put on garments of civilization, that somebody knocked at the door.

'Yes,' shouted Charteris. 'What is it? Don't come in. I'm changing.'

The melodious treble of Master Crowinshaw, his fag, made itself heard through the keyhole.

'The Head told me to tell you that he wanted to see you at the School House as soon as you can go.'

'All right,' shouted Charteris. 'Thanks.'

'Now what,' he continued to himself, 'does the Old Man want to see me for? Perhaps he wants to make certain that I've bathed my cheek in warm water. Anyhow, I suppose I must go.'

A quarter of an hour later he presented himself at the Headmagisterial door. The sedate Parker, the Head's butler, who always filled Charteris with a desire to dig him hard in the ribs just to see what would happen, ushered him into the study.

The Headmaster was reading by the light of a lamp when Charteris came in. He laid down his book, and motioned him to a seat; after which there was an awkward pause.

'I have just received,' began the Head at last, 'a most unpleasant communication. Most unpleasant. From whom it comes I do not know. It is, in fact – er – anonymous. I am sorry that I ever read it.'

He stopped. Charteris made no comment. He guessed what was coming. He, too, was sorry that the Head had ever read the letter.

'The writer says that he saw you, that he actually spoke to you, at the athletic sports at Rutton yesterday. I have called you in to tell me if that is true.' The Head fastened an accusing eye on his companion.

'It is quite true, sir,' said Charteris steadily.

'What!' said the Head sharply. 'You were at Rutton?'

'Yes, sir.'

'You were perfectly aware, I suppose, that you were breaking the School rules by going there, Charteris?' enquired the Head in a cold voice.

'Yes, sir.' There was another pause.

'This is very serious,' began the Head. 'I cannot overlook this. I –'

There was a slight scuffle of feet in the passage outside. The door flew open vigorously, and a young lady entered. It was, as Charteris recognized in a minute, his acquaintance of the afternoon, the young lady of the bicycle.

'Uncle,' she said, 'have you seen my book anywhere?'

'Hullo!' she broke off as her eye fell on Charteris.

'Hullo!' said Charteris, affably, not to be outdone in the courtesies.

'Did you catch your train?'

'No. Missed it.'

'Hullo! what's the matter with your cheek?'

'I got a kick on it.'

'Oh, does it hurt?'

'Not much, thanks.'

Here the Head, feeling perhaps a little out of it, put in his oar.

'Dorothy, you must not come here now. I am busy. And how, may I ask, do you and Charteris come to be acquainted?'

'Why, he's him,' said Dorothy lucidly.

The Head looked puzzled.

'Him. The chap, you know.'

It is greatly to the Head's credit that he grasped the meaning of these words. Long study of the classics had quickened his faculty for seeing sense in passages where there was none. The situation dawned upon him.

'Do you mean to tell me, Dorothy, that it was Charteris who came to your assistance yesterday?'

Dorothy nodded energetically.

'He gave the men beans,' she said. 'He did, really,' she went on, regardless of the Head's look of horror. 'He used right and left with considerable effect.'

Dorothy's brother, a keen follower of the Ring, had been good enough some days before to read her out an extract from an account in *The Sportsman* of a match at the National Sporting Club, and the account had been much to her liking. She regarded it as a masterpiece of English composition.

'Dorothy,' said the Headmaster, 'run away to bed.' A suggestion which she treated with scorn, it wanting a clear two hours to her legal bedtime. 'I must speak to your mother about your deplorable habit of using slang. Dear me, I must certainly speak to her.'

And, shamefully unabashed, Dorothy retired.

The Head was silent for a few minutes after she had gone; then he turned to Charteris again.

'In consideration of this, Charteris, I shall – er – mitigate slightly the punishment I had intended to give you.'

Charteris murmured his gratification.

'But,' continued the Head sternly, 'I cannot overlook the offence. I have my duty to consider. You will therefore write me – er – ten lines of Virgil by tomorrow evening, Charteris.'

'Yes, sir.'

'Latin *and* English,' said the relentless pedagogue.

'Yes, sir.'

'And, Charteris – I am speaking now – er – unofficially, not as a headmaster, you understand – if in future you would cease to break School rules simply as a matter of principle, for that, I fancy, is what it amounts to, I – er – well, I think we should get on better together. And that is, on my part at least, a consummation – er – devoutly to be wished. Good-night, Charteris.'

'Good-night, sir.'

The Head extended a large hand. Charteris took it, and his departure.

The Headmaster opened his book again, and turned over a new leaf. Charteris at the same moment, walking slowly in the direction of Merevale's, was resolving for the future to do the very same thing. And he did.

[9]

How Payne Bucked Up

I

It was Walkinshaw's affair from the first. Grey, the captain of the St Austin's Fifteen, was in the infirmary nursing a bad knee. To him came Charles Augustus Walkinshaw with a scheme. Walkinshaw was football secretary, and in Grey's absence acted as captain. Besides these two there were only a couple of last year's team left – Reade and Barrett, both of Philpott's House.

'Hullo, Grey, how's the knee?' said Walkinshaw.

'How's the team getting on?' he said.

'Well, as far as I can see,' said Walkinshaw, 'we ought to have a rather good season, if you'd only hurry up and come back. We beat a jolly hot lot of All Comers yesterday. Smith was playing for them. The Blue, you know. And lots of others. We got a goal and a try to *nil*.'

'Good,' said Grey. 'Who did anything for us? Who scored?'

'I got in once. Payne got the other.'

'By Jove, did he? What sort of a game is he playing this year?'

The moment had come for Walkinshaw to unburden himself to his scheme. He proceeded to do so.

'Not up to much,' he said. 'Look here, Grey, I've got rather an idea. It's my opinion Payne's not bucking up nearly as much as he might. Do you mind if I leave him out of the next game?'

Grey stared. The idea was revolutionary.

'What! Leave him out? My good man, he'll be the next chap to get his colours. He's a cert. for his cap.'

'That's just it. He knows he's a cert., and he's slacking on the strength of it. Now, my idea is that if you slung him out for a match or two, he'd buck up extra hard when he came into the team again. Can't I have a shot at it?'

Grey weighed the matter. Walkinshaw pressed home his arguments.

'You see, it isn't like cricket. At cricket, of course, it might put a chap off awfully to be left out, but I don't see how it can hurt a man's play at footer. Besides, he's beginning to stick on side already.'

'Is he, by Jove?' said Grey. This was the unpardonable sin. 'Well, I'll tell you what you can do if you like. Get up a scratch game, First Fifteen *v.* Second, and make him captain of the Second.'

'Right,' said Walkinshaw, and retired beaming.

Walkinshaw, it may be remarked at once, to prevent mistakes, was a well-meaning idiot. There was no doubt about his being well-meaning. Also, there was no doubt about his being an idiot. He was continually getting insane ideas into his head, and being unable to get them out again. This matter of Payne was a good example of his customary methods. He had put his hand on the one really first-class forward St Austin's possessed, and proposed to remove him from the team. And yet through it all he was perfectly well-meaning. The fact that personally he rather disliked Payne had, to do him justice, no weight at all with him. He would have done the same by his bosom friend under like circumstances. This is the only excuse that can be offered for him. It was true that Payne regarded himself as a certainty for his colours, as far as anything can be considered certain in this vale of sorrow. But to accuse him of trading on this, and, to use the vernacular, of putting on side, was unjust to a degree.

On the afternoon following this conversation Payne, who was a member of Dacre's House, came into his study and banged his books down on the table with much emphasis. This was a sign that he was feeling dissatisfied with the way in which affairs were conducted in the world. Bowden, who was asleep in an armchair – he had been staying in with a cold – woke with a start. Bowden shared Payne's study. He played centre three-quarter for the Second Fifteen.

'Hullo!' he said.

Payne grunted. Bowden realized that matters had not been going well with him. He attempted to soothe him with conversation, choosing what he thought would be a congenial topic.

'What's on on Saturday?' he asked.

'Scratch game. First *v.* Second.'

Bowden groaned.

'I know those First *v.* Second games,' he said. 'They turn the Second out to get butchered for thirty-five minutes each way, to improve the First's combination. It may be fun for the First, but it's not nearly so rollicking for us. Look here, Payne, if you find me with the pill at any time, you can let me down easy, you know. You needn't go bringing off any of your beastly gallery tackles.'

'I won't,' said Payne. 'To start with, it would be against rules. We happen to be on the same side.'

'Rot, man; I'm not playing for the First.' This was the only explanation that occurred to him.

'I'm playing for the Second.'

'What! Are you certain?'

'I've seen the list. They're playing Babington instead of me.'

'But why? Babington's no good.'

'I think they have a sort of idea I'm slacking or something. At any rate, Walkinshaw told me that if I bucked up I might get tried again.'

'Silly goat,' said Bowden. 'What are you going to do?'

'I'm going to take his advice, and buck up.'

II

He did. At the beginning of the game the ropes were lined by some thirty spectators, who had come to derive a languid enjoyment from seeing the First pile up a record score. By half-time their numbers had risen to an excited mob of something over three hundred, and the second half of the game was fought out to the accompaniment of a storm of yells and counter yells such as usually only belonged to school-matches. The Second Fifteen, after a poor start, suddenly awoke to the fact that this was not going to be the conventional massacre by any means. The First had scored an unconverted try five minutes after the kick-off, and it was after this that the Second began to get together. The school back bungled the drop out badly, and had to find touch in his own twenty-five, and after that it was anyone's game. The scrums were a treat to behold. Payne was a monument of strength. Time after time the Second had the ball out to their three-quarters, and just after half-time Bowden slipped through in the corner. The kick failed, and the two teams, with their scores equal now, settled down grimly to fight the thing out to a finish. But though they remained on their opponents' line for most of the rest of the game, the Second did not add to their score, and the match ended in a draw of three points all.

The first intimation Grey received of this came to him late in the evening. He had been reading a novel which, whatever its other merits may have been, was not interesting, and it had sent him to sleep. He awoke to hear a well-known voice observe with some unction: 'Ah! M'yes. Leeches and hot fomentations.' This effectually banished sleep. If there were two things in the world that he loathed, they were leeches and hot fomentations, and the School doctor apparently regarded them as a panacea for every kind of bodily ailment, from a fractured skull to a cold in the head. It was this gentleman who had just spoken, but Grey's alarm vanished as he perceived that the words had no personal application to himself. The object of the remark was a fellow-sufferer in the next bed but one. Now Grey was certain that when he had fallen asleep there had been nobody in that bed. When, therefore, the medical expert had departed on his fell errand, the quest of leeches and hot fomentations, he sat up and gave tongue.

'Who's that in that bed?' he asked.

'Hullo, Grey,' replied a voice. 'Didn't know you were awake. I've come to keep you company.'

'That you, Barrett? What's up with you?'

'Collar-bone. Dislocated it or something. Reade's over in that corner. He has bust his ankle. Oh, yes, we've been having a nice, cheery afternoon,' concluded Barrett bitterly.

'Great Scott! How did it happen?'

'Payne.'

'Where? In your collar-bone?'

'Yes. That wasn't what I meant, though. What I was explaining was that Payne got hold of me in the middle of the field, and threw me into touch. After which he fell on me. That was enough for my simple needs. I'm not grasping.'

'How about Reade?'

'The entire Second scrum collapsed on top of Reade. When we dug him out his ankle was crocked. Mainspring gone, probably. Then they gathered up the pieces and took them gently away. I don't know how it all ended.'

Just then Walkinshaw burst into the room. He had a large bruise over one eye, his arm was in a sling, and he limped. But he was in excellent spirits.

'I knew I was right, by Jove,' he observed to Grey. 'I knew he could buck up if he liked.'

'I know it now,' said Barrett.

'Who's this you're talking about?' said Grey.

'Payne. I've never seen anything like the game he played today. He was everywhere. And, by Jove, his *tackling*!'

'Don't,' said Barrett, wearily.

'It's the best match I ever played in,' said Walkinshaw, bubbling over with enthusiasm. 'Do you know, the Second had all the best of the game.'

'What was the score?'

'Draw. One try all.'

'And now I suppose you're satisfied?' enquired Barrett. The great scheme for the regeneration of Payne had been confided to him by its proud patentee.

'Almost,' said Walkinshaw. 'We'll continue the treatment for one more game, and then we'll have him simply fizzing for the Windybury match. That's next Saturday. By the way, I'm afraid you'll hardly be fit again in time for that, Barrett, will you?'

'I may possibly,' said Barrett, coldly, 'be getting about again in time for the Windybury match of the year after next. This year I'm afraid I shall not have the pleasure. And I should strongly advise you, if you don't want to have to put a team of cripples into the field, to discontinue the treatment, as you call it.'

'Oh, I don't know,' said Walkinshaw.

On the following Wednesday evening, at five o'clock, something was carried in on a stretcher, and deposited in the bed which lay between Grey and Barrett. Close scrutiny revealed the fact that it was what had once been Charles Augustus Walkinshaw. He was slightly broken up.

'Payne?' enquired Grey in chilly tones.

Walkinshaw admitted the impeachment.

Grey took a pencil and a piece of paper from the table at his side. 'If you want to know what I'm doing,' he said, 'I'm writing out the team for the Windybury match, and I'm going to make Payne captain, as the senior Second Fifteen man. And if we win I'm jolly well going to give him his cap after the match. If we don't win, it'll be the fault of a raving lunatic of the name of Walkinshaw, with his beastly Colney Hatch schemes for reforming slack forwards. You utter rotter!'

Fortunately for the future peace of mind of C. A. Walkinshaw, the latter contingency did not occur. The School, in spite of its absentees, contrived to pull the match off by a try to *nil*. Payne, as was only right and proper, scored the try, making his way through the ranks of the visiting team with the quiet persistence of a steam-roller. After the game he came to tea, by request, at the infirmary, and was straightaway invested by Grey with his First Fifteen colours. On his arrival he surveyed the invalids with interest.

'Rough game, footer,' he observed at length.

'Don't mention it,' said Barrett politely. 'Leeches,' he added dreamily. 'Leeches and hot fomentations. *Boiling* fomentations. Will somebody kindly murder Walkinshaw!'

'Why?' asked Payne, innocently.

[10]

Author!

J. S. M. Babington, of Dacre's House, was on the horns of a dilemma. Circumstances over which he had had no control had brought him, like another Hercules, to the cross-roads, and had put before him the choice between pleasure and duty, or, rather, between pleasure and what those in authority called duty. Being human, he would have had little difficulty in making his decision, had not the path of pleasure been so hedged about by danger as to make him doubt whether after all the thing could be carried through.

The facts in the case were these. It was the custom of the mathematical set to which J. S. M. Babington belonged, 4B to wit, to relieve the tedium of the daily lesson with a species of round game which was played as follows. As soon as the master had taken his seat, one of the players would execute a manoeuvre calculated to draw attention on himself, such as dropping a book or upsetting the blackboard. Called up to the desk to give explanation, he would embark on an eloquent speech for the defence. This was the cue for the next player to begin. His part consisted in making his way to the desk and testifying to the moral excellence of his companion, and giving in full the reasons why he should be discharged without a stain upon his character. As soon as he had warmed to his work he would be followed by a third player, and so on until the standing room around the desk was completely filled with a great cloud of witnesses. The duration of the game varied, of course, considerably. On some occasions it could be played through with such success, that the master would enter into the spirit of the thing, and do his best to book the names of all offenders at one and the same time, a feat of no inconsiderable difficulty. At other times matters would come to a head more rapidly. In any case, much innocent fun was to be derived from it, and its popularity was great. On the day, however, on which this story opens, a new master had been temporarily loosed into the room in place of the Rev. Septimus Brown, who had been there as long as the oldest inhabitant could remember.

The Rev. Septimus was a wrangler, but knew nothing of the ways of the human boy. His successor, Mr Reginald Seymour, was a poor mathematician, but a good master. He had been, moreover, a Cambridge Rugger Blue. This fact alone should have ensured him against the customary pleasantries, for a Blue is a man to be respected. It was not only injudicious, therefore, but positively wrong of Babington to plunge against the blackboard on his way to his place. If he had been a student of Tennyson, he might have remembered that the old order is in the habit of changing and yielding place to the new.

Mr Seymour looked thoughtfully for a moment at the blackboard.

'That was rather a crude effort,' he said pleasantly to Babington, 'you lack *finesse*. Pick it up again, please.'

Babington picked it up without protest. Under the rule of the Rev. Septimus this would have been the signal for the rest of the class to leave their places and assist him, but now they seemed to realize that there was a time for everything, and that this was decidedly no time for indoor games.

'Thank you,' said Mr Seymour, when the board was in its place again. 'What is your name? Eh, what? I didn't quite hear.'

'Babington, sir.'

'Ah. You had better come in tomorrow at two and work out examples three hundred to three-twenty in "Hall and Knight". There is really plenty of room to walk in between that desk and the blackboard. It only wants practice.'

What was left of Babington then went to his seat. He felt that his reputation as an artistic player of the game had received a shattering blow. Then there was the imposition. This in itself would have troubled him little. To be kept in on a half-holiday is annoying, but it is one of those ills which the flesh is heir to, and your true philosopher can always take his gruel like a man.

But it so happened that by the evening post he had received a letter from a cousin of his, who was a student at Guy's, and from all accounts was building up a great reputation in the medical world. From this letter it appeared that by a complicated process of knowing people who knew other people who had influence with the management, he had contrived to obtain two tickets for a morning performance of the new piece that had just been produced at one of the theatres. And if Mr J. S. M. Babington wished to avail himself of the opportunity, would he write by return, and be at Charing Cross Underground bookstall at twenty past two.

Now Babington, though he objected strongly to the drama of ancient

Greece, was very fond of that of the present day, and he registered a vow that if the matter could possibly be carried through, it should be. His choice was obvious. He could cut his engagement with Mr Seymour, or he could keep it. The difficulty lay rather in deciding upon one or other of the alternatives. The whole thing turned upon the extent of the penalty in the event of detection.

That was his dilemma. He sought advice.

'I should risk it,' said his bosom friend Peterson.

'I shouldn't advise you to,' remarked Jenkins.

Jenkins was equally a bosom friend, and in the matter of wisdom in no way inferior to Peterson.

'What would happen, do you think?' asked Babington.

'Sack,' said one authority.

'Jaw, and double impot,' said another.

'The *Daily Telegraph*,' muttered the tempter in a stage aside, 'calls it the best comedy since Sheridan.'

'So it does,' thought Babington. 'I'll risk it.'

'You'll be a fool if you do,' croaked the gloomy Jenkins. 'You're bound to be caught.' But the Ayes had it. Babington wrote off that night accepting the invitation.

It was with feelings of distinct relief that he heard Mr Seymour express to another master his intention of catching the twelve-fifteen train up to town. It meant that he would not be on the scene to see him start on the 'Hall and Knight'. Unless luck were very much against him, Babington might reasonably hope that he would accept the imposition without any questions. He had taken the precaution to get the examples finished overnight, with the help of Peterson and Jenkins, aided by a weird being who actually appeared to like algebra, and turned out ten of the twenty problems in an incredibly short time in exchange for a couple of works of fiction (down) and a tea (at a date). He himself meant to catch the one-thirty, which would bring him to town in good time. Peterson had promised to answer his name at roll-call, a delicate operation, in which long practice had made him, like many others of the junior members of the House, no mean proficient.

It would be pleasant for a conscientious historian to be able to say that the one-thirty broke down just outside Victoria, and that Babington arrived at the theatre at the precise moment when the curtain fell and the gratified audience began to stream out. But truth, though it crush me. The one-thirty was so punctual that one might have thought that it belonged to a line other than the line to which it did belong.

From Victoria to Charing Cross is a journey that occupies no considerable time, and Babington found himself at his destination with five minutes to wait. At twenty past his cousin arrived, and they made their way to the theatre. A brief skirmish with a liveried menial in the lobby, and they were in their seats.

Some philosopher, of extraordinary powers of intuition, once informed the world that the best of things come at last to an end. The statement was tested, and is now universally accepted as correct. To apply the general to the particular, the play came to an end amidst uproarious applause, to which Babington contributed an unstinted quotum, about three hours after it had begun.

'What do you say to going and grubbing somewhere?' asked Babington's cousin, as they made their way out.

'Hullo, there's that man Richards,' he continued, before Babington could reply that of all possible actions he considered that of going and grubbing somewhere the most desirable. 'Fellow I know at Guy's, you know,' he added, in explanation. 'I'll get him to join us. You'll like him, I expect.'

Richards professed himself delighted, and shook hands with Babington with a fervour which seemed to imply that until he had met him life had been a dreary blank, but that now he could begin to enjoy himself again. 'I should like to join you, if you don't mind including a friend of mine in the party,' said Richards. 'He was to meet me here. By the way, he's the author of that new piece – *The Way of the World*.'

'Why, we've just been there.'

'Oh, then you will probably like to meet him. Here he is.'

As he spoke a man came towards them, and, with a shock that sent all the blood in his body to the very summit of his head, and then to the very extremities of his boots, Babington recognized Mr Seymour. The assurance of the programme that the play was by Walter Walsh was a fraud. Nay worse, a downright and culpable lie. He started with the vague idea of making a rush for safety, but before his paralysed limbs could be induced to work, Mr Seymour had arrived, and he was being introduced (oh, the tragic irony of it) to the man for whose benefit he was at that very moment supposed to be working out examples three hundred to three-twenty in 'Hall and Knight'.

Mr Seymour shook hands, without appearing to recognize him. Babington's blood began to resume its normal position again, though he felt that this seeming ignorance of his identity might be a mere veneer, a wile of guile, as the bard puts it. He remembered, with a pang, a story in some magazine where a prisoner was subjected to what the light-hearted inquisitors called the torture of hope. He was allowed to escape from prison, and pass guards and sentries apparently without their noticing him. Then, just as he stepped into the open air, the chief inquisitor tapped him gently on the shoulder, and, more in sorrow than in anger, reminded him that it was customary for condemned men to remain *inside* their cells. Surely this was a similar case. But then the thought came to him that Mr Seymour had only seen him once, and so might possibly have failed to remember him, for there was nothing special about Babington's features that arrested the eye, and stamped them on the brain for all time. He was rather ordinary than otherwise to look at. At tea, as bad luck would have it, the two sat opposite one another, and Babington trembled. Then the worst happened. Mr Seymour, who had been looking attentively at him for some time, leaned forward and said in a tone evidently devoid of suspicion: 'Haven't we met before somewhere? I seem to remember your face.'

'Er – no, no,' replied Babington. 'That is, I think not. We may have.'

'I feel sure we have. What school are you at?'

Babington's soul began to writhe convulsively.

'What, what school? Oh, what *school*? Why, er – I'm at – er – Uppingham.'

Mr Seymour's face assumed a pleased expression.

'Uppingham? Really. Why, I know several Uppingham fellows. Do you know Mr Morton? He's a master at Uppingham, and a great friend of mine.'

The room began to dance briskly before Babington's eyes, but he clutched at a straw, or what he thought was a straw.

'Uppingham? Did I say Uppingham? Of course, I mean Rugby, you know, Rugby. One's always mixing the two up, you know. Isn't one?'

Mr Seymour looked at him in amazement. Then he looked at the others as if to ask which of the two was going mad, he or the youth opposite him. Babington's cousin listened to the wild fictions which issued from his lips in equal amazement. He thought he must be ill. Even Richards had a fleeting impression that it was a little odd that a fellow should forget what school he was at, and mistake the name Rugby for that of Uppingham, or *vice versa*. Babington became an object of interest.

'I say, Jack,' said the cousin, 'you're feeling all right, aren't you? I mean, you don't seem to know what you're talking about. If you're going to be ill, say so, and I'll prescribe for you.'

'Is he at Rugby?' asked Mr Seymour.

'No, of course he's not. How could he have got from Rugby to London in time for a morning performance? Why, he's at St Austin's.'

Mr Seymour sat for a moment in silence, taking this in. Then he chuckled. 'It's all right,' he said, 'he's not ill. We have met before, but under such painful circumstances that Master Babington very thoughtfully dissembled, in order not to remind me of them.'

He gave a brief synopsis of what had occurred. The audience, exclusive of Babington, roared with laughter.

'I suppose,' said the cousin, 'you won't prosecute, will you? It's really such shocking luck, you know, that you ought to forget you're a master.'

Mr Seymour stirred his tea and added another lump of sugar very carefully before replying. Babington watched him in silence, and wished that he would settle the matter quickly, one way or the other.

'Fortunately for Babington,' said Mr Seymour, 'and unfortunately for the cause of morality, I am not a master. I was only a stop-gap, and my term of office ceased today at one o'clock. Thus the prisoner at the bar gets off on a technical point of law, and I trust it will be a lesson to him. I suppose you had the sense to do the imposition?'

'Yes, sir, I sat up last night.'

'Good. Now, if you'll take my advice, you'll reform, or another day you'll come to a bad end. By the way, how did you manage about roll-call today?'

'I thought that was an awfully good part just at the end of the first act,' said Babington.

Mr Seymour smiled. Possibly from gratification.

'Well, how did it go off?' asked Peterson that night.

'Don't, old chap,' said Babington, faintly.

'I told you so,' said Jenkins at a venture.

But when he had heard the whole story he withdrew the remark, and commented on the wholly undeserved good luck some people seemed to enjoy.

[11]

'The Tabby Terror'

The struggle between Prater's cat and Prater's cat's conscience was short, and ended in the hollowest of victories for the former. The conscience really had no sort of chance from the beginning. It was weak by nature and flabby from long want of exercise, while the cat was in excellent training, and was, moreover, backed up by a strong temptation. It pocketed the stakes, which consisted of most of the contents of a tin of sardines, and left unostentatiously by the window. When Smith came in after football, and found the remains, he was surprised, and even pained. When Montgomery entered soon afterwards, he questioned him on the subject.

'I say, have you been having a sort of preliminary canter with the banquet?'

'No,' said Montgomery. 'Why?'

'Somebody has,' said Smith, exhibiting the empty tin. 'Doesn't seem to have had such a bad appetite, either.'

'This reminds me of the story of the great bear, the medium bear, and the little ditto,' observed Montgomery, who was apt at an analogy. 'You may remember that when the great bear found his porridge tampered with, he –'

At this point Shawyer entered. He had been bidden to the feast, and was feeling ready for it.

'Hullo, tea ready?' he asked.

Smith displayed the sardine tin in much the same manner as the conjurer shows a pack of cards when he entreats you to choose one, and remember the number.

'You haven't finished already, surely? Why, it's only just five.'

'We haven't even begun,' said Smith. 'That's just the difficulty. The question is, who has been on the raid in here?'

'No human being has done this horrid thing,' said Montgomery. He always liked to introduce a Holmes–Watsonian touch into the conversation. 'In the first place, the door was locked, wasn't it, Smith?'

'By Jove, so it was. Then how on earth –?',

'Through the window, of course. The cat, equally of course. I should like a private word with that cat.'

'I suppose it must have been.'

'Of course it was. Apart from the merely circumstantial evidence, which is strong enough to hang it off its own bat, we have absolute proof of its guilt. Just cast your eye over that butter. You follow me, Watson?'

The butter was submitted to inspection. In the very centre of it there was a footprint.

'*I* traced his little footprints in the butter,' said Montgomery. 'Now, *is* that the mark of a human foot?'

The jury brought in a unanimous verdict of guilty against the missing animal, and over a sorrowful cup of tea, eked out with bread and jam – butter appeared to be unpopular – discussed the matter in all its bearings. The cat had not been an inmate of Prater's House for a very long time, and up till now what depredation it had committed had been confined to the official larder. Now, however, it had evidently got its hand in, and was about to commence operations upon a more extensive scale. The Tabby Terror had begun. Where would it end? The general opinion was that something would have to be done about it. No one seemed to know exactly what to do. Montgomery spoke darkly of bricks, bits of string, and horse-ponds. Smith rolled the word 'rat-poison' luxuriously round his tongue. Shawyer, who was something of an expert on the range, babbled of air-guns.

At tea on the following evening the first really serious engagement of the campaign took place. The cat strolled into the tea-room in the patronizing way characteristic of his kind, but was heavily shelled with lump-sugar, and beat a rapid retreat. That was the signal for the outbreak of serious hostilities. From that moment its paw was against every man, and the tale of the things it stole is too terrible to relate in detail. It scored all along the line. Like Death in the poem, it knocked at the doors of the highest and the lowest alike. Or rather, it did not exactly knock. It came in without knocking. The palace of the prefect and the hovel of the fag suffered equally. Trentham, the head of the House, lost sausages to an incredible amount one evening, and the next day Ripton, of the Lower Third, was robbed of his one ewe lamb in the shape of half a tin of anchovy paste. Panic reigned.

It was after this matter of the sausages that a luminous idea occurred to Trentham. He had been laid up with a slight football accident, and his family, reading between the lines of his written statement that he 'had got crocked at footer, nothing much, only (rather a nuisance) might do him out of the House-matches', a notification of mortal injuries, and seeming to hear a death-rattle through the words 'felt rather chippy yesterday', had come down *en masse* to investigate. *En masse*, that is to say, with the exception of his father, who said he was too busy, but felt sure it was nothing serious. ('Why, when I was a boy, my dear, I used to think nothing of an occasional tumble. There's nothing the matter with Dick. Why, etc., etc.')

Trentham's sister was his first visitor.

'I say,' said he, when he had satisfied her on the subject of his health, 'would you like to do me a good turn?'

She intimated that she would be delighted, and asked for details.

'*Buy the beak's cat*,' hissed Trentham, in a hoarse whisper.

'Dick, it *was* your leg that you hurt, wasn't it? Not – not your head?' she replied. 'I mean –'

'No, I really mean it. Why can't you? It's a perfectly simple thing to do.'

'But what *is* a beak? And why should I buy its cat?'

'A beak's a master. Surely you know that. You see, Prater's got a cat lately, and the beast strolls in and raids the studies. Got round over half a pound of prime sausages in here the other night, and he's always bagging things everywhere. You'd be doing everyone a kindness if you would take him on. He'll get lynched some day if you don't. Besides, you want a cat for your new house, surely. Keep down the mice, and that sort of thing, you know. This animal's a demon for mice.' This was a telling argument. Trentham's sister had lately been married, and she certainly had had some idea of investing in a cat to adorn her home. 'As for beetles,' continued the invalid, pushing home his advantage, 'they simply daren't come out of their lairs for fear of him.'

'If he eats beetles,' objected his sister, 'he can't have a very good coat.'

'He doesn't eat them. Just squashes them, you know, like a police-man. He's a decent enough beast as far as looks go.'

'But if he steals things –'

'No, don't you see, he only does that here, because the Praters don't interfere with him and don't let us do anything to him. He won't try that sort of thing on with you. If he does, get somebody to hit him over the head with a boot-jack or something. He'll soon drop it then. You might as well, you know. The House'll simply black your boots if you do.'

'But would Mr Prater let me have the cat?'

'Try him, anyhow. Pitch it fairly warm, you know. Only cat you ever loved, and that sort of thing.'

'Very well. I'll try.'

'Thanks, awfully. And, I say, you might just look in here on your way out and report.'

Mrs James Williamson, née Miss Trentham, made her way dutifully to the Merevale's part of the House. Mrs Prater had expressed a hope that she would have some tea before catching her train. With tea it is usual to have milk, and with milk it is usual, if there is a cat in the house, to have feline society. Captain Kettle, which was the name thought suitable to this cat by his godfathers and godmothers, was on hand early. As he stood there pawing the mat impatiently, and mewing in a minor key, Mrs Williamson felt that here was the cat for her. He certainly was good to look upon. His black heart was hidden by a sleek coat of tabby fur, which rendered stroking a luxury. His scheming brain was out of sight in a shapely head.

'Oh, what a lovely cat!' said Mrs Williamson.

'Yes, isn't he,' agreed Mrs Prater. 'We are very proud of him.'

'Such a beautiful coat!'

'And such a sweet purr!'

'He looks so intelligent. Has he any tricks?'

Had he any tricks! Why, Mrs Williamson, he could do everything except speak. Captain Kettle, you bad boy, come here and die for your country. Puss, puss.

Captain Kettle came at last reluctantly, died for his country in record time, and flashed back again to the saucer. He had an important appointment. Sorry to appear rude and all that sort of thing, don't you know, but he had to see a cat about a mouse.

'Well?' said Trentham, when his sister looked in upon him an hour later.

'Oh, Dick, it's the nicest cat I ever saw. I shall never be happy if I don't get it.'

'Have you bought it?' asked the practical Trentham.

'My dear Dick, I couldn't. We couldn't bargain about a cat during tea. Why, I never met Mrs Prater before this afternoon.'

'No, I suppose not,' admitted Trentham, gloomily. 'Anyhow, look here, if anything turns up to make the beak want to get rid of it, I'll tell him you're dead nuts on it. See?'

For a fortnight after this episode matters went on as before. Mrs

Williamson departed, thinking regretfully of the cat she had left behind her.

Captain Kettle died for his country with moderate regularity, and on one occasion, when he attempted to extract some milk from the very centre of a fag's tea-party, almost died for another reason. Then the end came suddenly.

Trentham had been invited to supper one Sunday by Mr Prater. When he arrived it became apparent to him that the atmosphere was one of subdued gloom. At first he could not understand this, but soon the reason was made clear. Captain Kettle had, in the expressive language of the man in the street, been and gone and done it. He had been left alone that evening in the drawing-room, while the House was at church, and his eye, roaming restlessly about in search of evil to perform, had lighted upon a cage. In that cage was a special sort of canary, in its own line as accomplished an artiste as Captain Kettle himself. It sang with taste and feeling, and made itself generally agreeable in a number of little ways. But to Captain Kettle it was merely a bird. One of the poets sings of an acquaintance of his who was so constituted that 'a primrose by the river's brim a simple primrose was to him, and it was nothing more'. Just so with Captain Kettle. He was not the cat to make nice distinctions between birds. Like the cat in another poem, he only knew they made him light and salutary meals. So, with the exercise of considerable ingenuity, he extracted that canary from its cage and ate it. He was now in disgrace.

'We shall have to get rid of him,' said Mr Prater.

'I'm afraid so,' said Mrs Prater.

'If you weren't thinking of giving him to anyone in particular, sir,' said Trentham, 'my sister would be awfully glad to take him, I know. She was very keen on him when she came to see me.'

'That's excellent,' said Prater. 'I was afraid we should have to send him to a home somewhere.'

'I suppose we can't keep him after all?' suggested Mrs Prater.

Trentham waited in suspense.

'No,' said Prater, decidedly. 'I think *not*.' So Captain Kettle went, and the House knew him no more, and the Tabby Terror was at an end.

[12]

The Prize Poem

Some quarter of a century before the period with which this story deals, a certain rich and misanthropic man was seized with a bright idea for perpetuating his memory after death, and at the same time harassing a certain section of mankind. So in his will he set aside a portion of his income to be spent on an annual prize for the best poem submitted by a member of the Sixth Form of St Austin's College, on a subject to be selected by the Headmaster. And, he added – one seems to hear him chuckling to himself – every member of the form must compete. Then he died. But the evil that men do lives after them, and each year saw a fresh band of unwilling bards goaded to despair by his bequest. True, there were always one or two who hailed this ready market for their sonnets and odes with joy. But the majority, being barely able to rhyme 'dove' with 'love', regarded the annual announcement of the subject chosen with feelings of the deepest disgust.

The chains were thrown off after a period of twenty-seven years in this fashion.

Reynolds of the Remove was indirectly the cause of the change. He was in the infirmary, convalescing after an attack of German measles, when he received a visit from Smith, an ornament of the Sixth.

'By Jove,' remarked that gentleman, gazing enviously round the sick-room, 'they seem to do you pretty well here.'

'Yes, not bad, is it? Take a seat. Anything been happening lately?'

'Nothing much. I suppose you know we beat the M.C.C. by a wicket?'

'Yes, so I heard. Anything else?'

'Prize poem,' said Smith, without enthusiasm. He was not a poet.

Reynolds became interested at once. If there was one role in which he fancied himself (and, indeed, there were a good many), it was that of a versifier. His great ambition was to see some of his lines in print, and he had contracted the habit of sending them up to various periodicals, with no result, so far, except the arrival of rejected MSS.

at meal-times in embarrassingly long envelopes. Which he blushingly concealed with all possible speed.

'What's the subject this year?' he asked.

'The College – of all idiotic things.'

'Couldn't have a better subject for an ode. By Jove, I wish I was in the Sixth.'

'Wish I was in the infirmary,' said Smith.

Reynolds was struck with an idea.

'Look here, Smith,' he said, 'if you like I'll do you a poem, and you can send it up. If it gets the prize –'

'Oh, it won't get the prize,' Smith put in eagerly. 'Rogers is a cert. for that.'

'If it gets the prize,' repeated Reynolds, with asperity, 'you'll have to tell the Old Man all about it. He'll probably curse a bit, but that can't be helped. How's this for a beginning?

> "Imposing pile, reared up 'midst pleasant grounds,
> The scene of many a battle, lost or won,
> At cricket or at football; whose red walls
> Full many a sun has kissed 'ere day is done." '

'Grand. Couldn't you get in something about the M.C.C. match? You could make cricket rhyme with wicket.' Smith sat entranced with his ingenuity, but the other treated so material a suggestion with scorn.

'Well,' said Smith, 'I must be off now. We've got a House-match on. Thanks awfully about the poem.'

Left to himself, Reynolds set himself seriously to the composing of an ode that should do him justice. That is to say, he drew up a chair and table to the open window, wrote down the lines he had already composed, and began chewing a pen. After a few minutes he wrote another four lines, crossed them out, and selected a fresh piece of paper. He then copied out his first four lines again. After eating his pen to a stump, he jotted down the two words 'boys' and 'joys' at the end of separate lines. This led him to select a third piece of paper, on which he produced a sort of *édition de luxe* in his best handwriting, with the title 'Ode to the College' in printed letters at the top. He was admiring the neat effect of this when the door opened suddenly and violently, and Mrs Lee, a lady of advanced years and energetic habits, whose duty it was to minister to the needs of the sick and wounded in the infirmary, entered with his tea. Mrs Lee's method of entering a room was in accordance with the advice of the Psalmist, where he says, 'Fling wide the gates'. She flung wide the gate of the sick-room, and the result was that what is commonly called 'a thorough draught' was established. The air was thick with flying papers, and when calm at length succeeded storm, two editions of 'Ode to the College' were lying on the grass outside.

Reynolds attacked the tea without attempting to retrieve his vanished work. Poetry is good, but tea is better. Besides, he argued within himself, he remembered all he had written, and could easily write it out again. So, as far as he was concerned, those three sheets of paper were a closed book.

Later on in the afternoon, Montgomery of the Sixth happened to be passing by the infirmary, when Fate, aided by a sudden gust of wind, blew a piece of paper at him. 'Great Scott,' he observed, as his eye fell on the words 'Ode to the College'. Montgomery, like Smith, was no expert in poetry. He had spent a wretched afternoon trying to hammer out something that would pass muster in the poem competition, but without the least success. There were four lines on the paper. Two more, and it would be a poem, and capable of being entered for the prize as such. The words 'imposing pile', with which the fragment in his hand began, took his fancy immensely. A poetic afflatus seized him, and in less than three hours he had added the necessary couplet,

> How truly sweet it is for such as me
> To gaze on thee.

'And dashed neat, too,' he said, with satisfaction, as he threw the manuscript into his drawer. 'I don't know whether "me" shouldn't be "I", but they'll have to lump it. It's a poem, anyhow, within the meaning of the act.' And he strolled off to a neighbour's study to borrow a book.

Two nights afterwards, Morrison, also of the Sixth, was enjoying his usual during prep siesta in his study. A tap at the door roused him. Hastily seizing a lexicon, he assumed the attitude of the seeker after knowledge, and said, 'Come in.' It was not the House-master, but Evans, Morrison's fag, who entered with pride on his face and a piece of paper in his hand.

'I say,' he began, 'you remember you told me to hunt up some tags for the poem. Will this do?'

Morrison took the paper with a judicial air. On it were the words:

> Imposing pile, reared up 'midst pleasant grounds,
> The scene of many a battle, lost or won,

> At cricket or at football; whose red walls
> Full many a sun has kissed 'ere day is done.

'That's ripping, as far as it goes,' said Morrison. 'Couldn't be better. You'll find some apples in that box. Better take a few. But look here,' with sudden suspicion, 'I don't believe you made all this up yourself. Did you?'

Evans finished selecting his apples before venturing on a reply. Then he blushed, as much as a member of the junior school is capable of blushing.

'Well,' he said, 'I didn't exactly. You see, you only told me to get the tags. You didn't say how.'

'But how did you get hold of this? Whose is it?'

'Dunno. I found it in the field between the Pavilion and the infirmary.'

'Oh! well, it doesn't matter much. They're just what I wanted, which is the great thing. Thanks. Shut the door, will you?' Whereupon Evans retired, the richer by many apples, and Morrison resumed his siesta at the point where he had left off.

'Got that poem done yet?' said Smith to Reynolds, pouring out a cup of tea for the invalid on the following Sunday.

'Two lumps, please. No, not quite.'

'Great Caesar, man, when'll it be ready, do you think? It's got to go in tomorrow.'

'Well, I'm really frightfully sorry, but I got hold of a grand book. Ever read –?'

'Isn't any of it done?' asked Smith.

'Only the first verse, I'm afraid. But, look here, you aren't keen on getting the prize. Why not send in only the one verse? It makes a fairly decent poem.'

'Hum! Think the Old 'Un'll pass it?'

'He'll have to. There's nothing in the rules about length. Here it is if you want it.'

'Thanks. I suppose it'll be all right? So long! I must be off.'

The Headmaster, known to the world as the Rev. Arthur James Perceval, M.A., and to the School as the Old 'Un, was sitting at breakfast, stirring his coffee, with a look of marked perplexity upon his dignified face. This was not caused by the coffee, which was excellent, but by a letter which he held in his left hand.

'Hum!' he said. Then 'Umph!' in a protesting tone, as if someone had pinched him. Finally, he gave vent to a long-drawn 'Um-m-m,' in a deep bass. 'Most extraordinary. Really, most extraordinary. Exceedingly. Yes. Um. Very.' He took a sip of coffee.

'My dear,' said he, suddenly. Mrs Perceval started violently. She had been sketching out in her mind a little dinner, and wondering whether the cook would be equal to it.

'Yes,' she said.

'My dear, this is a very extraordinary communication. Exceedingly so. Yes, very.'

'Who is it from?'

Mr Perceval shuddered. He was a purist in speech. '*From whom*, you should say. It is from Mr Wells, a great College friend of mine. I – ah – submitted to him for examination the poems sent in for the Sixth Form Prize. He writes in a very flippant style. I must say, very flippant. This is his letter: – "Dear Jimmy (really, really, he should remember that we are not so young as we were); dear – ahem – Jimmy. The poems to hand. I have read them, and am writing this from my sick-bed. The doctor tells me I may pull through even yet. There was only one any good at all, that was Rogers's, which, though – er – squiffy (tut!) in parts, was a long way better than any of the others. But the most taking part of the whole programme was afforded by the three comedians, whose efforts I enclose. You will notice that each begins with exactly the same four lines. Of course, I deprecate cribbing, but you really can't help admiring this sort of thing. There is a reckless daring about it which is simply fascinating. A horrible thought – have they been pulling your dignified leg? By the way, do you remember " – the rest of the letter is – er – on different matters.'

'James! How extraordinary!'

'Um, yes. I am reluctant to suspect – er – collusion, but really here there can be no doubt. No doubt at all. No.'

'Unless,' began Mrs Perceval, tentatively. 'No doubt at all, my dear,' snapped Reverend Jimmy. He did not wish to recall the other possibility, that his dignified leg was being pulled.

'Now, for what purpose did I summon you three boys?' asked Mr Perceval, of Smith, Montgomery, and Morrison, in his room after morning school that day. He generally began a painful interview with this question. The method had distinct advantages. If the criminal were of a nervous disposition, he would give himself away upon the instant. In any case, it was likely to startle him. 'For what purpose?' repeated the Headmaster, fixing Smith with a glittering eye.

'I will tell you,' continued Mr Perceval. 'It was because I desired information, which none but you can supply. How comes it that each of your compositions for the Poetry Prize commences with the same four lines?' The three poets looked at one another in speechless astonishment.

'Here,' he resumed, 'are the three papers. Compare them. Now,' – after the inspection was over – 'what explanation have you to offer? Smith, are these your lines?'

'I – er – ah – *wrote* them, sir.'

'Don't prevaricate, Smith. Are you the author of those lines?'

'No, sir.'

'Ah! Very good. Are you, Montgomery?'

'No, sir.'

'Very good. Then you, Morrison, are exonerated from all blame. You have been exceedingly badly treated. The first-fruit of your brain has been – ah – plucked by others, who toiled not neither did they spin. You can go, Morrison.'

'But, sir –'

'Well, Morrison?'

'I didn't write them, sir.'

'I – ah – don't quite understand you, Morrison. You say that you are indebted to another for these lines?'

'Yes, sir.'

'To Smith?'

'No, sir.'

'To Montgomery?'

'No, sir.'

'Then, Morrison, may I ask to whom you are indebted?'

'I found them in the field on a piece of paper, sir.' He claimed the discovery himself, because he thought that Evans might possibly prefer to remain outside this tangle.

'So did I, sir.' This from Montgomery. Mr Perceval looked bewildered, as indeed he was.

'And did you, Smith, also find this poem on a piece of paper in the field?' There was a metallic ring of sarcasm in his voice.

'No, sir.'

'Ah! Then to what circumstance were you indebted for the lines?'

'I got Reynolds to do them for me, sir.'

Montgomery spoke. 'It was near the infirmary that I found the paper, and Reynolds is in there.'

'So did I, sir,' said Morrison, incoherently.

'Then am I to understand, Smith, that to gain the prize you resorted to such underhand means as this?'

'No, sir, we agreed that there was no danger of my getting the prize. If I had got it, I should have told you everything. Reynolds will tell you that, sir.'

'Then what object had you in pursuing this deception?'

'Well, sir, the rules say everyone must send in something, and I can't write poetry at all, and Reynolds likes it, so I asked him to do it.'

And Smith waited for the storm to burst. But it did not burst. Far down in Mr Perceval's system lurked a quiet sense of humour. The situation penetrated to it. Then he remembered the examiner's letter, and it dawned upon him that there are few crueller things than to make a prosaic person write poetry.

'You may go,' he said, and the three went.

And at the next Board Meeting it was decided, mainly owing to the influence of an exceedingly eloquent speech from the Headmaster, to alter the rules for the Sixth Form Poetry Prize, so that from thence onward no one need compete unless he felt himself filled with the immortal fire.

[13]

Work

With a pleasure that's emphatic
We retire to our attic
With the satisfying feeling that our duty has been done.

Oh! philosophers may sing
Of the troubles of a king
But of pleasures there are many and of troubles there are none,
And the culminating pleasure
Which we treasure beyond measure
Is the satisfying feeling that our duty has been done.

W. S. Gilbert

Work is supposed to be the centre round which school life revolves – the hub of the school wheel, the lode-star of the schoolboy's existence, and a great many other things. 'You come to school to work', is the formula used by masters when sentencing a victim to the wailing and gnashing of teeth provided by two hours' extra tuition on a hot afternoon. In this, I think, they err, and my opinion is backed up by numerous scholars of my acquaintance, who have even gone so far – on occasions when they themselves have been the victims – as to express positive disapproval of the existing state of things. In the dear, dead days (beyond recall), I used often to long to put the case to my form-master in its only fair aspect, but always refrained from motives of policy. Masters are so apt to take offence at the well-meant endeavours of their form to instruct them in the way they should go.

What I should have liked to have done would have been something after this fashion. Entering the sanctum of the Headmaster, I should have motioned him to his seat – if he were seated already, have assured him that to rise was unnecessary. I should then have taken a seat myself, taking care to preserve a calm fixity of demeanour, and finally, with a preliminary cough, I should have embarked upon the following moving address: 'My dear sir, my dear Reverend Jones or Brown (as the case may be), believe me when I say that your whole system of work is founded on a fallacious dream and reeks of rottenness. No, no, I beg that you will not interrupt me. The real state of the case, if I may say so, is briefly this: a boy goes to school to enjoy himself, and, on arriving, finds to his consternation that a great deal more work is expected of him than he is prepared to do. What course, then, Reverend Jones or Brown, does he take? He proceeds to do as much work as will steer him safely between the, ah – I may say, the Scylla of punishment and the Charybdis of being considered what my, er – fellow-pupils euphoniously term a swot. That, I think, is all this morning. *Good* day. Pray do not trouble to rise. I will find my way out.' I should then have made for the door, locked it, if possible, on the outside, and, rushing to the railway station, have taken a through ticket to Spitzbergen or some other place where Extradition treaties do not hold good.

But 'twas not mine to play the Tib. Gracchus, to emulate the O. Cromwell. So far from pouring my opinions like so much boiling oil into the ear of my task-master, I was content to play the part of audience while *he* did the talking, my sole remark being 'Yes'r' at fixed intervals.

And yet I knew that I was in the right. My bosom throbbed with the justice of my cause. For why? The ambition of every human new boy is surely to become like J. Essop of the First Eleven, who can hit a ball over two ponds, a wood, and seven villages, rather than to resemble that pale young student, Mill-Stuart, who, though he can speak Sanskrit like a native of Sanskritia, couldn't score a single off a slow long-hop.

And this ambition is a laudable one. For the athlete is the product of nature – a step towards the more perfect type of animal, while the scholar is the outcome of artificiality. What, I ask, does the scholar gain, either morally or physically, or in any other way, by knowing who was tribune of the people in 284 BC or what is the precise difference between the various constructions of *cum*? It is not as if ignorance of the tribune's identity caused him any mental unrest. In short, what excuse is there for the student? 'None,' shrieks Echo enthusiastically. 'None whatever.'

Our children are being led to ruin by this system. They will become dons and think in Greek. The victim of the craze stops at nothing. He puns in Latin. He quips and quirks in Ionic and Doric. In the worst stages of the disease he will edit Greek plays and say that Merry quite misses the fun of the passage, or that Jebb is mediocre. Think, I beg of you, paterfamilias, and you, mater ditto, what your feelings would be were you to find Henry or Archibald Cuthbert correcting proofs of *The Agamemnon*, and inventing 'nasty ones' for Mr Sidgwick! Very well then. Be warned.

Our bright-eyed lads are taught insane constructions in Greek and Latin from morning till night, and they come for their holidays, in many cases, without the merest foundation of a batting style. Ask them what a Yorker is, and they will say: 'A man from York, though I presume you mean a Yorkshireman.' They will read Herodotus without a dictionary for pleasure, but ask them to translate the childishly simple sentence: 'Trott was soon in his timber-yard with a length 'un that whipped across from the off,' and they'll shrink abashed and swear they have not skill at that, as Gilbert says.

The papers sometimes contain humorous forecasts of future education, when cricket and football shall come to their own. They little know the excellence of the thing they mock at. When we get schools that teach nothing but games, then will the sun definitely refuse to set on the roast beef of old England. May it be soon. Some day, mayhap, I shall gather my great-great-grandsons round my knee, and tell them – as one tells tales of Faëry – that I can remember the time when Work was considered the be-all and the end-all of a school career. Perchance, when my great-great-grandson John (called John after the famous Jones of that name) has brought home the prize for English Essay on 'Rugby *v.* Association', I shall pat his head (gently) and the tears will come to my old eyes as I recall the time when I, too, might have won a prize – for that obsolete subject, Latin Prose – and was only prevented by the superior excellence of my thirty-and-one fellow students, coupled, indeed, with my own inability to conjugate *sum*.

Such days, I say, may come. But now are the Dark Ages. The only thing that can possibly make Work anything but an unmitigated nuisance is the prospect of a 'Varsity scholarship, and the thought that, in the event of failure, a 'Varsity career will be out of the question.

With this thought constantly before him, the student can put a certain amount of enthusiasm into his work, and even go to the length of rising at five o'clock o' mornings to drink yet deeper of the cup of knowledge. I have done it myself. 'Varsity means games and yellow waistcoats and Proctors, and that sort of thing. It is worth working for.

But for the unfortunate individual who is barred by circumstances from participating in these joys, what inducement is there to work?

Is such a one to leave the school nets in order to stew in a stuffy room over a Thucydides? I trow not.

Chapter one of my great forthcoming work, *The Compleat Slacker*, contains minute instructions on the art of avoiding preparation from beginning to end of term. Foremost among the words of advice ranks this maxim: Get an official list of the books you are to do, and examine them carefully with a view to seeing what it is possible to do unseen. Thus, if Virgil is among these authors, you can rely on being able to do him with success. People who ought to know better will tell you that Virgil is hard. Such a shallow falsehood needs little comment. A scholar who cannot translate ten lines of *The Aeneid* between the time he is put on and the time he begins to speak is unworthy of pity or consideration, and if I meet him in the street I shall assuredly cut him. Aeschylus, on the other hand, is a demon, and needs careful watching, though in an emergency you can always say the reading is wrong.

Sometimes the compleat slacker falls into a trap. The saddest case I can remember is that of poor Charles Vanderpoop. He was a bright young lad, and showed some promise of rising to heights as a slacker. He fell in this fashion. One Easter term his form had half-finished a speech of Demosthenes, and the form-master gave them to understand that they would absorb the rest during the forthcoming term. Charles, being naturally anxious to do as little work as possible during the summer months, spent his Easter holidays carefully preparing this speech, so as to have it ready in advance. What was his horror, on returning to School at the appointed date, to find that they were going to throw Demosthenes over altogether, and patronize Plato. Threats, entreaties, prayers – all were accounted nothing by the master who had led him into this morass of troubles. It is believed that the shock destroyed his reason. At any rate, the fact remains that that term (the summer term, mark you) he won two prizes. In the following term he won three. To recapitulate his outrages from that time to the present were a harrowing and unnecessary task. Suffice it that he is now a Regius Professor, and I saw in the papers a short time ago that a lecture of his on 'The Probable Origin of the Greek Negative', created quite a *furore*. If this is not Tragedy with a big T, I should like to know what it is.

As an exciting pastime, unseen translation must rank very high. Everyone who has ever tried translating unseen must acknowledge that all other forms of excitement seem but feeble makeshifts after it. I have, in the course of a career of sustained usefulness to the human race, had my share of thrills. I have asked a strong and busy porter, at Paddington, when the Brighton train started. I have gone for the broad-jump record in trying to avoid a motor-car. I have played Spillikins and Ping-Pong. But never again have I felt the excitement that used to wander athwart my moral backbone when I was put on to translate a passage containing a notorious *crux* and seventeen doubtful readings, with only that innate genius, which is the wonder of the civilized world, to pull me through. And what a glow of pride one feels when it is all over; when one has made a glorious, golden guess at the *crux*, and trampled the doubtful readings under foot with inspired ease. It is like a day at the seaside.

Work is bad enough, but Examinations are worse, especially the Board Examinations. By doing from ten to twenty minutes prep every night, the compleat slacker could get through most of the term with average success. Then came the Examinations. The dabbler in unseen translations found himself caught as in a snare. Gone was the peaceful security in which he had lulled to rest all the well-meant efforts of his guardian angel to rouse him to a sense of his duties. There, right in front of him, yawned the abyss of Retribution.

Alas! poor slacker. I knew him, Horatio; a fellow of infinite jest, of most excellent fancy. Where be his gibes now? How is he to cope with the fiendish ingenuity of the examiners? How is he to master the contents of a book of Thucydides in a couple of days? It is a fearsome problem. Perhaps he will get up in the small hours and work by candle-light from two till eight o'clock. In this case he will start his day a mental and physical wreck. Perhaps he will try to work and be led away by the love of light reading.

In any case he will fail to obtain enough marks to satisfy the examiners, though whether examiners ever are satisfied, except by Harry the hero of the school story (Every Lad's Library, uniform edition, 2s 6d), is rather a doubtful question.

In such straits, matters resolve themselves into a sort of drama with three characters. We will call our hero Smith.

Scene : a Study

Dramatis Personae : SMITH
                     CONSCIENCE
                     MEPHISTOPHELES

Enter SMITH (*down centre*)

  He seats himself at table and opens a Thucydides.

Enter CONSCIENCE *through ceiling* (R.), MEPHISTOPHELES *through floor* (L.).

CONSCIENCE (*with a kindly smile*): Precisely what I was about to remark, my dear lad. A little Thucydides would be a very good thing. Thucydides, as you doubtless know, was a very famous Athenian historian. Date?

SMITH: Er – um – let me see.

MEPH. (*aside*): Look in the Introduction and pretend you did it by accident.

SMITH (*having done so*): 431 B.C. *circ.*

CONSCIENCE *wipes away a tear.*

CONSCIENCE: Thucydides made himself a thorough master of the conciscst of styles.

MEPH.: And in doing so became infernally obscure. Excuse shop.

SMITH (*gloomily*): Hum!

MEPH. (*sneeringly*): Ha!

Long pause.

CONSCIENCE (*gently*): Do you not think, my dear lad, that you had better begin? Time and tide, as you are aware, wait for no man. And –

SMITH: Yes?

CONSCIENCE: You have not, I fear, a very firm grasp of the subject. However, if you work hard till eleven –

SMITH (*gloomily*): Hum! Three hours!

MEPH. (*cheerily*): Exactly so. Three hours. A little more if anything. By the way, excuse me asking, but have you prepared the subject thoroughly during the term?

SMITH: My *dear* sir! Of *course*!

CONSCIENCE (*reprovingly*):???!!??!

SMITH: Well, perhaps, not quite so much as I might have done. Such a lot of things to do this term. Cricket, for instance.

MEPH.: Rather. Talking of cricket, you seemed to be shaping rather well last Saturday. I had just run up on business, and someone told me you made eighty not out. Get your century all right?

SMITH (*brightening at the recollection*): Just a bit – 117 not out. I hit – but perhaps you've heard?

MEPH.: Not at all, not at all. Let's hear all about it.

CONSCIENCE *seeks to interpose, but is prevented by* MEPH., *who eggs* SMITH *on to talk cricket for over an hour.*

CONSCIENCE (*at last; in an acid voice*): That is a history of the Peloponnesian War by Thucydides on the table in front of you. I thought I would mention it, in case you had forgotten.

SMITH: Great Scott, yes! Here, I say, I must start.

CONSCIENCE: Hear! Hear!

MEPH. (*insinuatingly*): *One* moment. Did you say you *had* prepared this book during the term? Afraid I'm a little hard of hearing. Eh, what?

SMITH: Well – er – no, I have not. Have you ever played billiards with a walking-stick and five balls?

MEPH.: Quite so, quite so. I quite understand. Don't you distress yourself, old chap. You obviously can't get through a whole book of Thucydides in under two hours, can you?

CONSCIENCE (*severely*): He might, by attentive application to study, master a considerable portion of the historian's *chef d'oeuvre* in that time.

MEPH.: Yes, and find that not one of the passages he had prepared was set in the paper.

CONSCIENCE: At the least, he would, if he were to pursue the course which I have indicated, greatly benefit his mind.

MEPH. *gives a short, derisive laugh. Long pause.*

MEPH. (*looking towards bookshelf*): Hullo, you've got a decent lot of books, pommy word you have. *Rodney Stone, Vice Versa, Many Cargoes*. Ripping. Ever read *Many Cargoes*?

CONSCIENCE (*glancing at his watch*): I am sorry, but I must really go now. I will see you some other day.

Exit sorrowfully.

MEPH.: Well, thank goodness *he's* gone. Never saw such a fearful old bore in my life. Can't think why you let him hang on to you so. We may as well make a night of it now, eh? No use your trying to work at this time of night.

SMITH: Not a bit.

MEPH.: Did you say you'd *not* read *Many Cargoes*?

SMITH: Never. Only got it today. Good?

MEPH.: Simply ripping. All short stories. Make you yell.

SMITH (*with a last effort*): But don't you think –

MEPH.: Oh no. Besides, you can easily get up early tomorrow for the Thucydides.

SMITH: Of course I can. Never thought of that. Heave us *Many Cargoes*. Thanks.

> *Begins to read.* MEPH. *grins fiendishly, and vanishes through floor enveloped in red flame. Sobbing heard from the direction of the ceiling.*
>
> *Scene closes.*

Next morning, of course, he will oversleep himself, and his Thucydides paper will be of such a calibre that that eminent historian will writhe in his grave.

[14]

Notes

Of all forms of lettered effusiveness, that which exploits the original work of others and professes to supply us with right opinions thereanent is the least wanted.

Kenneth Grahame

It has always seemed to me one of the worst flaws in our mistaken social system, that absolutely no distinction is made between the master who forces the human boy to take down notes from dictation and the rest of mankind. I mean that, if in a moment of righteous indignation you rend such a one limb from limb, you will almost certainly be subjected to the utmost rigour of the law, and you will be lucky if you escape a heavy fine of five or ten shillings, exclusive of the costs of the case. Now, this is not right on the face of it. It is even wrong. The law should take into account the extreme provocation which led to the action. Punish if you will the man who travels second-class with a third-class ticket, or who borrows a pencil and forgets to return it; but there are occasions when justice should be tempered with mercy, and this murdering of pedagogues is undoubtedly such an occasion.

It should be remembered, however, that there are two varieties of notes. The printed notes at the end of your Thucydides or Homer are distinctly useful when they aim at acting up to their true vocation, namely, the translating of difficult passages or words. Sometimes, however, the author will insist on airing his scholarship, and instead of translations he supplies parallel passages, which neither interest, elevate, nor amuse the reader. This, of course, is mere vanity. The author, sitting in his comfortable chair with something short within easy reach, recks nothing of the misery he is inflicting on hundreds of people who have done him no harm at all. He turns over the pages of his book of *Familiar Quotations* with brutal callousness, and for every tricky passage in the work which he is editing, finds and makes a note of three or four even trickier ones from other works. Who has not in his time been brought face to face with a word which defies translation? There are two courses open to you on such an occasion, to look the word up in the lexicon, or in the notes. You, of course, turn up the notes, and find: 'See line 80.' You look up line 80, hoping to see a translation, and there you are told that a rather similar construction occurs in Xenophades' *Lyrics from a Padded Cell*. On this, the craven of spirit will resort to the lexicon, but the man of mettle will close his book with an emphatic bang, and refuse to have anything more to do with it. Of a different sort are the notes which simply translate the difficulty and subside. These are a boon to the scholar. Without them it would be almost impossible to prepare one's work during school, and we should be reduced to the prosaic expedient of working in prep. time. What we want is the commentator who translates *mensa* as 'a table' without giving a page and a half of notes on the uses of the table in ancient Greece, with an excursus on the habit common in those times of retiring underneath it after dinner, and a list of the passages in Apollonius Rhodius where the word 'table' is mentioned.

These voluminous notes are apt to prove a nuisance in more ways than one. Your average master is generally inordinately fond of them, and will frequently ask some member of the form to read his note on so-and-so out to his fellows. This sometimes leads to curious results, as it is hardly to be expected that the youth called upon will be attending, even if he is awake, which is unlikely. On one occasion an acquaintance of mine, 'whose name I am not at liberty to divulge', was suddenly aware that he was being addressed, and, on giving the matter his attention, found that it was the form-master asking him to read out his note on *Balbus murum aedificavit*. My friend is a kind-hearted youth and of an obliging disposition, and would willingly have done what was asked of him, but there were obstacles, first and foremost of which ranked the fact that, taking advantage of his position on the back desk (whither he thought the basilisk eye of Authority could not reach), he had substituted *Bab Ballads* for the words of Virgil, and was engrossed in the contents of that modern classic. The subsequent explanations lasted several hours. In fact, it is probable that the master does not understand the facts of the case thoroughly even now. It is true that he called him a 'loathsome, slimy, repulsive toad', but even this seems to fall short of the grandeur of the situation.

Those notes, also, which are, alas! only too common nowadays, that deal with peculiarities of grammar, how supremely repulsive they are! It is impossible to glean any sense from them, as the Editor mixes up

Nipperwick's view with Sidgeley's reasoning and Spreckendzedeutscheim's surmise with Donnerundblitzendorf's conjecture in a way that seems to argue a thorough unsoundness of mind and morals, a cynical insanity combined with a blatant indecency. He occasionally starts in a reasonable manner by giving one view as (1) and the next as (2). So far everyone is happy and satisfied. The trouble commences when he has occasion to refer back to some former view, when he will say: 'Thus we see (1) and (14) that,' etc. The unlucky student puts a finger on the page to keep the place, and hunts up view one. Having found this, and marked the spot with another finger, he proceeds to look up view fourteen. He places another finger on this, and reads on, as follows: 'Zmpe, however, maintains that Schrumpff (see 3) is practically insane, that Spleckzh (see 34) is only a little better, and that Rswkg (see 97 a (b) c3) is so far from being right that his views may be dismissed as readily as those of Xkryt (see 5x).' At this point brain-fever sets in, the victim's last coherent thought being a passionate wish for more fingers. A friend of mine who was the wonder of all who knew him, in that he was known to have scored ten per cent in one of these papers on questions like the above, once divulged to an interviewer the fact that he owed his success to his methods of learning rather than to his ability. On the night before an exam. he would retire to some secret, solitary place, such as the boot-room, and commence learning these notes by heart. This, though a formidable task, was not so bad as the other alternative. The result was that, although in the majority of cases he would put down for one question an answer that would have been right for another, yet occasionally, luck being with him, he would hit the mark. Hence his ten per cent.

Another fruitful source of discomfort is provided by the type of master who lectures on a subject for half an hour, and then, with a bland smile, invites, or rather challenges, his form to write a 'good, long note' on the quintessence of his discourse. For the inexperienced this is an awful moment. They must write something – but what? For the last half hour they have been trying to impress the master with the fact that they belong to the class of people who can always listen best with their eyes closed. Nor poppy, nor mandragora, nor all the drowsy syrups of the world can ever medicine them to that sweet sleep that they have just been enjoying. And now they must write a 'good, long note'. It is in such extremities that your veteran shows up well. He does not betray any discomfort. Not he. He rather enjoys the prospect, in fact, of being permitted to place the master's golden eloquence on paper. So he takes up his pen with alacrity. No need to think what to write. He embarks on an essay concerning the master, showing up all his flaws in a pitiless light, and analysing his thorough worthlessness of character. On so congenial a subject he can, of course, write reams, and as the master seldom, if ever, desires to read the 'good, long note', he acquires a well-earned reputation for attending in school and being able to express himself readily with his pen. *Vivat floreatque.*

But all these forms of notes are as nothing compared with the notes that youths even in this our boasted land of freedom are forced to take down from dictation. Of the 'good, long note' your French scholar might well remark: *'C'est terrible'*, but justice would compel him to add, as he thought of the dictation note: *'mais ce n'est pas le diable'*. For these notes from dictation are, especially on a warm day, indubitably *le diable*.

Such notes are always dictated so rapidly that it is impossible to do anything towards understanding them as you go. You have to write your hardest to keep up. The beauty of this, from one point of view, is that, if you miss a sentence, you have lost the thread of the whole thing, and it is useless to attempt to take it up again at once. The only plan is to wait for some perceptible break in the flow of words, and dash in like lightning. It is much the same sort of thing as boarding a bus when in motion. And so you can take a long rest, provided you are in an obscure part of the room. In passing, I might add that a very pleasing indoor game can be played by asking the master, 'what came after so-and-so?' mentioning a point of the oration some half-hour back. This always provides a respite of a few minutes while he is thinking of some bitter repartee worthy of the occasion, and if repeated several times during an afternoon may cause much innocent merriment.

Of course, the real venom that lurks hid within notes from dictation does not appear until the time for examination arrives. Then you find yourself face to face with sixty or seventy closely and badly written pages of a note-book, all of which must be learnt by heart if you would aspire to the dizzy heights of half-marks. It is useless to tell your examiner that you had no chance of getting up the subject. 'Why,' he will reply, 'I gave you notes on that very thing myself.' 'You did, sir,' you say, as you advance stealthily upon him, 'but as you dictated those notes at the rate of two hundred words a minute, and as my brain, though large, is not capable of absorbing sixty pages of a note-book in one night, how the suggestively asterisked aposiopesis do you expect me to know them? Ah-h-h!' The last word is a war-cry, as you fling yourself bodily on him, and tear him courteously, but firmly, into minute fragments. Experience, which, as we all know, teaches, will in time lead you into adopting some method by which you may evade this taking of notes. A good plan is to occupy yourself with the composition of a journal, an unofficial magazine not intended for the eyes of the profane, but confined rigidly to your own circle of acquaintances. The chief advantage of such a work is that you will continue to write while the notes are being dictated. To throw your pen down with an air of finality and begin reading some congenial work of fiction would be a gallant action, but impolitic. No, writing of some sort is essential, and as it is out of the question to take down the notes, what better substitute than an unofficial journal could be found? To one whose contributions to the School magazine are constantly being cut down to mere skeletons by the hands of censors, there is a rapture otherwise unattainable in a page of really scurrilous items about those in authority. Try it yourselves, my beamish lads. Think of something really bad about somebody. Write it down and gloat over it. Sometimes, indeed, it is of the utmost use in determining your future career. You will probably remember those Titanic articles that appeared at the beginning of the war in *The Weekly Luggage-Train*, dealing with all the crimes of the War Office – the generals, the soldiers, the enemy – of everybody, in fact, except the editor, staff and office-boy of *The W.L.T*. Well, the writer of those epoch-making articles confesses that he owes all his skill to his early training, when, a happy lad at his little desk in school, he used to write trenchantly in his note-book on the subject of the authorities. There is an example for you. Of course we can never be like him, but let, oh! let us be as like him as we're able to be. A final word to those lost ones who dictate the notes. Why are our ears so constantly assailed with unnecessary explanations of, and opinions on, English literature? Prey upon the Classics if you will. It is a revolting habit, but too common to excite overmuch horror. But surely anybody, presupposing a certain bias towards sanity, can understand the Classics of our own language, with the exception, of course, of Browning. Take Tennyson, for example. How often have we been forced to take down from dictation the miserable maunderings of some commentator on the subject of *Maud*. A person reads *Maud*, and either likes it or dislikes it. In any case his opinion is not likely to be influenced by writing down at express speed the opinions of somebody else concerning the methods or objectivity and subjectivity of the author when he produced the work.

Somebody told me a short time ago that Shelley was an example of supreme, divine, superhuman genius. It is the sort of thing Mr Gilbert's 'rapturous maidens' might have said: 'How Botticellian! How Fra Angelican! How perceptively intense and consummately utter!' There is really no material difference.

Now, Talking About Cricket –

In the days of yore, when these white hairs were brown – or was it black? At any rate, they were not white – and I was at school, it was always my custom, when Fate obliged me to walk to school with a casual acquaintance, to whom I could not unburden my soul of those profound thoughts which even then occupied my mind, to turn the struggling conversation to the relative merits of cricket and football.

'Do you like cricket better than footer?' was my formula. Now, though at the time, in order to save fruitless argument, I always agreed with my companion, and praised the game he praised, in the innermost depths of my sub-consciousness, cricket ranked a long way in front of all other forms of sport. I may be wrong. More than once in my career it has been represented to me that I couldn't play cricket for nuts. My captain said as much when I ran him out in *the* match of the season after he had made forty-nine and looked like stopping. A bowling acquaintance heartily endorsed his opinion on the occasion of my missing three catches off him in one over. This, however, I attribute to prejudice, for the man I missed ultimately reached his century, mainly off the deliveries of my bowling acquaintance. I pointed out to him that, had I accepted any one of the three chances, we should have missed seeing the prettiest century made on the ground that season; but he was one of those bowlers who sacrifice all that is beautiful in the game to mere wickets. A sordid practice.

Later on, the persistence with which my county ignored my claims to inclusion in the team, convinced me that I must leave cricket fame to others. True, I did figure, rather prominently, too, in one county match. It was at the Oval, Surrey *v.* Middlesex. How well I remember that occasion! Albert Trott was bowling (Bertie we used to call him); I forget who was batting. Suddenly the ball came soaring in my direction. I was not nervous. I put down the sandwich I was eating, rose from my seat, picked the ball up neatly, and returned it with unerring aim to a fieldsman who was waiting for it with becoming deference. Thunders of applause went up from the crowded ring.

That was the highest point I ever reached in practical cricket. But, as the historian says of Mr Winkle, a man may be an excellent sportsman in theory, even if he fail in practice. That's me. Reader (if any), have you ever played cricket in the passage outside your study with a walking-stick and a ball of paper? That's the game, my boy, for testing your skill of wrist and eye. A century *v.* the M.C.C. is well enough in its way, but give me the man who can watch 'em in a narrow passage, lit only by a flickering gas-jet – one for every hit, four if it reaches the end, and six if it goes downstairs full-pitch, any pace bowling allowed. To make double figures in such a match is to taste life. Only you had better do your tasting when the House-master is out for the evening.

I like to watch the young cricket idea shooting. I refer to the lower games, where 'next man in' umpires with his pads on, his loins girt, and a bat in his hand. Many people have wondered why it is that no budding umpire can officiate unless he holds a bat. For my part, I think there is little foundation for the theory that it is part of a semi-religious rite, on the analogy of the Freemasons' special handshake and the like. Nor do I altogether agree with the authorities who allege that man, when standing up, needs something as a prop or support. There is a shadow of reason, I grant, in this supposition, but after years of keen observation I am inclined to think that the umpire keeps his bat by him, firstly, in order that no unlicensed hand shall commandeer it unbeknownst, and secondly, so that he shall be ready to go in directly his predecessor is out. There is an ill-concealed restiveness about his movements, as he watches the batsmen getting set, that betrays an overwrought spirit. Then of a sudden one of them plays a ball on to his pad. ' '*s that?*' asks the bowler, with an overdone carelessness. 'Clean out. Now *I'm* in,' and already he is rushing up the middle of the pitch to take possession. When he gets to the wicket a short argument ensues. 'Look here, you idiot, I hit it hard.' 'Rot, man, out of the way.' '!!??!' 'Look here, Smith, *are* you going to dispute the umpire's decision?' Chorus of fieldsmen: 'Get out, Smith, you ass. You've been given out years ago.' Overwhelmed by popular execration, Smith reluctantly departs, registering in the black depths of his soul a resolution to take on the umpireship at once, with a view to gaining an artistic revenge by giving his enemy run out on the earliest possible occasion. There is a primeval *insouciance* about this sort of thing which is as refreshing to a mind jaded with the stiff formality of professional umpires as a cold shower-bath.

I have made a special study of last-wicket men; they are divided into two classes, the deplorably nervous, or the outrageously confident. The nervous largely outnumber the confident. The launching of a last-wicket man, when there are ten to make to win, or five minutes left to make a draw of a losing game, is fully as impressive a ceremony as the launching of the latest battleship. An interested crowd harasses the poor victim as he is putting on his pads. 'Feel in a funk?' asks some tactless friend. 'N-n-no, norrabit.' 'That's right,' says the captain encouragingly, 'bowling's as easy as anything.'

This cheers the wretch up a little, until he remembers suddenly that the captain himself was distinctly at sea with the despised trundling, and succumbed to his second ball, about which he obviously had no idea whatever. At this he breaks down utterly, and, if emotional, will sob into his batting glove. He is assisted down the Pavilion steps, and reaches the wickets in a state of collapse. Here, very probably, a reaction will set in. The sight of the crease often comes as a positive relief after the vague terrors experienced in the Pavilion.

The confident last-wicket man, on the other hand, goes forth to battle with a light quip upon his lips. The lot of a last-wicket batsman, with a good eye and a sense of humour, is a very enviable one. The incredulous disgust of the fast bowler, who thinks that at last he may safely try that slow head-ball of his, and finds it lifted genially over the leg-boundary, is well worth seeing. I remember in one school match, the last man, unfortunately on the opposite side, did this three times in one over, ultimately retiring to a fluky catch in the slips with forty-one to his name. Nervousness at cricket is a curious thing. As the author of *Willow the King*, himself a county cricketer, has said, it is not the fear of getting out that causes funk. It is a sort of intangible *je ne sais quoi*. I trust I make myself clear. Some batsmen are nervous all through a long innings. With others the feeling disappears with the first boundary.

A young lady – it is, of course, not polite to mention her age to the minute, but it ranged somewhere between eight and ten – was taken to see a cricket match once. After watching the game with interest for some time, she gave out this profound truth: 'They all attend specially to one man.' It would be difficult to sum up the causes of funk more lucidly and concisely. To be an object of interest is sometimes pleasant, but when ten fieldsmen, a bowler, two umpires, and countless spectators are eagerly watching your every movement, the thing becomes embarrassing.

That is why it is, on the whole, preferable to be a cricket spectator rather than a cricket player. No game affords the spectator such unique opportunities of exerting his critical talents. You may have noticed that it is always the reporter who knows most about the game. Everyone, moreover, is at heart a critic, whether he represent the majesty of the Press or not. From the lady of Hoxton, who crushes her friend's latest confection with the words, 'My, wot an 'at!' down to that lowest class of all, the persons who call your attention (in print) to the sinister meaning of everything Clytemnestra says in *The Agamemnon*, the whole world enjoys expressing an opinion of its own about something.

In football you are vouchsafed fewer chances. Practically all you can do is to shout 'off-side' whenever an opponent scores, which affords but meagre employment for a really critical mind. In cricket, however, nothing can escape you. Everything must be done in full sight of everybody. There the players stand, without refuge, simply inviting criticism.

It is best, however, not to make one's remarks too loud. If you do, you call down upon yourself the attention of others, and are yourself criticized. I remember once, when I was of tender years, watching a school match, and one of the batsmen lifted a ball clean over the Pavilion. This was too much for my sensitive and critical young mind. 'On the carpet, sir,' I shouted sternly, well up in the treble clef, 'keep 'em on the carpet.' I will draw a veil. Suffice it to say that I became a sport and derision, and was careful for the future to criticize in a whisper. But the reverse by no means crushed me. Even now I take a melancholy pleasure in watching school matches, and saying So-and-So will make quite a fair *school-boy* bat in time, but he must get rid of that stroke of his on the off, and that shocking leg-hit, and a few of those *awful* strokes in the slips, but that on the whole, he is by no means lacking in promise. I find it refreshing. If, however, you feel compelled not merely to look on, but to play, as one often does at schools where cricket is compulsory, it is impossible to exaggerate the importance of white boots. The game you play before you get white boots is not cricket, but a weak imitation. The process of initiation is generally this. One plays in shoes for a few years with the most dire result, running away to square leg from fast balls, and so on, till despair seizes the soul. Then an angel in human form, in the very effective disguise of the man at the school boot-shop, hints that, for an absurdly small sum in cash, you may become the sole managing director of a pair of *white buckskin* boots with real spikes. You try them on. They fit, and the initiation is complete. You no longer run away from fast balls. You turn them neatly off to the boundary. In a word, you begin for the first time to play the game, the whole game, and nothing but the game.

There are misguided people who complain that cricket is becoming a business more than a game, as if that were not the most fortunate thing that could happen. When it ceases to be a mere business and becomes a religious ceremony, it will be a sign that the millennium is at hand. The person who regards cricket as anything less than a business is no fit companion, gentle reader, for the likes of you and me. As long as the game goes in his favour the cloven hoof may not show itself. But give him a good steady spell of leather-hunting, and you will know him for what he is, a mere *dilettante*, a dabbler, in a word, a worm, who ought never to be allowed to play at all. The worst of this species will sometimes take advantage of the fact that the game in which they happen to be playing is only a scratch game, upon the result of which no very great issues hang, to pollute the air they breathe with verbal, and the ground they stand on with physical, buffooneries. Many a time have I, and many a time have you, if you are what I take you for, shed tears of blood, at the sight of such. Careless returns, overthrows – but enough of a painful subject. Let us pass on.

I have always thought it a better fate for a man to be born a bowler than a bat. A batsman certainly gets a considerable amount of innocent fun by snicking good fast balls *just* off his wicket to the ropes, and standing stolidly in front against slow leg-breaks. These things are good, and help one to sleep peacefully o' nights, and enjoy one's meals. But no batsman can experience that supreme emotion of 'something attempted, something done', which comes to a bowler when a ball pitches in a hole near point's feet, and whips into the leg stump. It is one crowded second of glorious life. Again, the words 'retired hurt' on the score-sheet are far more pleasant to the bowler than the batsman. The groan of a batsman when a loose ball hits him full pitch in the ribs is genuine. But the 'Awfully-sorry-old-chap-it-slipped' of the bowler is not. Half a loaf is better than no bread, as Mr Chamberlain might say, and if he cannot hit the wicket, he is perfectly contented with hitting the man. In my opinion, therefore, the bowler's lot, in spite of billiard table wickets, red marl, and such like inventions of a degenerate age, is the happier one.

And here, glowing with pride of originality at the thought that I have written of cricket without mentioning Alfred Mynn or Fuller

Pilch, I heave a reminiscent sigh, blot my MS., and thrust my pen back into its sheath.

[16]

The Tom Brown Question

The man in the corner had been trying to worry me into a conversation for some time. He had asked me if I objected to having the window open. He had said something rather bitter about the War Office, and had hoped I did not object to smoking. Then, finding that I stuck to my book through everything, he made a fresh attack.

'I see you are reading *Tom Brown's Schooldays*,' he said.

This was a plain and uninteresting statement of fact, and appeared to me to require no answer. I read on.

'Fine book, sir.'

'Very.'

'I suppose you have heard of the Tom Brown Question?'

I shut my book wearily, and said I had not.

'It is similar to the Homeric Question. You have heard of that, I suppose?'

I knew that there was a discussion about the identity of the author of the *Iliad*. When at school I had been made to take down notes on the subject until I had grown to loathe the very name of Homer.

'You see,' went on my companion, 'the difficulty about *Tom Brown's Schooldays* is this. It is obvious that part one and part two were written by different people. You admit that, I suppose?'

'I always thought Mr Hughes wrote the whole book.'

'Dear me, not really? Why, I thought everyone knew that he only wrote the first half. The question is, who wrote the second. I know, but I don't suppose ten other people do. No, sir.'

'What makes you think he didn't write the second part?'

'My dear sir, just read it. Read part one carefully, and then read part two. Why, you can see in a minute.'

I said I had read the book three times, but had never noticed anything peculiar about it, except that the second half was not nearly so interesting as the first.

'Well, just tell me this. Do you think the same man created East and Arthur? Now then.'

I admitted that it was difficult to understand such a thing.

'There was a time, of course,' continued my friend, 'when everybody thought as you do. The book was published under Hughes's name, and it was not until Professor Burkett-Smith wrote his celebrated monograph on the subject that anybody suspected a dual, or rather a composite, authorship. Burkett-Smith, if you remember, based his arguments on two very significant points. The first of these was a comparison between the football match in the first part and the cricket match in the second. After commenting upon the truth of the former description, he went on to criticize the latter. Do you remember that match? You do? Very well. You recall how Tom wins the toss on a plumb wicket?'

'Yes.'

'Then with the usual liberality of young hands (I quote from the book) he put the M.C.C. in first. Now, my dear sir, I ask you, would a school captain do that? I am young, says one of Gilbert's characters, the Grand Duke, I think, but, he adds, I am not so young as that. Tom may have been young, but would he, *could* he have been young enough to put his opponents in on a true wicket, when he had won the toss? Would the Tom Brown of part one have done such a thing?'

'Never,' I shouted, with enthusiasm.

'But that's nothing to what he does afterwards. He permits, he actually sits there and permits, comic songs and speeches to be made during the luncheon interval. Comic Songs! Do you hear me, sir? COMIC SONGS!! And this when he wanted every minute of time he could get to save the match. Would the Tom Brown of part one have done such a thing?'

'Never, never.' I positively shrieked the words this time.

'Burkett-Smith put that point very well. His second argument is founded on a single remark of Tom's, or rather –'

'Or rather,' I interrupted, fiercely, 'or rather of the wretched miserable –'

'Contemptible,' said my friend.

'Despicable, scoundrelly, impostor who masquerades as Tom in the second half of the book.'

'Exactly,' said he. 'Thank you very much. I have often thought the same myself. The remark to which I refer is that which he makes to the master while he is looking on at the M.C.C. match. In passing, sir, might I ask you whether the Tom Brown of part one would have been on speaking terms with such a master?'

I shook my head violently. I was too exhausted to speak.

'You remember the remark? The master commented on the fact that Arthur is a member of the first eleven. I forget Tom's exact words, but the substance of them is this, that, though on his merits Arthur was not worth his place, he thought it would do him such a lot of good being in the team. Do I make myself plain, sir? He – thought – it – would – do – him – such – a – lot – of – good – being – in – the – team!!!'

There was a pause. We sat looking at one another, forming silently with our lips the words that still echoed through the carriage.

'Burkett-Smith,' continued my companion, 'makes a great deal of that remark. His peroration is a very fine piece of composition. "Whether (concludes he) the captain of a school cricket team who could own spontaneously to having been guilty of so horrible, so terrible an act of favouritismical jobbery, who could sit unmoved and see his team being beaten in the most important match of the season (and, indeed, for all that the author tells us it may have been the only match of the season), for no other reason than that he thought a first eleven cap would prove a valuable tonic to an unspeakable personal friend of his, whether, I say, the Tom Brown who acted thus could have been the Tom Brown who headed the revolt of the fags in part one, is a question which, to the present writer, offers no difficulties. I await with confidence the verdict of a free, enlightened, and conscientious public of my fellow-countrymen." Fine piece of writing, that, sir?'

'Very,' I said.

'That pamphlet, of course, caused a considerable stir. Opposing parties began to be formed, some maintaining that Burkett-Smith was entirely right, others that he was entirely wrong, while the rest said he might have been more wrong if he had not been so right, but that if he had not been so mistaken he would probably have been a great deal more correct. The great argument put forward by the supporters of what I may call the "One Author" view, was, that the fight in part two could not have been written by anyone except the author of the fight with Flashman in the school-house hall. And this is the point which has led to all the discussion. Eliminate the Slogger Williams episode, and the whole of the second part stands out clearly as the work of another hand. But there is one thing that seems to have escaped the notice of everybody.'

'Yes?' I said.

He leant forward impressively, and whispered. 'Only the actual fight is the work of the genuine author. The interference of Arthur has been interpolated!'

'By Jove!' I said. 'Not really?'

'Yes. Fact, I assure you. Why, think for a minute. Could a man capable of describing a fight as that fight is described, also be capable of stopping it just as the man the reader has backed all through is winning? It would be brutal. Positively brutal, sir!'

'Then, how do you explain it?'

'A year ago I could not have told you. Now I can. For five years I have been unravelling the mystery by the aid of that one clue. Listen. When Mr Hughes had finished part one, he threw down his pen and started to Wales for a holiday. He had been there a week or more, when one day, as he was reclining on the peak of a mountain looking down a deep precipice, he was aware of a body of men approaching him. They were dressed soberly in garments of an inky black. Each had side whiskers, and each wore spectacles. "Mr Hughes, I believe?" said the leader, as they came up to him.

' "Your servant, sir," said he.

' "We have come to speak to you on an important matter, Mr Hughes. We are the committee of the Secret Society For Putting Wholesome Literature Within The Reach Of Every Boy, And Seeing That He Gets It. I, sir, am the president of the S.S.F.P.W.L.W.T.R.O.-E.B.A.S.T.H.G.I." He bowed.

' "Really, sir, I – er – don't think I have the pleasure," began Mr Hughes.

' "You shall have the pleasure, sir. We have come to speak to you about your book. Our representative has read Part I, and reports unfavourably upon it. It contains no moral. There are scenes of violence, and your hero is far from perfect."

' "I think you mistake my object," said Mr Hughes; "Tom is a boy, not a patent medicine. In other words, he is not supposed to be perfect."

' "Well, I am not here to bandy words. The second part of your book must be written to suit the rules of our Society. Do you agree, or shall we throw you over that precipice?"

' "Never. I mean, I don't agree."

' "Then we must write it for you. Remember, sir, that you will be constantly watched, and if you attempt to write that second part yourself –" ' (he paused dramatically). 'So the second part was written by the committee of the Society. So now you know.'

'But,' said I, 'how do you account for the fight with Slogger Williams?'

'The president relented slightly towards the end, and consented to Mr Hughes inserting a chapter of his own, on condition that the Society should finish it. And the Society did. See?'

'But –'

'Ticket.'

'Eh?'

'Ticket, please, sir.'

I looked up. The guard was standing at the open door. My companion had vanished.

'Guard,' said I, as I handed him my ticket, 'where's the gentleman who travelled up with me?'

'Gentleman, sir? I haven't seen nobody.'

'Not a man in tweeds with red hair? I mean, in tweeds and owning red hair.'

'No, sir. You've been alone in the carriage all the way up. Must have dreamed it, sir.'

Possibly I did.

FOR THE BEST IN PAPERBACKS, LOOK FOR THE

In every corner of the world, on every subject under the sun, Penguin represents quality and variety – the very best in publishing today.

For complete information about books available from Penguin – including Puffins, Penguin Classics and Arkana – and how to order them, write to us at the appropriate address below. Please note that for copyright reasons the selection of books varies from country to country.

In the United Kingdom: Please write to *Dept E.P., Penguin Books Ltd, Harmondsworth, Middlesex, UB7 0DA.*

If you have any difficulty in obtaining a title, please send your order with the correct money, plus ten per cent for postage and packaging, to *PO Box No 11, West Drayton, Middlesex*

In the United States: Please write to *Dept BA, Penguin, 299 Murray Hill Parkway, East Rutherford, New Jersey 07073*

In Canada: Please write to *Penguin Books Canada Ltd, 2801 John Street, Markham, Ontario L3R 1B4*

In Australia: Please write to the *Marketing Department, Penguin Books Australia Ltd, P.O. Box 257, Ringwood, Victoria 3134*

In New Zealand: Please write to the *Marketing Department, Penguin Books (NZ) Ltd, Private Bag, Takapuna, Auckland 9*

In India: Please write to *Penguin Overseas Ltd, 706 Eros Apartments, 56 Nehru Place, New Delhi, 110019*

In the Netherlands: Please write to *Penguin Books Netherlands B.V., Postbus 195, NL–1380AD Weesp*

In West Germany: Please write to *Penguin Books Ltd, Friedrichstrasse 10–12, D–6000 Frankfurt/Main 1*

In Spain: Please write to *Longman Penguin España, Calle San Nicolas 15, E–28013 Madrid*

In Italy: Please write to *Penguin Italia s.r.l., Via Como 4, I-20096 Pioltello (Milano)*

In France: Please write to *Penguin Books Ltd, 39 Rue de Montmorency, F-75003 Paris*

In Japan: Please write to *Longman Penguin Japan Co Ltd, Yamaguchi Building, 2–12–9 Kanda Jimbocho, Chiyoda-Ku, Tokyo 101*

FOR THE BEST IN PAPERBACKS, LOOK FOR THE

PENGUIN OMNIBUSES

The Penguin Book of Ghost Stories

An anthology to set the spine tingling, including stories by Zola, Kleist, Sir Walter Scott, M. R. James and A. S. Byatt.

The Penguin Book of Horror Stories

Including stories by Maupassant, Poe, Gautier, Conan Doyle, L. P. Hartley and Ray Bradbury, in a selection of the most horrifying horror from the eighteenth century to the present day.

The Penguin Complete Sherlock Holmes   Sir Arthur Conan Doyle

With the fifty-six classic short stories, plays *A Study in Scarlet*, *The Sign of Four*, *The Hound of the Baskervilles* and *The Valley of Fear*, this volume is a must for any fan of Baker Street's most famous resident.

Victorian Villainies

Fraud, murder, political intrigue and horror are the ingredients of these four Victorian thrillers, selected by Hugh Greene and Graham Greene.

Maigret and the Ghost   Georges Simenon

Three stories by the writer who blends, *par excellence*, the light and the shadow, cynicism and compassion. This volume contains *Maigret and the Hotel Majestic*, *Three Beds in Manhattan* and, the title story, *Maigret and the Ghost*.

The Julian Symons Omnibus

Three novels of cynical humour and cliff-hanging suspense: *The Man Who Killed Himself*, *The Man Whose Dreams Came True* and *The Man Who Lost His Wife*. 'Exciting and compulsively readable' – *Observer*

FOR THE BEST IN PAPERBACKS, LOOK FOR THE 🐧

PENGUIN OMNIBUSES

Author's Choice: Four Novels by Graham Greene

Four magnificent novels by an author whose haunting and distinctive 'entertainments' and fiction have captured the moral and spiritual dilemmas of our time: *The Power and the Glory*, *The Quiet American*, *Travels with My Aunt* and *The Honorary Consul*.

The Collected Stories of Colette
Edited with and Introduction by Robert Phelps

'Poetry and passion' – *Daily Telegraph*. A sensuous feast of one hundred short stories, shot through with the colours and flavours of the Parisian world and fertile French countryside, they reverberate with the wit and acuity that made Colette unique.

The Penguin Complete Novels of George Orwell

The six novels of one of England's most original and significant writers. Collected in this volume are the novels which brought George Orwell world fame: *Animal Farm*, *Burmese Days*, *A Clergyman's Daughter*, *Coming Up for Air*, *Keep the Aspidistra Flying* and *Nineteen Eighty-Four*.

The Great Novels of D. H. Lawrence

The collection of the masterworks of one of the greatest writers in the English language of any time – *Women in Love*, *Sons and Lovers* and *The Rainbow*.

Frank Tuohy: The Collected Stories

'The time has come for him to be honoured for what he is: a great short-story writer, an absolute master of the form' – Paul Bailey in the *Standard*. From Poland to Brazil, from England to Japan, Tuohy maps the intricate contours of personal and racial misunderstanding, shock and embarrassment. 'Exhilarating fiction' – *Sunday Times*

The Nancy Mitford Omnibus

Nancy Mitford's immortal, unforgettable world in one scintillating volume: *The Pursuit of Love*, *Love in a Cold Climate*, *The Blessing* and *Don't Tell Alfred*.